1^{00} 7/11

⚐ **W9-BQT-424**

LARGE
PRINT

Girardi, Robert
  Madeleine's ghost.

MADELEINE'S GHOST

G·K
Hall
&Co.

This Large Print Book carries the
Seal of Approval of N.A.V.H.

MADELEINE'S GHOST

Robert Girardi

G.K. Hall & Co.
Thorndike, Maine

Library of Congress Cataloging in Publication Data

Girardi, Robert.
    Madeleine's ghost / by Robert Girardi.
       p.   cm.
    ISBN 0-7838-1507-7 (lg. print : hc)
    1. New York (N.Y.) — Fiction. 2. New Orleans (La.)
— Fiction. 3. Large type books. I. Title.
[PS3557.I694M3 1996]
813'.54—dc20   95-38049

This book is for my father —
SAM H. GIRARDI
1917–1992
— who told me stories.

It is history that teaches us to hope.
— ROBERT E. LEE

Part One:

A Saint for Brooklyn

Stones are falling from the ceiling of my apartment. First one, then two, then dozens. I take refuge beneath the kitchen table as they bounce and dance across every surface, denting the toaster, gouging into the old linoleum of the floor. The falling stones are like a rain of hail, but so absurd in this setting that I want to laugh.

The first stone hit five minutes ago with a solid thump on the arm of the orange Naugahyde easy chair in the living room, then rolled into my lap. It was egg-shaped and smooth and wet, as if it had just been dredged up from the bottom of the river. A second hit the television and fell behind the gas heater in the fireplace. I counted five more like warning drumbeats; then I ran for the table. Now they bounce and roll all over, making quite a racket. They don't seem to come from anywhere. There are no holes in the ceiling. The stones flash into air just below the tin egg-and-anchor molding and fall as if they are falling from a great height.

The whole manifestation lasts about ten minutes. I wait fifteen minutes more before emerging carefully into the daylight from beneath the table. The smooth stones lie in piles in the kitchen, in the living room across the rug, on the couch, and on the television set, which appears undamaged. There are no stones in the bathroom or in my bedroom, but I find the

*largest pile heaped up on the bare floor in Moles-
worth's old room when I push open the door.*

*I take about an hour and a half to remove all
the stones to the garden. The job requires five trips
with a full suitcase, which I empty in the corner
of the yard under the dry-rotted grape trellis. There
is quite a little mound out here now, enough to pave
a short walkway. I kick at it in frustration before
I go back upstairs to collapse on the couch.*

This is the second time in the last three weeks.

1

It is about two in the afternoon, Tuesday, mid-
June, with the sun hot on my back and the sky
seared and brown-looking above the island. The
collar of my shirt is soaked with sweat. Just a
block away the Manhattan Bridge creaks omi-
nously in the heat, its abutments age blackened
and massive as the pyramids. I am wearing an
unseasonable tweed jacket, swamp green cor-
duroy pants, a heavy powder blue oxford cloth
button-down, and a regimental stripe tie — the
only presentable outfit in my closet. I am shaved
and sober and calling on Father Rose in the rectory of St. Basil's Cathedral on Jay Street in
Brooklyn.

A flat-faced woman in thick spectacles answers
the door cautiously, pressing her nose against the
barred peephole like a deep-sea diver in an old-

fashioned brass helmet peering out at the ocean floor.

"I'm here to see the priest," I say.

"Father isn't seeing anyone right now. He's busy," she says, and goes to shut the peephole.

"Wait, I have an appointment."

"Step back," she says.

I step back, and a moment of silence follows in which the woman scowls and looks me up and down. I get the feeling she doesn't care for the striped tie. It's hardly the welcome one expects at the front door of a church, but I don't blame her. This neighborhood is bad, loomed over by the same projects to the east that threaten my derelict neighborhood just to the south.

At last she nods, slides the bolts, and opens the door. A dismal smell pervades such places, rectories and army barracks, places reserved exclusively for the use of men: ammonia and boiled cabbage dinners and long, terrible Sunday evenings without the sound of a woman's voice.

We go into a narrow hallway and up some stairs lined with dark paneling and hung with faded nineteenth-century prints of saints and Jesus praying in the Garden at Gethsemane, apostles sleeping the sleep of the craven behind Him in the weeds, and enter a small waiting room set with two rows of old pews and a few rump-sprung easy chairs. On an end table there are yellow copies of *Catholic Digest* and *Highlights for Children* magazine. I settle down to wait with the adventures of Goofus and Gallant in the latter as the woman goes to warn the priest.

Father Rose is lining up a putt when I am ushered into his chambers a few minutes later. He is hunched over the putter at one end of a mock putting green of Astro Turf, the hole opposing him an odd contraption that resembles a large aluminum daisy.

"Father Rose?" I say. "I'm Ned Conti, I called yesterday . . ."

This is not the moment to speak. The priest, hardly aware of my presence, follows through with the putt. The ball goes awry, hooks to the left, and rolls under a chair. He gives a small strangled sound, and his shoulders slump. Waiting for him to recover, I glance around the room. It is bright and cheery, free from the religious gloom that pervades the rest of the rectory. Golf trophies stand dustless in glass-fronted shelves to one side. Autographed photos of Jack Nicklaus and Arnold Palmer flank the abstract sixties-era crucifix hanging beside a window overlooking the handball courts in the asphalt park across the street.

"Putting is a gift from God," the priest says wearily, wiping the head of his putter with a handkerchief. He is a lean fellow, with a long face, and resembles a sort of amiable Charlton Heston. "It's like grace. The one thing in golf you can't really practice. You've got to have the knack, that's all."

He points the putter to a floral-print love seat against the wall. I sit, and he sinks back against the edge of his desk with the easy grace of a man who has spent his life on the links. His face is tanned; his wrists are specked with freckles. He crosses his legs, and I can see he's wearing expensive two-tone golf shoes, cleats unscrewed, though his black cassock is threadbare and traditional, pulled in with a simple square-buckled brown belt after the manner of the Jesuit Brothers at Loyola, who enjoyed the austerity of their priestly robes to the point of vanity. After all, there is nothing classier than basic black.

"Now, what can I do for you, Mr. Conti?" Father Rose says when we are settled.

"I came about your advertisement in the *U.S. Catholic Historian*," I say. "Historical research. That's my field. I'm a research historian. Have you gotten many responses?"

Father Rose frowns at his putter. "Are you a golfing man?"

I confess that I am not.

"I'm crazy about the game." He gestures at the trophy cases. "Maybe too crazy."

He pushes off the desk suddenly and strides back and forth across the room, putter held behind his back in one hand in a posture that I recognize immediately as characteristic.

"Last year," he says, "with the permission of the bishop, I took a few months off to join the PGA tour. I was quite the golf star in college, you know, but in our family it was traditional for the youngest son to join the priesthood. First time back in competition in something like

13

twenty-five years, and I made the cuts. All in all, for an old guy, I didn't do too badly, perhaps because I was careful to dedicate each ball to a different saint. After expenses, I came out of it with a net profit of five thousand seven hundred dollars. I have set aside these winnings for a special research project."

"Oh, yes," I say, trying to sound like I really don't need the money. "What sort of project?"

"It is of grave spiritual significance to the future of Brooklyn. This is all I will say for now."

2

We go down into the churchyard to walk in the heat among the graves. Father Rose examines my credentials for a few minutes in silence, putter under his arm, lips pursed in concentration, a posture that befits a man with weighty matters to consider.

"B.A., Loyola University of the South," he reads aloud from my curriculum vitae to the mortuary heat of the afternoon. "New Orleans is a little wild, they say. I hear the Jesuits have a pretty good time down there."

I shrug, noncommittal.

"Do you know that city well?" He looks over at me, shielding his eyes against the sun.

"It's been a long time," I say. "But I think I could still get around."

"I don't mind telling you that certain aspects of my project touch on New Orleans. A knowledge of the place might be useful."

"Then I'm your man," I say. "It's fate."

He ignores this and goes back to my résumé. "Catholic grammar school, Catholic high school . . . and now Ph.D. candidate in French history, Georgetown University. Well, an excellent Catholic education, Mr. Conti." He folds my CV into a pouch in his cassock. "You must be a man of sound convictions."

"I try, Father," I say, and give him the toothy smile of a used-car dealer. Actually my education is more a testament to my parents' faith than my own. I hated Catholic school. The nuns pulled on my hair and beat me with rulers. My mom forced me to go through the twelfth grade; Catholic scholarships paid for the rest.

"And how's your doctoral thesis coming along?"

"It's almost finished," I lie. "Another month, and I send it off to the committee."

The truth is, I started out right but got lost somewhere along the way. I haven't touched my thesis in nine months: *Shakos and Epaulets — Military Fashions and Ideas in the First Empire.* The grand title conceals a scratched over ream of half-baked theories and poor scholarship concerning the effect of fancy uniforms on the development of imperialist attitudes in Napoleon's France. It is strewn in a messy heap of footnotes, coffee stains, crumbs, and roaches across the kitchen table in my apartment. Each night I keep meaning to begin again, and each night I find some reason not to.

First it was the disruptive presence of my ex-roommate, Molesworth, a loud, obnoxious bayou-trash Louisianan with filthy habits and a beer gut the size of Lake Pontchartrain. Now I blame the series of strange disturbances which have manifested themselves in the apartment in his absence and which I can only ascribe to the actions of a poltergeist. I am a rational man, but how else to explain stones from the ceiling and other weirdnesses? It is impossible to concentrate on my work in the middle of a haunting. This is the only word I have for the horrible, oppressive feeling that has invaded my rooms. I was allowed six years to complete my thesis and defend it before the advisory committee at Georgetown. Time is running out; barely six months remain. Perhaps if the ghost would go away?

I consider mentioning the haunting to Father Rose. He might be able to do something, arrange an exorcism, if they still perform exorcisms. But I reject the idea. Undoubtedly it is bad form to discuss ghosts at a job interview.

We follow an uneven flagstone path between the graves and dead end at an elaborate monument topped with an obelisk of black marble that seems out of keeping with the humbler headstones surrounding it. I notice a worn inscription in French cut on the base before we turn back again. At last we sit on a flat grave marker by the gate, and Father Rose swats at the weeds growing up between the stones with his putter. The wall bordering Tillary is topped with broken glass and tangled razor wire. A plane booms overhead in the hot sky, lowering toward Kennedy.

"Every night from the windows of the rectory I hear gunshots," he says at last, weariness in his voice. "Last year two young black boys no older than twelve years old shot it out on the steps of the church with machine guns, just like in a gangster movie. One of them died in my arms. You can still see the bloodstains on the white marble. Then the young girls come over from the Decateur Projects bringing babies for baptism who have no fathers and no names. 'Are you Catholic?' I ask. They are not Catholic; they do not know a single prayer and have only vaguely heard of God. I baptize their babies on the sly, what can it hurt? But the situation is tragic. All around us ignorance and vice and poverty. There seems no solution except for the one God has in store for us all in the end."

He pauses, leaning on his putter like an old soldier. In the distance, the ceaseless rush of traffic on the BQE.

"Can I ask you a personal question, Mr. Conti?"

"Go ahead, Father," I say.

"After all those years of Catholic school, do you believe in God?" He seems to stop breathing as he waits for my answer. A dull light flickers in his eyes.

He has caught me by surprise. It is hard to lie about this one. I don't know what to say.

"Sometimes," I manage at last.

The priest wants more. I shake my head. In fact, until recently, like everyone else, I maintained a cynical skepticism regarding spiritual matters. I didn't believe in anything I couldn't see. The ghost in my apartment has started to change all that. It's still hard to extrapolate the existence of the deity from the presence of a single phantom, but one ghost, I suppose, could presage a whole unseen universe of ghosts, demons, saints, and miracles. The idea is frightening to me. I prefer the faceless charged particles of science, the big bang, the gaseous clouds of electrons and protons, the primeval soups of amino acids and so forth.

At last Father Rose puts a hand on my sleeve. "I think I understand your hesitation," he says gently. "God is too big an idea for most of us. How can you pray to a being that you can't imagine who is everywhere and nowhere? Even Christ in His faultlessness can be daunting. But think of the intercession of the saints! A saint is a human being who sinned, had problems, and overcame them to become one of God's people. What Brooklyn needs now is a saint. A saint who will hear our prayers and put in a good word for us with God."

I nod and try to look sincere, but I'm not exactly sure what he's getting at. Brooklyn needs a saint. I need the stipend mentioned in the advertisement in the *Catholic Historian*. I've been out of work for five months now, am flat broke, and rely on the odd day or two of temporary office work through an agency in Manhattan — filing, answering the phone, typing the occasional piece of correspondence into the word processor. Humiliating for a man of my dignity, a man who has completed all the course work necessary for a Ph.D. Though I have come to believe that dignity and a Ph.D. are liabilities in the world.

A moment later Father Rose rises with a sigh and brushes off the skirt of his cassock. He has an appointment to hear the confessions of two older members of the congregation. Everyone who comes to confession now is sixty if a day, he tells me. The young, it seems, no longer believe in sin.

We walk together to the heavy wrought-iron gate at the foot of the churchyard. He pushes back an iron bar as thick as my wrist and swings the gate open onto Jay Street. A bus goes chugging by, and we are overwhelmed with diesel fumes. He shakes my hand.

"You've got my phone number," I say, coughing.

I step through and am halfway down the sidewalk when he calls me back.

3

Tonight the ghost is an atmospheric disturbance, a storm on the horizon. The hand of the ghost is everywhere apparent as I walk around, a visitor in my own rooms: Clothes are pulled off hangers in the closet; coins atop my dresser are arranged in an oddly familiar crescent-shaped pattern; the furniture has been moved at right angles to the wall. The refrigerator door is hanging ajar, milk spoiled, cheese gone green at the edges.

I change into khaki shorts and T-shirt quickly and check the answering machine. I do not intend to stay long. These days I do little more than sleep and bathe here. The ghost brings a sick clamminess to the palms, knocks the gumption out of me. I need an antidote: One message from Antoinette would make all the difference, just the sound of her voice across the miles from New Orleans. Antoinette, I say out loud, Antoinette. It is a vain incantation. There are no messages on the machine. We are just friends now. She never calls.

In the last twenty minutes before dark I run out and take the F train into Manhattan and get drunk at the usual round of Lower East Side dives and then for a change stumble over to SoHo, where, at the wine bar of the SoHo Kitchen, I meet a blond businesswoman who believes in ghosts. She is an account executive at Carstairs and White and not too bad-looking if you squint your eyes. After a dozen or so glasses of a mildly piquant Pouilly-Fuissé, she is drunk enough to take me home with her, and I am drunk enough to go.

"It's the ghost," I explain. "I can't possibly

sleep in my apartment tonight."

She nods as if she understands, and we get in a cab and go up to her condo in a high-rise building at Ninety-third and Third. It is a well-appointed apartment on the forty-second floor, with a view of the lights of the city out a picture window that takes up one whole wall of the living room. After a little informal nuzzling on the couch, we resort to some sloppy and forgettable sex and then adjourn to the bed for more of the same. I fall asleep at last around dawn, happy to be away from the creaking of the old tenement and the ghost for one night.

But then I dream I am back in Brooklyn, and invisible hands are carrying me up the stairs into the darkness of my apartment. I am carried into the kitchen and set back at the table and forced to look around, and there, before the window, is a shapeless cloud full of despair in the same way that a thunderhead is full of hard rain and heat lightning. Then I see something white moving in the cloud and a pair of hands emerge, the white hands of a woman with rings on each finger, and my heart is filled with dread.

I wake up in a sweat to find that it is just past eleven in the morning and I am alone in the account executive's apartment. I get up, dress, and find a note and a business card set beneath a glass of orange juice and a cold buttered muffin on the glass table in the living room.

"Had fun last night," the note says. "Call me. Didn't want to wake you. Let yourself out."

As instructed, I let myself out and travel down forty-two floors in the elevator. The streets up here are neat and blinding. I wander this unfamiliar landscape for a few hours, feeling terrible and hungover and reflecting that the ghost has followed me into a woman's bed across the river and up ninety-three blocks through streets flooded with a blaze of brightness as dark and unforgiving as the tomb itself.

4

Looking back, I should have realized there was something wrong with the apartment from the beginning. My friend Chase Zingari found it for me five years ago, and she is an odd, tormented young woman who believes in ghosts, second sight, and demonic possession. She is half Romanian Gypsy and half blueblood WASP, with a bone deformity that has left her face a mess, something out of a cheap horror movie.

I had just moved to the city and was going through the hell of looking for an apartment to share out of the *Voice* when Chase heard about a rent-controlled two-bedroom in an obscure industrial neighborhood in Brooklyn called Molasses Hill. I still don't know how she found out about the place — an acquaintance, a stranger in a bar — but we got the key from the main office of a mob-run garbage concern on the Lower East

Side and went under the river on the F train to take a look.

I remember walking the empty streets in the first red light of dusk. After the clamor of Manhattan it seemed eerily quiet. Dark barges passed silently on the East River just a block down. Crickets chirped from weeds growing through the cobbles. The blood-colored sunset tinted shards of broken glass in the windows of abandoned warehouses. Along the three or four blocks of decrepit tenements across from the power plant, dying fig trees sagged against gravity, propped up with two-by-fours and wire stays. I saw a hummingbird dart off from the rotting fruit toward the light in the west. I was charmed. Fresh from Graduate Student Housing at Georgetown, I knew nothing of the violence and crime of South Brooklyn. And the rent was extremely low, almost a miracle in itself.

"So what's the catch?" I said to Chase.

We had inspected the apartment and stood in the empty living room, boards creaking beneath our feet. The smokestacks of the power plant out the window looked like the fingers of a giant hand.

"Does there always have to be something wrong?" Chase said. "For once in your life, believe." Then she did a sort of dance with the dust through the four vacant rooms and came back to stand beside me. "It's a fucking amazing bargain," she said, out of breath. "Three seventy-five for two bedrooms, one big, one teensy, a reasonable living room, a separate kitchen and bathroom sporting a full-length tub. And look out here. . . ." We stepped over to the bedroom window. The last light caught the ridges and scars of her *Phantom of the Opera* face as we peered through the dirty pane. "A backyard!"

Sure enough, there was a weedy fenced-in lot out back, with an overgrown garden patch, a square of grass, a broken-down grape trellis, and a crumbling brick barbecue pit. Beyond the fence and the nearest row of tenements, eight or nine massive residential towers stood black against the darkening sky.

"What are those?" I said.

"Those are the Decateur Projects, I think," Chase said, and danced off into the kitchen to light her cigarette at the gas burner.

"Wait, housing projects?" I followed her across the dirty linoleum to the stove. Moths flitted around the naked bulb dangling from the ceiling. "So how's the neighborhood?"

She shrugged. "Sort of melancholy. It suits you."

"I mean, how safe is it?"

"You're in New York now. Welcome to uncertainty and dread."

"What happened to the previous tenant?"

"He left."

"Chase . . ."

"Come on!" She gestured with her cigarette toward the fireplace in the living room. "Look at the one single thing the man left behind!"

Above the mantel, pasted to a piece of cardboard, hung a magazine reproduction of an unfinished portrait of the emperor by J. L. David. "Your hero, Napoleon!" Chase almost shouted. "That is a sign you should take this apartment! Now! Who cares about the neighborhood? We could all die tomorrow. Shit, you've got to move in, I can't explain it. I'm getting that prickly feeling up my legs. It's the right place for you, it just is!"

"Don't go intuitive on me," I said, calmly as possible. "Looks a little scary around here. That F stop at Knox . . ."

"Fine," Chase interrupted, "if you don't take the place, I will."

I moved in a week later.

Now I know that even in those first months, before Molesworth came up from Louisiana, I felt something in the apartment, a quiet expectation, the presence of an unseen something else.

But when Molesworth arrived, these vague inklings were drowned out by his vast human stink. Molesworth in himself was enough to obscure any apparitions, belonging as he does entirely to this world, mulchy stink of the Louisiana swamp still about him. He was much too solid for hauntings. His huge, rotund body sweated of earthly pleasures; the smell of his cigars curled out from beneath the door to his bedroom like his own sort of ectoplasm — even though I had expressly forbidden any cigar smoking in

25

the apartment. His bottles of Dixie beer, empty except for that little bit of backwash, piled up in the kitchen at the rate of a case and a half a week. And those women with big hair and gaudy jewelry brought home most Saturday nights from one bar or the next; their giggling and the squeals and groans of lusty play could be heard through the thin pressboard of the wall as I tossed alone on the other side in my narrow bed.

I suppose the ghost couldn't stand this noisy, squalid life. Perhaps it hid in the woodwork with the termites and the spiders or slept between the walls with the rats or disappeared into the fabric of the air.

Then, three months ago, Molesworth picked up and went back to Mamou, Louisiana, owing me one month's rent and six hundred dollars in long-distance phone calls. Of course, I will never see the money. I woke up one morning to find his room empty and what sounded like a prepared statement read into the memo function of the answering machine.

"Dear Coonass," came his thick backcountry drawl through the static of the tape, "circumstances beyond my control conspire to call me home to Louisiana. And if you ask old Molesworth's opinion, it's high time you yourself repair to other climes. Your life in New York has reached a dead end. You are drifting, Coonass, you have no agenda! Far be it from me to throw you a lifeline, but you might reconsider your old stomping grounds. I hope you will not take advantage

26

of my departure to masturbate too much. This is Lyle Molesworth signing off."

Molesworth had spent the two weeks just prior to his midnight exit from New York on the phone with a lawyer in Shreveport discussing wills and easements and liquor licenses. His grandfather Duploux died in January, and Molesworth inherited a bar on stilts in the middle of Bayou Dessaintes.

From all descriptions, it is a rough sort of place, which has been in his family for generations. There are no toilets, just holes in the floor opening directly into black water infested with alligator and cottonmouth, though for some reason the bar is patronized by a diverse group of folks that include from time to time Johnny Cash and the governor himself, as well as the usual host of Cajun brawlers and roughnecks from the oil fields. Legend has it that a drunken Hank Williams vomited on the stage there in 1947, and they preserve what passes for the great man's evacuated dinner — an indistinguishable lump gone green and black with age — in a mason jar on a shelf over the jukebox.

With Molesworth gone, the ghost started again where it had left off five years before. In the first few days there was nothing I could put my finger on, exactly. Just a renewed pressure in the wake of Molesworth's departure. A soft scraping no louder than leaves falling from a dead tree or breath leaving the mouth of a child. After a week or so I began to hear a sighing in the

27

moment before I entered a room to click on the lights at dusk, and once I caught an odd reflection in the green at the back of the mirror in the bathroom. But now it is already in the nineties every day, we are in for a hot, miserable summer, and the ghost has abandoned such subtleties. It is dropping stones from the ceiling, moving furniture. It has grown bolder with the rising mercury as if it thrives on the heat like a hothouse orchid. Now it blows through this apartment, a sour, vindictive wind.

What does the ghost want from me? Ghosts always want something. According to what I have read, they are the children of the spirit world, always tugging on the skirts of the living. They want comfort, they want attention, they want us to know how they died. And am I sure that it is a ghost? There are days when I have my doubts. Could it be an unusual sort of electrical phenomenon, a disturbance in the magnetic field of the apartment caused by the proximity of the power plant just across the street? The high-voltage transformers half a block up zap and fizz at regular intervals, throwing trails of blue static in the summer evenings.

Or perhaps the answer is more simple than all this. Perhaps I am going mad. It would be nice to go mad, absolutely insane, free of the mundanities and responsibilities of life, every day a holiday.

Unfortunately I am sane as a piece of toast.

5

The crypt of the church smells like old bones and camphor. We advance through the vaulted dimness past mortuary plaques, wilting flowers, and a heap of broken wooden chairs to a small unfinished chapel set off by an iron grate. A bare bulb hangs from the ceiling here over a battered wooden table. This place is full of moldering U-Haul boxes. About thirty of them are stacked against the walls of rough stone. Another dozen are lumped together in the center of the room.

"These are the records I spoke of," Father Rose says, pointing to the boxes with his putter. "They moved them over here when St. Catherine's was razed to make room for that Korean shopping mall."

I pull up the flap on one of the boxes. A dusty ledger, leather bound and edged in faded gilt, shows the date 1849; a letter written in the spidery handwriting of another era has fallen out of its envelope into a mess of other such letters. There are easily thousands of documents here, hundreds of thousands of manuscript pages in these boxes. Missalets, sermons, receipts, laundry lists, personal correspondence, accounts, you name it, all succumbing to the dampness and the years.

Father Rose pulls a rickety chair from the pile in the crypt, brings it in, and offers it to me. He crouches down, putter over his shoulder, and his eyes go half closed. When he speaks, his voice has an odd singsong quality, as if he is repeating something memorized by rote.

"A young nun came to this parish in 1846 from New Orleans. She was known as Sister Januarius. We don't know her given name. It was the rule of her order that the novitiates take the name of a male saint or martyr. In those troubled times it was much as it is now. Violence and poverty and ignorance. The neighborhood around the navy yard alone was home to a hundred-odd brothels and an equal number of grog shops and gambling dens. Because of the flood of unwashed Irish immigrants, anti-Catholic sentiment ran high. Murderous gangs of xenophobic hooligans called Know-Nothings roamed the streets at night, and no Catholic was safe. The parish priest was dragged off in the middle of mass, brutally beaten, and left naked and bloody in the middle of High Street, and the original wooden church was burned to the ground.

"Sister Januarius arrived two weeks after this incident. Because the situation was so bad, the bishop of New York asked that she return to her order, the Nursing Sisters of the Cross. She refused. She said that St. Benedict and St. Teresa of Ávila came to her at night in the form of hummingbirds and told her to stay. It is certain that she was seized by an irresistible religious fervor. She knocked on every door in the parish; she personally closed a hundred brothels with her proselytizing; and she won converts and doubled the congregation of St. Basil's in three months.

In one year a new brick church stood on the spot of the old one. In five years she was able to oversee the construction of the dome and steeple and the transepts. Five years after that she obtained a dispensation from Pope Pius the Ninth to create the cathedral you see now, the first on Long Island.

"These are the actions of an able administrator, you might say, an energetic woman. But Sister Januarius possessed other, more mysterious abilities. The sick came to her door and were healed with a touch. The hungry were fed by the hundreds on days when the church's larders were absolutely empty. After a lifetime of service to the parish, she died here at one hundred one years old in 1919, a peaceful death at vespers, and it was said by those present that angels hovered around her bedside just beyond the edge of seeing, ready to bear her soul to paradise. . . ."

At this, Father Rose straightens and swings the putter in my direction, his face lit by a sort of madness. A pinch of mortar crumbles from between the stone walls into a half open box of yellow papers.

"I'm not making all this up, Mr. Conti! A short monograph was written in the 1920s and privately published, containing the bare facts of her life and an account of a few of her many miracles. We had a copy in the library upstairs until recently. Somehow it has been misplaced, and I can't locate another one. But I'm hoping the rest of Sister Januarius's story might be buried in these papers here. I am particularly interested in contemporary accounts of miracles. It is my conviction that we have an unrecognized saint on our hands. One of the blessed, worthy of a cultus conveyed by the church. As I've said, Brooklyn needs a saint. Brooklyn is desperate, its jails are full; its people live without light. You are going to find us one, a saint who will intercede for us with the Almighty."

"O.K.," I say, trying to sound reasonable. "How do I go about finding you a saint?"

"It's a legal procedure. Ancient, time-honored. A suit of law is pleaded before the tribunal of the Congregation of Rites in Rome. This is a permanent commission of cardinals charged to investigate such matters, but of course, the supreme judge in cases of sainthood is the pontiff himself."

I don't think the pope more than a pious man in a funny hat, but I can't help it; the back of my neck prickles.

"The procedure is loaded with formalities and mysteries," the priest says after a breath. "The defense, if you will, must provide three distinct proofs of sainthood. First, a reputation for sanctity must be established. Second, the heroic quality of the virtues exhibited by the prospective saint must be shown. And third, of course, evidence must be gathered to establish the working of miracles."

I eye the thirty moldering boxes of paperwork, most of it more than a century old, illegible and dusty. Lately I've been developing allergies. Just the thought of this kind of work makes my nose itch. I pull my handkerchief out of my pocket in time to catch the sneeze.

"Bless you," Father Rose says.

"Seems like kind of a long shot, to be honest, Father," I say. "And there's no guarantees. History has a way of confounding our expectations."

He nods, strides to one end of the small room, putter behind his back, and strides back again.

"As a young priest," he says, "I remember coming across a letter in the archives at St. Catherine's that detailed a miracle performed by Sister Januarius. A child born blind was brought before her. Its eyes were turned inward, just a sliver of the cornea showing in the whites. In the presence of witnesses, Sister Januarius removed the child's eyes with her bare hands, replaced them correctly, and the child could see for the first time in its life. If this letter exists — and I remember it clearly — surely others exist as well. We need them as evidence for Rome. And there are probably newspaper accounts and perhaps other letters in private hands, but that's your business. Brooklyn is counting on you, Mr. Conti."

After he leaves, I am alone in the crypt, and I sneeze again, three times in a row. The stone walls sweat and flake, old mortar drifting through the cracks like sand. It would take six researchers a year to go through this mess thoroughly, to read every page, to dig between the lines. Father Rose believes in Divine Providence, in the intervention of the saints on behalf of a sinful humanity. I remain a skeptic.

I reach into the nearest box and extract a letter. Its thin, illegible sheets crumble in my hand.

6

Molasses Hill is abandoned to the heat and shadows of the afternoon. Old derricks rust quietly on the disused docks just ahead. The smokestacks of the power plant puff clouds of cottony white smoke into the blue sky. Sparkling in the sun, the East River looks fresh and innocent as a mountain stream.

My footsteps echo against the brick walls of the warehouses as I descend through the empty streets. The neighborhood seems innocent, appeased in this light. It is not. The Decateur Projects loom in the near distance like a malevolent deity about to demand the sacrifice of virgins. According to an article in *The New York Times Magazine* last month, those eight towers boast a higher casualty rate per capita than U.S. ground troops during the Vietnam War. There are sirens and gunshots in the near distance every night. Murder and muggings are commonplace around here. Bodies pop up at the rate of three or four a month.

Barely a week after I had moved in and unpacked my suitcases the cops found somebody's girlfriend hacked to pieces and stuffed in Hefty bags in the Dumpster around the corner. A couple of years later, smoking a cigar in his underwear on the stoop, Molesworth was knocked on the head by two gangsta youths with pantyhose pulled over their faces. They forced him upstairs at gunpoint, took the stereo, the microwave, and an unopened box of brown sugar–cinnamon Pop-Tarts. I've been lucky so far, cheated the statistics. My time will come. In any other city you would move. Not in New York, not at these prices, ghost or no ghost.

Last month, attempting to find a clue to the identity of the ghost, I spent half a week in the archives of the Brooklyn Library in Park Slope. I learned nothing about the ghost but a little more about the neighborhood. It was called Molasses Hill for the barrels of molasses once rolled by the thousands down the slight, cobbled incline to the river, loaded onto sailing ships, and traded somewhere along the chain of commerce for slaves. In the late 1840s Irish immigrants displaced the original mercantile Dutch and Anglo-Saxons. The Italians came just before the turn of the century. St. Cecelia's of Livorno, a rather grand Italian church full of marble and statuary, once stood two blocks up at the intersection of Jade and Blount.

A few of the remaining structures date from around 1820 and are among the oldest left standing in South Brooklyn, but of little interest to the architectural historian. They are not graced with embellishments of any kind, no Federal-style fanlights, no rococo iron railings. Low, plain-fronted, ugly dwellings of local brick and clapboard, they were built by ships' carpenters from the navy yard as rooming houses for dockworkers and sailors. Inside, the low ceilings, irregular doorways, and dim passages feel claustrophobic, like the hold of a ship. My haunted apartment occupies the top floor of one of these, an ancient green and white three-story building two doors down Portsmouth from Jade, at number 624.

Sometime in the late sixties, the last Italian families gave way to the current population of seedy, down-at-heel bohemians who infest the neighborhood like cockroaches: failed artists, alcoholic writers, photographers whose darkroom equipment has been stolen from vans long since sold to pay the rent, musicians who have not seen the inside of a club in years. These days the neighborhood has become a sort of terminus. The last place you fall to when you're falling, when your nerve is gone — cheap rents and failed promise, the place to brood on the wreckage of life, the mistakes, the missed opportunities, the woman that got away.

The mob-run garbage concern that owns most of the local property in absentia knocked down St. Cecelia's a decade ago, fenced in the property, and turned it into a garbage dump. This accounts for the rotten miasma that festers over us on the hot, airless summer days. But Chase was right. The atmosphere out here suits my disposition, the low-rent brand of melancholia, the petty inertias that have possessed my life since graduate school. Midway through life's journey, as the poet says, the true way was lost and I found myself in a dark and terrible wood . . .

Or just in Molasses Hill, Brooklyn, barely one stop out on the F from Manhattan. I'm not down for the count, I have only to finish my thesis.

Still, it's getting late.

7

The message counter reads 5, but the number is blinking, which is a sign of something gone awry. I hit the play button to find that the ghost has invaded my answering machine.

The first message is a long silence with eerie knocking noises in the background; the second a roaring like the inside of a seashell which ends with a small, childlike whimper. I listen to these, hair prickling on the back of my neck. For a moment I am sure there is someone standing just behind me. I spin around to the same empty room, the same dust thick on every surface.

This is unbearable. Then I hear the steady tap of a typewriter from the apartment downstairs. Rust is home.

Jim Rust answers the door barefoot, wearing the thick denim workshirt and jeans he wears all year round.

"Busy?" I say.

He shrugs, wipes his wire-rim glasses on his sleeve. "You look like hell. Better come on inside."

I step into the tiny, neat apartment. Its walls are lined with books carefully alphabetized, floor to ceiling. The only item of decor is an Indian blanket pegged over the fireplace. "Lakota Sioux, at least a hundred years old," he told me once. "Inherited it when my brother was killed by the U.S. government." And that's all he told me.

Like other westerners I've met, Rust never says enough and has a habit of squinting toward the horizon when he's turning something over in his mind, even if there's no horizon to be seen. He's got a wind-weathered, outdoor face set off by eyes the weary blue of cactus flowers. Born on a farm in Wyoming, he grew sugar beets, worked horses across one big empty state or another out West, worked the rodeo circuit in Mexico in the early seventies. Then, one day, he decided to write. He sold his pickup truck, his horse and trailer, bought a typewriter — an ancient Remington Rand noiseless, which is about as noiseless as a truck in third gear pulling up a grade — and moved to New York City.

Rust claims he loves this town, and I believe him. He loves it with the fierceness of someone raised in a place with too much sky. He bought a black leather jacket, a ten-year membership in the MOMA; he joined a socialist writers' group and attends the ballet at Lincoln Center and Noh theater performances at the Japan Society. But despite all this culture, he is still a good ex-cowboy at heart, and he couldn't bring himself to part with his hat or his boots. The hat, a battered black affair with a flat brim and tarnished silver coins strung around the crown, hangs above his sleeping bag and bookcases in the bedroom. The boots of red and black leather and lizard skin, wrought with fancy gold stitchery and comfortably worn, slouch in the corner like an old friend. There is a patched hole about the size of a .45 slug shot through just above the ankle of one of them. They were specially made for Rust during his rodeo days by a famous Mexican bootmaker in Durango. About the bullet hole he'll say nothing specific.

"Get yourself a beer," he says now, and gestures toward the battered Coleman ice chest in the far corner which he uses for perishables. He goes over to put away his work as I dig through the slush for a bottle of Vera Cruz.

"You?" I say.

"Why not? Guess I was about done," he says even though I know he's just pulled his writing gear out of the closet. He writes standing up, the typewriter sitting on an upended old steamer trunk, two stacks of paper, one covered with typescript, one blank, carefully arranged on either wing.

We settle cross-legged on the floor with our beers like two Indians. Rust lives in this apartment like he's camping out on the chaparral. No furniture, no stove, no refrigerator, no real possessions. Except for the books, everything he owns could fit on the back of a mule. Overhead the ceiling fan wobbles dangerously. We pop the bottles and drink, and the only sound in the apartment is the small slurp of beer.

"How's the novel coming?" I ask after a while. I set the beer down on the painted blue wood. It is a foolish question that I know Rust will not answer to any satisfaction.

"It's not exactly a novel," he says.

"So what is it?"

"Couldn't say. Writing. A mess of writing."

"So how's it coming?"

He pauses and squints toward the horizon. "Fair."

We drink some more, and out of politeness Rust asks me about my thesis.

"Can't concentrate," I say. "The ghost. Try writing your thesis in the middle of a haunting. It's impossible. And the silence. It's so damn thick. Pregnant if I may say."

"I've got a suggestion," Rust says, leaning forward. "Put on the radio, and you won't hear the silence. You'll hear the radio."

"Yeah, but the radio —"

"Classical station. A little Mozart. Vivaldi. One of those geezers. Works wonders, you'll be surprised."

Rust believes in the ghost, though in other matters he is a skeptic and a rationalist. It was he who put a name to the presence in the first place:

A few days after Molesworth's inglorious flight to Mamou, I asked Rust upstairs and shut him in the apartment while I waited on the landing, chewing on a cold piece of pepperoni pizza from his ice chest. He emerged ten minutes later, squinting at a horizon no one else could see.

"Well?" I said.

He nodded. "Something. Makes your ears pop."

"What do you think it is?"

"A ghost."

"Exactly."

Now Rust rolls a cigarette from the suede pouch of tobacco and fixings he keeps in his breast pocket. He offers one; I shake my head. That tobacco of his, a cheap Mexican blend a friend sends from Chiapas, tastes like burnt seaweed.

"I was staying in a cabin once in Colorado," he says, shaking out the match. "Place belonged to my uncle, my mama's brother. Don't remember what I was doing there, working, I guess, writing on another book. I stayed in this place four or five nights, up in the foothills above Tabernash. Cougar country, you could hear them big cats yowling at night from the pine bluff. And cold as hell, just about zero outside, too cold to snow, but I slept outside after the first night, wrapped in my bedroll and a half dozen buffalo skins. Was worse inside the cabin. Got this strange, thick feeling, just like the one you got upstairs. Couldn't sleep. Don't know how you sleep up there."

"I don't," I say. "Not well. Strange dreams.

41

A lot of tossing and turning."

"In any case, I find out that in this cabin supposedly some bastard killed a woman going back about thirty years. Cut her throat, gutted her, skinned her, hung her up to dry, and cured the meat. When they busted in on him, he was grinding her liver for sausages. Things like that, they linger in the air, you know?"

Rust has a way of hitting the nail on the head. The last mouthful of the Vera Cruz suddenly tastes like lead. What horrors were cooked up on my stove? I wonder. What terrible haunches stored in the refrigerator? And these morbid considerations lead to others. It strikes me suddenly that I don't take care of myself, that I am going to seed. That I am getting older, thirty-three in November, that I don't eat well, that I have no health insurance, that I have squandered my early promise, that there is no one in this city who loves me.

And just then, as if in dreadful affirmation, the power plant vents steam into the night sky. A rush of white rises beyond the window, and a great mechanical clanging rings out over Brooklyn like a scream.

8

Friday, dusk.

I am in Manhattan to pick up a last check

from my temp agency. Then, to escape the crush in the streets, I stop for a beer at the Crescent City Grill, a cheesy pseudo-Louisiana bar on East Broadway with an unaccountably reasonable happy hour. From 4:00 to 8:00 P.M. on Fridays, bottles of Abita are $2.25. As far as I know, this is the only place above the Mason-Dixon Line that serves Abita, which is New Orleans's hometown brew.

Louisiana is very trendy just now in New York. There are any number of imitation Cajun saloons, faux-Creole cafés, expensive East Side restaurants that feature down-home southern cooking at ridiculous uptown prices. New Yorkers are like the French in their childish attraction to what passes for genuine Americana; to country music, cowboy boots, deep-fried gator nuggets, sippin' whiskey, and all such redneck nonsense. This is because New York is really its own small nation; insular and provincial in the sense that New Yorkers do not know or care what's going on outside the five boroughs. Thus Dallas or Baton Rouge are as foreign and exotic to someone from New York as they would be to someone from Paris or Berlin.

The Crescent City Grill is Disneyland phony, with fake papier-mâché Mardi Gras heads and pressed rebel flags suspended from the ceiling, the severed bed of a 1959 Ford pickup for the DJ's booth. The bartender is an Irishman from Cork. But it is I who feel like an impostor here in my wrinkled thrift-store button-down and

stained tie among all the pressed happy hour yuppies hitting on each other over steaming mugs
of Bud Light. They could be anywhere, it doesn't
matter. A land of bar codes and spread sheets
and marketing strategies and units of merchandise.

Anywhere is a place I don't belong.

Later, at the intersection of Houston and Mer-
cer, pedestrians seem hushed beneath the strange
lavender twilight that blooms above the island,
moving in a dream. I stop and look up and can
almost feel it touching my face like the secret
ray shone upon a man visited by benevolent aliens
in a science fiction movie. This light is marvelous,
the color of longing and nostalgia, the devil's own
melancholy, the color of a woman's lips as you
are about to kiss them at midnight beneath the
neon of a deserted bar in a city you don't know
well.

After a few Abitas at Crescent City, I can't
help thinking of New Orleans and Antoinette;
though strictly sober, I try to resist the impulse.
Once I went and sang under Antoinette's window
in the Faubourg Marigny. A tiny trellis balcony
opened onto her bedroom. It was after 3 A.M.,
and we had agreed not to see each other that
night, but she came out sleepy-eyed in her slip,
and leaned lazy and smiling on the railing as I
yodeled "San Antonio Rose" in a passable Italian
tenor inherited from my father, and Molesworth
played straight-faced accompaniment, mandolin
propped against his gut.

" 'Moon in all your splendor,' " I sang, " 'so

lonely my heart. Call back my rose, rose of San
Antone. . . .' " The sky glowing not lavender
but green over New Orleans and Algiers, over
the Gulf, over Cuba and the Tortugas swimming
on the far horizon, as from the Mississippi in
that vanished hour the whistle of a tanker passing
like the thin wail of longing.

A small outdoor café has sprung up on the
asphalt triangle between Houston and East First,
not twenty steps from the yellow mouth of the
Second Avenue F.

Colored lights are strung above a dozen tables
in a roped-off square; a jazz trio plays against
the chain-link fence of the basketball courts.
Trucks roar down Houston toward the Gothic
crenellation of the Williamsburg Bridge; cabs
squeal in and out of traffic. A half dozen winos,
filthy and stinking of urine, congregate around
the perimeter, bumming cigarettes. It seems an
unlikely spot for a café, but most of the tables
are full of junkie-skinny East Village types in
retro-seventies outfits and platform shoes. Their
bell-bottoms flare from ankles I could encircle
with thumb and forefinger.

I decide to stop for a last beer, just for the
novel idea of drinking on a traffic island and because it is Friday night. The waiter, an English-
man with the usual mouthful of bad teeth, comes
over with a bottle of Fuller's ESB topped with
a plastic cup.

"It's all we've got right now," he says. "Either

this or water, and you can't drink water and sit here. You want to hear the music without drinking, you've got to stand outside with them." He thumbs toward the winos, the sad orange tips of their bummed cigarettes burning in the darkness. I nod, and the waiter sets the beer down and goes away.

The trio is plugged into a yellow extension cord stretched to a tenement building across the street. The lead singer, an overweight young woman with a Greek look to her sharp features, snaps her fingers and starts to breathe the lyrics of "Birdland" into the microphone when a spark flies from somewhere and the sound system goes dead. In a moment the colored lights flicker off, and we are sunk in the fluorescent gloom of the street.

An exhausted sigh goes up from the crowd. The English waiter stands on a chair and waves his hands. "Don't go anywhere, people," he says. "Just a question of fuses. Happened last night." Then he jumps down, dodges a cab, and disappears into the dark hallway of the tenement.

I look around in the dimness at my neighbors. To my left, a body-pierced woman with Auschwitz cropped hair smokes a cigarette like a European intellectual, the heel of her hand pressed to her chin. It's not hard to imagine her life. I have a vague picture: the cats, the boyfriend in an avant-garde band, the casual drug use, the vague artistic ambitions, the filth of a fifth-floor walk-up shared with six other young men and women much like herself. But what does she think about? She wears a large crucifix, yet it seems impossible that she believes in God. Does she instead believe in style? That what you look like is a better test of character than what you do?

I am lost in these heady considerations when I spot a familiar silhouette at a table against the far rope on the Second Avenue side. Those stooped shoulders and the odd angle of the neck, like a thick tube sticking straight up from the spine. And even from this distance and in the poor light and half turned away, you can see there is something wrong with that face. It is pushed in, uneven, a poorly executed mask. It is Chase.

She is tracing a despondent swirl in the gloom with her cigarette, underlining the words of a conversation I cannot hear. All I can make out of the woman sitting across from her in the shadows is one pale, bony, tattooed arm.

Chase has become extremely depressed of late. She turned thirty in the spring and — as she is fond of pointing out — has already lived four years longer than the poet Keats. When we first met, she had just graduated from Brown and was full of offbeat intelligence, nervous energy, irreverence, and spunk. You never knew what she would say next. The maudlin side was there, but submerged beneath a protective coating of youth. Now it seems the low moments are all she has. Her sole remaining topic of conversation involves how she is still a virgin, how her face has cheated her out of a life in the world.

In truth I have been avoiding Chase lately and have neglected to return the last three or four messages left on my machine. I feel guilty about this, but it is all I can do to keep myself afloat these days. Still, anything is better than drinking alone on Friday night. I step over to her table, Fuller's ESB and plastic cup in hand.

"Hey, Chase . . ."

She turns and registers my presence with a quick disapproving blink.

"Ned," she says without enthusiasm.

Her companion is a bone-thin young woman with an exquisitely sculpted face and pale blond hair. It takes me a moment to recognize Jillian Sumner, an old friend of Chase's from Brown. I am shocked. When I last saw Jillian, she was voluptuous and sexy and weighed at least forty pounds more than she does tonight. She looks like she has just gotten back from six months in a cave in Transylvania, living on bat wings and water.

"Some kind of style thing, Jillian?" I say. "Don't you know cadaver chic is a little passé?"

Jillian sneers up at me. "The bastard's here," she says, waving her cigarette toward the chair between them. "Sit down, bastard."

Chase shakes her head. "I'm not speaking to him right now," she says.

"Fuck that," Jillian says. "I like to talk to bastards every once in a while. Like to hear the bastard's side of the story."

I see they are both drunk. Jillian is slurring

48

her words. The table is cluttered with empty bottles of Fuller's. This is pretty potent stuff. Chase tells me they have been drinking since four in the afternoon.

"We were the first customers here," she says.

Jillian tugs at the seam of my khaki pants and pulls me roughly into the chair. It is an accepted fact among Chase's friends that Jillian and I despise each other. This isn't exactly true. It's more a question of aesthetic differences. Somewhere beneath the layers of bohemian cynicism and dread, I still believe in responsibility, honor, freshly mowed lawns, Manifest Destiny, and the virtues of married life — the old bourgeois song and dance. Jillian believes in nothing.

Her story is sad, typical of a certain kind of fucked-up rich kid: At nineteen she was a Grace Kelly-esque blonde from a wealthy family of *Mayflower* stock. She possessed classic looks, a large trust fund, a beautiful voice, and a bright future in professional opera. I once saw her give a recital from Puccini's *Madama Butterfly* at the Solarium in Providence. It was breathtaking, brought tears to my eyes. But all this promise seemed to rest on a foundation of darkness. Ten years later her trust fund is gone, she shoots heroin enough to be called an addict, works the peep shows along Eighth Avenue, and for smack money does an occasional porn film under the name April Storm.

A while back, for reasons I do not care to examine, I caught the afternoon show of Jillian's last film, *Anal Annie's Ecstasy Girls* at the Paramour on Forty-second Street. In one memorable scene she straps on a huge flesh-colored dildo, rolls a buxom redhead ass up, and proceeds to impale the squealing young woman with gleeful abandon.

One can only hope that Jillian's Pilgrim fore-fathers are mercifully shielded from any knowledge of such doings in the granite heaven which they have attained for their devotion to godliness. Had they only known what fate awaited their progeny on these green shores when they set buckled shoe to Plymouth Rock in 1620, they would have sunk the *Mayflower* with all hands in Massachusetts Bay in horror.

"We were just talking about you, bastard," she says now, turning away from me to light another cigarette, though the one she's got is still burning in the ashtray. In profile she still looks more like Grace Kelly than it is possible for anyone to look, and my heart sighs.

"What were you saying?" I ask, though I don't really want to know.

"We were saying how I've called you six fuck-ing times in the last two weeks," Chase says, "and you haven't called back once."

"I didn't get any messages," I lie.

"Bullshit," Chase says.

"Really, the answering machine's been messing up," I say. This at least is true; it has been invaded by a ghost.

"It was for the bastard's own goddamned good, that's what gets me," Jillian says to Chase. "Not only is he a bastard he is a selfish bastard."

"I'll leave you two drunks alone," I say, and am about to go back to my table when Chase puts a dry hand on my arm.

"Someone is trying to contact you from the Other Side," she says. Her eyes are dark and serious. The back of my neck goes cold. I haven't told Chase a word about the haunting, mostly because for years I have been scoffing at her belief in ghosts and other spiritual ridiculousness. Just then a half-ton pickup truck full of used wire coat hangers jounces over a pothole along Houston, and a few of the rusty metal things bounce clattering to the sidewalk. This gives me a moment to compose myself.

"What other side?" I manage. "You mean, New Jersey?"

"That's right, be a bastard about it, bastard," Jillian says, and she lurches up from the table. "I'm going to get some cigarettes."

"But you've already got cigarettes," Chase says, pointing to the butts burning in the ashtray.

"Whatever," Jillian says, and steps over the rope barrier and stumbles off into the night.

When Jillian is gone, Chase turns her dark eyes to me again. Her misshapen face looks like a skull in the yellow light of the street.

"I've been having these dreams," she says. "Very vivid, very clear. Someone wants to talk to you. I had six dreams and called you each time. Finally, in the last dream, I just wrote down your phone number and gave it to this hand stick-

51

ing out of a cloud. A woman's hand with a lot of rings. Get any weird calls lately?"

I hang on to the edge of the table to keep myself from shaking. "Just my bill collectors," I say through my teeth. "College loans. They're getting pretty aggressive."

"And she said something about you and her cousin. I couldn't quite get it. That's all I can tell you right now."

"Chase, can we talk about something else?"

At last the lights go back on, and the English waiter returns, and the music starts up again. We wait for Jillian to come back, but after two hours there is no sign of her; she has probably gone off to score some heroin. Then I am drunk and Chase is drunker, and we go over to Stella's on Second Avenue and then to the Telephone Bar and end up at Blue and Gold in one of the booths near the pool table. The balls crack across the worn felt, and ? and the Mysterians' "96 Tears" jangles from the jukebox, and on the walls in the faded hunting mural from the fifties the man in the hunting jacket is never any closer to bagging his bird, and Chase leans into me and tells me again that she can't stand her life.

"I mean it," she says. "I'm getting to the point where I want to jump off the Brooklyn Bridge and put an end to the whole miserable business." Then she asks me to kiss her, but I can't because her lips are all crooked, not really lips at all, but something the plastic surgeons made out of skin from her ass.

"It's O.K.," Chase says when I hang my head. "I don't blame you. Fuck it! In any case, we're all fucked, headed for something weird and terrible. That's another thing I got from my dreams. You and me and Jillian . . ." but in another instant the light in her eyes fades, and she passes out openmouthed against the back of the booth.

In the cab, on the way back to Brooklyn, the Haitian driver races downtown, swearing to himself, running red lights, and blasting voodoo music from the radio — they all hate taking fares across the bridges — but soon we are up Canal, and there is that familiar rumbling of tires on metal grating, and we are high above the river, New York spread out and dressed in false spangles and flickering lights on all sides, as pristine in the moonlight as St. Augustine's vision of the City of God. And for a single moment, despite Chase's dire predictions, it seems to me that the odds might be with us, it seems our lives might work out all right in the end.

Of course, the Manhattan Bridge has this effect: city glittering below, a small rush of optimism like a mirage at the summit.

9

Monday night again, just after eleven, and the sky is black with storms and the smokestacks of the power plant across the street, and I am sitting in my living room in the orange Naugahyde easy chair trying to eat a bowl of Froot Loops for dinner, but I am paralyzed by fear. The lights in the apartment have dimmed in a sort of supernatural brownout, and the ghost is at work shifting the furniture.

I was watching the eleven o'clock news when the television went to static and the furniture started creaking like the hull of an old ship. Now the hair on my arms stands on end, fear dances with the electricity on my skin, my ears pop. It is like being in the middle of a decompression chamber in which the pressure is fluctuating rapidly. To my left the desk chair falls over as if in a strong wind. Then the refrigerator door opens by itself with a small sucking sound. Ghoulish white light, illuminating ketchup, beer bottles, and day-old bagels, shines from within.

The poltergeist has moved furniture before, but I am not prepared for what happens next: The heavy bookcase across the room begins to bow and creak, books spilling across the floor. Suddenly it takes a short hop, then another, and all I can think of is animated dancing teacups in Walt Disney movies. Through a sickening sort of parody of human movement, the bookcase hops and splinters a good five feet in my direction, hesitates for a moment in a gesture that is somehow feminine, then falls face forward with a great crash. In the next second the lights flare up, and the pressure releases its grip from the back of my neck, and the television picture wobbles back into place with the news again, and everything is back to normal.

I sigh and take another mouthful of the Froot Loops, which have gone soggy in the bowl. Then it occurs to me that if the ghost can send bookcases full of history texts hopping across the room, it can just as easily send the same bookcases crashing down on my head. And with the finality of a key slipping into a lock, I realize that the ghost is growing stronger each day and that maybe it is trying to kill me.

10

At noon I find Father Rose practicing his swing in the churchyard. He is perched atop a low sepulcher, cleats of his golf shoes dug into the old sandstone slab, a nine iron in hand. The pouches of his cassock bulge with hollow practice balls. They make a whistling sound as he sends them arcing crisply through the air, a white blur in the hot wind till they bounce off their target, the black obelisk about twenty yards distant.

"Mr. Conti," he says as I ascend the narrow stairs from the crypt, "please don't think me disrespectful of those who lie here." He climbs down from the stone, pulls off golf gloves of Italian leather, and shakes my hand.

"The thought hadn't entered my mind, Father," I say. He winks at me. We have acquired a certain conspiratorial air, as if together he and I will pull something over on the pope.

"It's just that I think the dead don't mind a little company every now and then."

I blink in the strong light and sneeze. The sun is hard on my eyes after the dimness of the crypt. My allergies are going crazy. Each box of documents seems to have its own special species of mold spores. Some make my eyes water; some make me cough; some send me into paroxysms of sneezing. I sneeze again, and Father Rose blesses me and waves the nine iron in my face.

"You see this?"

"Yes," I say.

"A nine iron, I'm practicing my chip shot today," he says and assumes the lecturing, priestly tone he reserves for golf and God. "The chip shot is one of the least practiced shots, widely undervalued by good golfers simply because deep down, good golfers feel their game should consist only of the drive and the putt. You drive onto the green in one or two shots, you putt. Simple, right? Of course, even the best of us are not skilled enough to get the ball on the green in perfect drives every time. We land in the rough just shy of the green or, God forbid, in a trap. This is where the chip shot is our greatest ally. If the ball gone off course is like sin — you will allow me this clumsy metaphor — then the chip becomes a sort of necessary penance. And ignoring the chip shot is a great vanity, which is itself a mortal sin. Do you catch what I'm driving at?"

I say I do. Father Rose smiles, eyelids half closed, serene as a cardinal. Then he follows me back down into the crypt and installs himself in the broken chair for a status report. He is not a suspicious man, exactly, but he is careful and monitors my progress with the archives twice a week.

"So, how's it coming?" he says now.

I wade through the mess like a fisherman in hip boots. A fly buzzes around the bare bulb above as I hold a thick yellow sheet to the light.

" '. . . and though our life in this new country is a hardship,' " I read aloud, " 'and the depredations of the savages on nearby homesteads have been reported with increasing frequency, still my husband and I believe this open landscape is most nourishing to the soul. Better here, with savages and hoot owls and beasts of prey for company, than back East among the denizens of the false and wicked cities we have left behind. On Sundays, in the absence of a Church and Mass, I walk with my children upon the prairie surrounded by the works of the Divine Hand. . . .' Beautiful sentiment, don't you think, Father?"

He frowns. "What is that?"

"A letter from a member of the parish who emigrated to a frontier settlement around 1846. Of some interest as a historical document, I'd say."

"Written to whom?" The priest's eyes light up.

"Not sure," I say. "The first and last pages are missing."

"Ah." He turns to the table and leafs absently through a stack of gas bills from the 1880s.

"As you can see there, the rectory was converted to gas illumination in 1876," I say. "And wired for electricity rather late, in the teens of this century."

"All this is very interesting," Father Rose says, an impatient edge in his voice. "But not what we're looking for. I'm just starting to prepare the paperwork for the Congregation of Rites. I've got a letter in to the bishop. It's a very complex procedure. I need something concrete. Soon."

"Sorry, no miracles, Father. But I have gone through a lot of paper already." I gesture to the piles stacked neatly all around — "and I'm about to go through a lot more. And I've been to the Brooklyn Historical Society and to the archives of the archdiocese. It's almost as if history swallowed up our saint. I've even advertised in the historical journals. A call for letters, information, anything. Nothing yet."

I can see he is disappointed. He rises, takes a tentative step toward the iron gate opening into the crypt. Out there in the sepulchral gloom an old woman kneels before a memorial tablet set into the wall. An electric votive candle flickers in the alcove beside a black-and-white portrait of a young man encased in an oval of clear celluloid. In the background, always, even through these thick walls, the sound of traffic.

"Father?"

He turns back.

"I wonder if I could consult you on another matter?"

We go upstairs to his bright and cheery office on the third floor of the rectory and, surrounded by golf trophies, I tell him about the ghost. I am nervous talking about it and suppress an urge to kneel and say the act of contrition, like a ten-year-old at his first confession, as if the ghost has been brought on by my own unforgiven sins. He leans back in his chair and presses his fingertips together.

"Do you think this is a malicious presence?" he says at last.

"Hard to say, Father. First the stones, now the furniture. And I always feel there's someone looking over my shoulder. It's really very oppressive."

"Why do you tell me all this, Mr. Conti?"

"I thought you might have a suggestion as to how to get rid of it," I say. "A relocation, so to speak."

"You mean bell, book, and candle. Obscure Latin incantations."

I shift uncomfortably in my chair.

"Ghosts are no longer the province of the

church, I'm afraid. Only spirits."

"There's a difference?"

"Of course. You've heard of Vatican Two?"

"Sure."

"Vatican Two cleaned house on many archaic practices. Exorcism was one of them. I'm not saying they are no longer performed, ever. Just extremely rarely. And there is an unofficial policy disapproving of such activities. Currently it's up to the individual bishops whether or not to allow exorcisms to take place in their diocese. Bishop Allen frowns on them most definitely. These days the church believes in psychology and repressed memory. Our interests lie with Freud and therapy. Not ghosts and demons."

"What about saints?"

He ignores this. "If I were to authorize an exorcism in my parish, and word reached the bishop," he says, "I would be sent to a dude ranch in Arizona to recuperate with all those other wacko priests who can't keep their hands off the altar boys. And that's not the sort of company I care to be locked up with for ten or twelve months."

Sculptural light gleams off the polished trophies in their cases. Arnold Palmer smiles down benevolently. Here it is hard to believe in the haunted stillness of the apartment at 3 A.M., ghost frittering like a moth against the screen in the darkness.

Father Rose rises and takes his putter from the plaid golf bag in the corner.

60

"Anything else?"

I hesitate. "Advice? Helpful hints?"

He leans over and makes a pass at one of the practice balls strewn across the carpet. Then he straightens and fixes his sad brown eyes upon me.

"Yes. You live in a terrible neighborhood, in an apartment subject to unusual disturbances. My advice is very simple. Move."

11

On Thursday Rust and I take the train uptown to see a restored print of Nicholas Ray's *55 Days at Peking* on the big screen at the Gotham on Third Avenue.

The film is terrible, a misbegotten epic about the siege of the European community at Peking during the Boxer Rebellion of 1900, starring Charlton Heston, Ava Gardner, and David Niven. It is full of fifties-era hysteria, cardboard Chinamen, bad acting, and misapprehended historical facts, but I hardly notice.

I can't concentrate on the plot because I am still brooding over the priest's advice. I have been brooding over the priest's advice for two days now. I have checked and rechecked the classifieds in the *Voice*. The conclusion is inescapable. This is New York. They rent hallway space for five hundred dollars a month. And until I can save first and last and security deposit — about two thousand dollars — I cannot afford to move.

After the movie we wait on the empty station platform for the Brooklyn-bound F at Fifty-third Street, two levels down. We wait for a long time, but there is no sign of the F, not even the barest glimmer along the tracks. The stink down here is awful and the heat is intense. Rats scurry back and forth across the track bed between garbage and pools of black water. From somewhere comes a slow dripping sound. I feel like an extra in a Sergio Leone western, caught in one of those huge CinemaScope close-ups of desperadoes waiting for someone to kill on the Santa Fe express.

Rust scuffs along the platform edge. Then he spins on the heels of his boots to face me. We are discussing my dilemma.

"Let me tell you a story," he says.

I roll my eyes.

"Back about twenty-odd years I worked as a ranch hand at a hacienda in Mexico, Chiapas State. The owners were very rich. Old-time landowners. The deed signed by King Carlos of Spain hung in a big frame in the hall of the hacienda. Consuela, the daughter, had a spirit attached to her, a poltergeist, like you. When she was around, the thing would dump bowls of chili on people's heads, knock paintings off the walls, slam doors. Once tossed the cat into a tub of tequila punch at a dance they held in the ballroom. Would have been kind of funny except how the whole thing ended. One night, the girl vanished. She just wasn't in her room in the morning. A week we looked for her. They had us ranch hands combing the whole countryside. When it got dark, we took torches up into the hills. But that wasn't how we found her. We found her because of the birds."

"Birds" I say, a lump in the pit of my stomach. "What birds?"

"All of a sudden, there were vultures congregating on the roof of the hacienda. No one noticed till there were a half dozen up there, big, evil black birds staring down at us. Finally, Luis put a ladder to the eaves and climbed up and there she was, poor kid, what was left of her. Eyes and all the soft parts eaten out by the vultures. Clenched in her left hand was a bottle of rat poison from the kitchen. At the inquest they said that was how she died, her tongue was black with the stuff. They called it a suicide. But how she got onto the roof no one can say. There was no way up from the inside of the house. Not for a girl of thirteen. Some people say it was the ghost, the poltergeist, that took her up there somehow, that put the poison in her hand. I don't know. I do know that it's not healthy living with the damn things. Like living with a gas leak. Sooner or later there's going to be an explosion."

I open my mouth to speak but am overcome with exhaustion. I don't want to think about it anymore.

Now a few more passengers wait along the platform. An impeccably dressed old man talks to himself a mile a minute; two black teenagers wrapped in leather parkas despite the heat slouch over a boom box blaring rap; a thin, sad-looking woman stares with intensity at the third rail. Rust looks up suddenly, and in that instant there is a hot wind from the tunnel followed by a great roar. At this sound about twenty Puerto Rican youths pound down from the local track above, and the platform is full. But the train pulls into the station to groans and swearing from the crowd. It is a work train, its flat sides painted in yellow and black stripes like a plague ship, its windows barred.

The work train idles in the station inexplicably for the next fifteen minutes. Men in light blue transit uniforms mill about inside the single car. The caboose is a flatbed full of junk, mangled turnstiles, scrap iron. Finally another train pulls in on the upstairs track, and there is the tread of heavy boots on the stairs. Five transit workers, wearing sidearms and showing the brassy glint of extra cartridges from bandoliers, march quickly down onto the platform. They are escorting two nervous men in suits who carry small black suitcases. The doors open, the guards and men step into the yellow light, and in a moment the work train is gone, lurching off into the darkness of the tunnel.

I look over at Rust. He shrugs.

"New York," he says. "You never know what's going on. Not really. All we know is what they tell us. And they don't tell us much."

He is right. This city is one vast conspiracy, a riddle whose answer has been cleverly concealed from us. There is something we're not getting, though there are certain clues: Steam rises from the streets; the pavement rumbles; the bedrock beneath our feet is shot through with tunnels and secret passages, arteries leading into the gloom beneath skyscrapers to a secret terminus where the city's own heart is revealed beating and horrible, tended lovingly by transit workers like a queen by worker ants — the ventricles of its machine pump fueled by steam and blood and the dashed hopes of millions.

12

Sunday.

Chase is having a small dinner party in her loft just east of Carroll Gardens for Jillian. I almost refuse to attend, but Sundays are bad. Long, empty afternoons full of whispers and blank sunlight, followed by remorseless evenings, rearing up like a wall of ice.

It's not the food — Chase is an excellent cook, conversant in several obscure Asian cuisines. It's her friends, a motley collection of hipper-than-thou film professionals, acid heads, disaffected youths in jackboots, witches, Communists, performance artists. Rude bohemians with a passionate antipathy for table manners and the everyday

65

kindnesses that are the grease of bourgeois life.

As dark spreads up from the river, I walk up Tide and catch the F train at Knox to Bergen Street. The neighborhood here is mostly Hispanic now, but there is still a block or two of Italians left, a row of Italian restaurants, and a few safe streets, supposedly patrolled by Mafia henchmen. Chase's loft is at the corner of Smith and Baltic, in an old Episcopal church, St. John the Baptist. The church was converted to lofts ten years ago, when the last Episcopalian in Brooklyn fled or died.

The massive, studded doors on the Baltic Street side are equipped with an iron knocker of medieval proportions. Party lights shine through the Gothic stained glass window of Chase's loft, and I hear the crash and hammer of an old Sob Sister tape played at top volume.

After a few minutes Jillian comes down to answer the door, a snifter of whiskey in hand. Her blond hair is bleached white tonight and slicked back, and she looks unhealthy and even thinner than she did at our last meeting. She is wearing a long-sleeve knit top that fits like a wet suit. Her ribs stick out like the ribs in a Dürer painting of Christ crucified.

"Shit. It's the bastard," she says. For a minute it seems she is not going to let me in.

"Jillian, great to see you again," I say, shifting the bottle of cheap California Chablis and offering my hand.

"Whatever," she says, and gives a dismissive

wave and leaves me behind to shut and bolt the doors. I watch her bony butt wag up the stairs for a moment, and I am forced into a sad reflection upon its former luscious proportions. Another beautiful woman gone to the dogs on heroin and New York City. But this isn't exactly fair. Jillian's appalling new look is really the last stage of a general decline from ingenue through porn star to junkie that began many years ago. I blame everything on rock and roll.

At Brown in the early eighties, Chase and Jillian formed an all-girl thrash band called Sob Sister with an art student from the Rhode Island School of Design. Chase plunked the bass; Jillian picked up lead guitar and sang; the art student banged on things. In those days punk was the common language of the counterculture, and Jillian soon became known for her crude tattoos, dissonant shrieking, and disregard for common decency. During the performance of her infamous signature number, "Fuck Me Blind," she would strip naked and masturbate onstage with the head of the microphone. The most obscene part was the wet, squelchy sounds that came though the old Vox amplifiers.

For three years Sob Sister played a series of notorious gigs around Providence and in Boston. They were arrested eight times and briefly signed to the alternative Dischord label out of Washington, D.C. When it was all over, Jillian's voice — trained for opera by the finest coaches money could buy — was ruined beyond repair.

A long table composed of sawhorses and discarded doors is nicely laid out in the main loft space upstairs just beneath a Gothic icicle pointing down from the ceiling. I count twelve black octagonal plates, twelve sets of purposely mismatched silverware. An arrangement of black paper flowers floats in a stainless steel bedpan at the center. I pour some wine and walk down the row of seats, admiring the place settings. Each napkin is folded into a different sort of origami bird. Ashtrays stolen from a Japanese hotel in midtown are balanced on the doorknobs.

"Ever ask yourself what's going on with doors in this city?" I call over to Chase. "People just throw them away. You see them everywhere, in Dumpsters, alleys, just lying along the sidewalk. Then you rent an apartment to find every door has been removed, and you've got to hang up sheets for privacy."

Laboring over a huge wok full of vegetables behind the glass bricks of the kitchen area, Chase ignores me. She has made enough food to feed an army, but so far, besides Jillian and myself, there is only Byron Poydras. He is slumped on the leather couch against the far wall engrossed in a copy of *Gnarl*. Poydras is another bohemian friend of Chase's who does nothing I can put my finger on exactly. I stride across the bare wood expanse to the couch.

"Tell me something, Poydras," I say. "What do you do with your time?"

He looks up from the comic book, lazy as a cat. "Loiter, mostly," he says.

"Okay. Where do you loiter?"

An obscure shrug must pass for an answer.

He is a long-limbed kid of about twenty-seven, of the lanky, Ichabod Crane southern type. A shock of blond hair hangs permanently in front of his face; the buttons of his cuffs are always undone. They dangle limp as wet rags from his wrists. This drives me crazy. I want to button them up, take a comb to his hair. Instead I slump beside him and read over his shoulder. *Gnarl* is an avant-garde comic book that portrays Benito Mussolini as a canny panda bear and Gabriele D'Annunzio and the rest of the blackshirts as malicious raccoons.

"Ned," he says a few pages later, "don't read over my shoulder. It makes me nervous."

It's hard to imagine Poydras nervous about anything, but I move off to replenish my wine. Unlike most of Chase's friends, Poydras and I are on what passes for cordial terms in Bohemia. He hails from New Orleans and through an odd coincidence knew one of Antoinette's sisters at LSU. Though straight, he is heavily involved in the drag show scene that seems to be a staple of East Village life. I find that many transplanted Louisianans participate in these perverse spectacles, which culminate in the Wigstock Festival in Tompkins Square Park in August — a daylong extravaganza of transvestism, female impersonation, and sexual confusion of the first water. Perhaps it is the heritage of Mardi Gras that leads Louisianans in New York to such excesses. After all, in Carnival krewes for well over a century now, men have dressed like women and women like men to the delight of the drunks and tourists along Esplanade and other thoroughfares of that distant city.

We wait an hour, and no one else has shown up. Chase is too busy making the last preparations to notice, but at ten-thirty everything is ready, and she looks around her nearly empty loft, and her crooked eyes brim with tears.

"Not again," she says, a reedy, unhappy sound in her voice. "All this goddamn food."

"It's your lousy friends, Chase," I call out. "They don't show up as a matter of style. It's not cool to be where you say you're going to be when you say you're going to be there. There's a whole new generation of beatniks out there who think keeping appointments is a sign of latent middle-class tendencies."

"You are one uppity-fuck bastard." Jillian waves her snifter of whiskey at me from the other side of the room. For the last hour she's been pacing, jittery, swilling whiskey, and muttering to herself. Now her eyes are red and drunk, a nice contrast with the unhealthy green of her skin. She bounces over and jabs a finger in my face.

"What makes you think you're above the stink?" she says. "Because I've got news for you, you fuck. You've got about as much agenda as

70

the next hopeless bastard. You're choking on it just like the rest of us!"

I am taken aback by this and don't know what to say. For a moment all I can see are her eyes, red and accusing.

"Ha," she says, and throws up her hands, sloshing whiskey across the wood floor.

But at that moment Chase steps in. "Come on, you two," she says wearily. "Let's eat."

The meal tonight is Indonesian with a touch of Thai around the edges. We have a curried shrimp appetizer, lemon grass coconut soup, a cold broccoli and mussel salad, and twice cooked chicken Jakarta. A warm breeze blows on my neck from the stained glass windows tilted out at an angle to Baltic on their heavy pivots. The window closest to me portrays St. John the Baptist in his wild ass's skin in the desert; the other, St. Andrew strapped to his cross, rotating over a slow flame of colored glass. From somewhere outside the mournful sound of a tuba is carried on the wind.

"Listen to that," I say, gesturing over my shoulder with my fork.

"Listen to what?" Chase says.

"I've got to tell you," Poydras says suddenly from his end of the table. "I'm tripping. Took three hits before I got into the cab tonight." Then he smiles dully like a kid who has just peed his pants.

"Why would you drop acid before one of my dinner parties?" Chase says to him. "It wrecks the whole experience of eating. The food should stand by itself."

"The music," I say. "Can anyone hear the music from outside?"

Chase shakes her head. But my ears have always been very acute. I can hear babies crying a block away, couples making love in the next room quiet as church mice, clocks ticking steady as a metronome in the still hours of the morning.

For the next few minutes we eat without talking, dysfunctional family style. Then Chase notices that Jillian has not touched her food.

"Jillian," she says, sounding hurt, "you promised you'd eat something."

Jillian tosses back her snifter of whiskey with a dictatorial motion and pulls herself up from the table.

"Don't ride me, don't say another word," she spits out, a hysterical edge in her voice, and she heads toward the toilet, through Chase's bedroom at the far end of the loft. A moment later we hear the gasps and coughs of vomiting from behind the thin green curtain that shields the toilet from the world.

"Jesus," I say, food gone cold in my mouth, "what's wrong with her?" I think I know the answer, think it lies in the bloody tracks on her arms concealed by her long sleeves, but am surprised to find that it is something different altogether. Jillian has become an anorexic, and because of this can no longer make a living at the peep shows or in the porn movies. Worst of all, Chase says, the affliction has forced poor Jillian to appeal to her rich parents for help with the rent.

"An anorexic?" I say. "What happened to the heroin?"

Chase almost smiles. "That's old news. She gave up heroin a year ago. Doesn't do anything except single-malt scotch. Doesn't even do food. She drinks one of those Vita-Plus cans of vitamin supplements every once in a while, usually mixed with whiskey. It's like milk, only thicker and nastier."

"Let me get this straight," I say. "You threw a dinner party for an anorexic?"

Chase shrugs. "I thought I could get her to eat. She said she would try. I was wrong."

Fifteen minutes later Jillian emerges from the bedroom and sits down quietly as if nothing has happened. Chase is serving the dessert, saffron ice cream, and Vietnamese coffee sweetened with condensed milk.

"I just got off the phone with Inge," Jillian says. "Inge's coming over for a bite. I figured with all the leftover food . . ."

Head down, meek as a servant girl, Chase nods and settles back into her chair at the end of the table.

Inge is a large German woman in her mid-twenties. A redhead with very pale skin, an uneven, toothy smile and breasts the size of the Matterhorn. She thumps up the stairs, kisses Jil-

lian on the lips, gives a Teutonic nod to the rest
of us, throws herself down at the table, and begins
to eat with gusto.

Jillian smiles watching Inge eat. Perhaps Inge
eats for the both of them. Withdrawn, Chase sits
with her coffee behind a cigarette, two fingers
propped against her forehead. Conversation,
which has been dismal, stops completely, and we
all watch Inge eat. Every now and then she looks
up and smiles at us and goes back to eating.
Her appetite is enormous. She finishes off a huge
plate of chicken and is halfway through the mussels and broccoli when I remember where I have
seen her before, and I am just drunk enough to
say so.

"You made a film, right?" I say. "You and
Jillian. I saw it at the Paramour. Definitely a
fine performance from the both of you."

"*Ja*," Inge says. "We did one scene together
in a fack film. That's how we met," and she
leans over to kiss Jillian's sunken cheek.

Chase glares at me through the smoke of her
cigarette, but Jillian does not seem to mind.

"You didn't jerk off to us doing it?" Jillian
says, and looks me right in the eye.

"No," I say, wincing. "Of course not."

"I mean I could understand if you jerked off
because Inge and I were pretty hot together."

"*Ja*," Inge says, smiling.

"Turns out, Inge loves it like that, from behind." Jillian goes on. "When they turned the
camera off, she wanted me to keep doing it. So

74

that night we went to dinner at Florent and I took her home and we tried it without the crew and lights. You'd be surprised how many women like it like that. From behind."

"Very good for facking," Inge agrees.

"Faxing?" I say, perplexed.

"Facking."

"What?"

"Fucking, for chrissakes, Ned," Chase says, annoyed, stubbing her cigarette out in the ashtray.

"Oh."

Just then the sound of slow, mournful music reaches us again from down the street. It sounds like a funeral procession in a Mexican village.

"Hey, Ned," Poydras says, his eyes bright and crazy in an instant. "I hear it now. I hear the music!"

The music gets louder, seems to be advancing up Baltic Street, a melancholy dirge — tuba and trombone, the steady booming of a drum, the decorous clink of triangles. As if on cue, we all get up from the table and go to the windows, Inge still chewing her food.

It's midnight, and below an Italian religious procession has just turned the corner. I see a small brass band, a dozen big-haired Italian girls dressed in tight black dresses, a little wobbly on their three-inch heels. Following them, six or seven guidos in big-shouldered suits bear along a plaster statue of the Virgin fifteen feet high on a bier draped in black and hung with cheap silvery trinkets. Struggling painfully along on their knees in the wake of this holy effigy are a few shrunken old Italian ladies bent over their rosaries.

"Wow," Poydras says.

"What is it, a mob funeral?" Chase says. "Look at those bimbos with the hair."

"It's the festival of the Virgin of Palermo," Jillian says quietly. "It was started by a humble shoemaker in Sicily a few hundred years ago. His children were kidnapped by bandits as part of a vendetta, and he went into the local basilica and prayed to the Virgin Mary that if his children were returned to him safe and sound, he would do the tour of the city on his knees saying the rosary.

"Well, the children were returned to him, but all chopped to pieces like so much flank steak. So he put their bloody bodies in a wheelbarrow and wheeled them into the basilica during mass the next day, to the shock of the parishioners, and he got on his knees and prayed to the Virgin that they be restored to life. Before the eyes of the whole congregation, the bloody pieces came back together again, and the children hopped out of the wheelbarrow, spry as Pinocchio, smiling and laughing and good as new."

"The shit that people will believe," Chase says.

Jillian shrugs. "When this was an Italian neighborhood, there used to be thousands of people in the streets following that statue, most of them on their knees. Not anymore. The Ricans don't

76

care for the Virgin of Palermo. They have their own saints."

"How do you know all that?" Poydras says, awed.

"I read it in the metro section of the *Times* this morning," Jillian says.

As the procession passes just below our windows, I recognize the music. It is an old Italian melody appropriated for a famous aria in an opera by someone or other.

"Hey, Jillian," I say, "do you know that tune? It's from —"

"Yes, Massenet's *A Girl of the Streets.* 'The Whore's Apology.' "

She pulls a chair over from the table, stands on it, and begins to sing in a high, clear soprano that reaches the procession in the street. They look up, startled, and when they see Jillian singing in the light of the church window, a small cheer goes up from their midst. For a few seconds, her voice rises like a prayer, clear as a bell. I watch her face, and seem to see powerful emotions pass there: regret, shame, a longing for purity.

But I am a sentimentalist. It is only the effort of the singing. After a moment her voice cracks, and she falters, gasping for breath, and then the procession marches past us and is gone into the night.

13

Rain sweeps across Brooklyn tonight. The river smells like a wet dog. Mosquitoes hop and dance across the walls, but I am too tired to go after them. I find myself drowsing over an old rerun of *Star Trek*, and I fall asleep in the orange Naugahyde chair in front of the television in the living room and have a very vivid dream.

In the dream I am standing on the upper gallery of a great house overlooking another river, this one brown and moving slowly in the distance. A long drive bordered on either side by live oak leads up to the levee, and farther off, men and women in white clothing work in the fields. The sun is bright overhead and casts the thick black shadows of columns along the polished wood of the gallery. A party of men on horseback assemble where the steps sweep down to the drive. I can hear the breaths and snorts of the horses and the men talking and laughing, and an unpleasant cloud of cigar smoke rises up to me in the stifling air. It is very hot, and my heart is beating so fast. I hold my breath and feel the pounding in my ears.

Soon the men move off, the hooves of their horses sounding hollow in the dust, halters jingling. I am glad when they are gone, because I am waiting for someone else to come. I wait for an hour, hiding in the hot shadows under the eaves, and there is such a dreadful anticipation that I feel faint and dizzy, and the heat is awful.

At last I spy a lone figure on horseback coming along the road. He rides up to the house, and I step out from the shadows and put my hand on the railing, and it is here that I see my hand is white and delicate with elaborate rings on the two middle fingers, one a ruby of antique cut surrounded by diamonds that glitter smartly in the sunlight. It is a woman's hand. Then there is the sound of the man mounting the stairs and his voice calling my name, and my heart is wild with it, absolutely wild because it seems I have been waiting so long for him, so long. . . .

At this point I wake up to the television playing the national anthem, and my neck and shoulders are wet with sweat. There is a small rustling noise behind me, but I do not turn around, afraid of what I will find there. I stay in the orange chair, immobile and stiff, until the rustling noise stops. Then I get up very carefully, still without turning around, and get into bed and pull the sheets over my head, and I do not turn off the lights in the living room or the television, which pops and hisses out there till morning.

14

Tide Street is a long, dark canyon. Two working streetlights flicker a dull purple in the gloom. The rest are out. Coming home from work late, I hug the dark bricks of the warehouses, take a left along the cobbles, turn down Tyler to avoid the bums and wild dogs that live off the week-old pita pockets in the Dumpster of the Damascus Bakery, and walk the narrow alley between the parked bread trucks, silent and black as hulks.

There is a thing that grips your heart at this point, not fear exactly, but the certainty that you will not make it, that tonight will be the night, a few faceless thugs, a bullet with your name on it — and now, as I step out of the shadows, my heart drops: I make out a figure, maybe two, halfway down, moving toward me in the shadows between the trucks.

I freeze. Then I hear a familiar growling sound, and the shapes become more distinct. To my great relief it is the Scared Guy with Dogs. This was Molesworth's appellation for a perennially frightened neighbor whose real name is Geoff Pulaski. He is a tall, skinny man in his late thirties, always dressed in black leather no matter the season, with a startling shock of prematurely gray hair that stands up from the top of his head and a white, uneasy face straight out of a woodcut by Edvard Munch.

Geoff reins in the animals as we come abreast and peers at me in the dark. The dogs growl and claw the paving stones, tugging at their chains to get at my throat. They are Alsatian mastiffs bigger than rottweilers and more deadly, bred for bear hunting in eighteenth-century France. For reasons of his own, Geoff named them Manny, Moe, and Jack after the Pep Boys of automotive retailing fame. There are many such animals in the neighborhood. Big Savoyards and Russian wolfhounds and even a few Great Danes, all kept for protection by nervous bohemians with barely enough money to feed themselves, let alone animals that eat their weight in ground meat every two days.

Rather than walk the rest of the way home alone, I decide to accompany Geoff to the dog run in Brooklyn Heights. We will skirt the neighborhood and arrive back on Portsmouth near the apartment. He understands implicitly. Unfortunately it is not possible to walk in silence. We must converse to keep up the illusion that we are friends, not just scared rats banded together for safety's sake. As we turn back up Tide Street to the warehouses, Manny, Moe, and Jack sniffing the sour, bready wind, I ask politely about his job. Geoff is an assistant producer for a news magazine show aimed at gay teens on the Aramco Group Cable Network in Manhattan. His job is fine. He asks about my job. My job is fine.

Then the conversation turns as it always does to the only real subject we have in common, the neighborhood and the safest routes in and out. Everyone has a theory, backed up by intuition or hard experience or hearsay. There are two ways in: the F train at Knox, then down Tyler to Tide, or the A into Brooklyn Heights and along the rutted streets down to Portsmouth. Geoff supports the school that avoids the F train at Knox, which is the closest subway stop, a ten-minute walk through deserted streets. In his view, hooligans from the projects ride the train and prey on passengers getting off at Knox in the shadows under the Manhattan Bridge. But the A, he says, another seven minutes farther off by foot, is not subject to this sort of hooligan traffic.

In truth it's all a crapshoot. Your fate will find you when it wants to find you, on A or F or along any of these dark streets. Still, we find theories comforting; it gives us the illusion of control.

"You know Ang Dong, right?" Geoff says. "Lives two doors down from you. He's a Korean artist, makes sculptures out of coffee grinds."

I nod, though I have never heard of this person.

"Ang was like you, he thought the F was O.K. It's a well-traveled train, right? Always crowded. Wrong. They don't call it the death train for nothing. He got careless, came home on the F after dark last week, and they got him. You know how they are about mugging Koreans. But they got him anyway."

It is a widely accepted yet untested fact among us that the hooligans don't like mugging Koreans because unlike white people, who have more money than guts, Koreans are often well versed in the martial arts and are known to put up a good fight. I don't believe this, but still, I am shaken.

"Maybe it was dark. Maybe they couldn't see he was Korean," I say.

"Oh, no. They knew it all right. They got him anyway. Reached out, crooked him with an elbow around the throat, and he was out cold. It's getting worse. You heard about the Irish, of course. Hell, they live in your building. . . ."

This puts us in a gloomy silence. It is true. Reports of muggings have increased lately. Gerry and Ian, the illegal Irish poet-bricklayers who live in the basement, were both mugged in two separate incidents last month. They got Gerry just off the F and Ian not a block from the apartment. In that uncertain hour when afternoon turns to dusk, two kids from the projects came at him out of the alley off Tide with a Chinese-made Kalashnikov assault rifle. They found only ten dollars in Ian's pockets and gave him a good crack with the butt of the gun for their trouble.

Now Geoff and I come beneath the great arch of the Manhattan Bridge, its closed walkways hung with orange construction netting. Once you could cross here to Canal Street in Chinatown, just as you can cross on the Brooklyn Bridge from the Heights to the financial district. The old pedestrian walkways of the Manhattan Bridge hang over the river on a level lower than the main span, and there are disused observation bays on either side of the towers, semicircular terraces set in days past with iron benches and lit by elaborate gas lamps. I have seen old photographs. There is still a terraced park off Jay Street leading to the approaches, but the park is closed off behind barbwire and heaped with rubble, and the wooden boards of the walkway vanish halfway across, high above the choppy waters of the East River.

Before we reach Pearl, one of Geoff's mastiffs stops short of the curb, lets out a low whine, and in a moment the three of them erupt into a cacophony of barking — a vicious noise that resounds against the abutments of the bridge. Geoff can barely restrain the monsters. Sweat breaks on his brow; he rolls his eyes at the darkness, the very caricature of fear.

Just then two emaciated black women emerge from the jumble of cable and vandalized machinery beneath the arch twenty yards to the right. They circle toward us warily and stop just out of range of the dogs.

"Oh, my God," Geoff whispers to me. "What if they've got guns?" It is truly an absurd thought. The women are skin and bones and weak as children. One wears a pair of jeans torn below the knee and a dirty T-shirt that proclaims "Virginia is for Lovers." The other wears a sort of quilted housecoat and carries a plastic garbage bag. With an eye on the dogs, this one dumps the garbage bag across the cobbles. I see some men's clothes, a belt, a pair of blackened running shoes.

"Wanna buy a shirt," the one in the shorts says. "Got a nice shirt here for y'all." She picks an indistinguishable rag out of the mess.

"Absolutely not!" Geoff seems genuinely offended, as if no one ever asks him for money in New York.

"Those doggies bite?" the other one says in a high, frightened voice.

The woman in shorts kneels and rummages through the pile of clothes to find a yellow striped button-down, once a quality shirt but now stained and ragged. "Come on, mistah, how about this? Two dollars. Can't spare two dollar, from where y'at?"

I recognize her accent immediately. It's the Ninth Ward. "Are you from New Orleans?"

She looks up from the pile of clothes, suspicious. "Who wants to know?"

Geoff sighs, irritated, and maneuvers the dogs around the pair onto the cobbles.

"I'll meet you up ahead," he says and goes off down Pearl.

"Long way from home," I say to the woman, and wonder at the strange destiny that has brought her here, the drugs, the wrong decisions, the bad luck, the desperate poverty. How far am I from her lot, how far any one of us?

The woman stands quietly for a moment, clutching the shirt. "Yes, suh, long way from home," she says in a cracked voice. "Never thought I'd come up North like this. I'm not from New Orleans proper, mind you, born Algiers way. But we moved 'cross the river when my mama die. Lived with my grandpap. He used to play squeeze box and slide trombone in a band in the Quarter. The old M'ssippi's red as mud or green sometimes, depending on the rain. Not like this one . . ." She waves the shirt toward Manhattan, floating in light across the gulf, immune, unreachable. "No, suh, this here river's got a black heart, black as night. . . ." She trails off and looks me in the face, her eyes milky and sick in the dim light. "Don't you miss New Orleans?"

I nod, feeling an odd pang. "I do. I'm not from there. But I do miss it."

"People are nice down Louisiana way," she says. "They got time, you know? You ought to go back. Lots of pretty girls down there for a lucky young man like youself. I can't go back. But what about you?"

It's a question I don't care to answer. I end up buying the shirt for five dollars, and the two women fade back to their unimaginable life under the bridge.

"What were you talking about with that creature?" Geoff says when I catch up a block down, ragged shirt clenched in my fist.

"She gave me some good advice," I say, and leave it at that.

15

Tonight the projects glow out the back window of the apartment, lit up like a pirate ship, and there is a funny sweet scent hanging in the hot air, a scent like a woman's perfume. The scent lingers for a few days, moving from room to room, and I puzzle over its source until I realize it is a phantom odor, the work of the ghost. I don't mind the scent that much — it smells of freshly washed skin and clean hair and magnolia blossoms and verbena — but there is something about it that reminds me strongly of Antoinette, and this is bad for my disposition.

Suddenly my life seems unbearable. I cannot remember a happy day, a happy hour, a minute when hope seemed anything other than a torment. Then I think about calling Antoinette in New Orleans two thousand miles away, but I do not call her. What good would it do? We would have a friendly conversation, as we do every now and then, laugh a bit over old times, and afterward I wouldn't sleep for days.

But the smell only gets sweeter and stronger and more familiar, and the longing gets worse, and Antoinette's presence becomes more palpable than the ghost's in the apartment, and I place a call in an hour of the afternoon when I know she will not be home, just to hear the phone ring in her apartment in the Faubourg Marigny. I haven't been back to New Orleans in ten years. In New Orleans I was happy. The world seemed a benevolent place, and I was in love. This last decade has been hard, a series of struggles and disappointments, failed relationships, and dead ends.

After this foolish call, there is no helping myself,

so I take a six-pack of Koch's Golden Reserve
up to the roof and stretch out in the lawn chair
I keep up there for such melancholy purposes,
and I pull my old New Orleans Saints cap down
low over my eyes and abandon myself to memory.

Part Two:

New Orleans and the Past

oday, as the sun sets over Brooklyn, I am thinking of New Orleans. I am thinking of the iron filigree A and P and cupid's bow woven into the railings of the Pontalba Apartments, I am thinking of the river moving brown and sluggish in the rain and the green sky over the city. I am thinking of Antoinette. We are lying beneath the mosquito netting in her four-poster together, and we have just made love. It is hurricane season. Ominous yellow light glows through the louvers of the shutters, and out along the Faubourg Marigny the whine of traffic is thin and hollow like sound effects in a play. . . .

1

In those days Molesworth and I lived in a peeling pink shotgun house on the corner of Mystery and Fortin, dead against the chain-link fence of the Fairgrounds. It was a dissolute little place, with a weedy backyard mostly full of a rusted 1949 International Harvester pickup that belonged to one of Molesworth's city cousins. There was one small bedroom, a miserable kitchenette with a two-burner gas stove new during the lifetime of Kingfish Huey Long, and a sticky-flued fireplace that never did much more than belch smoke during the tepid Louisiana winters. At one end of the narrow living room, a dirty bay window overlooked the cracking asphalt of Mystery Street.

Through some leverage I can't remember now, I got the bedroom and Molesworth installed himself on the fold-out couch in the living room. But within days of moving in, he had taken over, his stuff everywhere, even in the bathroom and kitchen: unread textbooks and dirty underwear and beer bottles and cigarette butts and roach clips, yellowing piles of the *Times-Picayune*; and the occasional cheap porn magazine whose grisly black-and-white photos displayed from all vantages some of the ugliest naked women I had ever seen. After a week I gave up cleaning after him, and we lived in typical undergraduate squalor, dishes piled up in the sink, garbage rotting in bags on the back porch. We had been roommates freshman year at Loyola, one of those odd pairings of fate that can change the course of a lifetime. When given the choice as sophomores to move off campus, Molesworth found the house through his cousin, and we split the rent of $180 a month, which included water and electricity. That seemed expensive to me then. Everything is expensive to a student.

For the next three years all we did was drink. I remember hangover mornings late for class, loudspeaker from the Fairgrounds announcing the third race a distant booming, and the thud of the horses and the bright silks of the jockeys in my shallow dreams. Drinking was Molesworth's hobby and his passion. Other men have golf or racquetball or building ships in bottles. Molesworth liked to sit in bars and drink. He collected bars as others would collect stamps. No establishment was too mean or too far out of the way. It was impossible to live with Molesworth and not join him on his drinking expeditions. Like all men with a passion, he could be very eloquent and very persuasive; but he was no alcoholic. Drinking was not a thing he liked to do alone or in secret.

Somewhere along the way he acquired a battered old British Land Rover, similar to the one in the sixties television show *Daktari*. An original open-sided, right-hand-drive model, it possessed an ill-fitting canvas top and cloudy plastic windows that snapped over the doors. When it rained or the temperature dipped below fifty, we had to take the spark plugs out and heat them in a frying pan on the stove. In this rickety, uncertain vehicle we bombed all over New Orleans and surrounding parishes, looking for the right draft of Jax and bourbon side at the right price.

Because I had tested out of a good dozen basic requirements as a freshman, I finished my B.A. a semester early, but a scholarship and considerable stipend offered by the history department induced me to stay at Loyola for graduate school, and life continued much as before. More bars and late nights and the trumpet calling the thoroughbreds to post in the bleary calm of noon just beyond my window. If I ever came to own a racehorse, I vowed, I would name the beast Tylenol.

Recently I found among my papers a partial list of the bars we visited, scrawled on the back of a cocktail napkin: Clayton's, Laffite's Westpark Grill, The Arabi Ale House, St. Bernard's, The Broad Street Tap, Tad Bourbon's Bourbon Street, The Loyola Blue Jay, The Sazerac House, Feret's, Tchoupitoulas Inn, Bar Les Reves, The Natchez Parlor, The Paris Lunch, Mulaudon's Café, The Seminole Trail, St. Claude's Cocktail Hour, The Happy Time, Club Tomorrow, The Academy Grotto, Cafe Girod, The Melpomene Café, Claudelle's Toledano Street Saloon, Harry's Louisiana Emporium, The Irish Channel, The Gin Mill, Beauregard's Rest, The Contreras House Bar, Prytania Station, McDonough's Pelican North, McDonough's Pelican South (Lakeside), The Louisiana Drinking Society, The Pup and Oyster, Mad Jack's Bayou Getaway . . .

The list goes on. The rest is unreadable, blotted out by the round, telltale stain of some dark and spirituous liquor many years gone. There is much to be learned of life from Louisiana bars. A whole education for the liver, of course, but also something else that cannot be qualified. The grace that comes drunk at 4:00 A.M. slumped in a booth with a sly blonde from Gretna you didn't know two hours before; the moment before last call when anything seems possible.

2

At midnight, in the middle of a rainy week toward the end of my first year as a graduate student, Molesworth took me to Spanish Town.

Spanish Town was a new bar opened the month before by a friend of Molesworth's from Bayou Dessaintes. It stood alone in a rutted street of warehouses near the river where Tchoupitoulas runs into the levee at Felicity. A brick arcade went the length of the facade, and a row of Harley-Davidsons glistened in the rain out front, all chrome and bulbous gas tanks. Dark figures loitered there beneath the arches, their cigarettes glowing a threat or a promise, as lightning bugs are said to hover over unmarked graves across the fields of the South. From the open doorway, curtained off with cheap plastic beads, the thump and jangle of zydeco blared at top volume out across the levee.

The barroom seemed rough and half finished. A bucket of pitch and a stack of two-by-fours stood in the entryway, and the familiar beer piss stench of redneck bars had yet to overwhelm the smell of caulk and paint. I had half expected castanets, sangria, flamenco, but there wasn't anything at all Spanish about Spanish Town. Instead it was the sort of dive for badass boots and brawling swamp trash. A half-varnished old bar full of cherubs and carved mermaids, gilt rubbed off their scales, rose improbably at the center of the large, airy warehouse space like a wooden fort on the prairie. The blue pelican flag of Louisiana and an eight-by-fifteen-foot Elvis rug hung from pipes in the ceiling.

There was a fair crowd for a Wednesday, all pushed up against the rail. I settled at a table near the door, and Molesworth came back from the bar with two bottles of Jax. He handed over my bottle and settled heavily into the chair, which creaked under his bulk. Even then he weighed more than twelvestone.

"I'll grant you one thing. That coonass has got a good thing going here, but he's got it going for all the wrong reasons."

"Which coonass are you talking about, Molesworth?" At times he could be quite obscure.

"I'm talking about that coonass Dothan," he said.

Dothan Palmier was Molesworth's friend from the bayou, the owner and founder of Spanish Town, a mysterious tough character I had heard stories about but never met.

"That sombitch had a nice little place out on the bayou and a nice little business cutting up stolen Porsches and selling them for parts to Mexico." Molesworth leaned forward, resting his forearms as big as Popeye's on the table, beer dribbling off his red beard. "Plus he sold a shitload of dope to the locals. Cajun homegrown, good stuff. He had these fields on islands out in the middle of the swamp. Dug channels around them and filled the channels with alli-

96

gators. Man, what a setup!"

"So maybe he wanted to go legit," I said. "What's wrong with that?"

"You're not getting it. Dothan sold his share to his brother, came on down, and opened this whole damn bar, just chasing a woman. If that isn't the worst reason to do anything."

"Beautiful?"

"Not to my tastes, but decide for yourself." Molesworth jerked his head. "Dothan's got her behind the bar these days."

I looked over but could only see the leather and plaid-shirted backs of the drinkers. "Everyone needs a weakness," I said.

Molesworth grunted, knocked back his beer in what seemed like a single gulp, and went back for another round. I sipped mine and considered. I was living with a man who kept the company of thieves and drug smugglers. His presence at Loyola was perplexing. He was in his sixth year now and showed no signs of finishing soon. He had always seemed too loud for the staid Jesuit school, and his grades were not up to snuff. I asked him once how he had managed to get admitted with a tuition waver. It was one of those arrangements Louisiana is famous for: Apparently, his uncle, the pastor of a seedy little church in Plaquemines, had some dirt on Bishop Mulready of Orleans Parish who held a prominent seat on Loyola's board of visitors.

Five minutes later Molesworth came back with two Dixies and motioned me to a door in the far dark corner. In shadows back there stood a stuffed grizzly which I hadn't noticed before, reared up on its hind legs, claws out, teeth bared. From beneath the door, a thin line of yellow light.

"Get up," Molesworth said. "Let's go talk to Dothan."

But as we passed along the fringes of the crowd, a howl went up, and a young woman stepped from behind the bar onto the tin countertop. She wore a white rose tucked between her breasts, a tight red dress that fell two inches above her knees, and black cowboy boots. She flicked her cigarette toward one of the wooden mermaids with something like contempt and began to dance up there to the song just coming on the jukebox. I recognized it, a lively number by Papa Languenbec and his Cajun Allstars about a boy who loves his mother to distraction, full of accordion and fiddle and bawdy double entendre sung in a nasal, incomprehensible Cajun French.

I paused just within reach of the bear's paws to watch her dance. Beyond the arcade windows of the facade, where bales of cotton once steamed in the summer heat of another era, it had stopped raining, and there was a sort of green halo above the river. Framed against this faint illumination, the young woman swung her hips and swung her thick black hair from side to side and stamped her black boots into the tin of the counter in time to the music and shook what she had to shake, which was God's own plenty. She had *duende*. She put the Spanish in Spanish Town.

The rednecks and bikers at her feet whistled and cheered and threw money and pounded the bar with fists the size of ham hocks. I thought of the perfect frenzy of John Singer Sargent's *Gypsy Dancer*, and bareback riders, and circus acrobats dangling high above the sawdust in sequined tights. Her bare skin was covered with a thin sheen of sweat. A tiny fleck touched my lip when she flung out her arms.

Then I felt Molesworth's hand heavy as the law on my shoulder. He pulled me around and shook his head.

"Is that her?" I said, but I couldn't keep the wobble out of my voice.

"What do you think?"

"Christ, how could you say she's not beautiful? She's —"

"I didn't say that, Coonass." He cut me off. "I just said she wasn't to my taste, which means I don't fancy a shotgun between the eyes."

I followed him reluctantly through the door and into a vast unfinished kitchen area, flooded with fluorescent light. Steel pots big as bathtubs sat here and there. A huge exhaust fan and two stoves still in crates were pushed at angles to the wall, packing material strewn all around. I tripped over an open box of spoons as long as my arm.

"Dothan's going to do a little bit of catering," Molesworth explained. "He's thinking about exporting some of his jambalaya to sell up North. Chicago or New York or something. You know how they go for that sort of thing up there."

Dothan Palmier sat hunched at a card table in the cramped office going over the accounts with all the pencil-biting intensity of a ten-year-old doing math homework. A thin gun slit of a window gave out on the levee and the lights of Marrero across the river. He looked up narrow eyed when we came in and closed the big red ledger.

"Hey, Dothan," Molesworth said. "How's it going, you old coonass?"

"Lyle," he said. He stood up, shook Molesworth's hand, and gave a grimace that passed for a smile. He wore tight black jeans, pointy cowboy boots curled up at the toes, and a plain white shirt, sleeves rolled over thick biceps like a farmer's son showing off his muscles.

Molesworth introduced us, and I stepped forward, and we shook hands. His hands were oversized from heavy work, hard, and scarred. The tattoo of a python curled out of the jungle of wiry black hairs on his left wrist and beneath the gold band of his watch. He was probably thirty-five, attractive in a dark, sideburned Cajun sort of way and short, about five feet six inches. But something else made him hard to ignore; a dangerous, unpredictable quality. He seemed coiled tight as a spring.

Dothan brought a bottle of Early Times and three lowball glasses out of a battered file cabinet near the window and poured a shot in each.

"Good-looking place you've got here," Molesworth said, and raised his glass. "Let's drink to that."

"I've got a long way to go, shit, check the wreck out there." He waved toward the kitchen. "Don't want to jinx it. Better drink to you finishing up that schooling of yours before the end of the decade."

Molesworth shook his head and laughed, a deep, rumbling sound from the belly. "No way," he said.

"Wait," I said, "let's drink to the beautiful girl behind the bar. She's amazing."

They both looked over at me. Molesworth seemed stunned, his jowls sagging like a St. Bernard's. Dothan studied me for a moment, unblinking, expressionless.

"You mean Antoinette," he said quietly.

"He don't know, Dothan," Molesworth cut in. "He don't know for shit."

"It's all right," Dothan said. "She is a beautiful woman. Any fool can see that."

"Well, then" — I raised my glass — "to Antoinette . . ."

We drank. Dothan drained his glass and, after a minute or so of strained chitchat with Molesworth, turned back to his account books abruptly. "If you boys will excuse me," he said.

Molesworth and I went down through the kitchen and out into the bar. "You're a real coonass," he said when he was sure we were safe. "That old boy stuck a knife in a man in a club

101

in Chalmette for less than what you did back there."

"Don't be ridiculous," I said. "In any case a woman like that is worth a little trouble."

"Now you're talking crazy," Molesworth said, and turned hulking toward the street door.

"Another round," I said. "I'll buy."

Molesworth hesitated for an instant, then shrugged and made a place with his bulk at the rail. He was a practical man. He would accept a free beer from the devil himself.

A few minutes later Antoinette came down to our end of the bar, a cigarette, half ashes, curled in the corner of her lip. Without removing it, she leaned across and kissed his fat cheek.

"Hello, Lyle," she said.

Molesworth nodded. "Antoinette."

"What can I get you gentlemen?"

"Hell, this coonass is buying," Molesworth said. "Make mine something fancy and expensive, from the blender."

"All right, a Frozen Bastard . . . what about you?"

She passed her eyes over me in a quick evaluation. I sat back, a little surprised. New Orleans is like London; you can place any native within a street or two if you know what to listen for. I had expected deep bayou, like Dothan's Lafayette Parish drawl, but what I heard was polished, urbane: St. Jerome's Academy for Girls, the Garden District, and summers on a forty-five-foot Camper-Nicholson in the Gulf.

"Well?"

"Frozen Bastard," I croaked.

Then she smiled unexpectedly and did a quick pirouette to the blender down the bar.

We all have our moments. There are those rare nights when reach exceeds grasp and the implausible becomes as real as the coins in our pocket. When Antoinette brought the drinks — two embarrassing pink concoctions with paper umbrellas and pineapple slices — I made a few offhanded cracks, and she laughed and lingered in banter as Molesworth brooded next to me like a disgruntled genie. Down the bar rednecks waved twenty-dollar bills, trying to catch her attention. She was the darling of the place, the resident deity. She ignored them, had all the time in the world. Outside the obvious symmetries shared by all beautiful women, there was something familiar about her face. Then it hit me, a stroke of genius.

"In the Presbytère," I said, actually snapping my fingers, "the Louisiana State Museum . . ."

"The museum's in the Cabildo," she said, "but what about it?"

"They've got these historical paintings, you know. One I remember — a pretty young woman in a white dress, circa 1825. God, she looks just like you. She could be your sister. I can't remember the name. But . . ."

Antoinette seemed impressed. "I know the one you're talking about," she said. "I've got a photograph of it on the wall in my apartment. They found that painting stuffed at the back of the attic in my aunt Tatie's house on Esplanade in the Vieux Carré. Loaned it to the museum when Aunt Tatie went off to the old folks' home. The woman in the painting is some ancestor. We're Creoles, one hundred percent. My mother's family's been here for always. Had plantations down river, the whole deal. A couple of people have told me there's a resemblance, but I don't see it."

"It's the eyes mostly. She's got the same eyes. What color are your eyes?" I reached for her hand suddenly and leaned close across the bar.

Antoinette was startled, but she did not pull away. "Sometimes blue," she said almost in a whisper, "sometimes gray. Depends on the mood."

"No," I said. "They're the color of rainwater."

There was a pause, my nose a half inch from the smoldering end of her cigarette. Molesworth groaned audibly to my left. Antoinette's hand felt cool and small in mine. She disengaged gently and stepped back.

"Your friend here is drunk, Lyle," she said to Molesworth. "Drunk but cute. Bring him back when he isn't so drunk." Then she turned to the clamor at the far end of the bar.

"You are one dumb sombitch," he said when she was gone. "I wash my hands of the consequences," and he made a hand-washing gesture.

I laughed, something like joy in my heart, and

tipped up my Dixie and drank, and I tried not to mind when Molesworth gave me a sharp elbow in the ribs and I turned to see Dothan standing just outside the doorway to the kitchen, a dark figure beneath the paws of the bear in the hard yellow light.

3

In matters of the heart, luck is everything. I have never been a lucky man, which is to say circumstances conspired in my favor once, then never looked my way again.

Two weeks after Molesworth took me to Spanish Town, I happened across Antoinette in the museum in Gibson Hall at Tulane. A dull gray sky stretched tight as a drum over Audubon Park, palm trees along St. Charles drooping listlessly against it. It rained; then it didn't rain; then it rained again. There is nothing to do in such oppressive weather, impossible to concentrate, so I wandered over to look at the yellow skulls and Indian relics in their dusty glass cases. The museum is a strange, unkempt little place, not much visited and full of mismatched oddities: dingy bones of mysterious provenance, the perfect glass beads of the Mound Builders, two Egyptian monkey mummies from the Middle Kingdom, codices written on human skin, and gold ornaments stolen by the conquistadors — perhaps by stout Cortez himself — from the bloody cities of the Aztecs.

Antoinette stood before a case of Aztec artifacts in an unseasonable sleeveless flowered dress, shivering, her hair in wet curls down her back. There were bruises on her bare arms, and when I got closer, I saw she was soaked through to the skin.

"Antoinette?" I said.

She turned toward me with a zoned-out stare. Her pupils looked dilated. I had been back to Spanish Town twice since the first visit, each time making a point to talk to her, but I could see she did not know my face.

"At your bar," I said. "I've been in a few times —"

"Dothan's bar." She frowned, an edge in her voice. She was too sedated to show any real anger, but I felt a wicked thrill when I considered that something might have happened between them.

"Are you all right?" I stepped closer. "Is there something wrong?"

She ignored the question and pointed at the case. "Check this stuff out," she said. "It's really wild."

Behind the thick glass, a large obsidian blade, strands of gold wire still wrapped around the haft, lay on a strip of red velvet. I read the tag and shuddered.

"The Aztec priests used it to cut out the hearts of their sacrificial victims," she said in a dull monotone. "They believed that the sun was a feeble old man who needed human blood to survive and rise the next day. So they'd force the people to line up at the base of those stone temples, thousands of them. Then, one by one they'd be dragged up to have their hearts cut out with that bit of polished rock. Then the priests would roll their bodies down the other side, where acolytes would flay the skin and wear it like a coat, until it rotted. Shit, imagine having your heart cut out while you were still alive. You'd be able to see them lift it over your head — this bloody hunk of meat — in the last split second before your eyes went black." She turned to me, expecting a reasonable response.

"Gruesome," I said, making a face.

"No. Not really. Hell, I would have gone voluntarily. I think it would be a good thing to have your heart cut out. Who needs a heart?"

"Everyone needs a heart," I said as if talking to a child.

She shook her head and opened her mouth to speak but instead leaned forward and put her hands and her forehead flat against the glass and gave a small moan.

"Oh, man," she said. "This is bad. I'm coming down. Fast." Then she began shivering in quick little spasms. I touched her bare shoulder and felt the spasms go through her like electric shocks, and I became alarmed. Her teeth began to chatter. I put my books on the floor and took off my coat and put it around her shoulders and stood there for a moment in the dim light of the museum, unsure of what to do next. From a case nearby the black monkey faces of the mummies leered at me through the glass and from across the distance of three thousand years.

"We've got to take you to a doctor or something," I said at last.

She clamped her jaw shut in an effort to stop the chattering noise. "No," she said. "This has happened before. It's just a bad trip. Listen, you've got to help me get home. Will you help me get home?" Then she pushed off the glass and stood woozily on her feet for a second before she slumped back into my arms.

4

Antoinette lived in the Faubourg Marigny at North Villere, one block from Elysian Fields. The St. Roche shrine was visible through the round window of the stairwell. I lugged her with some effort up the two narrow flights and into the apartment, where she crawled onto a worn yellow satin Victorian fainting couch in the living room and covered herself over with a quilt that lay crumpled in a heap on the floor.

The place was a wreck. A bit worse, if that was possible, than my own pink house on Mystery Street. Clothes lay in piles in every corner and the expensive-looking oriental carpet was filthy, strewn with glossy French fashion magazines, open lipsticks, apple cores, half-eaten Healthy Choice dinners, empty cups of low-fat yogurt, and other junk. A waterless fish tank, gravel at the bottom, sat on the floor, filled with shoes. A large framed photograph of the portrait of the antebellum lady I had seen in the Cabildo hung at a crooked angle between the French doors that opened onto the balcony fronting Marigny.

Antoinette's lips had a white, parched look, and she watched me through glassy eyes, quilt tucked up to her chin, as I rummaged around in the kitchen cabinets, looking for anything that would help: aspirin, a bromide, tea. Reaching onto a top shelf, I knocked a jar of dried red beans onto the tile floor. It shattered, beans and glass shards everywhere.

"Please," she said from the couch, her lips barely moving. "Come here."

I left the mess and went to kneel beside her. She shivered visibly beneath the quilt.

"A doctor might not be a bad idea," I said. "You look terrible." But it wasn't true. Even sick and shivering, she was one of the most beautiful women I had ever seen.

"No," she said in a harsh whisper. "A doctor might go to the police or, worse, to my parents. I took one hit too many. It's Dothan's stuff. Homemade, by this half-crazy chemist up in Dessaintes Parish. You can never tell how you'll react. This time it's like a block of ice. It's like I'm sitting naked on a block of ice." Then she put an arm out from beneath the quilt, took hold of my wrist, and pulled me close. Her breath was foul. "I want to ask you something, and you've got to tell me the truth."

I nodded.

"You have a nice face, but so do a lot of people who aren't so nice. Can I trust you?"

"I'm Molesworth's roommate," I said. "If you don't remember."

"Yes, I remember, but that's not my question. Are you a gentleman?" She asked this without a trace of irony, in the same tone perhaps that the woman in the portrait on the wall would have used 150 years before.

"Yes," I said. "A gentleman."

She closed her eyes. "O.K.," she said. "I can't get up. I can hardly move. I'm frozen solid. You're going to have to do something for me. . . ."

I went into the bathroom and stood gawking for a second. Built for the ablutions of another era, the bathroom was as large as the rest of the apartment put together, with an old claw-foot tub, a bidet, and a sink with dual faucets, one for cold water, one for hot, worn brass fish-head fixtures all around. Turn-of- the-century tilework wound around the walls halfway up. A fanlight overlooked the traffic of the faubourg. I cracked the louvers a little, just enough to admit the gray afternoon and ran a bath hot as I could make it without burning my elbow. Then I went back into the small living room and stood over her.

"All right," I said. "Your bath."

"You're going to have to —"

I shook my head.

"Please," she said, sounding pitiful.

"Do you always rely on the kindness of strangers?" I said, but the reference escaped her, and with great effort, she held up her arms.

I helped her into the bathroom and showed her the greenish bathwater steaming under its fish-head spigot.

"There," I said with an airy wave of the hand.

"I can't do it." She turned toward me, teeth chattering. "My clothes. Please . . ." Her skin looked gray in the gray light and felt like ice.

I began to undress her, squinting as if peeling an onion. She stood stiff and unblinking as I undid the zipper on her dress and it fell to the floor. Then I knelt and unbuckled her shoes and held her ankles and pulled her cold feet out of them and stood and backed away.

"The rest," she said. "What's the difference now?"

"O.K.," I said. "Think of me as your doctor." But when I undid the clasp on her bra, she closed her eyes, and she kept them closed as I rolled her panties down the curve of her hip. Her nakedness gleamed against the dull tiles of the bathroom. I tried not to think at all, and I took her hand and led her to the tub. She lifted one foot over the water, but when her toe broke the surface, she pulled back with a small cry.

"I can't," she said. "It's too hot."

"You've got to," I said.

"I can't."

"Slowly."

Breathing through her teeth, she put one foot in the water, a millimeter at a time. Then, hand on my shoulder, she put in the other. A tear rolled down her cheek and splashed lightly on the surface. Still holding on to my arm, she crouched down, steam rising from her cold flesh. I tried not to look; it was impossible. I looked away and still saw her reflection in the silvered mirror, her breasts floating in the water. She slid under finally, her black hair spreading on the surface like ink. A bubble rose, then another, and at last she pushed up, breathing hard, and leaned her head back against the tub.

"O.K.," she said. "I think I'll be O.K. now."

"Good," I said. "I draw the line at scrubbing your back."

I went out of the bathroom without a word and put on my coat and gathered my books. From inside the bathroom now came that bath sound of splashing water and the sound of her breath.

"Antoinette," I called in, "I'm going to take off."

The bath sounds stopped for a beat. "No, please," she called. "Wait till I get out. Please."

She was in there a long time, soaking. I heard the water run again, and again after that. I settled on the couch in my coat and tried to read my history text, *France and the Age of Napoleon*, by Hervé Surgère for an upcoming exam. It was dry reading, written by a man who had no feeling for the grandiose color of the era, but there were a few unforgettable anecdotes.

112

I read how the emperor, upon his return from Elba for the Hundred Days that culminated in Waterloo, began his march toward Paris, gathering supporters along the way. The new royalist government sent an army to stop him, composed of veterans of Austerlitz and Marengo and other campaigns, now led by foppish aristocratic officers who had emigrated in 1793 and returned at the emperor's abdication like a swarm of locusts descending on France. They met up at a field near Grenoble, Napoleon and his few hundred followers facing an army of thousands. Alone, the emperor walked across the open ground till he was within range of the opposing guns. There he stopped, spread his arms, glanced up at the blue sky and the peaks of the Massif Central in the distance. Then he stared down the muzzles of the muskets aiming for his heart.

"Soldiers!" he cried. "Would you fire upon your emperor?"

"Fire!" the officers ordered. "Fire!" But the men threw down their guns and ran to him, tears in their eyes.

From the bathroom came more watery sounds and a tuneless sort of humming. I closed the book with a sigh and poked around the apartment. It had once been part of a much larger place, perhaps a Creole gentleman's pied-à-terre in the 1850s. Plaster medallions in the ceiling were interrupted by cheap presswood partitions; fanciful grape leaf molding circled the walls until cut off by the pasteboard walls of thoughtless remodelers.

In the tiny bedroom there was barely enough room for the ancient four-poster of dark wood. It had the heavy, solid look of furniture made by slave artisans. From between the mashed pillows, a stuffed brown bear protruded feetfirst. On the bureau, an ormolu box spilling over with earrings and piles of makeup. Behind this, ranks of framed family photographs going back several generations. Also, there was one of those plastic photograph cubes filled with pictures of Dothan: Dothan and Antoinette on a Gulf beach in the sand. Dothan astride a big Harley panhead, his tattooed hand at the throttle, his eyes hidden behind mirror frame shades. Dothan shirtless, one foot on the fender of an old yellow pickup, the butt of a twelve-gauge shotgun resting on his hip, a tar paper shack and the green riot of the swamp behind.

I picked up the cube with the tip of my fingers and held it to the light just as Antoinette stepped into the room barefoot and sober, wrapped in a thick white terry-cloth robe, her hair twisted into a turban with a blue towel.

"That's Dothan," she said, leaning in the doorway. "But you know that."

I replaced the cube carefully among the other photographs. "Are you feeling better?"

"I'm fine," she said a bit sullenly, and picked her way through the rubble to the bed. She approached it knee first, swung around, and in a quick movement was sitting cross-legged in the sheets, hands gripping her elbows. An awkward silence followed in which I heard the metallic rush of traffic heading up Marigny to the Pontchartrain Expressway.

She spoke first. "I know what you're thinking —" she began.

"Forget about it," I interrupted. "If you're straightened out now, I'll be leaving."

I pushed off the dresser and started for the door.

"Wait!" she said, but when I stopped and turned toward her, she looked away and bit her lip, a flush to her cheeks.

"I just want you to hold me for a little please before you go," she said in a small voice after a minute. "Please. This is the last thing I will ask you to do."

I went over to the bed and sat down and reached for her. Then she leaned forward and put her head against my coat, pressing her face into the tweed and put her arms around me. We stayed like that for about fifteen minutes without talking, listening to the traffic and the rain, the gray light of afternoon deepening to dusk. I felt her warm, damp body through the terry cloth, and I felt her trembling. Then she was still, and for a moment I thought she was asleep. But she stirred at last and took my hand and kissed it lightly and sat up.

"It's late," she said. "You'd better go."

I didn't know what else to say, so I said, "O.K., I hope you feel better," and I got up and went out into the rain along Villere, and I tried not to think of her body and her black hair and the way she looked naked and shivering in the bathroom. Then I walked over into the Quarter to a place generally known as Twenty Naked Girls, because of a neon sign out front to this effect, where they have strippers on the stage with nothing but G-strings between themselves and the world. I ordered a watery bourbon and watched a woman with a mass of cheap-looking blond hair and huge breasts take off her clothes and run her hand between her legs, but it made me feel rotten, just rotten. I left without finishing my drink and walked up Orleans Street and through Congo Square up to Broad, where I caught the bus to the corner of Gentilly and Marepas, the stands of the Fairgrounds rising just beyond.

Molesworth's Land Rover was gone from the drive when I got home, and the house was empty. I went to my room and lay on my bed in my coat and stared into the darkness. Outside, the rain passed in squalls over the muddy track beyond the chain-link fence, and passed over the cars on their way across the causeway to Covington, and passed over the upright tombs reflecting in the lagoon in the cemetery at Metairie. And there was rain, I knew, on the flat roof of Antoinette's apartment as she slept in her big bed, her flesh damp beneath her robe, and rain on the brown waters of the river rolling down, oblivious, to the sea.

5

Two days later, Friday afternoon, there was a knock on the door at our pink house on Mystery Street. Molesworth heaved himself off the couch with some suspicion, as our only regular visitors were bill collectors and officers of the court attempting to serve subpoenas on the previous tenants. But on the stoop stood a teenage delivery boy from Marche Florists, his arms full of two dozen yellow roses wrapped in cellophane. The delivery boy looked at Molesworth, bare-chested in his tattered plaid robe, and Molesworth looked at the delivery boy, who wore a pressed white shirt and green apron with "Marche Florists" printed across the front.

"I think you got the wrong house, pardner," Molesworth said, and made a motion to close the door, but the boy insisted.

"Two twenty-four Mystery Street, right? Mr. Ned Conti, is that you?"

"Coonass," Molesworth called over his shoulder, "boy here's got something for you."

I came out from the kitchen, munching on a grilled cheese sandwich, signed for the flowers, and stood rather stupidly in the middle of the living room, flowers in my arms, the antics of Wile E. Coyote blaring from the TV in the background. No one had ever sent me flowers before, and I couldn't think what to do with them.

"First you cut the stems," Molesworth said

calmly. "Then you put them in some water. Then, most important, you read the card and see who was stupid enough to send you that mess of posies."

I did what he said. I cut the stems and put them in our plastic water pitcher out of the refrigerator and set them on the mantel, where they gleamed like hope amid the squalor of the place. Then I read the card.

"These are for you," the card said in a female hand. "I'll be at the Napoleon House at eight tonight."

"Well?" Molesworth said, looking up from the TV.

"They're from my, uh, mom," I said.

"Your mom?" He raised an eyebrow; then he shook his head. "Have it your own way, Coonass," he said, and went back to his cartoons.

6

At eight the streets of the Quarter were crowded, full of tourists and horse drawn carriages. I took the bus down to the corner of Dauphine and St. Louis and walked the rest of the way through the crowds. The Oyster Houses were packed to capacity; the bars spilled patrons onto the street. Drunken midwestern businessmen on a spree, honeymoon couples arm in arm, tipsy after two Hurricanes at Pat O'Brien's, and a little dazed by it all. Though barely five years in the city, I had acquired the native's scorn for these pasty-faced legions who couldn't hold their liquor. Show me a Louisianan, and I'll show you someone who can drink even an Irishman under the table.

A mild evening, the windows of the Napoleon House stood open onto Chartres Street. I went in and ordered a Sazerac cocktail just for the hell of it and sat at the bar and waited. At about eight-thirty one of the waiters, an ancient black man in a stained red jacket and crooked bow tie, came up and tapped me on the shoulder.

"You Mr. Ned Conti?" he asked.

"Yes," I said, surprised.

"Follow me, please."

I took my drink and followed him around the bar, down a peeling corridor and past a sign that said *Patio Closed,* and into the courtyard. An iron fountain out there stood dry for the winter. Banana trees and other shrubs in large earthenware pots surrounded a half dozen empty black iron tables like a jungle. A curving staircase led to upstairs galleries — apartments once prepared for the emperor himself on the eve of a failed plot to rescue him from the arid and windswept rock of St. Helena, where he died in exile.

Antoinette sat at a table on the far side of the fountain, a martini before her. Two candles in old cognac bottles lit her face and sparkled off the rhinestone pins at the shoulders of her green velvet cocktail dress. She looked fine, her eyes shining, without a trace of the distress of a few

119

days before. We were alone in the courtyard.

"Here you are, suh." The waiter gestured to a chair across from her.

Antoinette looked up and smiled. "Thank you, Henri," she said to him. "Hello," she said when I sat down.

"Can I get you anything, suh?" the waiter said.

"Yes, another Sazerac, I guess," I said, looking into my drink.

Antoinette made a face. "You're some kind of tourist," she said. "Sazerac."

"Yeah, I don't know what got into me. I had a taste for something fancy," I said, trying to ignore her breasts in the low-cut dress.

"Hmm . . ." She pursed her lips, then turned to Henri. *"Au bon goût, Henri. Lo vrai fai por loui. Et lo même por moi,"* she said in what sounded like Gombo French, the dying old dialect of New Orleans. I'd never before heard anyone speak it.

"Bon, bon, 'zelle Toinette." Henri nodded and moved off slowly across the courtyard toward the bar.

"I told him to make you a good one," Antoinette said. "None of that nasty-ass bottled stuff. From scratch, you know."

"You seem to have some pull around this place," I said, looking around at the empty tables and the dripping balconies. "Looks like they opened up the patio just for you."

"Papa proposed to Mama right here in this courtyard," she said. "I was practically born here, you could say. Food's not so good anymore, but I love the place."

When Henri brought the drinks, I tasted the Sazerac, and it ran like fire down my throat.

"Damn," I said, "this is one hell of a drink."

He smiled, pleased, and went away.

"Henry used to be head bartender here till they figured he got too old," Antoinette said. "But he's one of the few can still make a Sazerac from scratch. You know, absinthe, bourbon, sweet vermouth, sugar, bitters. The secret is you take the absinthe, swirl it around the glass, and throw it out, then add the other stuff. That's the secret. Of course, you can't get absinthe anymore. Pernod's a decent substitute."

I nodded dumbly.

Antoinette pulled her metal chair close. It made a scraping sound on the old bricks of the patio. "Let me taste that," she said. She tasted the Sazerac and grimaced. "Packs a wallop," she said. Then she put her hand on my arm and lowered her voice. "Listen, I want to get this over with right now, because the whole thing's a little embarrassing. I really appreciate what you did the other day. I was really out of control, and I needed someone to help me, and you were there, and I really, really —"

"You don't . . .." I began.

"Please, let me finish. I really appreciate what you did and how you did it — so sweetly. So, this is for that. . . .." She leaned forward and kissed me on the lips, her hand still on my arm, and I was too dumbfounded to kiss her back.

"You taste like Sazerac," she said, but when I didn't say anything, she leaned back and watched me through narrowed eyes, waiting. I must have looked white as a sheet, because after a while she said, "Shit, I didn't mean to scare you."

"No, you just took me by surprise."

"If you don't like me to kiss you, just let me know."

"That's not it," I said, and in a rush I reached for her and kissed her hard on the lips and kissed her again and tried to pull her close, but instead knocked her martini shattering to the bricks.

"O.K." She laughed and pushed me back, hand flat against my chest. "You be careful now."

In retrospect it was advice I should have heeded. But instead, as she went for Henri, I leaned back in the metal chair and stared up at the sky above the courtyard, such a shade of marvelous green it seemed a miracle.

7

Sometime around 4:00 A.M., after drinking and dinner and more drinking at a half dozen tourist bars across the Quarter, we ended up at Lafitte's, its old blackened walls of slave-made brick sunk four feet below the level of the banquette. It was a piano bar now, with fancy neon over the baby grand and chrome-rimmed glass tables and red leather booths. But once, in another age, the place had been a front for the pirate Lafitte's illegal slaving operations, and it still held the low-down feel of crime's past.

Antoinette and I leaned into each other at the booth in the corner, half-drunk bottles of Dixie on the table before us. The oversize brandy snifter on the piano across the room was stuffed full with dollar bills, and the woman there wailed her last number, but it was still an hour away from last call, a bare hint of dawn over the city.

"There's a few little things I want to tell you," Antoinette said.

"Shoot."

"But you won't remember. You're drunk."

"Don't worry," I said. "I'll remember."

"The Quarter," she said. "All of these tourist bars. Why do you think I wouldn't leave the Quarter tonight? Do you think I like drinking down here?"

"I know," I said. "The bar at the Hyatt. Those plastic alligators hanging from the ceiling. Christ."

She took hold of my arm in a firm grip, and her voice was serious all of a sudden.

"My friends don't drink here; your friends don't drink here. Dothan doesn't drink here. Do you see what I'm saying?" She bent her face toward the table as I considered this. Her neck showed white and smooth as ivory in the dim light. Her black hair curled around the pearls in her ears. Along the street a trio of drunks stumbled by. All I saw of them was their shoes through the low window.

"I'm saying that it could be dangerous for you at first." Antoinette continued quietly. "Dothan doesn't always react rationally, and he's done some crazy things in the past. We're going to have to sneak around a little. Not that I like sneaking around. Just till I can figure out how to go about breaking it off. I'll be totally honest with you because I like you and you're a nice guy. I've been trying to get away from Dothan for a while now. He's just too much for me. He wants too much. But I'm weak, and I can't do it by myself. I call him when I've told him that we're going to cool it for a while, because I get lonely and bored. And when he's not around and when I'm lonely and bored, I do stupid things, like the other day, all that acid. That was really stupid. So I need your help." She wouldn't look at me, and when I pulled her face up, there were tears in her eyes.

"But I'm not promising anything," she said. "I want you to remember that. But I want . . ."

I held my breath.

"I want you to be my lover. Will you be my lover?"

I should have been thinking about the things she said, but I wasn't thinking at all. Instead I took her in my arms and I kissed her face.

"The devil himself," I whispered. "For you, I'd face the devil himself," and out in the green firmament above the city there was the long

124

demon howl of a departing freight, the Illinois Central north to St. Louis and Chicago, pulling through the swampy darkness along the river.

8

We were careful. We went to tourist bars where no one we knew would be caught dead and made love in hotel rooms in the Quarter — the Lasalle, the Landmark French Quarter, the Monteleone — coming and going amid the businessmen on convention and the housewives from Akron with balding husbands in tow who wore their mortgages on their sleeves.

I liked to stand in the shadows and watch her sitting at the bar of the Bienville House or the Bourbon Orleans waiting for me. They made way for her; they gawked. Antoinette was the girl on the poster waving from a speedboat bouncing along the blue waters of the Gulf — "Louisiana, Sportsman's Paradise!" — hanging on the walls of travel offices in some gray city of the North. Once a middle-aged CEO, old enough to be her father, offered eighteen hundred dollars for one night. She turned him down with firm politeness. Another time a hustling young pharmaceutical salesman from New Jersey offered her four hundred dollars for a blow job. She dumped a cup of coffee in the lap of his Armani suit.

The hotels were much alike. Hard double beds,

125

wall-to-wall carpeting, blue movies for an added fee, bad paintings of flowers on the wall, the smell of anonymity, the lights of Algiers across the way through the thick plate glass. We had our routine and our subterfuges. She'd leave a message in a copy of Th. Flournoy's *Des Indes à la planète Mars* in my study carrel at the Fr. Dupuis Library at Loyola. (At the time I was doing a research project on the phenomenon of automatic writing in the nineteenth century, and this is a famous work written supposedly by an otherworldly entity *à la planchette,* as they used to say.) The messages — which I was instructed to memorize and destroy like somebody out of *Mission Impossible* — were little scraps of yellow paper bearing the name of a hotel, an hour of the day or night, a room number, and signed only with a scrawled heart.

She made all the arrangements, put everything on a credit card I never saw, and was always waiting for me in the hotel bar or in the room, freshly bathed, with her hair wrapped in a towel like Scheherazade when I came up, coat smelling of the outside world. Then we'd fall on each other, two healthy young animals.

For a while this was enough. I asked no questions, and we didn't talk about Dothan. For a while there was just her body, and the smell of her and the feel of her hair in my hands, and afterward, smoking like two characters in a foreign movie and ordering room service: bacon cheeseburgers or tepid filé gumbo at 3:00 A.M.

I was young then and not so experienced with women, but I knew from the beginning that there was something missing, that her heart did not follow her body when we made love. That she was possessed by a reserved spirit, cold and watching at the center of it all. I am not saying that she lacked enthusiasm. She had plenty of that, and I learned a few things in bed that stood me in good stead with paler women later, but something vital was missing, a piece to the puzzle not in place. Then, one night following the act, Antoinette drowsing against my shoulder, it hit me: We weren't making love at all; we were fucking.

I woke her up and told her so.

She looked at me through sleepy eyes. Then she leaned up, gave me an ironic sort of kiss at the side of the mouth, and said, "Baby, just go to sleep."

But I wouldn't go to sleep, and I sat up brooding over it until dawn.

A few days later, in bed in room 247 of the old River Mark Hotel, I brought up the subject again. Through the thin walls of the place came the hooting and catcalls of a bachelor party. They had a stripper in the suite next door. I'd seen this buxom creature coming up in the elevator, wrapped in a long raincoat, accompanied by a man the size of an outhouse. We could hear the drunken howls every time the girl squatted down to pick dollar bills out of someone's teeth with her vagina, and then the sound of breaking glass.

In our room the television was on to static to drown out the sound of this neighboring bacchanal.

"You might as well shut off the TV," Antoinette said at last, turning on her hip away from me. "It's not working."

I got up and turned it off, but instead of getting back into bed, I sat down naked in the desk chair across from her.

She blinked at me curiously. Her gray eyes shone like a cat's in the dim light of the desk lamp. The hooting surged from next door, and from the opposite side, the sound of a toilet being flushed.

"I'm sorry this is a crummy hotel," Antoinette said, and put the pillow over her head. When she came up for air and saw me still sitting there, she held out her arm for me to come to her.

I shook my head. "We need to talk," I said.

She was quiet a moment. "O.K., why don't we talk in bed?" she said at last.

"That won't work."

Then she sighed and rolled over onto her back, her breasts fleshing out on either side like a river overflowing its banks. She clasped her hands between them, a saint in repose. She was never an easy woman to talk to; she did not trust words. She held back so much of herself that reticence became a habit.

"All right, if everyone's going to talk," she said, staring at the ceiling, "why don't you put on your pants?" It did seem strange to have a serious talk in the nude, so I stood and put on my jeans and pulled on my T-shirt and sat down again in the chair.

"O.K., go ahead."

I hesitated, looked out toward the city, elusive in the green light, and looked back at Antoinette, still staring at the ceiling. The hotel seemed terribly quiet all of a sudden. I knew I had everything to lose, but I couldn't stop myself. "I'm tired of hotel rooms," I said. "This whole thing's beginning to seem a little cheap."

"I'll admit this place is a shithole, but it's all I could get tonight, baby," she said. "The Quarter was booked solid. But you like the Holiday Inn Château LeMoyne, right? They've got that huge Jacuzzi tub in the bathroom, remember?"

"You're missing the point, Antoinette," I said. "First, all this is really expensive. Hotel rooms three, four nights a week. My God! And it just vanishes on your credit card. That's not right."

"Money," she said with a dismissive wave. "Don't you worry about that."

The party next door was fading in and out like a bad radio station. "Antoinette," I said softly, "next time let's go to your apartment or mine."

"No," she said.

"Why not?"

"You're pushing me on this. Stop. Just let it go for a while."

"Antoinette, are you still sleeping with Dothan?"

"Don't ask me that," she said sharply. "That's none of your goddamn business."

"O.K.," I said, "I should go." I don't know where I got the courage to get up, to dig around in the mess of clothes on the floor, to pull on my socks and tie my shoes, to buckle my belt, to get my coat and step over to the door. I put my hand on the knob and half turned back toward her. She lay motionless in bed, hands still clasped tightly between her breasts, eyes fixed on the water-stained acoustic tiles of the ceiling.

"I'm crazy about you," I said. "You know that. But I need something. A word. Something to keep going with this. Otherwise it's just fucking. And I suppose I'm still too much of a Catholic to believe that's a good thing."

I stood there like a fool, watching her. She wouldn't say anything. After a while I turned the knob and went out into the carpeted hall, and got into the elevator again with the stripper and her bodyguard. This girl, a year or two younger than Antoinette, was no doubt on her way to another gig at another hotel across town, and I snuck a good look at her in the hard white light. Her hair was in place, her makeup newly applied, mascara and eyeliner perfect. Calm, pale, composed, she did not show a single drop of sweat or any outward sign of her recent performance.

9

I waited all week for Antoinette to call. She didn't call. It was one of the hardest weeks of my life.

I alternated between curses and self-congratulation on my handling of the situation. I was tough all right, I said to myself, real tough. But then I'd break down and pray to some secret god of lovers that Antoinette would come back to me. This didn't seem like a matter for the Catholic God, the God of chastity and abstinence and punishment, the God on the cross, who never laid a finger on Mary Magdalene and who spoke through the apostle Paul to tell us that physical love, even confined to the sacred bonds of marriage, was at best a lewd compromise with the evils of the flesh. Instead I prayed with intensity and despair to another being entirely. A female deity in her hidden velveteen bower in the humid shade. A goddess of laughter and music and the rustle of silk under silk, and long afternoons in the arms of a woman whose husband was elsewhere. A goddess whose famous name I did not care to pronounce, adding another broken commandment to the long list we acquire before we leave our mother's house.

To pass the time, I drank. Molesworth was the architect of this escape. I'd present myself to him like a penitent in the red evenings after class, and he'd fire up the Land Rover, and we'd do the town till 3:00 and 4:00 A.M., undergraduates again. He was a man who asked no questions. At some point in his distant past all the natural curiosity had been beaten out of him by one of his backwoods relations, or perhaps he was one of the lucky few content not to know. But a man who asks no questions often gets answers despite himself.

We were ensconced in one of the foul, beer-sticky booths all the way out at the Stew Pot, sunk in gloom over two bottles of Jax with bumps, when I spilled my guts. Molesworth had traveled this far afield to score a few bags of homegrown weed from his connection, a suspicious ex-con known only as Sawyer, who hung out in the bathroom there. The deal went down in one of the stalls while I kept an eye on the door for the local police, drank my beer, and tried to look as innocent as possible, given the circumstances.

The Stew Pot is a little-visited dive out on the fringes of Belle Chasse on the other side of the river and typical of the establishments found in Plaquemines Parish. The usual chewy Cajun crocodile bits deep fried in congealed fat as bar food, the usual morose country songs on the jukebox and Confederate flag–mounted fish decor, with one remarkable exception: A full-length portrait of Judah P. Benjamin in frock coat and gray beard painted sometime before the Civil War hung over the bar. The portrait was stained and blackened with age and torn at the corner, but still a museum piece. How it ended up at the Stew Pot was beyond imagining. I asked the redneck

132

bartender if he knew anything about it when he came over with another round.

He shrugged. "Jest a picher of some old fart," he said.

"Where did it come from?"

"Hell if I know, been here since I been here."

"That's Judah P. Benjamin," I said.

"Who?"

"He was a Jew."

The redneck's jaw dropped and he turned to the portrait with suspicion. "Huh," he said. "A Jew."

When he went away, Molesworth raised an eyebrow.

"Judah P. Benjamin, though a Jew in a day of much anti-Semitism, became secretary of state of the Confederacy under Jefferson Davis," I said. "He was often called the Brains of the South. He led a wandering life, full of temporal successes, but sad somehow. Born in the West Indies, the son of a rabbi, he went to Yale, went into exile after the war rather than swear an oath to the Union. He eventually became a famous barrister in England and died in France in the arms of his French mistress on an estate outside Paris. He never returned to New Orleans, a city he dearly loved."

"So who cares?"

"It's history, Molesworth. You should care. Everyone should care. Judah P. Benjamin at the Stew Pot. Amazing."

"I don't give a damn," Molesworth said. "Let's get out of here."

"Where?"

"Back to civilization. Let's go to Spanish Town. Haven't been there in a while. We can say hello to Dothan and that beautiful bitch he's got behind the bar."

I went white. "No," I said. "I can't go to Spanish Town."

"Can't?" Molesworth said, surprised.

"Don't ask."

Molesworth shrugged and went back to his beer, tipping the butt end of his bottle toward Judah P. Benjamin, who seemed to nod back, his bearded lip touched with a smile of benevolent patriarchy.

After a while I said, "Aren't you going to ask?"

He shook his head. "Nope."

"O.K.," I sighed. "I'll tell you." I told him everything, sparing only those intimate details which discretion forbids the gentleman from repeating in a barroom.

After I was done, he set his beer down on the table with a wet, decisive click, something like disappointment in his eyes. "Have I taught you nothing, Coonass?" he said. "All these years, and you're still the same Yankee coonass you were when you moved into the dorms. You've gone and done it this time, all right." Then he made an inarticulate gesture with his thick hand.

"Gone and done what?" I said, trying to keep the panic out of my question.

He leaned close, his voice a deep gravel now, his breath smelling like beer and careless brushing. "There are badasses, and there are badasses. Dothan is one of the latter, from a family full of badasses. I'm not saying he isn't a decent sort. He's fully rational, not like his brother Curtis. But Christ, when the sombitch gets mad . . ."

On the way back to town, up the Belle Chasse Highway, through Fort St. Leon and the greenish mists of 10:30, a large blue snipe flew low across the grille of the Land Rover and swung off into the darkness on its big wings toward the Bayou Barrierre Country Club. Molesworth honked the horn at the big clumsy bird and gestured with a Styrofoam go-cup full of bourbon and soda. In those days, before intrusive national legislation, Louisiana was one of the few states civilized enough to allow its citizens to drink and drive and carry a gun in the car at the same time.

"If I were an ancient Roman," Molesworth said, "I'd take that bird as an omen. A bad omen."

"You're not an ancient Roman, Molesworth," I shouted over the carbon monoxide roar of the engine.

"Augury, you know, the prediction of the future from the flight of birds. The ancient Romans were into that sort of thing. Think, when was the last time you saw a snipe flying at night?"

"I have no idea," I said.

"They're diurnal birds, not nocturnal. Everyone knows that." Molesworth, though he knew little else, knew the wildlife of the Louisiana swamps

135

in a detail unequaled since the day John J. Audubon set up an easel in the Barataria wilderness. "And they're river birds. We're a good way from the river out here. An omen, Coonass!"

"O.K.," I said. "I'll bite. What does that particular bird tell you?"

He paused, took a sip of his bourbon, and nodded a toothy grimace at the dark windshield, faint glow of the instruments in his face. On the short-wave now, the plaintive wail of Cajun violin from a station clear across the state in Bayou Laforce.

"That little bird tells me you're a fool, Ned." There seemed for a moment an unusual note of sympathy in his voice that scared me more than anything I had heard tonight. "It's bound to end badly for you. A woman like that. What kind of fool rushes to meet disaster?" He wouldn't say any more.

For a while we drove on in silence except for the sound of the truck. When we slowed down coming into Gretna and the West Bank Expressway, I took advantage of the lessened roar to say, almost in a whisper, "But she's beautiful. She's the most beautiful woman I've ever seen. Without her the days drag by, empty, dull. She's like the sun, Molesworth. Without her the whole city is dark, the whole state. Dark, empty streets full of strangers."

"Very pretty, Coonass," Molesworth said. "But let me tell you a little story. There was this Greek Coonass named Paris for some reason, though why they named a Greek after a French city will

136

always escape me. In any case, he ran off with this high-class chick who was some other poor sombitch's wife. But Paris, he had a choice in this matter. It's not like people don't have choices. He could have chosen to be the smartest man in the world, the richest man in the world or to run off with this chick. He picked the chick over all of that. Shit, you know what happened next. The rest is history, which is your field. A whole shitload of trouble."

We didn't say anything more about it. He finished the go-cup and crumpled it and tossed it on the floor with the rest of the garbage, and soon we were on the New Orleans Bridge, running at full bore toward the city whose light, if Molesworth's augury was to be believed, illuminated a tragic destiny.

10

Two days later came another knock at our door on Mystery Street, and the boy from Marche Florists delivered a second armload of roses from Antoinette. These were white, to show the purity of her intentions, and the card said, "I'm sorry about everything. Been missing you. I'll try. Please come to my apartment tonight at 8:00. 177 Marigny, No. 3, if you don't remember. — A."

Molesworth was out somewhere, so I hid the

roses in my bedroom beneath a sheet, and I went and got a haircut at a Salvadoran place on Esplanade at DeSoto, where for five dollars you emerge looking like a gaucho in an old movie. Then I went home and dressed and walked over to the Delgado Museum and mooned absently around the galleries there till it came time to take the bus downtown. Traffic was sparse along the streets of the faubourg. A pale and inviting light showed through the shutters of Antoinette's apartment. She buzzed me up without speaking, and I took the narrow steps two at a time. The door was open, a deep, slow jazz coming from within. It was eight o'clock exactly.

I saw the gleam of silverware and crystal as I entered and took off my coat. The small table in the living room was set for dinner. Just then Antoinette came out of the kitchen with a bottle of wine and two glasses. She smiled.

"I knew you'd be on time," she said. "But look at me, I'm not even dressed." She wore a new red plush robe that fell all the way to the floor, and her hair was loose and damp about her shoulders. There was something different about the place. I looked around for a beat, saw the fainting couch, its yellow pillows plumped up, the oriental rug, the photograph of the painting hanging straight between the French doors.

"Wow, you cleaned," I said. "Just for me."

"Well, sort of. I got a maid."

She went over to the table to open the wine, but I stepped up and took the bottle from her and put my hand on her breast under the robe and kissed her and started pulling her toward the bedroom.

"Hey," she said, "we've got to eat dinner. It's almost ready. Crayfish Étouffée, salad, wine . . ."

I stopped in the doorway and leaned her back against the frame. She put her face on my neck and lay there, silent for a moment, and there was the fragrance of perfume and soap and shampoo and the ready smell of her.

"So I guess you forgive me," she said, her face still in my neck.

"Sure," I said, and I reached around and tugged the robe down off her shoulders, and pulled her back into the bedroom, closing the door behind, even though the apartment was empty.

11

Later we lay in each other's arms in the rumpled sheets of her four-poster and listened to the hush and murmur of the darkened city beyond the shutters. The jazz record on the turntable kept repeating. Lassitude prevented us from getting up to turn it over. I pushed my face into her armpit and inhaled the pleasant bitter smell of her body.

"Hey," she said, and slapped me lightly on the nose with the back of her fingers. Out in the living room the record player picked up and went back to the beginning again. "Someone's got to change that," she said.

"Unh-huh."

"And my étouffée is going to be ruined."

"We'll eat it for breakfast."

"Aren't you hungry?"

"Yeah," I said, "but not exactly for étouffée."

She smiled and reached for me.

After we made love again, Antoinette sat up in bed and lit a cigarette from the pack on the night table. She offered one, but I shook my head.

"Reminds me of those motel rooms," I said.

"Oh." She stubbed it out quickly in the ashtray and put her head on my chest.

"There's still no promises. I'll try to make things different. I want you to know that," she said. "But you'll need to show me what to do, because I'm new at this. What do you want me to do?"

I thought for a moment. Then I said, "I want you to tell me about Dothan."

She went stiff and rolled off me and was quiet for a long time, but then she said, "All right, I'll tell you about Dothan," and went on in a small voice. "Dothan and I had a talk on Wednesday. He's off on a tour of South America for the next three months. Colombia, mostly. Then Venezuela and Peru. I don't know what he's doing down there, and I don't want to know, but I can guess. In any case, we're supposed to think about things while he's away, and we're supposed to have this big talk when he gets back."

"What will you say to him?"

"I don't know."

"Did you tell him about me?"

She hesitated. I couldn't see her eyes in the darkness.

"Did you?"

"Yes."

"Was it hard?"

She reached for another cigarette, lit it, and blew the smoke out her nose like a tough chick in a bar. In the few seconds it took her to light the cigarette her mood had changed.

"There's a lot you don't know about Dothan and me," she said a little harshly.

"O.K."

"I mean, I have loved him. I have loved him very much."

"Do you still love him?"

"Do you really want the whole story?"

"Yes."

"All right, shut up and listen, since you want to hear it," she said, and took a deep breath of the cigarette smoke. "Papa has a place up in Bayou Dessaintes near Mamou. A fishing place not much more than a shack, really, with an outhouse — there's electricity now, just got it a couple years ago — but Papa loves the place. He's never happier than when he's up there fishing or carrying on away from Mama's society friends and all that shit in the Garden District. Out of us girls I was his favorite. He told me once that I reminded

141

him of his sister who died when she was still beautiful and young in high school with the nuns.

"In any case, Papa always took me up there with him when he went for the weekend. He'd fish, and he'd let me drink beer and smoke. Once, I was about ten, I remember, and he fed me two beers and I was drunk off my ass. Papa just laughed. Then he'd have these poker parties with some of the local boys, and I'd sit in a chair in my nightgown — nothing very revealing, just an old flannel thing buttoned up to here — I'd sit beside Papa and watch him and tell him what cards to keep and what cards to put down. Hell, they'd play till four in the morning, old Cajun stuff on the radio, Hank Williams, whatever, and drink and talk like bayou men do, and crack dirty jokes, but Papa didn't mind because they were always respectful to me. To this day, I'll tell you, I'm a pretty good poker player. I can bluff with the best of them, and I'm a good fisherman, too. I can tie a lure, and I can fix an outboard with a rubber band, gum, and some spit. You got that?"

"Huntin', fishin', cardplayin'," I said. "Yes, ma'am!"

She elbowed me for my sarcasm and went on.

"So one summer Papa and I went up to the cabin for two months because he'd been working real hard and needed to get away for a while. By this time, understand, I'm thirteen, and already pretty well developed. Just about as busty as my sister Jolie, who was seventeen and in her last year at St. Jerome's Academy. You could say I divide my life into distinct categories, B. B. and A. B. — that is, before breasts, when I was a girl, and after, when I grew up pretty fast and did a few things maybe that should have waited for later."

She paused here, said, "Wait a minute," and set her cigarette on the lip of the ashtray on the night table and went out and turned the record over. It began to rain suddenly, as it will in South Louisiana, rain sweeping up from the direction of Algiers and across the low neighborhoods of the city, the drops beating lightly against the shutters. Before she got back into bed, Antoinette pulled the curtains wide and opened the window to the deluge, leaving the shutters closed. Damp air entered the room, and with it the smell of the river and mud and the fecund bayous of the delta. There was a slight chill on her body when she crawled back in beside me.

"Hold me," she said.

I held her until she was warm, watching the cigarette over her shoulder on the nightstand smolder down to its filter and wink out. A few minutes later she rolled away from me, took a breath, and went on.

"So there was this younger guy that started showing up at Papa's poker parties, a kid compared to the rest of them, about twenty-five then, I guess, but he was one hell of a good poker player and my God! one of the most beautiful single human beings I had seen outside of Peter Frampton with his shirt open on the cover of

143

Frampton Comes Alive, who I had a serious crush on back then. This poker-playing boy was the son of Claude Palmier, a Cajun tracker out of Mamou Papa used when he took friends from New Orleans on hunting trips. Dothan was his name. A weird name, some biblical thing, but he looked like a combination of Elvis and Richard Burton, and there I was, thirteen with these brand-new breasts and feeling sort of wild whenever he came into the room. Papa stopped letting me hang around in my nightgown that summer, because as he put it, 'I was growing into too much of a lady.' But keep in mind this is the seventies. Instead of my coverall flannel nightgown, I wore jeans cut down to here and a midi-halter top thing, and my hair's parted down the middle like Laurie Partridge, and I'm hanging out all over. All in all, the nightgown would have been less revealing.

"So after a while I caught Dothan sneaking looks at me over his cards, but not so anyone else would notice. He was very smart about it. Picked his moments. I tried not to look back, but it was impossible. There he was with these black eyes staring like he knew things about me I didn't know myself. He probably didn't figure me for thirteen, but I don't think it would have mattered much to him anyway. Then, one night when they were playing pretty hard, Dothan sat out a hand to use the outhouse. He went out on the porch and into the yard, but he came back real quietly a half minute later and stood just the other side of the screen door. Something made me look up, and he smiled and beckoned and stepped back out of the light. I said something about being hot and went out on the porch and found him there smoking in the shadows. He threw the cigarette away and pushed me against the side of the house and started kissing me like that, and his hands were all over me, and his belt buckle pressed into my bare stomach, and he was saying stuff in my ear I had never heard before. Finally I crooked my elbow around his neck and pushed up against him like I had been doing it all my life and kissed him back, and he probably would have done me right there against the side of the house except for the men playing cards inside."

"Jesus," I said, slightly shocked. "Were you scared?"

She paused for a moment. "No, I wasn't scared," she said. "I knew exactly what he wanted and what I wanted to give him. I'm the youngest of five sisters, and you know how sisters are."

"So when did it happen?"

"Why am I telling you all this?"

I shrugged. "Because I'm interested?"

"You're dangerous. Women lay in bed and they tell you things that they shouldn't tell you. . . ." Then, for a minute or so, it seemed Antoinette would stop, but she didn't.

"It happened two weeks later in the back of his pickup on some blankets," she said. "He got me drunk on wine and I wanted to do it, so

145

we did. Afterward I was scared finally, and I cried because I knew there was no going back. But he kissed me and told me he loved me and said he wanted me and would always want me because I was beautiful like the stars to him, and he swore he would marry me and take me away from Papa and we would live together in a big house in the bayou, and by God, he meant it. All of it. Dothan may be a hard-ass sometimes and a little bit of a smuggler and what not, but when he says a thing, he means it.

"So we made love all that summer, and I got to like it. I would sneak out of the cabin just before dawn, just after Papa went to bed, drunk from the card game, and Dothan and I would make love in his truck parked on one of the trails in the bayou. Or in the ruins of the old Spanish fort, sun coming up over the crumbling brick walls. When I went back to New Orleans in the fall, Dothan drove down in his truck for the weekends, and we'd get hotel rooms out in Arabi or someplace. I told my parents I was sleeping over at one friend or another's, and we'd go to redneck bars out there in the suburbs, where they're not too picky about IDs, and Dothan would tell the rednecks that I was his wife. . . ."

Antoinette was quiet for a while, smoking, her eyes dark and far away. "Do you want me to go on?" she said at last.

"Yes."

"Of course, my parents found out, finally. I had built this web of lies, and it all came crashing

146

down on me. Jolie told them, that bitch. She said she did it for my own good, but I think she did it because she was jealous. Because she wanted a boyfriend as beautiful as Dothan. When Papa found out it was Dothan, he was furious. He told me I could never see him again. Ever. There I was, his favorite daughter, a slut or something, and there was Dothan, ten years older and worse; a Cajun, for chrissakes, a bayou rat. Not good enough for his daughter, no way in hell. There's always been this thing between the Creoles and the Cajuns in Louisiana. You know that, right?"

"Vaguely," I said.

"The Creoles were aristocrats, descendants of Spanish and French nobility, all that crap. Plantation owners. And the poor backwardsass Cajuns, well — redneck peckerwoods. Possum-eating scum who ran down from Canada when the Brits got too tough on them."

"Plantation owners?" I raised one skeptical eyebrow, a habit acquired from Molesworth. "Did your family really have a plantation once?"

"Hell, yes. Had a big old place down past English Turn on the river. Slaves, the whole nine yards."

"What happened?"

"Burned to the ground during the Civil War, that's what happened, like everything else. We've still got a bit of land down there, all tangled over with kudzu and Spanish moss. Keep in mind this is Mama's family. Papa's family wasn't much different from Dothan's really. They were Creole, but poor Creole. Fishermen or something out on Grand Isle. Papa came up the hard way. Went to the army in World War II, went to engineering school on the GI Bill. Made a lot of money in the oil fields by inventing this drill bit thing, I don't know. The house on Prytania Street, all the dumb old pictures, and dusty old books, that's Mama's stuff. You ever see the house?"

I shook my head.

"You will," she said, and she leaned over and kissed me lightly on the lips and continued her story. "After he found out about Dothan, Papa wouldn't speak to me, not a word. For three weeks I stayed in my room. I wouldn't go to school. I hardly ate. I just cried and cried. It was terrible. Mama came in to talk to me, but I wouldn't talk to her. I wouldn't talk to anyone. I just cried because they were watching me all the time and I couldn't get to Dothan. Finally I managed to sneak a phone call to him from a pay phone, and he came down in his pickup truck and parked right out front and knocked on the door. I saw him through the window, but I stayed in my room. I could hear the yelling from downstairs and glass breaking. Dothan told Papa he wanted to marry me. Today I think how ridiculous this was, but then it seemed like something right out of *Romeo and Juliet*. I was barely fourteen, a freshman at St. Jerome's Academy. Shit! Of course, Papa said no. Papa said if he ever saw Dothan again, he'd get the police and have him locked in jail for statutory rape. Then he threw a half full bottle of Old Grand-Dad at something Dothan said, but Dothan ducked, and it crashed into Mama's china closet and broke a whole lot of her precious antique crockery.

"I watched him drive away, but I had stopped crying because I knew what I was going to do. A week later I decided to go back to school, and a few days after that Dothan was waiting for me with his truck. I was in my school uniform. I still remember it: dress blue blazer with the cross and crown on the pocket, white shirt and bow tie, blue plaid skirt, saddle shoes. I just put my books on the curb and got in the truck without a second thought. Jolie saw us drive away and ran after, screaming for us to stop, but I didn't look back. We drove down to the river near the grain elevators off the levee and made love right there in the cab. Then we drove off to Baton Rouge. Dothan had already rented an apartment there in Spanish Town, not far from LSU. That's why he called the bar Spanish Town, after the six months we spent there, living together like we were married."

"Six months? What about your parents?"

"My poor parents were frantic. They called the police, they called the FBI; they called everyone. There was an APB out on Dothan. The state troopers were looking for him all over. It was even in the papers and on TV. They called it a kidnapping, but Dothan wasn't afraid. We would live together for three years, he said. Then, when I was seventeen and old enough to consent, we would get married. He sold the truck, got some phony name and phony driver's license from one of his crooked friends, and got a job working in an electronics store, selling stereos. Dothan in an electronics store, crazy just to think about it.

"We had fun for a while. Dothan played husband and I played wife, and we smoked pot and ordered out fried chicken and pizza every night and went to the bars and made love afterward. But I was too young for it, really. I missed my family and my friends at school. So one Saturday, when Dothan was out scoring some weed, I called Mama, and she cried and cried. She loved me, she said, she missed me. She wanted me to come home. Then Papa got on the phone, too, and he cried. It really shook me up, hearing Papa cry. It was terrible. I made a deal with him right then and there. 'Let me keep going out with Dothan,' I said, 'don't get him in trouble, and I will come home and go back to school.' They agreed. They just wanted me home.

"The next day Dothan packed up my things and drove me back to New Orleans. He was scared, but Papa kept his word and called the police and squared things somehow so Dothan wouldn't get in trouble. Dothan and I have been together ever since, going on ten years now. I mean, we've had our ups and downs. Didn't even speak to each other for almost a year once. I went on a few dates, even brought a few of them

150

around to the house, but they were nothing compared to Dothan, and when we got together again, it was great. And it's been great up till recently. Till he moved down from Mamou and opened up his bar. And that's pretty much the whole story. The end."

Antoinette was quiet for a few minutes afterward, smoking her cigarette and blowing the smoke through her nose. The rain picked up outside, and wind rattled the shutters. She got up and closed the window, pulled on her robe, and turned to look at me through narrow eyes.

"Let's go eat some étouffée," she said.

I got up and put on her spare terry-cloth robe, and we went into the living room and she brought out the étouffée and the salad. The étouffée was dried out from sitting on the stove all that time, and the rice was sticky; but the salad was good, and the wine was fine. It was a silent meal. The candles burned low. Side two of the jazz record kept repeating itself. At last, during the salad, Antoinette looked up at me.

"O.K.," she said. "What else? There's something else."

I looked down at my plate. "What is he like?" I said.

"You're jealous?"

"No. A little."

She took a sip of her wine and sighed. "He's wild. He just does whatever the hell he wants, and the rest of the world be damned. You've got to realize I grew up with him. I did everything with him. Before Dothan, I was a little girl. He does a lot of drugs, more lately, so I've done a lot of those, too, because for a while there we did everything together. I don't really see them as bad, especially pot, as long as it's recreational and doesn't take over your life."

"Is he dangerous? Molesworth says he's dangerous."

"I suppose he can be mean. He's never been mean to me. He's never hit me. Lord knows, I've hit him a hundred times. Gave him a black eye once after I heard through the grapevine he went off with some bimbo in Shreveport. I love him. I'll always love him. It's just that . . ." Her voice trailed off.

"What?"

"He's the same. He's always the same. I don't think he'll ever grow up. He'll just stay the same hell-raising good old boy forever. I started out younger than him, and he knew everything. Then I caught up with him, and for a year or two we had the best time. But now I'm older than he is. I've been to college, more or less — that is, I've got a year or so left at Dominican. I know things he doesn't know, and I see now that a lot of the things he does are just plain stupid. We're becoming different people now. He'll never change. I think change is a good thing. He doesn't. And I'd like to go out with someone else for a while."

She leveled her pale eyes at me, and I saw that she meant what she said, and I felt a twinge in my heart for this man who loved her and had loved her from the beginning. Men can be like that, constant and blind, their women changing in the dark hours when they are not looking, just when they think everything is safe. Mutating, growing new limbs, turning away, becoming utterly unrecognizable in the space of two weeks, a day, an hour. I might not be the one she'd settle on in the end, but she was through with Dothan, that was plain to see.

Antoinette put her wineglass down, leaned across the table, and took hold of my hand.

"Now that I've told you all this," she said, "I want you to forget it. I want you to make love to me and keep making love to me for the next three months. And when Dothan gets back, I want to be as far away from him as possible. I want to be gone. O.K.?"

I started to say something, but Antoinette said, "Shh!" and put her lips over mine and took my hand, and we went into the bedroom and got back into the high four-poster bed, where we stayed for the next three days. Making love and talking softly in the soft light as rain swept across the low neighborhoods and the brown river frothed and boiled up the sides of the levees and sandbags broke in the lower delta and water spread across the black, rich earth of cottonfields beneath the wild yellow hurricane sky of the season.

12

Suddenly, from the furtive life of motel rooms and French Quarter tourist bars, I entered a world I barely knew existed. The way Antoinette handled her credit card and a comment or two from Molesworth had led me to believe her parents were well off, but in fact, they were better than this. They were filthy rich. According to *Louisiana Magazine*, Antoinette's father, Charles Gaston Rivaudais, was the major shareholder in the Louisiana Gulf Company, and one of the dozen richest men in the state. Her mother, Helene d'Aurevilley Rivaudais, was the last-surviving offspring of a prominent Creole plantation family who had come to the region not ten years after the Sieur de Bienville caused his surveyors to lay out the streets of a new city at a defensible bend in the river.

Her full name was Antoinette Marie Jeanne d'Aurevilley Rivaudais, a marvelous mouthful. She had four older sisters — Elise, Manon, Claudine, and Jolie. All of them attractive, though none as downright beautiful as Antoinette. Elise, the oldest and most responsible, had married an engineer out of the University of Texas at Austin who now managed the Biloxi branch of her father's firm. They had two girls, a four- and a five-year-old hellion with blue eyes and hair the color of straw.

Manon, the bohemian of the family, met an Irish jazz musician while attending Juilliard in

New York and had married him the year before in a quick ceremony at City Hall in Manhattan. Then they moved home to New Orleans for no particular reason and lived in a restored nineteenth-century Creole-style raised cottage on Carrollton Avenue, a wedding present from Papa. The Irish husband drank whiskey professionally, smoked Turkish cigarettes, and occasionally gigged at clubs around town. Manon's specialty was the harp, that damnably bourgeois instrument. She gave recitals twice a year with a quartet that played chamber music in the bandshell in Audubon Park and lived without a qualm of conscience off her trust fund.

Claudine and Jolie were just a year apart, three and four years older than Antoinette. They were the ambitious ones. They had gone to LSU together, both majored in political science, and now lived in Washington, D.C., in a neatly appointed town house on the Hill, not far from the ugly white wedding cake of the Capitol. Claudine worked in some minor administrative capacity for Republican Congressman Robert Essex, who represented the uptown wards of New Orleans and was coincidentally, a large shareholder in the Louisiana Gulf Company; Jolie worked as a lobbyist for the National Rifle Association. They were both part of the contingent of attractive, preppy, harddrinking Louisianans that enliven our staid capital.

I admired the Rivaudais family. I admired their style and their complacency and the grace with which they went about the world, the grace that comes from belonging to a specific place, from belonging to its streets and its skies, from knowing you are home. I had the wanderer's appreciation for those things they took for granted: family portraits, tombs in old cemeteries all over the city full of their familiar dead, stories of a hundred years past, ancient photographs, trunks full of musty letters.

For their part, the family didn't seem to like me much. I didn't really fit in. It was a question of attitude. I am ill at ease in company, sarcastic, cynical, sentimental. A northern temperament, Antoinette called it once. A temperament born of gray afternoons and sleety rains and melancholy, though I am a native of Washington, D.C. — technically south of the Mason-Dixon Line — where my father worked for the Bureau of Indian Affairs.

But worst of all, to the Rivaudaises' way of thinking, I was an intellectual. They regarded ideas as unnecessary, even dangerous. They were old-fashioned Creole pragmatists, happy with good food, strong drink, nice clothes, beautiful things — the fruits and sweetness of life.

13

In January, an icy wind blowing down across Lake Pontchartrain from the north, her parents took Antoinette and me to Commander's Palace for dinner in one of the private rooms there. They wanted to get a closer look at me, confirm the unfavorable opinions formed at our first meeting. Though relieved to find she had given up Dothan, they were suspicious of my motives. How could I tell them I didn't give a damn for their money, that it was only their daughter I wanted? Their daughter unadorned, naked, and asleep in my arms at three o'clock in the morning.

It was an expensive, excellent meal, full of awkward silences and stilted conversation. Antoinette, stiff beside me, looking marvelous in a tight dress of crushed velvet, rarely lifted her eyes from the plate. At last Mama, a big, handsome woman of about sixty, with hair still as black as her daughter's, rose and went off to the powder room. Antoinette flashed me a weak smile and followed demurely, and I was left alone at the table with the big man, Papa himself. He seemed an assured, robust figure in possession of an amazing mass of white hair and a mustache as thick as a hussar's. But there was a certain tiredness around his eyes and a disappointed droop to his lower lip. He looked like a Confederate general in retirement after the war. Like P. G. T. Beauregard at Contreras House before the White League riots, like Lee at Lexington in 1870. A man who had lived long enough to see his secret certainties confounded, his best hopes dashed by unfortunate circumstance.

He finished his cognac and studied me from

beneath his bushy eyebrows as I fidgeted. In the background, the clink of glasses, the hushed murmur common to expensive restaurants everywhere. Our waiter, who had introduced himself as Remi, approached in the uniform of the place — black trousers, a spotless red apron and starched tuxedo shirt and bow tie, his feet encased in a pair of those ridiculous glossy black tux slippers. He carried our check on an ebony tray. Papa waved him away without even looking.

"Not yet, Remi," he said.

Remi withdrew without a peep. I am always impressed by men who command the respect of waiters and bartenders, by men who know that money means prompt, efficient, and obsequious service.

Then Papa took a cigar sealed in an aluminum tube out of the inside pocket of his jacket, unscrewed the cap, and removed the dark, fragrant log within. He ran it beneath his nose, smiled, clipped the end carefully with a fancy device on his key ring, and lit it off the candle. In a moment the air of our little dining room was heavy with cigar smoke.

"Now you see why they put us in here," he said. "They know I like a good cigar after a meal, and people these days hate cigar smoke." This was dissimulation. The private rooms at Commander's Palace were reserved weeks in advance for special guests at a considerable surcharge over the main dining room.

For the next few minutes, absorbed in the cigar,

drawing on it, blowing smoke rings at the ceiling, Papa seemed to forget about me. I sat absolutely still, hands in my lap as if awaiting judgment. Finally, when I reached for the last of the wine, he made an exaggerated show of remembering my presence.

"Forgive my manner," he said. "I've got another one if you'd like to join me." He pulled a second aluminum tube out of his pocket and pushed it across the table. "They're actually Cuban. Have them imported through Panama with Jamaican labels. Here."

I shook my head.

He nodded, as if to say he knew as much, then went back to enjoying the cigar. In his houndstooth sports jacket and open-collared white shirt, cigar in mouth, he was the very image of the southern patriarch at his ease. Then he put the cigar in the glass ashtray and leaned forward so abruptly I started.

"Let me ask you something, Ned," he said, a sudden edge in his voice.

"O.K., Mr. Rivaudais," I said.

"What is it that you want from us?" It was an accusation.

I felt the back of my neck begin to sweat. For a moment I imagined being dragged outside by thugs from the bayou, my legs broken over the curb. But I can be just as pugnacious as the next guy. I looked down, drumming the tablecloth with my fingertips for dramatic effect. Then I looked up to confront him.

"I'll tell you what I want from you, Mr. Rivaudais," I said. "Not a damn thing."

He leaned back, a bit surprised. I wondered how many of his daughters' hapless suitors he had tried this with. I didn't blame him really. The world is full of scoundrels, and he had five attractive daughters and no sons. The poor bastard.

"So you're a student," he said at last.

"That's right. A graduate student."

"Studying some kind of history."

"French history, yes."

"And what is it you expect to do with that?"

"Become educated," I said.

"And then?"

"Then, to paraphrase Samuel Johnson, I will be fit company for myself."

"Unh-huh." He jabbed his cigar in my general direction. "Of course, it hasn't occurred to you that I am one of the wealthiest men in this state and that a union with my daughter would allow you to keep yourself company for life without doing much else."

This was a bit much. No wonder Antoinette had run away with a Lothario from the bayou. I told him so.

"You know about that," he said, looking a little crushed.

"Yes," I said, my voice raising. "And let me tell you something, sir. I don't care about that, and I don't care about your damn money. In fact, money to me is a strike against your daughter that I'm willing to overlook because I'm crazy about her. And for your information, all this is not my style at all." I waved to include the restaurant, the slippered waiter, the bejeweled customers in the main dining room. "I'd just as soon eat a po'boy at Nick's than put on a tie and swallow your crap."

"I didn't see you protesting when I brought you in here, son," he said calmly. "I would say quite the opposite. You seemed downright pleased to be walking through the door of Commander's Palace for a free meal."

"It was not my intention to abuse your hospitality," I said. Then I stood, almost knocking over the chair, and rang the bell for the waiter. In two seconds Remi entered on slippered feet with the check and made to hand it to Papa.

"No," I said, "I'll take that." He looked at Papa, who clamped the cigar between his teeth and shrugged.

"You heard the boy," he said.

The waiter nodded apologetically, handed the check to me, and left the room. The total came to $575, not including tax and tip. One of the bottles of wine Papa had ordered was listed at $125. I went white, slumped back in the chair, and went fumbling for my credit card with the dazed motions of a man who has just been told he has six months to live.

Then Papa began to laugh and laughed for the next few minutes till cigar smoke came out of his nose.

"I don't appreciate that, sir," I said stiffly.

He wiped his eyes on his napkin. "Your face," he managed. "When you saw that check! Priceless." Then he reached for it.

"No," I said weakly, "I'll pay."

But he made an unseen gesture and in a beat the waiter was there and the check was signed for and it was over.

"Don't worry about it. I've got an account here," he said. "And this is a legitimate business expense to me. Trying to marry off my daughter. Hell, I was a student myself once, if you can believe it. Scraping after every penny. I know how it is." Then he leaned forward and put a conciliatory hand on my arm. "Listen, let me give you a piece of advice. Please."

"O.K." I looked him in the eye. They were blue and watery, a sadder reflection of Antoinette's.

"What you need, Ned, is a sense of humor. Because if you're going to deal with my daughter, there's no other way. A highly developed sense of humor."

I thought he was probably right, so we shook hands.

A few minutes later Antoinette and her mother came back in, hand in hand, their eyes shining, the stink of oranges on their breath. They had been at the bar, drinking Cointreaus.

"You two men have a nice talk?" Mrs. Rivaudais said, and leaned to kiss her husband on the forehead. Antoinette came around and sat beside me and put a hand on my knee.

"Yes," I said. "We had a fine talk. Mr. Rivaudais tried to get me to smoke one of his cigars, but I turned him down."

"Good for you," Mrs. Rivaudais said. "Lord, those things do stink," and she gave her husband a drunken punch on the shoulder, and everyone laughed. Then Remi came in with a nightcap on the house, and everyone talked at once, and things were much more relaxed between us. But at the last of it I glanced over to see Papa, a weary sadness in his gaze, studying me from beneath his eyebrows.

14

A week later, out of money from a student loan, I bought a beat-up 1960 MGA for eight hundred dollars from a doctor in Gentilly who was selling his house, and took Antoinette along the Gulf Coast on a trip to Biloxi. Wind whistled through the holes in the tattered convertible top, the twin SUs stuttered and burped, but on the curves the old sports car flexed and held the road like a living thing, and the loud thrum of the engine at open throttle sounded a strange sort of harmony not available in newer vehicles.

Antoinette loved the old car from the first. She stretched out happily, feet against the dash like a teenager, and kept her hand on my thigh as

I racked through the gears with the grim determination of Stirling Moss himself. She wore cat-eye sunglasses, a silk scarf over her head and shouted over the engine's shudder to tell me I had won the first round.

"Papa said you stood up to him," she said. "Papa likes that, when people stand up to him. He said you've got backbone. He likes backbone."

Then she put her hand on top of mine on the gearshifter and kissed my ear, and that night we made love with particular intensity in one of the crumbling old rooms at the Biloxi-Stanton Hotel, windows open to the cold, salty air.

This was the first of several trips we took together in the three months between Thanksgiving and Mardi Gras, after I bought the car. Though Dothan was gone on his unspeakable journey south, the city still held his shadow. To escape it, we drove to Natchez and Opelousas and Galveston, and we went on smaller jaunts, just driving out of a Sunday. We drove a hundred miles along the River Road, stopping at Ashland and Destrehan and Oak Alley, where we strolled arm in arm down the famous approach of live oaks to the great house with the tourists, its twenty-eight columns gleaming in the winter light. We drove up to Oxford to visit Faulkner's home and up to Jackson for a Christmas party given by one of Antoinette's old classmates from St. Jerome's. Then we drove to Gulfport and Mobile. Christmas we spent with Antoinette's family — all five girls, husbands and broods, and a few aunts and uncles — in the Rivaudais condominium on St. Eustatius, Leeward Islands. I sent a sarcastic postcard to Molesworth from this idyllic tropical isle, showing a topless babe knee-deep in turquoise water with the caption "Wish you were here!" On the back I wrote, "Not really," and left it at that.

New Orleans in winter is mild, but there is a bite to the damp that can get into your bones. The furnace in our pink house went out in the middle of November, and there was frost in the yard. I never felt the chill that year. It was impossible to be cold with Antoinette around, her warm voice in my ear or just on the other end of the phone line. I did my best to forget about Dothan. Antoinette got a few postcards from the other hemisphere, sanitized tourist views of Caracas, of Bogotá and Lima, which she refused to let me read, and there was one long phone call full of silences in the middle of the night. I didn't mind.

She had taught me to live in the moment. For the first time in my life I gave no thought to the future or the past.

15

Now I remember the Mardi Gras party at Antoinette's parents' house on Prytania Street with some bittersweetness. It was the high point of my brief, bright life with her. I wandered the well-dressed crowds a dazed man, not daring to believe my luck, expecting the ceiling to come crashing down on my head at any moment.

The Rivaudais house was an amazing place, built in 1857 by a wealthy English cotton exporter, Albert Douglas, with the use of slave labor, fifteen varieties of indigenous hardwood and lavender marble from Carrara, Italy. Two raised galleries ran the length of the front and back, sheltering enormous high-ceilinged rooms filled with antiques and paintings. Historic houses often have the stiff and slightly lurid appeal of wax museums. Not so with the Rivaudais house, which managed to be both elegant and comfortable. Antoinette, wearing the same low-cut green velvet dress she had worn that night at the Napoleon House, rhinestone pins sparkling at her shoulders, gave me the tour just before the party started. In my rumpled fifties-era thrift-store tuxedo, I felt like a servant being shown the busing stations. But I nodded and smiled and cracked jokes and tried not to let on how badly outclassed I felt.

We poked our heads into the downstairs salon, where a jazz quartet warmed up in the corner, looked into the vast brick-walled kitchen crawling with caterers. Then we went up the wide staircase of polished maple, past age darkened portraits of ancestors — Spanish grandees and ladies of France dead two or three centuries, overlaid with the layers of varnish and fine skein of cracks that are the years. We ended up in the library on the second floor just as the downstairs began to fill with guests. Out the tall windows, expensive cars pulled up the circular drive to the red-jacketed valet parkers at the front steps, who in turn pulled them down again and parked them under guard along Prytania Street.

From above the mantel in this room the portrait of an especially forbidding ancestor glowered down at us. It showed a middle-aged man with olive-toned Spanish skin and a hawkish, unforgiving face. He wore the Byronic coat and high collar of the 1820s; his hand rested on a table upon which there were some charts, a brace of pistols, and a few heavy ledgers, probably lists of slaves and indigo and horses. Beyond a drape to his right a plantation house overlooked the river in the near distance. It was built in the early Creole style like Destrehan, with a horseshoe-shaped staircase leading to the galleries on the front, and walls an unusual shade of pale blue.

"Another ancestor of Mama's," Antoinette replied to my question. "They're all ancestors of Mama's. Father's people were too poor or too decent to have their portraits painted. Supposedly this guy was one real son of a bitch. Just a real mean bastard. Famous for his duels — that's why he had the pistols painted in. Looks Spanish, doesn't he? Like the Grand Inquisitor or something. Those eyes. Always scared the shit out of me when I was a girl. I used to be afraid to come in here alone." She shivered, though there was a fire going in the grate, and I put my arm around her bare shoulder.

"And the house?" I pointed to the distant blue mansion.

"That was the plantation I told you about. Along the river down past English Turn. Belle something. They're always called Belle something." She shrugged, oblivious to this lost patrimony. From downstairs now came the sound of voices and the thrum of the jazz quartet. I had never been in such a well-appointed room with such a beautiful woman. The world seemed a marvelous place. I turned to Antoinette and kissed her, happy and blind. We nuzzled for a few minutes on the couch until the door opened and Jolie pushed in, breathless.

"Hey, you two," she said, "some other time for that shit. Nettie, Papa wants you downstairs before the house is too packed to move."

"What for?" Antoinette said, annoyed, pulling away from me.

"You know, pictures. Up!" She snapped her fingers, and Antoinette rose with a sigh and smoothed out her dress.

"I am not in the mood for this fucking shit," she said to Jolie. Between themselves the girls used the cheerfully obscene language of truck drivers.

"What pictures?" I asked as we swept down the stairs to the crowds waiting below.

"Some Papa thing," Antoinette whispered. "He's got magazine people coming. *Southern Liv-*

ing. They're doing a spread on the party, on the house."

"On us," Jolie said with a sharp smile. "It's going to be about us."

A half hour later I slumped hands in pocket against the wall near the door and watched the family pose on the stairs. First the parents — Papa, ruddy-faced and slightly drunk, ill at ease in a tuxedo of magnificent cut; Mama, wearing a blue tulle gown of amazing proportions, sapphires at her throat — both of them the picture of success and earthly contentment, battles won, wine in the keg. Then the girls, arranged shortest to tallest, from Jolie to Antoinette, all cocktail dresses and bare shoulders and youthful promise, showing healthy teeth to the flash and whir of the camera and the applause of the guests gathered in the foyer: Louisiana's first citizens, residents of the Garden District, patrons of the most prestigious Carnival krewes.

It was hard to reconcile this Antoinette, smiling and elegant for the pages of *Southern Living*, with the other ones: the acid-dropping bar girl dancing above the drunks at Spanish Town or the jaded lover, who, even in my arms, wore her past like an extra layer of skin. Suddenly I felt a little dizzy. The spectacle was too much for me. I wandered the party alone for the next hour or so, drink in hand, catching glimpses of Antoinette engaged in conversation with well-dressed people I didn't know, her glossy hair reflecting light, the sound of her voice full of laughter floating an octave above the party chatter.

At last, a little drunk, I found myself out on the back patio. A semicircle of rough brick opened onto the garden encircled on all sides by a high hedge of English boxwood and a half dozen live oaks. It drizzled slightly, rain making a soundless trickle in the thick, dark leaves.

The caterers had set up a shrimp scampi station out here. It was a miscalculation, little patronized because of the weather. The fry chef dozed in a director's chair beneath the eaves against the old bricks of the house, a rather comical figure in his clown whites and tall hat. The gas fire from the burners fizzled a tepid yellow. His Teflon frying pans, large and purposeful as bicycle wheels, sat idle on the chopping block, beside Tupperware containers full of deveined translucent shrimp and bottles of olive oil. The sky showed a green glaze above the darkened garden. A cold wind picked up the rain suddenly and blew it in on us. The cook, snoring openmouthed, shivered in his sleep.

A soft soughing through the live oaks whispered a warning I could not hear.

16

The end came sooner than I expected.

Five days after Mardi Gras, on the first Saturday of Lent, the city scrubbed and penitent after the bacchanal, I stopped at Antoinette's apartment on my way home from the library. A 1958 Chevy Apache pickup was parked in a red zone at a crooked angle to the curb on Marigny directly in front of Antoinette's door. Its dented sides were painted submarine yellow. The tires, wide and knobby-treaded, were the sort of things for muddy back roads through bayou country. I put a hand on the big bell hood and felt the warmth there, the engine still ticking. The windows of Antoinette's apartment stood open to the street, shutters closed. From within, the vague rise and fall of voices.

For a moment I hesitated. Best come back later, I thought, when Antoinette had things sorted out. But I felt ashamed of my cowardice. I took a deep breath and went up the narrow stairs with the heavy, resigned step of a condemned man mounting the scaffold. From the landing I could hear the muffled sound of an argument. I let myself in with the key Antoinette had given me and put my books on the couch. They were in the bedroom. I paused a minute and listened. When I had heard enough, I called out to her.

Silence.

Finally Dothan said, "Who the fuck is that?"

"Oh, God," Antoinette said.

Then, in a moment like the eye of the hurricane, Antoinette emerged in her red robe, and I saw she was naked underneath.

"Ned," she said. She was puffy-faced from crying, and her eyes held a strained whiteness. She seemed surprised, though I often dropped by in the afternoons on my way home. "This is not a good time."

"What's going on in there?" I said quietly.

"Nothing, O.K.?" and she began to push me back toward the door.

But I looked down at the robe and her bare feet, and I said, "Have you been making love to him?"

From the bedroom came the hurried metallic clinking of a belt buckle and the sound of boots on hardwood. In a moment Dothan appeared in the doorway, his shirt in one hand. He was as brown and muscular as an Indian. A whitish scar crossed his chest with a diagonal line, and a tattoo of the Greek letter *omega,* showed red on his shoulder. His eyes were black. He pointed at me with one long, sinewy arm.

"Who the fuck is that?" he snapped. "Get that motherfucker the fuck out of here."

"Just a friend." Antoinette turned to him, an admirable calm in her voice. "He came to drop off some notes. I told you I was thinking about going back to school. . . . Thanks, Ned," she said to me, and again tried to back me toward the door, but I stepped out of the way.

"Dothan," I said, "my name is Ned Conti. We need to talk."

"Wait a minute, I remember you now, motherfucker." He advanced, menacing. "You're that fat shit's roommate."

172

"Yeah, and Antoinette told me all about you," I said.

"Yeah?" He stepped up till he was quite close. His underarms stank, and there was something else, the faint ammonia smell of lovemaking. He had let his sideburns grow, and now they reached down like two hairy hands on either side of his jaw. I choked down a quick burst of panic. There was no way out of this.

"So what did she say?" Dothan breathed his foul breath into my face. I could almost see his muscles tense.

"She said it was over between the two of you," I said. "She said she was crazy about me." This was a lie. Antoinette had never said anything of the kind, never made so much as a single promise.

Dothan swung toward her. "Is this true?" he hissed.

Antoinette lowered her eyes and said nothing. Light the color of stone came through the shutters in dull slashes. In the apartment next door a shower went on, and there was the murmur of a television.

"Is this true?" Dothan repeated. "Was there anything between you and this runty little motherfucker?"

She opened her mouth to speak, then closed it and shook her head.

"She's lying," I said. I looked at her, but she would not meet my eyes. "I'll put it so you can understand. We've been fucking for the last four

173

months. Since before you went to buy drugs in Colombia."

I was still looking at Antoinette when the blow came, it seemed out of nowhere, an explosion in my left eye. I went crashing back over the couch, blind, and Dothan was on top of me, quick as a monkey, flailing with his fists. I took it in the jaw and in the eye again. I don't remember much except for the hiss of Dothan's curses in my ear and the raw stink of him. It was a smell that clung to me for days. Then I heard Antoinette's voice screaming his name, and she came up behind, pulling at him to stop, her robe open, her breasts hanging down, the nipples red and swollen as the teats of a dog. He swung back and hit her across the face with a quick backhand and she fell away from him with a cry. But in another moment, I'm not sure how, he was off of me and the two of them were twisted together, weeping, in a heap on the floor, Dothan kissing her hair, her face.

"I'm sorry, baby," he sobbed. "I'm sorry. I'm so sorry. I ain't never hit you before. I didn't mean to hurt you. I'm a fucking asshole. I'm an asshole." Then he twisted away from her and slammed his fist into the tough old oak of the floor, once and again and again until I heard a sickening cracking which was the cracking of bone.

"Don't, Dothan! Stop it, please! Please!" He stopped, his face contorted in pain, and she took his broken hand and put it between her breasts and leaned over it and wept. He pulled her to him with his other hand, and they collapsed like that, weeping and petting each other on the floor.

I saw all this as a vague blur out of one good eye as I staggered up, my face bloody, my lip broken, the taste of blood in my mouth. Somehow, I gathered my books from the couch and stepped around them writhing there in private ecstasy and stumbled down the narrow stairs. Out in the faubourg the wind was cold and the pain in my eye was terrible, but it did not hurt enough to make me realize what a fool I'd been all along.

What a fool.

17

A week later the third and final bunch of roses was delivered to my home on Mystery Street. Red this time, symbolic of blood and suffering. The delivery boy waited sympathetically as I fished in my wallet for a tip.

"Man," he said, "who hit you over the face with a board?"

"Ran into a door," I said.

"Yeah, mighty big door."

"You could say that."

"I been here before, right? You the only people get flowers in this neighborhood."

"Yes," I said, and I gave him three dollars.

"Good luck, man," he said, and got back into

the Marche Florist van and drove out of my life.

"I can't tell you how very sorry I am about everything," the card said. "I would like to see you if that's O.K.," and it named a neutral, touristy meeting place, Café du Monde in the old French Market on Jackson Square and a time later that afternoon.

An unforgiving wind swept up from the river, but, hunched in our coats, we sat outside behind one of the thick beige columns. The waiter brought two café au laits and a paper plate of beignets covered with powdered sugar and went back inside, shivering.

My eye had been swollen shut for three days and was just opening up again. The skin around the eye was an amazing shade of purple, and my eyebrow still sported a lump the size of a quail egg.

Antoinette wore a short coat of faux leopard skin, long gloves of red kid leather, and a fancy scarf wrapped around her head. Cat-eye dark glasses hid her expression. She looked like an Italian starlet going incognito. She drank some of the coffee and put her hands in her pocket.

"Wow," she said. "Your eye."

"Yes," I said.

"Does it hurt?"

"Not too much anymore."

"Sorry," she said.

"About what?"

"About your eye." She didn't sound too sorry,

really. Pigeons perched on the equestrian statue of General Jackson in the park; tourists in rain slickers loitered in the arcade of the Cabildo. On the steps of the St. Louis Cathedral, two priests stood deep in discussion — arguing theological matters, one would like to think. From the river came the long, hollow whistle of a tanker docking at Algiers.

Antoinette looked away. "You need to know a few things," she said. "First, I love Dothan."

"But you're tired of him, you told me so yourself. You wanted to end it, to get away." I must have sounded a little desperate.

She held up her hand to stop me. "Please," she said. "He needs me. He's always needed me. We're probably going to get married. At least we're talking about it. He's just got to clean up his act a little bit. You were a lot of fun. But it's only been three months —"

"Four."

"Whatever. Dothan and I have been together ten years. You can't throw that sort of thing away without trying to work it out first." There was something missing in her voice, a certain depth that had been missing all along. She started to say something else, but I stood suddenly, and my chair fell over and clattered on the brick pavement.

"Enough," I said.

She looked up at me. I couldn't see her eyes through the dark glasses.

"Take off your glasses," I said.

177

She took them off. Her eyes were steely blue today, resolved.

"O.K.," I said. "Have a nice life."

Then, trying not to feel too ridiculous, I turned and walked down the square, past the pigeons and the tourists, and the ornate railings of the Pontalba Apartments, built by the philanthropic baroness in 1849. Antoinette called my name once, I think, but it is to my credit that I did not look back.

18

I have always been best at endings. I am an expert in tying up my affairs and disappearing into the night. The roots that hold me anywhere are never strong enough. I have a few acquaintances, fewer friends, a stick or two of furniture, a suitcase of clothes, eight boxes of books. Nothing indispensable, nothing real. Is one moment of bliss worth a lifetime? the poet asks. All the years since then I have made do with those few months in New Orleans with Antoinette. Every happy moment pored over, tattered and torn now at the creases like a letter from an old lover you will never see again. The pages are yellow, the ink faded to a whisper. Only the signature remains in a fluid, half-remembered hand.

Three days after our last meeting at Café du Monde, I was ready to go. The MGA packed, bills paid or discarded. I took a leave of absence from the history program at Loyola, citing a fictitious death in the family. I sold my books to Ribari's, the used-book place on Carondolet, and I gave my mattress to Molesworth. On the last afternoon he and I went in the Land Rover for one last drink at Saladin's, a little run-down place on Gentilly Boulevard.

We sat at the dusty table near the window and drank two Dixies apiece in gloomy silence and stared out at the traffic. Spring was on its way. The buds on the magnolia trees along the neutral ground looked like little white buttons from this distance. "I still think you're making a mistake, Coonass," Molesworth said. "Running out of town just because Dothan beat the shit out of you. Hell, if all the people that old boy beat the shit out of decided to leave town, there'd be a traffic jam on the Pontchartrain Expressway."

"Don't worry, Molesworth," I said. "I'm paid up through the end of the month. That should give you enough time to find another sucker."

"That's not it." He frowned and went on in a serious manner unusual for him. "Letting a woman chase you out of town is bad for your soul. So what if you move somewhere else? She'll always be there at the back of your mind, every time you look in the mirror, like a ghost. Why do you think I left Mamou, went to school? Hell, did you figure me for the academic type?" He turned his big face toward me, and I saw for the first time a deep sadness in his eyes.

"Molesworth," I said, shocked. "You?"

He nodded. "Takes people by surprise, don't it? Old Molesworth's a human being."

"Who was she?"

"Makes no difference now," Molesworth said in a tired voice. "It's over now. She's married. Three kids. Shit. Every time I go home it tears my heart out. If I had stayed, I might have been able to face it down, to reclaim my own town. Instead I ran. Big mistake."

"Too late, Molesworth," I said. "These streets are like poison to me. The green skies, the river. I can't stay another day."

"Where will you go?"

"D.C., my mom's for a while. After that wherever my credits will transfer. I'll finish the degree, do my thesis, then" — I shrugged — "life will engulf me. One city or the next, it doesn't matter. Maybe New York. New York is a good place for exiles."

"You're a morbid bastard, you know that?"

We finished our beers in silence, and he drove me back to the peeling pink house on Mystery Street and watched from the porch as I put a few last things into the MGA. When I was done, I stepped up and shook his hand.

"This is it, Lyle," I said. "God bless you, I guess."

"You, too, Coonass."

Then I got into the car and drove off, down Mystery to Esplanade and over to the expressway. Soon, within fifteen minutes, I had left the city behind, racing along the dark pavement, whine of the MGA in my ears, the choppy waters of Lake Pontchartrain away to my left, small planes descending toward the airport out of the gloom, and ahead now through the dirty windshield, only the gray prospect of northern cities.

19

But the past is the past, and despite our best intentions, life goes on.

Two and a half years later, in another spring, during exam week at Georgetown, I called Antoinette for no reason, on a whim. We talked for hours that night, not as lovers but as old friends. I am genuinely interested in her life, she in mine. We have stayed in touch sporadically since then, with the occasional call and the less than occasional postcard or letter. I finished the course work for my Ph.D. at Georgetown, then moved to New York for a paid research assistant-ship at the New-York Historical Society, which ended three years ago. Molesworth found me in Brooklyn when obscure events forced him to leave the state of Louisiana, and after an interval of six years he once again became my roommate.

Antoinette never finished college. She dropped out of Dominican to open up a vintage clothing boutique called Antoinette's Vintage Armoire, which is on Treme on the fringes of the Quarter.

It is a popular place, and she does a good business, especially around Carnival time. I have even seen her face-to-face a few times over the years. She comes up to New York now and then to shop for clothes for her store. On her visits we go to Domsey's, the used-clothing warehouse in Williamsburg, and I help her pack the boxes of mold-smelling clothes to ship back South, where they will be cleaned and repaired and sold for ten times what she paid. Then we go to dinner and stay out drinking till all hours in East Village bars. She looks beautiful still, though I am careful to keep my hands to myself. We are in our thirties now, and wiser. The years, if anything, have added an attractive patina of world-weariness that she wears well, like one of the 1940s-era dresses she sells in her store.

Somewhere along the way she dropped Dothan. We never talk about it. She is unmarried and not dating anyone seriously at the moment; of course, I get the impression that there are always plenty of men around. I am in love with her still, but that is no matter. This is a world in which the heart's desire, once achieved, can become bitter and sad and ugly. I have my life. There have been other women. One day I will finish my thesis and find someone else. New York is a city made up of lonely people like me. They are its bricks and its mortar.

Now, on these empty red evenings in Brooklyn, power plant bristling across the street, rank odor of the emulsion factory wafting through the window, broken glass on the pavement reflecting the last light over the island, I think Antoinette is better like that. As a memory. As a dream of her city, New Orleans, asleep and surrounded by its bayous between the river and the lake, beneath the green skies of the past.

Part Three:

A Séance on Portsmouth Street

1

A faint parrot flush of green shows in the sky over Brooklyn this afternoon, and now a congenial breeze from the south reminds me of New Orleans and better days, so I decide on a solitary barbecue in the crumbling pit at the back of the garden. Every summer I try to barbecue a few times down there, because it is a shame to let a garden go to waste in New York, no matter how tangled and abandoned, but so far this summer I have not had the chance. Mary and Todd, the vegetarian couple in the first floor apartment, have taken over the garden for their nude meditation.

Most afternoons since the beginning of June I've seen them squatting in the lotus position on a blanket in the weeds, faced off in their nakedness, searching for nirvana in each other's eyes. The first time I stopped and got an eyeful from the dusty window on the landing, but now the sight of them is nothing new. And if I may say, they are two rather unremarkable, vegetable-skinny human specimens. Todd is all elbows and ribs and stringy hippie hair, his penis thin as a finger hidden in the pale tangle between his legs. Mary is brown-nippled and stoop-shouldered and has the kind of long hippie-girl horse face that appeared on album covers in the sixties. These last few days they have taken to playing a sort of Tibetan gong music from their tape box during meditation and burning joss sticks stuck in the old flower bed. The smell of this stuff reaches my apartment in nauseating cinnamon gusts, mixing in with the foul wind from the emulsion factory around the corner.

They are out there now, naked as ever, their long hair tied back with identical headbands covered in Chinese characters, but I do not intend to let them stop me. Not today. I've got a couple of quarts of Pete's Wicked Ale in the fridge, a nice piece of meat from Key Food marinating in a bowl, and fixings for a salad and home fries. I am standing at the stove in the kitchen, drinking one of the beers and cooking up the home fries, when the Tibetan gong music from the backyard gives way unexpectedly to a woman's voice raised in song. This is surprising. I have never known my neighbors to sing before. It is a pleasant old tune that I can't quite place because I can't hear the words, so I walk over to the window to take a look.

Now I can't make out the hippies downstairs, because their blanket lies just below my kitchen, which juts out over the yard, but I see they have been joined by a friend, and it is she who is singing. In the center of the weedy square of garden a young woman nude to the waist is washing her hair in a wooden tub. Her back is bent away from me, but I can see that she is made of different stuff from Mary and Todd. Her arms are fleshy and supple; her breasts hang, faint heavy globes in the shadow her body makes on the grass. Her skin gleams white, almost incandescent, as if she never goes out into the sun. And her hair is amazing. Thick and black, there must be enough of it to reach to her waist. She leans down over the tub, washing vigorously; she flips up to wring it out with both hands, twisting the hair into a thick black rope. Her chemise and corset lie strewn about her in the grass.

Of course, there are bathrooms for such activities, but this is truly a charming scene, and I watch for a while entranced, as the woman washes and wrings again, sometimes singing, sometimes humming this soft, familiar tune. I hope that she will turn her head so I can see her face in the sunlight and maybe catch a better view of her breasts, but she does not. Then a burning smell calls me back to the stove, and I must tend to the home fries before they are ruined. At last I gather my meat and salad and fries together and lug a bag of charcoal out of the basement. Todd and Mary look up, cow-eyed, when I step out the steel door into the brightness of the garden.

"Hello," I say, and pass quickly to the barbecue pit. I am already spreading out the coals when Todd pads up behind, naked and rubbery-skinned as a chicken.

"Uh, excuse me, man," he says. "Like, what are you doing?" His voice has the kind of California drawl associated with skateboard punks and surfers that a certain class of bohemian has been affecting of late, as if they all had picked it up at the same commune in Oregon.

"I'm barbecuing, Todd," I say. "That's what I'm doing," and I go back to spreading the coals.

"Look, we're meditating out here, O.K.?" he says. "If you could come back later and cook your dead meat some other time?"

I swing toward him angrily and poke the air between us with the barbecue fork. Todd steps back alarmed.

"You people have monopolized this garden all summer with your meditation and your nudity," I say, my voice rising an octave. "The garden doesn't belong to you; it belongs to the house. Half the summer is gone, and I haven't barbecued once! And if you want to have a conversation with me, put on some goddamned clothes!"

He blinks, his eyes an indeterminate sandy color, and appears to hesitate. But there is the barbecue fork and the fact that he is naked. "Man, you are really uptight," he says at last, and retreats to the blanket for more meditation.

Later the smell of cooking meat proves too much for them, and wrapped in their blanket like two Indians, they come to sit across from me at the warped old picnic table beneath the fig tree to watch me eat.

"Is that good?" Todd says, nodding at my steak.

"What do you think?" I say, chewing with gusto.

"No, seriously, we haven't eaten steak in ten years," Mary says. "We've totally forgotten what it tastes like."

"It's very good," I say, mouth full. "Excellent, in fact."

"But what does it taste like?" Mary insists.

"Like meat," I say.

"Oh."

They look hungry, so I break down and offer some of the home fries, which they eat off my plate with their fingers.

"Look, man," Todd says, "we didn't mean to monopolize the garden. It's just that we're really trying to practice our meditation skills. We're getting ready to go to this ashram in Colorado for a month, and we want to be ready."

"Yeah?" I say, trying to sound interested. "How did you pick Colorado?"

"It's a kind of vacation," Mary says. "There's this travel agent in the Village puts together these meditation packages. You can meditate anywhere in the world."

"Even in Paris?" I say.

"Why not?" Todd says.

Then, though I do not want them to know I was watching out the window, curiosity gets the better of me.

"So who was your friend?" I say.

"Friend?"

"The woman out here washing her hair."

"When?"

"Oh, a half hour ago."

They look at each other puzzled.

"Yeah," I say. "She had long black hair and she —"

"Sorry, man." Todd shakes his head patiently. "Just us, all day. We've been out here alone."

Mary wags her head in agreement. "Better to meditate when there's no one else around. It's a vibe thing."

I have a hard time swallowing the piece of meat in my mouth.

"All day, alone," I say in a small voice. "Are you sure?"

I give them the remainder of the home fries and salad and toss what is left of the steak over the yard for the vicious guard dogs that patrol the neighbor's backyard. Then I take my quart of Pete's in hand and go upstairs to the apartment and collapse shivering on my bed, despite the heat of the afternoon.

Something has happened. An escalation. I have seen the ghost.

2

The trains are full, the taxis four deep on Second Avenue, streaming downtown. The bars of the East Village already reek of cigarette smoke as the last sun glints red off the million windows of the financial district. It is Saturday night, and the city vibrates like an engine at full throttle.

I board the crowded Manhattan bound F at Knox and find a seat at the back of the car. If the color range is from mocha to deep chocolate here, I am the single dollop of whipped cream on the side. This is common on the subway, especially in the hottest months of summer, when the city stinks like an old mattress and white flight to the beaches is at its peak. Across from me now a group of Latin youths and their dates chatter and squawk in a mixture of Spanish and English that will probably become the American idiom of the twenty-first century. The boys have perfectly slicked-back hair with the sides shaved in zigzag patterns, and the girls wear gluey, stiff pompadours matched by thick red lipstick and huge, barbaric-looking gold earrings.

Then I change at Delancey to the Essex Z and step into a car filled with Chinese families. The air is thick with the smell of ginger. I hear the sound of several dialects and the complaint of babies crying. When we stop in the tunnel for a few minutes between Canal and Chambers, a Korean man comes through with a shopping bag full of cheap plastic toys for sale. He squats in the middle of the car and demonstrates. He has a top that plays "The Yellow Rose of Texas" when you spin it, illuminated pumpkin globe headbands left over from Halloween, and a cute windup dog that arfs and somersaults when you set it on the floor. The Korean winds up one of the dogs and puts it down to do the backflip. This is the demonstrator model, its white paws black from the grime of a hundred subway cars. An elderly Chinese woman to my right buys a half dozen illuminated pumpkin headbands, a young mother buys a top to quiet her child, and on a whim I buy one of the somersaulting dogs for eight dollars.

Later, pushing my way through the crowds of Chinatown past hot duck and dumpling stands, I feel rather foolish carrying the dog, which will not fit in my pocket. It is a gift for Chase, a peace offering. We have not spoken since her dinner party, when I said or did something that caused her to write me off. Of course, she is always writing people off, then writing them back on again. We have negotiated through answering machines, and tonight she is waiting for me at the bar at Le Hibou.

3

Le Hibou is one of the strangest clubs in Manhattan. It is tucked away two blocks from Confucius Place in the dark angle of Doyers Street, which was the scene of many lurid murders during the tong wars of the 1920s. This is the traditional heart of Chinatown, more like Shanghai than New York, but in the last few years Albanian Gypsies have begun moving into the neighborhood. Now in Doyers Street, side by side with dim sum parlors and cheap Asian gift shops, there are Gypsy palm-reading salons and a few greasy holes in the wall that serve Albanian and Bulgarian cuisine. Le Hibou sits at the middle of the block, a weird light showing through windows stenciled with golden owls.

The place was originally opened as a country-French restaurant by an Albanian Gypsy who had once worked as a sous chef at the Crillon in Paris. Inside, it is still set up with plastic vine leaves, maps of the Auvergne, and posters for Edith Piaf at the Olympia. But who in their right minds would look for French food in Chinatown? The restaurant failed, the Albanian had taken out the wrong loans from the wrong people, was found in a Dumpster with his throat cut, and the place immediately reopened as a Gypsy club without a single change in decor. Now it is notorious, a hangout for Gypsy cabdrivers, hoodlums, and hustlers of various sorts, a place where tribal disputes are settled with a quick thrust of the knife and women are bought and sold for a handful of C notes on the dance floor.

Chase is sitting at the far end of the bar over a snifter of blood-colored liquor when I come up. I wind the dog and set it down at her elbow, and it arfs cheerfully and does a neat somersault on the sticky counter.

"Hey, that's a pretty cute doggy," Jamal, the bartender, says. "Where did you get it?"

"On the Z train," I say.

He is not surprised. Almost anything can be had on the subway, he says. Once, on the 3, he saw a man in a dirty butcher coat and a white hard hat selling raw steaks wrapped in plastic.

"Wow," I say. "On the West Side."

"Yeah, but don't ask me where that meat came from," he says. "Or what kind of meat it was."

"Did you buy any?"

"Are you kidding?" He is a big man with a stiff, pointy mustache like the kaiser and a thick head of black hair. He speaks to me because he knows I am a friend of Chase's. Non-Gypsies, unescorted, are not tolerated at Le Hibou.

Chase has yet to say anything. She looks from me to Jamal and back again and frowns.

"It's for you," I say, pointing to the dog when Jamal turns away.

"Why?" she says.

I shrug and decide to be honest. "I need your help with a problem."

Chase picks up her dog, and we go and sit at a table beneath the arbor of plastic grape leaves, on the little terrace reserved for couples on Saturday nights. From here we have an unobstructed view through the glass partition of the front door and the pool table, where a quartet of Gypsy men lounge sullenly, pool cues in hand, cigarettes dangling from lower lips, their black hair shiny with mousse. It is still early, and there isn't much of a crowd yet. By midnight the place will be full of Gypsy men in Armani knockoffs, and their hard women in fuck-me heels and spandex. The knife fights usually start about one, after everyone has got a good gut full of arak.

Chase is in a glum mood tonight, which is nothing new for her these days. She will not meet my eyes. From time to time she winds up the dog and lets it do a somersault on the tablecloth.

As efficiently as possible, I relate everything that has happened with the ghost. I feel rather silly about my confession because I have spent all the years of our relationship denying the existence of the supernatural. But the recent visual manifestation has got me really shaken up. It is time to make a serious effort to get rid of the ghost, and Chase has Gypsy relations with connections on the Other Side. Her great-aunt, known as Madame Ada, runs a sort of tearoom-tarot parlor in downtown Brooklyn. The woman was once a friend of Aleister Crowley, the famous diabolist, and is widely known as a great spirit doctor and medium. About a year ago I saw a feature story on her on the eleven o'clock news. She is incredibly old and rather crazy and will not see anyone new without an introduction.

Chase is quiet awhile when I am done, staring into her glass.

"So, my dreams were right on target," she says. "Someone was trying to contact you from the Other Side. And I've been right all along about the Spirit World. You admit that now?"

"Yes," I say, cringing a little, but she is not gloating.

"Thing is, you let a haunting go on too long, and it's like cancer," she says. "Can be too late to operate. The ghost gets into the grain of your life, and you're stuck. You have to do whatever it wants you to do. No other way out."

"You're sure about that?" There's a heavy feeling in the pit of my stomach.

"Yes. Why didn't you tell me sooner?"

"Pride, I guess."

"Is that it?"

"And all those years of scientific rationalism," I say. "Modern people just don't go around talking about ghosts. I guess I was in denial, hoping it would turn out to be something else. Rats in the walls. Electrical disturbances. Insanity, anything."

"But you told Rust."

"Yes."

"It's all right," Chase says in a small, sad voice. "People don't trust me. Why should they? I found the apartment for you in the first place. I thought it would be a good place for you. I was wrong. I fucked up. No wonder people don't trust me."

"Don't say that."

She waves me away. "How can you trust somebody with a face like this? Give me your hand."

She has managed to turn the conversation to her favorite topic. I give her my hand reluctantly, and she takes it and passes it up her chin and across her reconstructed cheeks, and an involuntary shudder passes through me.

"See," she says. "It even feels bad. Sort of unfinished. I blamed my mother for a long time, but she was a drunk when Father married her. A rich socialite drunk from a family full of drunks. He married her because she was white, you know, and he was a Gypsy boy on scholarship.

198

He thought she looked like Jackie Kennedy. Shit. See what they got." She points at her face with two fingers.

"Chase . . ."

"You think I'm drunk," she continues. "For once I'm sober as a judge. The Greeks have a little parable I want you to hear. They sent their greatest warriors to capture Silenus, the wise centaur, because he was the only one who knew what all the Greeks wanted to know, the answer to the question, What is the greatest thing of all? When they finally got him in the nets and demanded the answer under pain of death, he warned them. 'You're not going to like what you hear,' he said. But they kept at it, and finally Silenus gave in. 'The greatest thing of all is to never have been born,' he said. What do you think of that, Ned?"

I am saved from a response by the noisy arrival of a long white limousine in the street out front. Disco music blares from its open moonroof as a group of Gypsy men in shiny suits and a few women in gauzy dresses descend and enter the club to a wave of applause and whistles. Jamal leaps over the bar to embrace one of the newcomers, a dark, striking-looking young man with perfect hair and a profile that reminds me of portraits I have seen of Lord Byron. Even from this distance it is possible to see his eyes are predatory and piercing and black as coal.

Chase stands from her chair, excited. "It's Ulazi!" she cries, plucking at my sleeve. "Ulazi's back!" Then she is around the table and into the crowd and in the arms of the young man with the profile. She gives him a bear hug. He smiles thinly and avoids kissing her face. In a moment they approach the table arm in arm and sit down. They are followed by a pouty-looking big-haired blonde got up like Miss America in a strapless minidress of red, white, and blue spangles, who takes a seat beside me.

"I've told you about Ulazi," Chase says to me. "Ulazi, this is Ned Conti. A friend of mine from Brooklyn."

"Oh, yeah." Ulazi shakes my hand with a grip of iron. His black eyes are veiled and dangerous, and for a moment I am reminded of Dothan Palmier.

Then Jamal comes over from the bar with a bottle of arak and some glasses.

"On the house, my friends," he says to us. Then he leans forward and whispers a few words of Romany in Ulazi's ear.

"I'll be there in a minute," Ulazi says angrily in response. "You tell them I'm talking to my sister."

Jamal withdraws, and Ulazi pours four hefty shots of the arak into the glasses. This stuff is blue-tinted and nasty as shoe polish and illegal in the United States.

"To my sister," Ulazi says. Chase raises her glass and smiles dumbly. She can't seem to take her eyes off him. Suddenly she is a different person, docile, happy, and starstruck.

"But, honey," the blonde says to him, "you know I can't drink your nasty old liquor. I want a bourbon and water. Can't you tell the boy to bring me a bourbon and water?"

"You will drink what we drink, Cheryl," Ulazi says in a hard voice. "You will not insult me in front of my sister. That is final."

"Oh, shit," Cheryl says, but she puts her nose into the glass and wets her tongue like a cat. Her accent sounds like the hills of North Carolina. I take a good look at her. I would like to say that she is not attractive, but this is impossible. I've seen girls like her lounging away the summers on Myrtle Beach by the thousands, busting out of gold bikinis that are little more than scraps strung together with thread, their makeup melting in the sun, and despite myself, I wanted every one of them, at least for an hour. New York is full of Cheryls. Big-boned southern girls with a certain native beauty who leave Asheville or Winston-Salem for the lights of the city. The best of them after brief careers on the kick lines of off-Broadway shows end up as the wives of Italian construction subcontractors or police sergeants from the Bronx. The worst of them end up with men like Ulazi.

I remember now the few things Chase told me about her stepbrother: He is an actor, a gigolo and a thug, something of a celebrity in the Gypsy community here. After a bit of modeling work in New York, he went out to Hollywood to make his fortune in the movies and does supporting roles as a heavy in the Mexican soap operas produced in Los Angeles. He is the son of the Spanish Gypsy whom their father married after divorcing Chase's mother. Chase dotes on him; this is plain to see. A few years back she hid him out in Providence when he was wanted by the NYPD in connection with fraud and assault charges brought by a wealthy widow of Fifth Avenue. After sleeping with the unfortunate lady for six months at two thousand dollars a week, there was a falling-out, and Ulazi hit her and took some jewelry; we never got the full story. Eventually the charges were dropped.

We drink a few more toasts of the arak. The stuff tastes like lighter fluid. Cheryl almost chokes getting it down and pounds her breastbone with her fist.

"Damn," she says. "Damn."

"How have you been, little brother?" Chase says. She has a tight hold on his arm to keep him from escaping. "I haven't heard from you all year. Did you get my Christmas card? I sent you some expensive socks for your birthday; they were real cute. Did you get the expensive socks?"

Ulazi nods, somberly, lifts his leg, and pulls up his trousers to show off the socks. This particular pair is embroidered with tiny shields bearing the fleur-de-lis of the arms of France.

"I meant to call," he says. "You know how it is."

Chase gives a girlish laugh that is shocking. I have never seen her like this. "You never call,

202

you never write," she says as if it is a good thing. "That's just you."

The spectacle is a little painful, so I turn to the blonde.

"You're from North Carolina?" I say.

She smiles, showing a mouthful of even white teeth. "Hey, that's pretty good," she says. "How did you guess?"

I give out a mysterious smirk. "You and Ulazi here been going out for a long time?"

"Around a year now," she says. "Ully and I see each other every time he comes to New York, and that's pretty often. About every other month."

"Oh!" Chase looks over at the blonde with a hurt expression, then looks back at her brother. "You mean, you've been coming to New York for a year and haven't managed to see me?"

At this Ulazi nods sharply to Cheryl, who gets up quickly, pulling Chase with her.

"Let's go to the little girls' room, honey," Cheryl says nervously. Chase is too confused to resist, and I am left at the table alone with the brooding Gypsy. There is a moment of silence. Then Ulazi turns his odd black eyes on me.

"Are you hustling my sister?" he says.

I give him a blank look.

"You know what I mean. Is she paying you to fuck her?" He is serious.

"No," I say, aghast. "We're just friends."

He stares at me, his eyes narrowed. "O.K., I believe you," he says at last. "Given the way she looks, you'd have to be a real weirdo to fuck her, money or no money. You look a little cheap, but you don't strike me as a weirdo."

"Hey, thanks," I say.

"But you never know. It takes all kinds. I ran into a guy in L.A. who will only screw amputees. He's a good-looking guy, too. Strange, huh? Don't get me wrong. Chase is a great kid. It's just hard for me to hang out with her because of my career. You never know when you'll run into someone from the fashion magazines or some producer, and it helps to be seen with a certain kind of woman. Someone more like Cheryl. Ugliness, just like bad luck, it rubs off, you know?"

I think this despicable but consider it best not to tell him so.

A minute or so later the girls return, and after another round of arak, Ulazi and Cheryl rise and take their leave.

"Nice meeting y'all," Cheryl says brightly.

"Yeah, we've got to hang out with a couple of business acquaintances," Ulazi says. "You know, business." He flashes a false, perfect-toothed grin.

"Will I see you soon?" Chase says, panic rising in her voice. "Come to dinner. Why don't you come to dinner?"

He shakes his head. "I'm really busy this time, Chase," he says. "I'll call you."

Then they disappear through a padded door to the private party rooms in the back.

An hour later Chase and I walk up Doyers Street through Columbus Park, its concrete bandshell quiet at this hour, and up Baxter to a Vietnamese Pho place at Canal where the soup is cheap and good. But when we try the door, it is locked from the inside. The last couples sit finishing their spring rolls at the small tables, and the proprietor wags his finger at us through the glass.

"We close," he says.

Chase turns away and takes out a cigarette. For a moment she stands on the sidewalk, blowing smoke up toward the banner of the Italian and American flags strung between Forlini's and the sushi place across the street.

"I can't believe he's been coming to New York all this time," she says to the burnt-out sky over Manhattan. "And he's never called me. Not once. I sent him money every month till he got established out in L.A., and these were in the days when I could barely make my rent. Then I wrote him letters, so many letters. You know, I don't think he even bothered to read them. The bastard."

We walk up to Canal to catch a cab but stand lingering on the corner as the traffic shoots down to the bridge.

"It's the fucking banquet," she says. "I'm denied a place at the banquet of life. All these years I thought I could fight my way in. I thought style or toughness would be enough. No. The banquet is open only to the beautiful. There's a guy out front who checks your face."

"Don't be hard on yourself because your step-brother's a jerk," I say, but she has stopped listening. I flag her a cab and, as she bends toward the door, lean down and kiss her gently on the lips.

4

The clock ticks heavily in my room. Across Portsmouth the power plant grumbles in the yellow night. Bolts of blue static zap between the transformers. Out the bathroom window Manhattan seems rimmed in fire, burning against the sky, cables of the bridges strung glittering like blown glass over the dark river.

The apartment is like an oven tonight. Sleep is impossible. Yesterday the temperature reached 102 Fahrenheit in Times Square. The weatherman on the radio says we're in the middle of one of the worst heat waves the East Coast has seen in over a hundred years. In Philadelphia fifteen people have already died from heat-related illnesses. In New York they're not saying.

These conditions seem to please the ghost. The other night there were two new noises: a flapping sound and a very distinct cough. The flapping sound could have been the curtains in Molesworth's old room, but the cough? Also, when I stumbled to the bathroom in the dark, my hand came to rest for a second against what felt like a ladder-back chair in the middle of the living room. It only occurred to me the next morning that I have no such chair. I was half asleep, so I am not entirely sure of this incident.

But I can't discount it either.

5

One hundred and one in the shade, and I am sitting on a bench in the sun across from the Cost-Less shoe store, eating a bag of peanuts, sweating profusely and watching the crowds. This stretch of the Fulton Street Mall in downtown Brooklyn looks like pictures of Nairobi or Timbuktu I have seen in the pages of *National Geographic*. The same dark throngs and run-down buildings and women carrying bundles on their heads. Afrocentric ware is spread across blankets on the sidewalk. On the nearest one I see vials of liquid incense, wooden zebra statuettes, and hardcover books about Malcolm X, Tina Turner, and the blackness of the Pharaohs of Egypt.

At last I spy Chase exit the subway at Clark Street, two blocks down. She waves at me and pauses to look in the window of Cost-Less.

"They really do cost less," she says when I reach her side. "Look at those." She indicates a pair of black clumpy platforms with large chrome buckles, passable imitations of expensive models sold for hundreds of dollars at fashionable boutiques in Manhattan. "Twenty-nine ninety-five. Seems like a bargain. What do you think?"

"Yes," I say. "But you get what you pay for." This statement would have made my mother proud.

We stand there for a minute longer, staring at the shoes. Chase is wearing a short summer dress and Birkenstock sandals today and a pair of big Italian sunglasses that have the effect of making her look like a bug in a cartoon, but she is in a rare good mood.

"O.K." She flashes me a crooked smile. "Ready for the Spirit World?"

We walk around the corner to Madame Ada's Gypsy Tearoom on Livingston. The place is one flight up, over a Korean deli that features a salad and hot lunch buffet. A plastic-lettered sign in the deli window gives today's specials as Beef Lo Mein, Bratwurst and Sauerkraut, Chicken Lasagna. The greasy smell of these disparate offerings haunts us until we step into Madame Ada's parlor. This place has a powerful smell all its own, the reek of cats and cloying perfume and incontinent bowels and baby powder, an old woman's smell.

I settle on the sofa in the hallway in a cloud of dust and wait as Chase goes through the curtain into the back to fetch her great-aunt. After a moment I hear the sound of arguing, and it seems it will take a while, so I go on into the tearoom, which is done up in what can only be described as Gypsy kitsch: The walls are covered with brocade fabric and framed 3-D pictures of the Last Supper and the Statue of Liberty. A yellow parrot blinks somnolently from a pagoda-shaped cage. A black lacquer celestial globe rests idly on its axis, ringed with fanciful personifications of the constellations. There is actually a crystal ball on a Turkish table, surrounded by low, carpet-covered Turkish couches. A poorly executed plaster statue of the Muse Calliope flexes her breasts in one corner. Of greater interest is the bookcase overflowing with ancient wide-backed tomes on various extraphysical topics, a few of them familiar to me from the research paper on automatic writing done in my abandoned year of graduate work at Loyola.

With a twinge of nostalgia I make out a copy of Flournoy's *Des Indes à la planète Mars*, the volume in which Antoinette once left love notes in another life. There is also Charles Linton's *The Healing of the Nations*, J. Murray Spear's *Messages from the Spirit Land*, and rare copies of Joseph Glanville's *The Vanity of Dogmatizing* and *Sadducismus Triumphatus*, containing Glanville's account of the séance that roused the infamous knocking drummer of Tedworth in 1661. I am surprised to find both are original seventeenth-century editions, worth a small fortune. As I examine them, the curtains part and Chase wheels her great-aunt into the tearoom.

Stuffed into her wheelchair, Madame Ada is

quite a sight. She has the jowls of Winston Churchill, a head the size of a basketball and is of an indeterminate age between 60 and 90. A big person to begin with, but bloated by years of overeating and no exercise, she must weigh more than Molesworth. The woman is not a cripple — Chase has told me this — just someone who does not like to walk. For a horrible second I imagine her inner organs, her heart encased in fat like a canned ham. With some effort Chase pushes her great-aunt up to the table.

"Auntie, this is Ned," she calls out, and then collapses into a doilied armchair across the room.

The old woman in the wheelchair looks me up and down with eyes black and hard as marbles. "Young man, put the books back where you got them, very carefully, and sit down," she says. Her voice booms from somewhere out of all that flesh.

I replace Glanville on the shelf and sit carefully on the Turkish couch, so low I am staring up at Madame Ada's knees. She is wearing the heavily embroidered skirt and shawl of her tribe. A circlet of Greek coins is stuck to her forehead with sweat. She stares at me for the next few minutes in silence, fixing her black eyes with a concentration that sends a chill down my spine. I start to speak, but Madame Ada puts a finger to her lips, and there is nothing but her eyes and an odd catlike humming from her barrel throat. Then, suddenly, she claps her hands. It is a loud, meaty, popping sound, and I almost jump off the sofa.

"Do you know how long you were out?" she says.

"What do you mean?" I say.

"It's been ten minutes," Chase says from across the room. "Auntie had you in a trance for ten minutes. You sat on that couch stiff as a board with your mouth hanging open."

"Hush, girl!" Madame Ada says. "You didn't feel it?" she says to me.

I shake my head, confused, and Madame Ada shrugs and turns to Chase.

"There is nothing I can do for your friend," she says. "The knots are tied too tightly around him."

"Wait a minute," I say. "You haven't done anything. You haven't even heard about the ghost yet."

"We don't use the word *ghost* here," she says sharply. "The word *ghost* is offensive to the spirits of the departed. We use the word *spirit,* or *presence* or *apparition,* or, if you must, *shade* or *phantasm,* but never *ghost.* Also, the words *phantom* and *entity* are discouraged."

I frown and say nothing.

"Why can't you help him, Auntie?" Chase says from her chair.

"Listen, how about we just forget the whole thing?" I stand up to go, annoyed.

"Sit!" Madame Ada brings her black eyes to bear like cannon.

I sit.

"I don't need to hear about the spirit from

you because I can see the spirit. Right there."
She points to my head with a knobby finger made
crooked by arthritis.

"Where?" I say.

"There, in your aura."

"You mean, right now?"

"Yes. She's with you always. Not just where
you live but wherever you go. And she has been
with you for some years. Waiting."

"She?" I begin to sweat. "Did Chase tell you
about the, uh . . . spirit?"

The old woman shakes her head. "Chase told
me that you were sharing your apartment with
a restless presence, and that you found this arrangement uncomfortable. Nothing more."

Chase sits forward in her chair across the room.
Now I see that her eyes are like her great-aunt's,
only dimmer, much less powerful.

"So you are aware the spirit is that of a
woman?" Madame Ada says. "You have seen her.
Am I correct?"

"Maybe," I say.

"And let me tell you something else. Your people, they often see the dead. This mark is upon
you. A certain melancholy tone in the outer edge
of your penumbra. A sadness that enables you
to grope a little way into the gloom. Am I correct?"

"My mother," I mumble. "She was a little
weird. She had these migraines; she would see
colors, hear things . . ."

"And?"

"Once, when I was a kid, she said our cat, Miss Kitty, came scratching on the kitchen door to be fed. She fed the cat, and out it went again. Thing is, I saw Miss Kitty run over by a car two weeks before that."

"Of course. Your mother. And you have denied your own spirit sight time and again, am I right?"

"I don't know," I say, my voice the barest croak.

"So you felt something when you moved into the apartment?"

"Not really." I look down. I can barely meet the old woman's eyes. "A whisper, maybe."

"A whisper!" She shakes her massive head in disgust. "If you had cultivated your gift, you wouldn't have moved into the apartment in the first place. You would have felt the presence there and found somewhere else to live."

"Chase found the place," I say. "She said it suited me —"

Madame Ada gives an impatient wave. "And maybe it does. Maybe your own destiny is tied up with the restlessness of this female spirit."

"Who is she?"

Madame Ada wheels her chair over to me, takes hold of one knee in a painful grasp, and closes her eyes. I feel a slight tingling sensation emanating from her fingers. Her lower lip begins to tremble and sweat, and when her voice comes out, it is an octave closer to the ground.

"I see a white dress. A woman in a white dress," she says. "Not from here. From far away, a

213

warmer place. Proud and arrogant. Ruled by terrible passions. Revenge. She paid dearly for what she did. She is still paying. She needs your help to find rest. Her cousin . . ." Then she lets go, her eyes fluttering open. "There, that's all I can tell you."

"Please, how can I get rid of her?" I say, desperate. "Are you telling me that it's not the apartment, it's me? What if I move to Alaska? Will the ghost follow me there?"

"Even to the ends of the earth," Madame Ada says, with grim satisfaction. "In your dreams."

"But why?" I'm almost shouting now.

"This spirit has been waiting for you for a long time. Now she won't let go till she gets what she wants. You are at the center of a complicated web of circumstance. Many choices in your life have led you to the spirit, and the spirit to you. You have chosen each other from out of the billion souls."

I feel sick. The smell of the place is overpowering. It all seems so unreal, so ridiculous, but my heart knows what Madame Ada says is true.

"I've got to get rid of it," I say weakly at last. "Please."

The old woman shakes her huge head. "The spirit must be coaxed far enough into the light for you to see her clearly. Only then will she answer your questions, tell you who she is, what she wants from you. You need a séance. I am too old for such things. You need a good medium. I might be able to give you a referral."

The yellow parrot shifts its weight on the perch and screeches, the first sound it has made in an hour.

Before I can ask another question, Chase stands behind the wheelchair and puts her hands on the old woman's massive shoulders.

"I'll do it," she says.

Madame Ada twists backward, the coins on her forehead jingling.

"You will not," she says, and appears to leave no room for argument, but Chase is adamant.

"You told me once that I had a talent with the dead, Auntie," she says. "You told me they would speak to me if I tried. I've never really tried. Look in my face now. I'm halfway there already."

The old woman studies her great-niece for a quiet moment, then takes her hand. After a while she lets it go, and her shoulders droop sadly. "Yes, I see," Madame Ada mutters, and the bird shrieks again in its cage in agreement.

"All right, Ned," Chase says to me. "You can take off. Auntie and I need to talk some shop."

I am at a loss for words. Chase is making a sacrifice I do not understand. "Are you sure about this, Chase?" I say to her.

She smiles.

"Madame Ada, is this dangerous?"

The old woman shrugs. When I reach the door, she calls me back.

"You're forgetting something, young man," she says.

I look at her blankly.

"My fee. I am a psychic consultant. My services are not free. You owe me two hundred fifty dollars." And she holds out one fat paw.

"It's less than most lawyers charge," Chase says. "Think of it that way."

I have no choice. I walk out into the equatorial heat of the afternoon and wait in line for the money machine at the Chemical Bank on Flatbush. It is rush hour; cars inch by, radiators boiling over, bound for scattered unimaginable neighborhoods on the ocean side of Long Island. The acrid stench of antifreeze and burned brake lining fills my lungs. On the way back I squint up into the haze through my sunglasses till my eyes hurt. The light in the sky is so hot it makes me stupid.

My pocket is full of money to pay a woman about a ghost.

6

The morning of the séance is pale blue and bright, with white fleecy clouds hanging high above Manhattan, Oz-like across the river, and the sun shining cheerily off the twin monoliths of the World Trade Center. I would prefer gray skies and rain, an unseasonable coolness in the air, but the weather will not oblige with such theatrics. It is a good day for the beach, reasonable humidity and temperatures in the low nineties, and I hear on the radio that routes to the Jersey Shore are jammed with cars and it's standing room only on the LIRR to the Hamptons.

I spend the day cleaning the apartment, which has not been thoroughly cleaned since Molesworth's departure. At about four o'clock I walk up to the Heights and purchase a bottle of wine and two twelve-packs of Genesee Cream ale, which is on sale at Key Food on Montague Street. A séance is a somber occasion, I know, but this one feels like a party. A séance, Chase has warned me, must be pursued sober and on an empty stomach, like holy communion during mass. I resist the temptation to buy buns and ground meat for the grill.

At six Chase rings the doorbell and comes upstairs. She is lugging a suitcase full of gear and is done up in Gypsy regalia — embroidered skirt, shawl, headdress of silver coins. She looks ridiculous and small in this elaborate outfit, but her eyes are clear, and she seems rested. I have already downed a couple of beers, and I give her two kisses on the cheek, French style, perhaps a little overenthusiastic.

She steps back, sniffing disapprovingly. "You've been drinking," she says.

I shrug.

She sets her suitcase down and looks around the apartment. "And you've cleaned." Her tone is sour.

"I figured since I'm having people over . . ." I say.

"It's not good to clean. Better to have everything just as it was during the haunting." She walks over to the windows and stares out at the power plant. The sheer brick wall of this structure extends up about thirty stories. High in the facade there is an opening the size of a garage door where workmen can be seen moving about at odd hours of the night, small as ants.

"I'm going to explain only once," she says to the window and the beautiful afternoon. "This is not a game; this is not a party; this is not a little bit of summer fun. We are dealing with matters of ultimate seriousness here, life and death and the misery of souls trapped in the physical world unable to move to the next. Your apartment is possessed by an entity that has attached itself to you. If we weren't having a séance tonight, I'd put the whole damned place under psychic quarantine — that is, no one in, no one out except you, because for you it's too late. I don't want any ghost jokes or cracks, and I don't want any drunkenness. I have been working hard with Auntie for the last two weeks, I have been going without sleep and dinner, and I have been meditating and preparing for this thing, which is my destiny."

When she turns to me from the window, her face is white and dramatic, and there is a peculiar drawn expression about her eyes. She gives me the benefit of this attitude by posing there in

218

her black against the light of the window, stiff as a lady in a daguerreotype, but it doesn't work. She doesn't have the psychic power of her aunt, not by half. Embarrassed, I nod in agreement, but I know it is impossible to face this thing sober. When she is not looking, I grab another beer from the refrigerator, which I pour into a coffee mug.

"Coffee?" I say to her, waving the mug, but she shakes her head, annoyed, and commences a thorough inspection of the apartment. She raps on walls, opens doors, squats first in one place on the floor, then another. She goes into my bedroom, turns down my sheets, goes into the bathroom, and stands in the shower stall, her hands braced against the tiles.

"You may wonder what I'm doing," she says from the bathroom. "But think of the Fox sisters. You have to be very careful."

"Eh?" I say, and take advantage of her preoccupation with the shower stall to refill my mug full of beer.

"The Fox sisters were American spiritualists from upstate New York, the original mediums. They were the ones who started the whole spiritualist craze in the 1840s — you should know that, you're the historian. The knocking noises everyone heard at their séances seemed to be coming from nowhere, true spirit voices. Then someone discovered that Kate, the younger sister, could make the noises by dislocating her knee and popping it back into place again. They had a series of other gimmicks, too. Wax hands, secret compartments in the floor. I just want to make sure you're not pulling any of that stuff, that we've got a genuine case here."

"Come on, Chase," I say, but I let her continue the inspection. She finishes in Molesworth's old room, where she lingers for a few minutes, then comes out a little red in the face.

"It's definitely in there," she says. "That's where the presence is strongest. That's where we're going to have the séance."

"What the hell," I say. "Molesworth was such an utter pig. The stench! The man only washed his clothes every six months. This ghost must have a pretty strong stomach for filth."

"You'll have to move those boxes." She points to a few boxes of junk Molesworth left when he skipped town. I move the boxes out onto the landing and pull in the threadbare rug from the living room because there are not enough chairs and we all will be sitting on the floor in here.

Chase continues to pace restlessly, and I notice now that there is a slight wobble in her walk and that she is favoring her left leg.

"Is there something wrong with your leg, Chase?" I ask her at last.

She stops pacing and sits down heavily on the gas heater. "No," she says. "It's my hip. It hurts."

"Why?"

She hesitates and looks away. When she speaks, she does not look at me. "It's part of my condition," she says quietly. "It's not just my face, you know. It's the rest of me, too. It's a bone thing."

"Is it bad?"

"There's work to do. I don't want to talk about it now."

I respect her wishes.

Chase takes her suitcase into Molesworth's room and closes the door. An hour after dark she emerges and ushers me in. The walls are now hung with purple silk banners sewn with stars and moons and symbols like hieroglyphics.

I ask her what they mean.

"Those are just for effect," Chase says, "to help create the proper mood. The proper mood is very important." On the rug she has set a wide circle of white candles in elaborate holders. At the center of this circle sits a flat wooden board on a sort of swivel stand with a system of cogs and weights suspended underneath. A large pad of butcher paper is affixed to the old wood. Several grease pencils poke out of a brass holder.

"Do you know what that is?" Chase points out the board with obvious pride.

"No," I say, though I recognize it immediately from my researches at Loyola.

"It's a planchette," Chase says. "Genuine nineteenth century, used for automatic writing. It once belonged to the famous Neapolitan medium Eusapia Palladino. Auntie says that I'm not experienced enough to have the spirit speak through me and that this is the best thing. With the aid of the planchette, the spirit will guide my hand and send written messages from the Other Side. Go ahead, check it out."

I step carefully inside the circle of candles and press a thumb against the polished veneer. Under a bare minimum of pressure the board sways up and down and side to side in a fluid gyroscopic movement. Outside now, the square lit windows of the projects and the faint glow of light in the basalt sky. From the planchette comes the muted whir of gears that is the sound of a sinister and ancient machine at work.

7

The séance is scheduled for midnight. By eleven-thirty only five of the thirteen invited participants are present. There's Rust and Todd and Mary, the vegetarians, and Ian, the Irishman from the basement, wearing a gaudy blue-and-yellow Hawaiian shirt, and Geoff, his dogs tethered and sniffing the wind in the backyard. None of Chase's bohemian friends, unreliable as ever, has bothered to show. And despite her efforts, the gathering has taken on a distinct party atmosphere. The radio in my bedroom is switched to NPR's "Bluegrass Saturday Night." Jaunty fast fiddle music fills the apartment, followed by banjo picking and yodeling.

"It's spook night at the Grand Ole Opry," Rust

says, and everyone laughs.

When the beer is gone, Ian, the Irishman, fetches up a bottle of whiskey from the basement. We pass this around the room as Chase, arms crossed, fumes silently on the couch.

Geoff, perched nervously beside her, his prematurely white hair pointing stiffly to the ceiling, upends the bottle and gags.

"Eagh!" he says. "I really can't drink this without some sort of mixer. Do you have anything like Mountain Dew, Ned?"

The Irishman is scandalized.

"That's good single-malt stuff," he says, seizing the bottle. "Smooth as milk!" He takes a hit and offers it over to Rust, sitting in the orange Naugahyde chair. Rust shakes his head and points, grinning, to Todd and Mary, who squat at his feet wearing Guatemalan ponchos and thong sandals.

"I think I'll go with a little of the wacky-baccy tonight," Rust says. "In keeping with the occasion."

I take a step closer and see that the vegetarians are in the process of fixing up a power hitter, and soon the seaweed bitter smell of pot fills the living room. After Todd and Mary smoke their fill, Rust takes the small inlaid box and brass screw in his hand and inhales. Then the Irishman kneels to join them, leaving his bottle of whiskey on the mantel. One toke suffices to make him a philosopher.

"You know, I don't deny the existence of spirits

and the like," the Irishman says, rocking back on his heels, his pot-red eyes set off by the blue and yellow of his Hawaiian shirt. "Quite the contrary. Years ago in County Clare my grandmother was haunted by a Fer Darrig, a bog spirit — that is to say, the spirit of a man drowned in the bog and denied the comforts of consecrated burial. The bleedin' thing tore slate off the roof, broke a lot of dishes and cups, and was responsible for all sorts of related mischief. Frightened the old woman half to death. But what puzzles me is the whys of it. Why the hell would someone come from as far away a place as death to rap on wood and make noises and break crockery and such? Don't they have enough crockery of their own in the next world?"

This is a good question. We look at Chase, who shakes her head in disgust, pushes herself off the couch, and goes muttering into the kitchen. Just then there is the sound of automatic-weapons fire from the projects, matched a minute later by sirens coming down Knox. In the backyard Geoff's dogs begin to howl.

"You've got to love this town," the Irishman says. "Some poor bastard getting murdered every ten seconds."

At a quarter to twelve Chase moves us into Molesworth's room, and we take our places in a circle around her on the carpet. She wants us to spend a few minutes in quiet meditation before the séance to help sober up the atmosphere.

"Think about someone you love who is dead

now," she says when we close our eyes. "Think of cold nights in the tomb. Think of the work of the worm. Think of old bones in the ground so long they turn to powder. Think of moths fluttering in the twilight. Think of the mutilated bodies of children left to rot in the woods. Think —"

"Jesus, Chase." I interrupt. "Do you have to be so gothic about this thing?"

"Shut up," Chase says, and is about to continue, but then the buzzer sounds, and I go and bring Inge and Jillian up for the séance.

"Sorry we're late," Jillian says when they step into the room, smelling like cigarettes and the outside world. "We were at the Pyramid and lost track of time."

"*Ja*," Inge says. "Quite a scene tonight. Top-notch drag show. The Lady Bunny was there, and RuPaul was supposed to come but did not."

"Gee, that's too bad," I say, and am about to make a crack about RuPaul, a tall gay black man whose sole skill consists of wearing high heels and a wig about as well as someone's gawky aunt, but Chase narrows her eyes at me. When everyone is settled, she drops her head, puts her hands out in an oracular gesture, and kneels before the planchette for several minutes. I take this opportunity to get an eyeful of Jillian. She looks better tonight, wearing a sheer blue dress and dangly earrings. It seems she has put on a little weight. Her cheeks have regained some of their lost bloom; her breasts conform to a single supple

225

curve beneath the blushed velvet.

"Been eating lately, Jillian?" I say.

Jillian ignores me, but Inge is her simple Bavarian self. "Eating is not so good," Inge says. "I have been making her to drink beer. Good German beer. Makes you strong. Puts meat on the bones."

"Yes," I say. "Nothing like beer to make a human being out of you."

Jillian scowls at this and is about to snap back when Chase rears up suddenly and screams. The sound is bloodcurdling. We all blink in her direction, startled.

"All right," Chase says. "Now that I have your attention." She proceeds to engage the company in what she calls a spiritual exercise. Each of us is to tell the very saddest thing that comes to mind. This will help the mood and make us think of death, which will in turn help summon the ghost. Chase starts with Rust, to her left, and goes around the circle.

"The Trinidad Massacre," Rust says. "They were strikers protesting inhuman conditions in the copper mines of Trinidad, Colorado. This is about 1914. One hundred and seventy-five men, women, and children shot down by federal troops with the cooperation of the United States government. They killed my grandmother, a fifty-caliber shell right through the forehead. She was a beautiful young woman, nineteen years old with two kids. No one remembers. But I remember. I'm writing a book about the whole thing. Been

226

working on it for the last five years."

I am surprised to hear the nature of Rust's mysterious project so revealed, but do not have the time to comment. Chase moves her white finger to Ian, who looks up sad-eyed, his whiskey-red face sagging.

"My mother," the Irishman says. "I never got to say good-bye to her. She died two weeks after I left for America."

"The rain forest in Brazil," Todd says next. "Millions of species are disappearing every day so they can raise beef for McDonald's hamburgers. We're eating the rain forest as Big Macs and Quarter Pounders with cheese. It's like a fucking tragedy."

"Yeah, meat is murder," Mary says. "And that's my big sad."

"No, murder is murder," Geoff says, in a strained voice. "What's sad is we can't walk the streets of New York without worrying about being shot by some thug with a Glock nine millimeter. I love this city, it's the greatest city in the world, and it scares me half to death just to go out of my house every morning. That's sad as hell."

"I have nothing sad to say," Inge says. "I am quite a happy camper," but her lower lip trembles.

"I'll tell you something sad," Jillian says. "When I was ten years old, at the beach on Block Island, my father raped me. I was wearing a red bathing suit with yellow ducks on it. He tore it off and raped me in the changing cabin. My mother found the bathing suit and the bloodstains, and she must have known what happened, but she never said anything. Not a word, not ever."

After this revelation there is an embarrassed lull, but Chase waves us on. "All right," she says. "Now you."

"I don't know," I say. There is a funny feeling in my throat. "The Holocaust, I guess. Think of all those Jews. Six million, they say. Stolen from their lives and stuffed into ovens."

"My father was in the SS," Inge says so softly at my elbow she is barely heard. "He belonged to a unit responsible for many war crimes. I found out quite by accident. I always thought he was such a good man. . . ."

"Yes," Chase says to me. "The Holocaust is terrible, sad, but it's not your sad. You've got to be honest here, Ned. This whole thing is for you."

"All right," I say, feeling foolish. "Antoinette Rivaudais, a girl I knew in New Orleans a long time ago. That's sad. I still love her. I think about her every day. It's like my life continued down there without me. Walking down the same streets at her side, up the stairs into her apartment in the Faubourg Marigny like a ghost. God, I miss her."

"Now," Chase says, almost smugly. "Here's something real sad: The doctors at St. Vincent's told me ten days ago that my condition has worsened. I'm real sick. I was born with a degenerative bone disease called osteospyroplasia.

Starts with your face and extends to other joints and finally reaches the spine, which fuses together stiff as a broom handle. In a few years, no matter what, after a whole lot of excruciating pain, I'll be dead."

I am shocked into silence. Chase going to die? It seems impossible. Despite the depression and the medical problems, she seems too stubborn for that.

"My God," the Irishman says, "is it the whole truth?"

"Yeah, because that's a real bummer," Mary says.

"You're kidding, right, Chase?" Jillian says, her eyes worried.

"Please," Chase says, "I don't really want to talk about it."

"You can't just pass over something like that," Jillian says.

"We're here to do a séance," Chase says. "Mostly because I want to find out what it's like."

"What what's like?" I say.

"What it's like to be dead," Chase says. Then she goes around, lights the candles, and turns off the overhead, which is like the houselights going down for the feature presentation, and the room is cast into flickering shadow.

"Join hands," she says. On one side I take Inge's hand, which is warm and sticky; on the other, Rust's, calloused and hard as sun-dried mud.

"There is a spirit here in this room," Chase

says, her voice high and strange. "A restless spirit. Now, all of you. Close your eyes and look into the darkness."

I look into the darkness and see the flickering of the candles against the back of my retina, then nothing at all, and there is a long period of silence, the only sound the grinding of the power plant across the street and the hush of nine people breathing. At last there is a strangled coughing sound, and I open my eyes to find everyone staring at Chase. I gasp. She definitely seems possessed by something. She rocks back and forth in a quick, jerky motion, her hands curled into claws on her knees. Her eyes are closed, but her eyeballs can be seen making rapid movements beneath lids that seem thin as paper. Her mouth convulses, trying to form words. Nothing emerges. We are transfixed, in the presence of an otherness. She begins to move faster, to shake like a rag doll in the hands of an angry child. From the kitchen now comes the faint rattle of pots, and in the living room the furniture begins to creak.

"Wow," Mary says.

"Wow," Todd says.

"What's happening?" Geoff says in a scared voice.

"The spirit," Inge says. "It has a hold of her."

I am used to these displays, but everyone else in the room is stiff and petrified.

"We should stop this thing," Jillian says, "before it gets too late, before Chase gets hurt."

"No," Rust says. "Let the girl go through with

it, let the ghost say what it's got to say."

Suddenly the candles flare up brightly as if someone has turned up the gas, and the butcher paper on the planchette wags and rumples. One of the grease pencils flies from its brass keeper into Chase's hand. Her lids flutter open to reveal a blank expanse of white, flutter closed, and she leans over the planchette and begins writing furiously. At first just a wide, jagged scribbling, page after page of it, then there are letters and words too quick to read, the pages turning a mile a minute.

"Ask your questions, Ned," Rust yells at me from the opposite side of the circle. "Now's your chance!"

For a moment I feel an enormous pressure on my temples and I can't think. "Why are you here?" I shout finally. "What is your name? Why don't you just leave? I've got news for you! You are dead, leave me alone! Leave!" This is all I have to say, but Chase keeps writing, and we can see that this work is becoming a terrible strain on her. She is covered with sweat now, and her breathing is labored. She is like a long-distance runner in the last mile of the marathon. Any minute it seems she will collapse. We watch her for a bit longer, unsure of what to do.

"Someone's got to stop this thing," Jillian says. "It will kill her!" Chase's eyes flutter open again, and we get another flash of white. Inge gives a little cry at this and faints, her plump hand slipping from mine. A moment later the paper on the planchette is used up, but Chase continues to scribble, a black greasy scrawl across the old wood.

"Stop it!" Jillian screams. "Stop!"

Rust and I look at each other, then he lunges forward. He catches Chase around the shoulders in a half nelson. I grab on to her arm, which is writing frantically in the air. I try to pry the grease pencil from her fingers. Her grip is strong, and it breaks off in my hand. Suddenly she jerks her head toward me, and with a face somehow not her own, she hisses out a few quick words that I can't make out, that sound like French: *"C'est vous!"* is all I get.

Startled, I drop her arm and rear back, and in that moment a strong, unseen wind gusts through the closed room, billowing the purple banners like sails. The candles blow out in one hot breath of wax and sulfur, and in the darkness that ensues there is panic and much screaming. From the living room I hear an unearthly pounding not made by any of us. Then the door is flung open, and as the others fall out, in the half-light I see Chase lying still and white as death in Rust's arms.

The séance is over.

8

Not until three days later do I have the chance to enter Molesworth's room and clean up. I take down the purple banners, fold them carefully, scrape up the candle wax, and gather the ghost-scribbled sheets of paper into a pile. I have examined them several times now. Covered with frenzied layers of scrawl, each sheet is heavy as a palimpsest and absolutely illegible. Sheet after sheet of weird whorls and loops, without so much as a word or a name or even a single letter. From a results standpoint, the séance was an utter failure. But I don't have time to think about these things now. The last seventy-two hours have been awful. Chase has disappeared, and I fear the worst.

After the séance she was revived with a whiff of Clorox, and taken by Jillian via car service to the loft in Carroll Gardens. I paid for the car service. It was the least I could do. On the way home, according to Jillian, Chase rambled incoherently about green lights and big blue houses and a lady in a white dress who was beautiful, and she said a few more words in French, a language that, to my knowledge, she did not have the use of. When they got up to the loft, Chase was fed a couple of Valium, put to bed, and then Jillian fell asleep on the couch. The next morning Chase was gone. Jillian found the futon in Chase's bedroom an empty mess of rumpled sheets, the stained glass window angled open to the street, and the steel and chain fire escape ladder hanging down to the sidewalk.

"Chase must have let that ladder down very slowly and very carefully," Jillian said to me during the course of a calm, denunciatory phone call. "Otherwise she would have woken me with the rattle of the chain. I can't imagine why she didn't use the door, why she didn't tell me where she was going or even leave a note."

I knew the answer to these questions, but Jillian's calm fury would not allow me a word. Perhaps rightly, she blames me for everything. Chase left the way she did because her aim was not just to leave. Instead she wanted to make her escape completely and utterly. She didn't want a bit of fresh air, a change of scenery. She wanted a new life. All the years since birth she had been a prisoner whose sole design it was to break out of the prison of her flesh.

At Jillian's insistence, I went down to the Eighty-fourth Precinct at Gold and Tillary to file a missing persons report, but the desk sergeant, after hearing the circumstances, did not look too seriously on my request for immediate action.

"You're all a pack of loonies," he said. "A séance! Come back in seven days, and if she still hasn't shown up, we'll talk. But if I had my way, I tell you, pal, I'd throw all youse kids in jail just for being weirdos."

The cop was probably a year or two younger than I, but there is something about the law enforcement mustache and the rattle of cuffs at the belt that gives a man an air of maturity beyond his years. I left the precinct house, tail between my legs, without uttering another word.

After that I checked all of Chase's usual haunts

on my own. I went to the Arcadia and the Lobster and Club 219. I tried to contact her brother through Jamal, the bartender, at Le Hibou. I went over to Madame Ada's tearoom on Livingston, but the place was closed. A hand-lettered sign on the door read *Gone Fishing*. I called a few friends of hers who live in Providence. They hadn't seen her in years. Now there is nothing more to do but wait. I wait.

At last the call comes on Tuesday as I am packing the purple banners and elaborate candleholders back into Chase's suitcase. Jillian's voice is strained and stiff on the other end of the line, and despite her inbred Anglo-Saxon reserve, I know immediately something is terribly wrong.

"They found Chase," she says slowly, "floating in the East River. She committed suicide. The cops talked to some homeless women who live under the Manhattan Bridge who saw her jump. Just thought you might like to know, you bastard." Then she hangs up with a sharp click, and I am left with the dead buzzing of the line like the ring of conscience in my ear.

An hour later I go down Pearl Street to the wide cobblestone triangle where the abutments of the Manhattan Bridge rise up like a dark fortress.

"Hey!" I call into the rubble of construction equipment and wire spools jammed under the arch. "Hey, you, the lady from New Orleans. I want to talk to you! Hey!" Then I sit down on the curb, chin on my knees, and wait. Ten minutes later the black woman, emaciated, worn, and yellow-eyed, emerges from the perimeter of junk but stands warily a little ways off like a skittish animal.

"What you want, mistah?" she says. "I already done talk to the police."

"I'm not the police," I say. "I bought a shirt from you a few weeks back. I just want to ask a couple of questions."

"Oh, yeah, I remember. You from New Orleans too." She comes a little closer and squats down on the cobblestones. Her knees bulge out from her narrow shins, like the knees of starving Biafran children in magazine ads.

"The girl who jumped, she was a friend of mine. I'd like to know what happened," I say.

The woman nods solemnly. "All right," she says after a beat. "I'll tell you. It was about ten o'clock this past Sunday morning, and Bernice and I, we see this white girl coming down Jay Street over here. She moving in a funny way, like in a dream or something, and she wearing a bathrobe or a nightgown and she ain't got no shoes on her feet. Looks like a white crackhead, Bernice says, but I'm not so sure. Then the white girl, she climbs the fence up yonder and gets onto the bridge like she's going to walk over to the city. But the bridge is busted, been busted for years, anyone can see that. Check it out." She points up to the disintegrating planks of the walkway overhead.

I look up and nod.

"So the white girl walks along till she comes to the place where the boards end, you know, and she stands there for a minute. Then she holds out her arms and just kind of leans forward. Man, she fell like a stone straight into the water, and she didn't come up again."

I am quiet for a few minutes after this terrible account. Then I rise and offer the woman a ten-dollar bill, but she shakes her head.

"I don't want any money," she says. "Sorry to hear about your friend is all."

"Thanks."

She pushes up off the cobbles and stands for a moment, knuckles jammed into the pockets of her dirty cutoffs. "It's this damn city," she says. "You know what's best for you, you get on home to New Orleans, where you belong."

Then, as if on cue, we turn to Manhattan, moored across the river in the near distance like the dark hulk of a prison ship.

9

The service for Chase is a quiet affair at a Gypsy funeral chapel in Manhattan on East Seventh, across from the Café Deanna. As usual, the incessant pounding of drums comes from Tompkins Square Park, one block over. The facade of the place, otherwise a normal tenement, is distinguished by two faded plaster urns painted to resemble pink marble, and a tiny storefront window decorated only with a dusty plaque that reads "Gragogian Bros. Embalmers. Romany Spoken Here."

Inside, at one end of a narrow wood-paneled room, a cheap urn filled with Chase's ashes rests on a table draped in black. In death, as in life, Chase cannot rely on her friends. Now, at the final hour, out of all of them — for Chase was a woman who cultivated many friendships — there is only myself and Jillian. Jillian has gained a few more pounds and looks very good in a tight suit of black satin, a black veil hanging from a little hat over her eyes. She sits in the front pew between Madame Ada in her wheelchair and Ulazi, gangsterish as George Raft in a high-shouldered double-breasted suit. Seated behind them are a half dozen or so Gypsy relations, dark men in dandruff-flecked pinstripe suits from the seventies and rotund women draped in layers of black chenille.

I arrive a few minutes late and slip into a pew at the back and, to my relief, am joined a minute later by Byron Poydras. He is half shaven, literally: One side of his face is smooth, the other stubbled, and there is the faint trace of purple eye shadow and mascara ringed around one eye. The nails of his left hand are painted with purple glitter nail polish. Metallic flecks flash in the dim light.

"In a drag show last night," Poydras whispers when he sees me eyeing his painted fingers.

"There was, like, a gender role theme. We had to come as she-males or he-shes, a half man–half woman thing. Then we had to get on stage and try to fuck one half with the other half. It was wild."

I feel it best not to question the logistics of this perverse spectacle and lend an ear to the old priest mumbling over Chase's ashes up front. But he is speaking in Romany, the indecipherable language of the Gypsies, and I can't understand a word. When he is done, Ulazi stands, gives a thuggish tug on the front of his suit, takes a fiddle from a case beneath the table, and begins to play. It is an old Gypsy melody, that sounds like wagons rolling through the tall grass at dusk and the smoke of campfires and the faces of peasants seen for a moment in the half-light along the roadside; that sounds like all the sadness and beauty of life. Ulazi plays with a passion and feeling unsuspected in one so shallow, violin tucked tightly under his chin, eyes closed. He finishes with a flourish, wiping tears from his cheek with the back of his hand like a child.

"Ozun tula bagran tu-da!" he says in a choked voice, and the statement is repeated in a murmur by the other Gypsies present. I recognize the phrase. A traditional Gypsy farewell, translated once for me by Chase, which means "Oh, when shall we cease our wanderings!" An admirable sentiment, which drives Ulazi to despair. He flings the fiddle to the floor with practiced melodrama and throws himself against the bulk of his great-

239

aunt. She wraps her arms around him, and he weeps copiously there into her skirts as the priest says a few final words. Then the urn is lowered into a plywood box and handed to Jillian, who steps forward with as much dignity as Jackie accepting the flag from JFK's coffin at Arlington.

Afterward the small party of mourners assembles in the foyer of the funeral chapel, which is decorated with yellowed black-and-white photographs of unknown men in suits, framed under glass with borders of black crepe paper. Everyone is going to Le Hibou for the funerary meal, a Gypsy tradition, where the departed is toasted with arak and toasted again till all participants are dead drunk. Ulazi and another Gypsy are trying to heft Madame Ada out of her wheelchair for the short walk down to the curb as I approach.

"I am truly sorry," I say to the large, old woman. "Chase was a good friend, and I will miss her sorely. If you don't mind, I'd like to come along to Le Hibou."

Standing behind the wheelchair, Jillian jerks her head to me, eyes flashing. "Get away from here, you swine!" she hisses. "Haven't you done enough damage already?"

At this, Ulazi jumps forward with a cry and knocks me to the ground. I feel the hard tilework meet my assbone and the wind rush out of me.

"You bastard!" He stands over me, waving his fist. "You bastard! I should kill you!" But this is all he can manage before he chokes up and throws himself once again against Madame Ada's formidable bulk.

"It's a pity you didn't show such concern for your stepsister when she was alive," I say, and get up off the floor and dust my trousers with as much dignity as possible. The Gypsy relations stand watching stone-faced, their dark eyes moving from Madame Ada to me and back again. One nod from her, I get the feeling, and it's a knife in the back.

"Honestly, ma'am," I say to the old woman, "I didn't know it would end like this, I —"

But she cuts me short. "My grandniece's death was not your fault," she says, her eyes hooded. "I saw that she was sick and would take her own life the day you two came into my parlor. There were dark flames all around her, and I knew it would not be long. That is not why we do not want you to join us at the meal in which we will remember her. We do not want you there because you are an unlucky person and Gypsies are superstitious and do not like to be around unlucky people. Your bad luck is written all over your face and in the palm of your hand." She reaches up and grabs my hand, frowns into it for a moment, and thrusts it aside. "Yes," she says. "Just as I expected. Only a miracle will help you to evade your fate."

At this, she turns away. The Gypsies wheel her over to the front door and help her down the stairs. A graffiti-scrawled van, fitted with a hydraulic lift, rumbles at the curb.

"Loser!" Jillian hisses as she passes with the rest.

The street door is shut in my face, and I am left alone in the quiet foyer, the eyes of the dead Gypsies in suits staring down at me from behind their panes of glass, quiet, accusatory, and still as memory itself.

10

I am drained of life; I am cold, shivering in the air-conditioning of the subway. The car is full of poor wretches who live without this amenity in New York. For them the subway is the only place they can come to get cool on hundred-degree days that blast this city like a blowtorch. They are easily recognized. Old men who live in back-alley tenements with a single window open on the airshaft where no wind stirs. Here on the F, they sit in their shorts and sandals, reading the paper, jolting sideways, loose as puppets when the train comes to a stop and when it starts up again. They are going nowhere. To Coney Island and back in the dull yellow glare.

When I exit the long tunnel at Knox in the grainy twilight, I know there is something wrong. I am being followed.

They are two black youths, about fifteen, dressed in full-blown gangsta style: Jeans ten sizes too big droop around skinny thighs to balloon over unlaced two-hundred dollar sneaker-boots; matching gold dollar signs dangle from necklaces of thick gold rope; the plastic straps of X hats, worn backward, sweat into their foreheads. They've got that low-balanced street walk, the loping swagger of someone who has just been released from the joint. They're hooting and hollering back there; they don't care who hears them in this neighborhood. There's no one around, no place to run. They're looking for trouble, and I know the trouble is me.

I got a good look at them earlier on the platform at Broadway and Lafayette. With each stop, they made their way back through the cars, entering mine at Delancey. By East Broadway they came to sit across from me, and as the train gathered speed for the long run under the East River, they were making loud comments designed to instill fear into the average commuter. But I am not the average commuter, and I have a secret weapon for such moments.

I removed my weapon carefully from the back pocket of my khakis, made a great show of bending it out, smoothing the crinkled pages. Then I began to read. It is an old orange-and-black Penguin copy of Alan Moorehead's *The White Nile*, curved to the shape of my ass, and dog-eared from much use, which I carry with me wherever I go in New York. This fading text gives me the courage I need to walk the streets of the city, to board subway and bus heedless of the dangers, to order an egg salad sandwich from the angry Ashanti behind the counter at the Kwanzaa Deli on Montague Street and ask, steel-eyed, for extra onion.

The book narrates the British exploration of Central Africa in the nineteenth century and is full of the brave and foolish exploits of men who overcame incredible odds, surmounted many dangers, and mostly returned to good old England to tell about it: There is Mungo Park, determined to find the source of the river Niger, who had himself deposited on the shores of an unknown continent wearing a top hat and carrying a valise; Burton and Speke, who discovered the source of the Nile; Baker and Stanley and Livingstone, who traipsed across Africa wearing flannel suits; and the great General Gordon, who met his end at the hands of the Mahdi's dervishes at Khartoum in the Sudan.

Whenever I am feeling particularly outnumbered, I turn to the general's sad story. Surrounded by a fanatical enemy, he held out for months in the Citadel at Khartoum, praying for a relief column that came three days too late. Food gone, water low, no hope left, as out in the fragrant desert night a hundred thousand dark faces waited for the final assault. The Mahdi sent a message at the last minute under a flag of truce. Gordon would be allowed to leave with his personal possessions if he abandoned the city to the slaughter. Otherwise he would suffer the unspeakable fate of all unbelievers. Leave and Allah will spare you! The Mahdi made this generous offer in his capacity as the right hand of that inscrutable deity.

But Gordon did not hesitate. The offer was rejected without a second thought. "When God was passing out fear in the world," Gordon told the messenger, "He came to Gordon and there was no fear left. Tell the Mahdi this! When God created Gordon, He created him without fear." O brave General Gordon! How many of us will muster such composure at the end? For the tiniest breath of that courage now!

The two youths follow me down Knox, past the corrugated graffiti-scarred fence that conceals a big empty hole in the ground. They slouch about twenty paces behind, trading loud mothafuckas back and forth. I start to sweat. In a second my shirt is stuck to my back. I hear the sound of a bottle smashed, and another bottle, but I do not turn around. It is like the surface tension that keeps water poured a little too high from overflowing the glass. Look at it wrong, and the stuff spills over the sides.

Shadows deepen along the warehouses now. From somewhere comes the plaintive cry of a car alarm. At this, they quicken the pace, unlaced sneaker-boots flopping like clown shoes against the glass-strewn pavement. Then the talk stops all at once. Their silence is worse. On the warehouse just ahead a rusty sign from the fifties announces the manufacture of men's and boys' hats. The sky is all blue shadow and beautiful, with just a hint of moon. This is the moment that all New Yorkers dread, the moment they wait for all their lives. What will you do?

A moment later one of the youths is at my side, and an almost friendly arm crooks around my neck. I look up, my nose a half inch from his nose. His breath has the sweet reek of cheap malt liquor, and his eyes are wild. He smiles. We could be two old friends passing each other on the street.

"Hey!" I say.

"What you looking at?" the youth says, hostility in his voice.

"You, I guess," I say, and duck out from under his arm and begin to run, but the other one is already crouched like a fullback between the Dumpsters of the Damascus Bakery and the head of Tide Street. I try to dodge around him; he leans into it and catches me up with his sneaker-booted foot, and I go sprawling across the cobbles. It is that simple. Before I can get up, I hear an unmistakable ratcheting sound.

"Freeze!" one says, and the other one comes around and pulls the wallet out of my back pocket. They find nothing, just a cash card, driver's license, and a few sentimental odds and ends: a bit of old ribbon from an ex-girlfriend's hair, a couple of hopeful fortune cookie fortunes, a four-leaf clover sealed in clear tape that my father plucked once from among more mundane clovers in the front yard of our suburban bungalow just outside of Washington, D.C.

"What is this shit, Dano?" one says, dropping the contents of my wallet to the ground.

"Looks like shit to me, McGarrett," the other says. "Better get this cracker-ass on his feet." They are playing a game; they are characters from *Hawaii Five-0*.

Dano reaches down, pulls me up by the scruff of the neck, and twists me around. I am facing the business end of a Garibaldi nine millimeter pointed between my eyes. This gun is made by the Italians from a carbon compound and designed to pass undetected through metal detectors at airports. I hold my breath and hope they cannot hear my heart beating against the inside of my ribs. They look me up and down for a moment, eyes narrow with power. They are at that dangerous age. Despite all evidence to the contrary, they cannot imagine their own mortality.

"What do you think?" Dano says. "Should we shoot the guy? What do you think, *guy?*" he says to me, emphasizing the word.

"Definitely not," I say. "Wo Fat wouldn't like it."

"Think you funny?" McGarrett says, tapping the gun against my forehead.

"No," I say.

"Then gimme your money! We know you got money!" the other one shouts, and I jump and go fumbling in my pocket for my change purse, which contains three dollars and some change. Dano empties it out into his hand and stares at the wadded bills and pennies with disbelief, and it is then I remember something Geoff told me: Always carry fifty dollars in your pocket for the muggers. Anything less, and they're likely to kill you.

"O.K.," I say. "Let me tell you a story. It's about Gordon of Khartoum. Do you know Khartoum? It's in the Sudan, a straight shot down the river from Cairo. Do you know about Gordon? He was governor-general of the Sudan and tried to stop the slave trade there." I am talking fast, in a voice all quivery around the edges.

"Huh?" McGarrett says.

Dano looks up from the pittance in his hand. "What you saying?"

"Listen, when he knew there was no hope left, when the dervishes were climbing over the palace wall, Gordon retired to his chambers and put on his dress uniform, the white one covered with gold braid, and he put on his fez, and he buckled on his sword and walked out to the top of the stairs to face them. They crowded into the court-yard, thousands of them, their bloody spears poised, half afraid to come up, because he had the reputation of being a man who talked with gods and devils. There was a moment of silence. There often is at such times. Gordon just stared down at them with his blue eyes. He had these blue eyes, you see, ice-cold steel. He had been known to stop riots in dusty desert towns with just one look. Then he made a gesture like this" — I give them an ambivalent movement of wrist and elbow — "some say a gesture of contempt, others say resignation — who knows, does it matter? And you know what happened then?"

The two youths look at each other, then look back at me.

"What happened?" Dano says.

"Well," I say, frowning, "one of the dervishes shouted," *'Mala oun el yom yomeck!'* which means 'Accursed one, thy time has come!' in Sudanese, and then they, um, hacked him to pieces and threw the pieces down a well."

"Say what?" McGarrett says.

"What the hell kind of story is that?" Dano says.

"It's history," I say.

"Fuck history," McGarrett says. "Enough of this shit."

"Right. This all you got, Mr. Gordon of Cartoon?" Dano says, pushing the crumpled bills under my nose.

I nod miserably.

"Then we got to do it to you; it's one of the rules," McGarrett says.

"Do what?" I say.

"Fuck you up, that's what," Dano says.

"You don't got enough money," McGarrett says, shrugging in an affable way, "you get fucked up. Just business."

"Yeah," Dano says. "It's the nature of the beast. Especially these days when people walk around with too much plastic. People these days got cards to take a shit, you know? We need to put the word out you don't carry enough cash money on you, you going to get fucked up."

"Think of it as a sort of street tax," McGarrett says. "The IRS in this case being us."

"Really, you —"

I don't have the chance to say anything more. In another second the blunt carbon side of the Garibaldi is slammed hard against my head, and I catch a last oily whiff of it before I sink, blank, to the cobbles.

11

The street at eye level is like a gray moon landscape, all peaks and valleys and thick with dust in the cracks between the cobbles. Overhead the streetlight flickers green, an orbiting eye, the moon's moon. My head is stuck to the pavement with dried blood. I unstick myself with some effort and much pain and gather my scraps and stumble back to the apartment.

In the bathroom I am afraid to look in the mirror. Is there an eyeball hanging out? No, just the face of a man scared half to death, a purple knot swelling three inches to the north-northwest of his ear. I wash the wounded area delicately with a blue facecloth, administer iodine to the cut, then run a hot bath and soak for an hour and try to consider myself lucky. But the truth will not be soaked out of me: My life hangs by a thread. Only the thinnest of possibilities separates me from disaster. It's this city, yes. But is it different elsewhere? Is there a corner of America safe from this murderous nonsense, the dance of the haves and the have-nots? O Arcadia! Then I think of Chase and her watery doom, and I am sad and scared.

An hour later I am lying on the couch, watching the news, when the phone rings. I let it ring. Then it stops ringing and rings again a few seconds later, and I pick it up even though I don't feel like talking to anybody.

"Hello?"

"Ned?"

"Yeah."

"My God, you sound awful!"

I'm not sure for a moment about the identity of the woman on the other end of the line. Then it hits me with a little jolt.

"Hello, Antoinette," I say in a flat voice. I haven't spoken to her in six months, but tonight my head hurts, and I can't work up any enthusiasm. Somehow, I can't even imagine her face.

"Are you all right?" she says.

On the news right now they are pulling three bodies wrapped in sodden bedsheets out of the East River. The newslady, a spunky, attractive Korean girl named Kim Sung, is on the scene, trying to suppress her glee over covering such a great gruesome story. It's amazing how cheery tragedy makes us, as long as it happens to someone else.

"As we speak, they're pulling a couple of bodies

out of the river on the other side of the Brooklyn Bridge," I tell Antoinette in the same flat tone. "I'm watching it on the TV. The newslady says that some underwater cables kept the bodies from drifting into the harbor. The bedsheets they were wrapped in got tangled up in the cables. They've been floating there for three days with holes in their heads, like seaweed, like fucking kelp. Two kids and a woman. They suspect the husband, who is wanted for questioning. This is happening as we speak."

Antoinette is silent on the other end. I can hear the distance crackling between us, the long miles of countryside, the wide sweep of the continent down past New Orleans to the Gulf.

"Why don't you tell me what's wrong, Ned?" Antoinette says at last. She sounds concerned.

"All right," I say, "here it is in random order — last week my friend Chase committed suicide by jumping off the Manhattan Bridge, I can't seem to finish the thesis for my Ph.D. which just might get me a real job, I haven't slept with anyone I care about in years, I have no money to speak of and no health insurance, I live like a pig in a crummy apartment in one of the most dangerous neighborhoods in New York, and this evening, coming home from the subway, I got mugged." For some reason I don't tell her about the ghost.

There is another silence as Antoinette absorbs all of this. My forehead is hot. I find I am clutching the receiver so hard my hand hurts.

"Listen to me, Ned," Antoinette says now. "Did they hurt you? Are you hurt?" Practical girl that she is, she seizes on the most immediate of my sorrows.

"Pistol-whipped, I think that's the word," I say. "Two hooligans with a gun. A big gun. My head hurts, maybe a mild case of shock. But I'm O.K., I guess."

"Ned, you need —"

"Yeah," I interrupt. "I need a million bucks; I need a house in the country; I need a vacation. But all I've got are a couple of shirts, a few battered books, and a lot of squalor." I regret this self-pity immediately. It doesn't do to whine to Antoinette, who always maintained a cheery distance, even when we were sleeping together, but there it is. Suddenly she clicks into place like a slide in a slide show, and I feel an unwelcome tug at my heart. She is sitting in her slip on the old yellow Victorian fainting couch in her apartment in the Faubourg Marigny, cigarette in hand, comfortable mess strewn around her, the aquarium full of shoes, the piles of clothes on the floor waiting for the maid, and out the window the St. Roche shrine a dark silhouette against the green sky.

"Ned, I think I can help you," she says quietly now.

"Forget about it, Antoinette," I say. "Didn't mean to go off like that."

"Shut up and listen to me. Are you listening?"

"Yes."

253

"I can't do anything about the million bucks; things haven't been real good with the store lately. But I can help you with the vacation and the house in the country."

What is she saying? The miles fizz and pop between us. From the power plant across the street there is the loud echoing scrape of metal expanding against metal.

12

It is almost impossible for someone to disappear completely from history. Even the least fortunate leave some scrap behind, a faded letter, a line or two in a police blotter, a few bones in a desiccated pine box buried in the ground beside other pine boxes, each corresponding to a number in a ledger on the dusty shelf of a rectory library. Not so for Sister Januarius, whom Father Rose wishes to declare a saint before the Congregation of Rites in Rome. This woman has left nothing, not a crumb, not a postcard or a dentist's bill. Catholics are usually very good record keepers, especially when it comes to their own. Think of the Venerable Bede, of the chroniclers and the ecclesiastical historians, of those monks who for centuries copied books by hand and candlelight, and the parish priests who, with a weary flourish of pen, recorded deaths and births and baptisms. This nun lived and died a bare hundred years ago, but her life seems as distant and obscure as Ptolemy's.

I have begun to have my suspicions. Perhaps Sister Januarius is a figment of Father Rose's imagination. Still, excepting the obsession with golf, he strikes me as a sane man. It seems more plausible that someone went through the records and destroyed every document pertaining to the woman. But what about her bones? Catholic dogma is explicit on the subject. Catholic bones must be interred in Catholic ground!

I leave the crypt and the contents of box number twenty-two — bundle after bundle of 1920s-era business correspondence half eaten by termites — mount the stone stairs and follow the passage that leads beneath the rectory to the parish house. This Gothic stone building was once the site of St. Basil's School before the Irish families who formerly inhabited this section of Brooklyn departed for the suburbs. The narrow, locker-lined corridors still smell of chalk and the unwashed flesh of children. At one end of the main hall, behind a mesh screen, a life-size plaster polychromed Jesus suffers in detail on the cross. The screen was put up, Father Rose once explained, to keep schoolchildren from sticking their gum to the bottom of Christ's feet. The Savior's elongated toes hang about thirty inches off the floor, just elbow level for a nine- or ten-year-old.

Father Rose is delivering a pre-Cana lecture in the old auditorium two doors down from the caged crucifix. His audience, three bored Hispanic couples, sit clumped together, front row center. It is a wide, airy room with arched windows, redolent of Christmas pageants long gone, eighth-grade graduations, and basketball games against Gonzaga pulled out a second before the last buzzer. I take a seat at the back and wait for Father to finish. Up on the stage he is pointing at a word writ large upon the blackboard. The word is *RE-VIRGINIZATION!* The Hispanic couples stare up at him, confusion and embarrassment on their faces.

"The church realizes that many young people have not been able to hold themselves aloof from the promiscuity and corruption of this corrupt age," Father Rose says, tapping on the blackboard with his pointer, "and that they have fallen from the state of grace conferred by virginity. But the church also believes that it is possible to become a virgin again!"

At this the Hispanic couples exchange confused looks, and there is some quick whispering in Spanish.

"The state, if you will, of re-virginity, is attained through prayer and by practicing abstinence for at least three months before the marriage. Many couples find that they emerge from this process totally inexperienced in sexual matters even after long years of illicit liaisons. There have even been one or two cases where the woman's hymen has been found miraculously restored, and she has actually, physically become a virgin again —"

256

One of the Hispanic men raises his hand. "Yes, Cipriano?"

The man rises. He looks angry. Angry veins stand out in his forehead. "So what you are saying, Padre," he says in a choked voice, "is our women, the women we are going to marry, the women we are going to take home to our mothers, these women are whores?" His fiancée, an attractive girl no more than eighteen, wearing a childish dress of blue chiffon and lace, hangs her head and begins to weep.

Father Rose is flustered. He looks from the word on the blackboard to his students in dismay.

"Not at all, Cipriano," he says quickly. "I am just giving you a possible situation here. I am not trying to suggest that it necessarily applies to you. If your fiancée is a virgin —"

Cipriano explodes at this. "If!" he shouts. "If — !" But he is too excited to speak. He shakes his fist at Father Rose, makes an incoherent gesture to his companions, and they rise in a single movement and follow him to the door. One of the young women does a curtsy as she leaves the auditorium, but Cipriano pulls her back roughly.

"Marriage classes!" he calls from the hallway. "We don't need no stinking marriage classes!" Then the door slams, and they are gone.

On the stage Father Rose sighs and wipes the offending word from the blackboard. He gathers his notes and comes down and sits heavily beside me on a rusty folding chair.

257

"I'm fine with the usual Ten Commandment stuff, Mr. Conti. You know, adultery and thy neighbor's wife and all that. But it is foolish of the church to require priests to act as counselors in more specific sexual matters," he says. "We are men who have renounced the sensual in favor of the spiritual. It's like asking a golfer to play baseball. Other than the fact that we both wear shoes with cleats, there's no comparison."

I'm not sure what he means by this metaphor, but I nod and express my sympathy. Then, as I turn toward him, he notices the swollen lump on my temple.

"That's a good solid bump you have there," he says. "An accident?"

"Mugged," I say.

"In the neighborhood?"

"Yes." He doesn't seem surprised.

"I'll pray for you," he says simply.

"Thanks."

After a moment he stands, smooths out his cassock. It's obvious I've come about something important.

"Well?" he says.

"Bones," I say.

13

I am pledged to absolute secrecy. Father Rose makes me swear on the great gilt-backed Bible at the altar in the church. Then he makes me swear again on the chalice used for the communion wine during mass, the vessel in which takes place the sacred miracle of transubstantiation. When he is satisfied with the sincerity of my vow, he takes me downstairs to the crypt and unlocks a nondescript door I hadn't noticed before. We descend a short flight of steps and come to a halt in front of another more impressive door inlaid with the Chi-Rho initials of Christ, in a yellow metal that might be gold.

"This is the secret of St. Basil's," he says, in a solemn Charlton Heston voice, and I can't help feeling a tingle at the back of my neck. "I turned down a posting as assistant golf coach at Holy Cross to accept this charge. I could have instructed generations of young men in the art of the sport, but I chose to come here instead. Do you understand?"

I am suitably impressed by his sacrifice, and I tell him so, but I am more impressed by what I see when he unlocks the door and we step into the inner chamber: At the center of the windowless stone room sits a glass coffin containing a mummified body in a nun's habit. I approach in awe. It is like something out of a B-grade horror movie. Sharp brown teeth grimace out of the collapsed leathery face; wax eyes, an artificial shade of blue, stare from lidless sockets. A few twists of white hair curl from beneath the wimple gone green with age. Bony hands clutch a thick black Bible which has long since fallen to one side. A string of Christmas lights around the ceiling lends the final garish touch. A small spider, I notice, is making a web in between the clumpy nun shoes.

For what seems like five minutes I cannot take my eyes off the shriveled corpse. Father Rose stands at a respectful distance. At last he approaches.

"This is Sister Januarius," he says as if introducing us. Then he sinks to a faded velvet kneeler, says a brief prayer, crosses himself, and leads me back up the stairs to his sunny office on the third floor of the rectory. Even here, surrounded by golf trophies and cheery flowered wallpaper, I cannot quite shake the maudlin atmosphere of the hidden crypt. Hands clasped thoughtfully, Father Rose steps over and sits in the big leather swivel chair behind his desk. This is the first time I have seen him use this corporate-looking piece of furniture, and our conversation is a little like an interview with the chairman of IBM.

"Granted, the presentation down there is unfortunate," he says. "I go often to the chapel of Mother Cabrini in Washington Heights and envy her beautiful wax work, the crystal sarcophagus, the modern chapel, and wonder why our Sister Januarius is so neglected. Of course, the answer is a simple one. Our saint is still a secret. To this day the bishop does not know, the cardinal does not know. Do you understand?"

"I'm not sure I do," I say. Suddenly I picture

Snow White asleep and waiting for the kiss of Prince Charming in her glass coffin, and it seems the brown mummy downstairs is waiting for a kiss from me to wake from her catacomb slumber. A dry historian's kiss on those desiccated brown lips. How horrible.

"As you know, the establishment of a cultus for a saint is strictly regulated by the Holy See," Father Rose says, "and is dependent on the decision of the Congregation of Rites in Rome. Any veneration of relics, any preservation of the body must follow the granting of this status. What you saw downstairs, what was done here with the earthly remains of Sister Januarius by Pastor John McCarty nearly a hundred years ago was outside the laws of the church and punishable by excommunication. But Father McCarty acted on faith. Sometimes the wheels of the church grind too slowly for the true believer. He knew Sister Januarius was a saint, had in fact witnessed miracles, and wished to act before the body disintegrated —"

"Excuse me, Father," I interrupt. "You once mentioned a monograph written on this subject. I have spent many hours searching libraries for that monograph. Now I find out the whole thing's a big secret from the pope. My guess is the monograph does not exist, that I've been on a wild-goose chase all this time."

Father Rose is silent at this accusation. He folds his hands and looks down at the polished surface of his desk. Sunlight gleams off the golf trophies in the cabinets and laps like the waters of a tropical lagoon against the flowered wallpaper. Outside a summer haze is settling over Brooklyn. At last he looks up.

"You're right," he says, and swallows hard, a guilty glottal sound in his throat. "There is no monograph. I'm sorry. A white lie. The story I told you concerning Sister Januarius was handed down from pastor to pastor in the oral tradition, you might say. When I took charge of this parish from old Father Carello, I was made to memorize every detail. I couldn't let you know this because of the secrecy involved. Each pastor selects his successor carefully on the basis of devotion to the cult of the saints. And each pastor must keep the secret in his own way until the day when all secrets can be revealed at last."

"And when is that?"

Father Rose shrugs and goes to the window. "Anytime short of Judgment Day, that's up to you and your research," he says. "For a long time the pastors here were content to keep all this to themselves, to keep Sister Januarius as a sort of private saint. But saints are for people, Mr. Conti. People who have need of their intercession. When I saw that letter in the archives years ago, I thought the possibility of building a case for the beatification of Sister Januarius before the Congregation in Rome just might exist. Where there was one letter, there were bound to be others."

"So the letter was real?"

262

Father Rose turns to me now, a little indignant. "The letter is there in the archives somewhere. It's just a question of perseverance and faith."

"Faith."

"Yes."

There follows an uncomfortable silence in which we hear the grunts of the handball players sweating on the blacktop of the park below.

Then I tell him that I am planning a short working vacation in New Orleans. I'm going down to visit an old friend, I say, and will consult the archives of the Nursing Sisters of the Cross, supposedly Sister Januarius's order. They still maintain a convent in that city, in the Vieux Carré.

Father Rose seems pleased with this plan and comes over to clap me on the shoulder with his calloused golfer's hand. But when I rise from the love seat, I rise a skeptic.

"You went to college in New Orleans, am I right?" he says as he sees me to the door.

"Yes," I say, "Loyola."

"How long has it been since you've been back?"

"Ten years, Father."

14

My suitcase is packed; everything is ready. A sliver of laconic moon rises over Manhattan, and a wind fragrant of salt and oil stirs from the river. It's the night before I leave for New Orleans, and I can't sleep. Never could sleep the night before a trip. Who can? The power plant is grinding out a merry tune, and every time I close my eyes, I see Antoinette's face framed against the darkness. Despairing of sleep, I rise at 3:00 A.M. to clean the apartment. There is nothing worse than coming back to the same mess and squalor, and I haven't really touched the place since the séance.

I get on my hands and knees in pajamas and rubber gloves and scrub the kitchen floor, I wash all the dishes, I clean out the refrigerator. In the bathroom I scrape mold from the grouting in the shower stall with a screwdriver and have a go at the commode and sink with the kind of foaming action cleanser they advertise with animated bubbles on TV. The ghost seems to approve of my activities. The toilet brush, which has been missing for some time, mysteriously appears in its old place in the corner by the commode. Same with the two-pronged converter plug for the vacuum cleaner, which I find in the sugar bowl in the kitchen.

When I fall asleep at last on the sofa at dawn, I dream of the wax eyes of Sister Januarius's mummy staring up into the darkness in her locked tomb beneath the altar, and I dream of a brown river that might be the Mississippi, and I dream of Antoinette. I wake late at 7:00 A.M. and must rush to catch the Carey bus to La Guardia. But on my way out the door, I stop, place the suitcase on the landing, and sit a minute in the morning light of the clean apartment. It is an old Russian custom, adopted from a Tolstoy novel: Before taking a trip, you pause a quiet moment to consider where you are going and where you are leaving and what will be different on your return.

So I think of New Orleans — it seems impossible that I will see it again in a few short hours — and I think of Brooklyn and the mundane run of my life here, but I fail to imagine the future, which is imponderable as ever. Then I rise and exit, closing the door on the sunlight and the dust beneath the radiator that will never be vacuumed and the apartment full of silence that is the sound of the ghost at work in the walls like a termite.

Part Four:
To the Bayou

1

New Orleans appears out of the gray afternoon as a patch of green on the horizon. Rain beads the thick goggle of window; the plane dips a wing toward Lake Pontchartrain, and we bank for the final descent. I see the gray-blue waters of the lake, touched with little whitecaps and the white dots of sailboats, and farther off, rising from the river, the flash of heat lightning. Then, I see the green oval of the infield at Jefferson Downs, and the streets of Kenner like lines on a map, and as we lower toward Moisant Field, silver water tanks in backyards, and the shallow blue of pools and cars moving like flecks of gold in an uncertain light on the Eastern Expressway, and here and there, the pale buttons of magnolia flowers.

At last there is the pressure in my ears, and the rough bump as the wheels hit the grease-burned tarmac, and the flaps-down shriek of brake. My heart is in my throat as we taxi along-side the Duncan Canal and approach the terminal, and for a moment I wonder what is wrong — I have flown before, many times — but then I look out the thick window past the drops of rain and see the familiar green-and-white profile, the scrub pines and jasmine, the shaggy tops of the palms nodding over the flat pastel neighborhoods, and even in the pressurized cabin it seems I can smell the thick, loamy richness of bayou and lake beyond the tangle of city, and it hits me — New Orleans. I am back after ten years.

2

Antoinette is waiting at the baggage terminal. She is wearing a nice tan and a red polka-dotted one-piece pants suit outfit from the forties, scooped down low at the back. Her black hair, curly because of the humidity, is twisted over one shoulder. She searches the crowds for me, stepping around a group of Japanese tourists, pausing to ask one of them a question I can't hear. She towers over the man; he stares up, wide-eyed. But he shakes his head, makes the international sign for no understand, and stoops to retrieve a plaid golf bag from the baggage carousel. I watch from an oblique angle, admiring her profile, as another Japanese man, judging her an excellent specimen of the local fauna, asks to take a photograph. When this is done, I come up quietly behind.

"Antoinette," I say.

She spins around, and I see that she is carrying a bunch of pink roses wrapped in green tissue paper — what does the pink represent, I wonder, possibility? — but I don't have time to think. She lets out a small cry and in a moment has me in a healthy bear hug, crushing the roses between us. She kisses me full on the lips, then leans back, hand on her hip to get a good look at me. A pair of expensive Italian sunglasses is propped in her hair. She adjusts these with an expert gesture and gives me a long, gray-eyed look. From far above, the airport loudspeaker crackles unintelligible flight departures.

"Hmm, you're looking white as a fish, boy," she says, and pushes a finger into the paste-colored skin of my arm. "We need to get you out in the sun, that's for sure."

I shrug. She is right. I've spent the summer in a crypt with thirty boxes of decaying documents, not a stone's throw away from a mummified corpse with wax eyes. But she looks marvelous. Healthy and athletic yet elegant in that casual way she always had. Antique earrings of bloodstone and silver bump against the muscles of her throat.

"I sure as hell better look good," she says to my compliments. "Cost me enough. I've got a personal trainer, can you believe it? This gorgeous black man, used to play for the Saints, comes over twice a week and gives me one hell of a workout. Here, check this out." She flexes her free arm. "Go on," she says.

I give it a squeeze and feel the muscle stiffen and bulge beneath the flesh. "Very nice," I say.

"And that's not all, feel this!" She puts her foot on the steel lip of the carousel, pulls up the flared leg of her slacks and stiffens her calf muscle. I hesitate; she takes my hand and presses it against her calf, which feels warm and smooth.

But when I bend toward her, my hair falls away from my face and she sees the purple bruise and zigzag laceration on my temple.

"Honey," she says, concerned, "is that where they got you?" She pulls me up and touches it gently with her fingertips.

"Yeah."

"New York. What the hell are you doing all the way up there?"

There is not enough time to answer. My shoulder bag comes crashing out of the chute, and as soon as I've got it, she pulls me toward the sliding doors and out into the thick, buttery heat of New Orleans in August.

"I'm parked illegally," she says. "Come on. Oh, and these are for you." She turns and thrusts the pink roses into my arms.

"Welcome back," she says, and leans over and kisses me on the cheek.

3

The car is new and impressive, a red convertible Saab Turbo with brushed aluminum alloys and an interior of white Italian leather. Antoinette kicks off her shoes and drives the thing barefoot, carelessly, as if she were driving a battered old pickup truck. There is already a ding or two in the bright enamel. We're dodging in and out of traffic on the Airline Highway, headed toward the city in the light flow of Saturday traffic.

"Nice car," I shout over the rush of hot wind.

"I guess so, if you like your cars all modern," she shouts back. "Papa got it for me last year. I didn't want the car, really. I wanted a big old 1959 pink Cadillac convertible, and I had one lined up for ten thousand dollars — this old boy I knew who used to work with Dothan at Spanish Town. But Papa said he didn't feel comfortable with me driving around in a thirty-year-old car no matter how big it was, and he goes out and buys me this thing. Didn't even ask me. I hate it, if you want the truth. Makes me feel like a sorority girl just out of Ole Miss. Need a bow in my hair to drive this thing."

Now the clouds seen earlier from the window of the plane break with a crack of thunder, and it begins to rain. Antoinette's got the top down. Raindrops hit the windshield, but because of the rake of the car, we stay dry. I've never driven with her before, and it's a frightening experience. Her idea of driving seems to involve the quickest way of getting from point A to point B, and damn all the niceties in between. She looks over at me, teeth clenched in the front seat, and laughs.

"Hey, haven't lost a passenger yet," she says. When the rain picks up and I begin to feel a few drops, she fishes up an LSU hat from the junk in the backseat and tosses it my way. "Put this on if you don't want to get wet," she says, and she bears down on the accelerator and we go barreling in and out of traffic till downtown rises, a gray and green swath, through the windshield. She's got the radio on now, a station that plays country oldies. She sings along with this, a song full of slide guitar and broken hearts, as we intersect with the Pontchartrain Expressway. The streaked metal walls of the Superdome glint dull and ugly just ahead, like the walls of a futuristic prison.

"How do you feel about a beer?" Antoinette puts a gruff fist on my knee. I am hunkered down in the seat like a ten-year-old.

"I'm game," I say.

"But just one. Because we need to stop by the store so I can borrow some money from myself; then we've got to hit the road. The whole family's waiting for us. O.K.?"

"Sure."

We exit the freeway at Dryades and head over to Perdido. Antoinette leaves the Saab parked at the corner of Perdido and Carondolet right beside a fire hydrant. Half a block down, just before the dead end of Carroll Street, there is a neon martini glass lit against the gray sky. It fizzes a pleasant blue in the rain. Antoinette jumps out of the Saab in a short athletic hop, without opening the door. She's done this before. I can see scuff marks and grass stains on the armrest.

"Aren't you going to put the top up?" I say.

"Don't you worry about my car," she says, annoyed, and is already halfway to the bar. She's inside before I have quite disentangled myself from the seat belt. I leave the pink roses on the backseat, where they will benefit from the rain, and hurry after her. She is acting a little strangely now, slightly awkward as if she doesn't want to make too much of my arrival after the initial enthusiasm at the airport.

The cocktail lounge is long and dark, decorated in a nautical theme. Prints of sailing ships hang in the dark booths; a polished wood ship's wheel hangs over the bar, and nets with glass floats are nailed to the ceiling. I get a vaguely illicit fifties atmosphere. Close to the federal buildings and businesses on Canal, it's the sort of place you would bring your secretary if you were having an affair. Antoinette is already sitting on a red vinyl stool at the bar, smoking a cigarette and drinking a gin and tonic. She points to another one of these, sweating on a paper cocktail napkin. A lime and a lemon perch on the edge of the glass.

"Drink up," she says. "We're already late. The rest of them got there this morning."

I climb on the stool, somewhat dizzy. I had forgotten the heat of New Orleans in the summer, the air like a hot bath, then the frozen atmosphere of air-conditioned places. And there is something else — a strange disassociation, a transparency. I feel like a man haunting his own past, and it seems I can almost see through my own hand as I pick up the glass. O damned insubstance!

"You look a little sick," Antoinette says. "A little green around the gills. You sick?"

"No," I say. "It's just been so long, I —"

"Oh, come on now." She gives me a stiff punch on the shoulder. "Don't go misty-eyed on me. You're back, that's all. You've been gone too long. This is your vacation. Climb out of your head for me and try to relax. Can you do that? Come on, try," and she reaches over and raps on my head with a sharp knuckle.

I decide to take her advice, for fear I'll return to New York with more bruises than when I left. She knocks back her gin and tonic and orders another round, though I have barely touched mine. Then she snaps open her small rectangular purse and removes an antique pillbox. She takes a yellow pill out of the box, curls it onto her tongue, and swallows with a mouthful of gin.

"What's that?" I say.

"Didn't get much sleep last night," she says. "Just a little something to keep me going."

"Unh-huh."

"Don't ask."

We are silent for a minute, and Antoinette slurps her second drink as I finish my first. Then she pauses and looks at me through her lashes, an unreadable expression on her face.

"Out with it," I say.

"Nothing," she says. "You're too sensitive." Then she tells me about the family gathering, which I will be attending. It's a Rivaudais tradition. Her parents have a sort of fishing camp downriver between Pointe de la Hache and Jesuit Bend that twice a year they fill with daughters and husbands and grandkids and crayfish boils and barbecues.

"When I talked to you on the phone, you sounded so low," she says. "This thing might be a little boring, but anything's better than New York, right?"

"Right."

"We've been going down to the camp about the last ten years now. Ever since Papa gave up his cabin on the bayou outside Mamou. You know, he just never could stomach that place after the whole Dothan thing. I think he always blamed himself for taking me out with him, unsupervised, as it were, and for everything that happened. Though to tell you the truth, it would have happened just the same anywhere else. I was a little piece of something ripe in those days."

Suddenly she seems very nervous. Cigarette going in the corner of her mouth like a truck driver, she begins to tap her fingers in a drumbeat on the bar, and then her foot is going, and I realize that the yellow pill has kicked in and that it is speed. She tries to say something but shakes her head. Her thoughts are racing faster than her tongue. I try to slow her down.

"So whatever happened to Dothan?" I say, and she stops jittering for a second, as if someone has just closed a gate in her face.

"Dothan, huh," she says. "I don't know where the hell he is now, and I don't care. We broke up for good about three years after you blew town. The bastard gave me a nice fat black eye, just like the one he gave you. Not too long ago

277

I heard the state troopers got him for some drug thing. They had him up at Angola for a couple of years on the prison farm. He was a tough guy, but that place is full of tough guys. I heard a couple of things from Leroy Threefoot, this half-blood Choctaw used to work at the bar, the same guy I almost bought the Cadillac from. Leroy told me that Dothan took a little black boy lover like they all do up there and that somebody broke both his arms and stabbed him in the lung, which he recovered from. When he got out, he left for Texas. That's all I know. But I'll tell you what, Texas is where he belongs. A state full of red-necks, no-class shitheels, and rattlesnakes. Dothan ought to fit right in."

Antoinette finishes her drink, mouths a cube, spits it back into the glass, takes her purse, and slides off the stool. There's something unfamiliar about her, something I can't quite put my finger on, a layer of weariness perhaps, or sadness, beneath the tanned sexy look and the speed, but I do not know enough yet to say for sure.

"You ready?" she says.

It is not a question. She's out the door, and I swallow half a glass of gin in a choking second and follow.

Antoinette's store is on Treme, on the block closest to the park. It occupies the ground floor of a late-nineteenth-century three-story town house built in the Creole style, with wrought-iron balconies and painted a vivid shade of pink common in New Orleans.

"Up there you've got two apartments," Antoinette says, pointing to the balconies of the upper floors. "Pretty nice one-bedrooms with a little shared garden in the courtyard out back. Two gay couples, but I'll say one thing — except for the occasional marital spat, they're neat and quiet. I really ought to kick them out, renovate a little, jack up the rent, which is dirt cheap, and move in some yuppies. But you know how I am about money. Never could abide the stuff."

"You own the building?" I say.

"Now I do. Papa had the deed made over in my name last year on my birthday."

"Nice of him."

"Yes."

Antoinette double parks the Saab on the narrow street and we go into the store. Inside the small foyer there is hardly enough room to move. It smells like mold, clove cigarettes, and mothballs and is jammed floor to ceiling with old clothes — suits, dresses, jackets, coats, hats, shoes, purses. The flotsam and jetsam of the last four decades.

"This is the sale room," she says. "Everything here is fifty percent off, or two for one." A hand-lettered sign over one rack reads 70s! HIP! STYLISH! ON SALE! I see ugly polyester dresses, maxicoats, and the fuzzy rabbit fur jackets that I remember from the fast girls of my youth.

"The seventies are so hot right now," Antoinette says, pulling out a disturbing green sweater-dress hemmed with a green feathery substance.

"I know," I say. "It's all over the East Village. Clumpy black platforms and bell bottoms. The stuff was ugly then, it's ugly now."

She frowns, and we pick our way around piles of clothes on the floor to the next room. Here there are counters and glass display cases and framed black-and-white photos of people from the 1920s. I stop before one of these, a pretty woman with the glossy black bobbed hair of the era. The resemblance is striking. The same cheekbones, the same insouciant smile.

"That's my aunt Tatie," Antoinette says. "Something of a wild woman in her day apparently. Had lovers, never got married."

"Runs in the family, I guess."

"Shut up." Antoinette shoots me a glance. "She was so sweet. She died a couple of years ago in the home. I miss her."

The register, manned by three hard-looking high school girls, is set on an antique planter's desk against the far wall. Antoinette introduces them as Sticky, Polly, and Emmy-Lou. The girls eye me blandly. I don't impress them.

"How'd we do yesterday?" Antoinette says.

Polly shrugs. "All right."

They all wear exaggerated makeup and are dressed in clothing from the store. They look like little girls who have gotten into their grandmother's cedar closet. Two of them smoke clove cigarettes, and a noxious cloud of this stuff hovers in the air over their heads. Speed metal shrieks at volume from a tape box on the shelf behind them. It is too easy to predict the lives that await them: At nineteen, one will marry a bassist in a rock band and after a roller coaster ride of drugs and distant gigs will divorce, bereft of youth and prospects, at thirty. The other will die of an overdose or in a drunken car accident in the next five years. But the third, she might surprise us. I see a rapprochement with her parents and finally law school. Between them, seven abortions.

I am drawn from these uncharitable speculations by Antoinette's jittery nervousness. She knocks a box full of glass beads off the counter, and Sticky sighs and stoops with her to clean up the mess. Then I look around the store while Antoinette opens the register and counts up the previous day's receipts. There is a back room, full of an odd assortment of men's clothes. I count nearly a hundred pairs of khaki jodhpurs, regulation for the pre–World War U.S. Army, racks of Depression-era double-breasted suits, ten boxes of wing tips, curled up at the toes. I try on a moth-eaten Knights of Columbus bicorne hat. Its silver braid cross still glitters beneath a layer of dust. As I am posing Napoleon style in the peeling oval mirror, Sticky approaches me from behind.

"Hey, mister," she says.

I jump around, embarrassed, and go to remove the hat, but she waves me off.

"Don't worry," she says. "Everyone likes to try on that hat. Most people look stupid in it, but it looks good on you, I think."

"I can't very well walk down the street looking like one of Napoleon's marshals," I say.

"Why not?" she says, and she is serious. Then she glances over her shoulder to where the others are busy with the cash and lowers her voice. "I want to talk to you. Out here." She pulls me out the back door onto the porch overlooking the courtyard garden. She is wearing a frilly pirate shirt, bloomers, and riding boots, a bandanna tied over her blond hair. Still in my Knights of Columbus hat, I have the odd feeling that we are two characters out of H.M.S. *Pinafore.*

"I want to talk to you about Nettie," she says. Her expression beneath the makeup is earnest and without guile.

"You mean Antoinette?"

"Listen, are you her boyfriend or something?"

"No," I say.

"Well, she was talking about you like you're her boyfriend."

"What?" I feel a light tingling at the back of my neck. "Antoinette talks about me?"

"Yeah, she was saying that you were coming

282

down from New York and that she hadn't seen you in a while, and she seemed real excited about it, so I thought you were her boyfriend. But you're not her boyfriend."

"Not that I know of."

"But you are her friend, right?" She plucks at my sleeve for emphasis.

"Yes."

"O.K. I just want to say that I'm worried about her. I mean, I don't know her family or anything, or I would tell them — Nettie's been doing a lot of speed lately. I mean, a lot of speed. She got depressed when all this stuff happened with Victor last year —"

"Who's Victor?"

She makes an impatient gesture. "Nettie's old boyfriend. So she was sleeping a lot — you know how it is when you're depressed, you just lie around in bed all day and smoke cigarettes and sleep — and to get herself out of it, she started doing speed. It's a classic, right? She hasn't ever really gotten off of the stuff since then. And lately she's been coming into the store and taking money from the cash register, like today. I don't have to tell you that's bad for business, right? We used to make real good money here; the store's a very popular place, one of the only real vintage places in New Orleans. But now I think we're losing money, and I wonder . . ." She looks over her shoulder again to make sure no one has crept up on us. "I wonder if she's starting to get back into coke again."

"You mean . . . ?"

"Oh, yeah, cocaine. She and Victor used to take baths in the stuff. Maybe I'm paranoid, but I see the telltale signs. Anxiousness and such. It's none of my business; it's just that someone close to her ought to know. That's all."

Sticky is slightly out of breath when she finishes. I am silent for a moment, taking all this in. Then we hear Antoinette calling from inside.

"Sticky? Need to ask you about some receipts."

"O.K., that's me," Sticky says. "I don't want to be an alarmist, but Nettie's great and she needs some help maybe, and if you can help her out, that would be great. O.K.?"

Antoinette calls again and the girl ducks away and I am left on the porch in my bicorne hat, grave as the emperor himself, arms crossed and musing over the green garden wet with rain just below.

5

The sun is out now, and the sky, clear of clouds, shows an unremitting blue. That's the way it is down here. Rain in the morning, then clear and hot in the long hours that extend from noon till dusk. Antoinette's got her Italian shades down, and we're racing along the Belle Chasse Highway, a glittering red bug against the dark asphalt. Soon the highway banks sharp to the right, and there's the river, a brown lazy snake on the other side of the levee.

"What did you think of my girls?" Antoinette calls over the Swedish-aluminum whine of the Saab.

"In the store?"

"Yes."

"They're in an awful hurry to grow up. Bohemians, junior version. They remind me of some people I know in New York. I can see them in the Village in a couple of years, making the scene. But clove cigarettes? I thought clove cigarettes went out years ago."

Antoinette grins. "Not with these chicks."

"Actually I thought one of them made some sense. The girl in the pirate's outfit. A good kid."

"Sticky? Oh, yeah. Sticky's great. She loves me."

"I'd say she's worried about you, too. The pills —"

"Shit. I can't believe she said anything about that." Antoinette frowns into the windshield, and when her lips pull down, I see sharp worrylines around her mouth.

"What about the pills, Antoinette?"

"The pills are nothing, forget the pills. They're not much stronger than the average espresso."

"And what about cocaine? Doing any of that?"

She shakes her head and gives the wheel an impatient tap. "Let's drop it, O.K.?"

"Antoinette . . ."

"Later," she says. "The afternoon is too beautiful. Let's not spoil it right now."

She's right. We pass Jesuit Bend, and there is a high flush of cirrus in the blue sky and the smell of the open country. Soon we are rolling alongside miles of orange groves interspersed with odd-looking squares of magnolia and live oak that were once the site of great plantation homes.

In the days before the Civil War, when a single white man could own as many as seventeen thousand black slaves, this country of the Plaquemines delta was the center of a fantastically opulent plantation culture built on the sweat of others. Rice, sugarcane, and indigo grown in fields reclaimed from the swamp were traded upriver for the luxuries of the world: Carpets and Sèvres china and books from France, bolts of silk and spices from the Orient, dueling pistols and silverware and beaver hats from England, even Renaissance paintings from Italy. Each planter then was monarch and law on his land and owed allegiance only to the profit margin and his own bad conscience. But all of it came to an end in 1862, when Admiral Farragut's gunboats crashed through the chain the Confederates stretched across the mouth of the river. The Federals bombarded Fort St. Philip and Fort Jackson into submission, then steamed past the plantations to New Orleans, which capitulated without a fight.

About five miles south of Naomi, Antoinette turns off the highway onto an access road that leads through an orchard of orange trees into the bayou. There is the buzzing of many bees here and the smell of honey, and down one of the green shaded alleys between the trees, I catch a glimpse of a man in overalls and a mesh veil tending to rows of square white boxes that are the hives. A few of the yellow and black insects splat against the windshield before we pass off the gravel and onto a narrow road marked "Private — No Trespassing." It is paved with shells and just wide enough for one vehicle to pass. The air here is live with gnats and mosquitoes. On both sides of the road the terrain falls away to swamp, and all around is the green press of vegetation. I see sap willow and pine, cypress, magnolia, and low, scrubby bushes punctuated with the occasional burst of wildflowers: wild Creole lilies, camellias.

"Alligator," Antoinette says as we cross a new wooden bridge, and I turn quickly to see what looks like a mossy log sink beneath the green surface of the bayou. The shell pavement ends here. She bumps the Saab none too gently onto a rutted track, and I have to reach out and push branches away from the car as we pass. Now there is only the green light through the trees and the noisy hush of the swamp.

"Jesus," I say, "this is . . ." But I am too awed to finish.

"Not New York," she says, and she smiles.

6

The Rivaudaises' fishing camp occupies a clearing on a rise overlooking the still waters of a lagoon. This dark, oblong body of water drains into a navigable creek which meanders through the bayou to the Indiana shaped lake known as the Pond, which is in turn connected through a complicated series of bayous to the open waters of Lake Salvador. At one end of the Pond is the small town of Coeur de France. There's a bait and tackle shop, a saloon that is also a general store and post office, a Catholic church built by the Spanish two hundred years ago, a jail, and a few dozen shotgun houses raised from the sandy soil on cypress stilts. It is the closest bit of civilization, about three hours by pirogue through the bayou.

"They used to have dances there all summer long," Papa Rivaudais says. "Real country-French dances. Had a kind of dance hall attached to the old church. But that was a long time ago. Before the girls came along when we were still a young married couple, Mrs. Rivaudais and I, we spent all our weekends down here. Come Saturday afternoon, we'd hop in the pirogue and paddle all the way out to Coeur de France, dance all night, then hop in the pirogue and paddle all the way back again. But a hurricane came through — oh, sometime in the late fifties — and knocked that dance hall right out of there. The priest, he was a superstitious old buzzard, and he decided God didn't want any more dancing at the church, and that was that. Never did rebuild the place. Otherwise I'd tell you, latch on to Nettie, get the pirogue, and get on over to Coeur de France. Dancing's just about the best thing two young people can do to get acquainted. Know what I mean?"

I am sitting with Antoinette's father at the end of the small landing that juts about twenty yards out into the black water of the lagoon. Papa Rivaudais is supposed to be fishing. But in actuality he is just slumped in a canvas-backed folding chair, staring out at the lagoon, a dull expression in his faded blue eyes. The expensive-looking fiberglass reel is propped loosely in one hand. At his feet, a Styrofoam cooler of alcohol-free O'Doul's, a tackle box, and an empty wicker basket for the fish. The years have finally caught up with the man, still one of the twelve richest citizens of the state of Louisiana. His hand trembles upon the pole; one eye droops, the legacy of a stroke the year before. His white hair floats in wisps from underneath his long-billed fishing cap, and the once handsome mustache is thin and yellow-looking. I remember the robust patriarch of ten years before, a man still in grips with life, and I am sorry. Papa Rivaudais has become old. He survives on a bland salt-free diet and a shoe box full of medications. Even as we speak, his lungs are filling up with fluid.

He leans over and spits cottony white phlegm

289

into the black water of the bayou. It is a messy business. He wipes his mouth with a red bandanna that he stuffs back into the pocket of the long-sleeve plaid shirt he wears, even in this stifling heat.

"You'll have to excuse me," he says now. "When the stuff comes up, the stuff comes up. My doctor says it's better to spit than swallow."

"That's O.K.," I say. Then we settle down to a long silence. From somewhere nearby there is the cry of a loon.

The three cabins, arranged on a rise overlooking the lagoon, are connected by covered walkways and surrounded by a raised wooden patio. The center cabin with an old-fashioned porch, stone chimney, and sash windows probably dates from the twenties. The two side cabins with sliding glass doors and air-conditioning units are new additions, just a couple of years old. Still, there is a rustic feel about the place. This is the way the first French settlers must have lived, it seems to me, before slaves and plantation opulence, when they came to the province in the wake of the Sieur de Bienville and his soldiers. Then there was just the trees and the sky and the Indians off in the bayou. The primeval purity of frontier life.

From the cabins now I hear the high shriek of a child's laughter and a baby crying and the sound of women's voices. I look over my shoulder to see Antoinette and her sisters emerge onto the patio. They are preparing to barbecue. I recognize

Jolie, though her hair is dyed blond. She's got a baby in one hand and a bottle of Abita in another. Also, there are two little girls, twins from this distance, pulling each other's hair.

"You don't mind sitting with an old man, do you?" Papa Rivaudais says, looking up at me. "Unless you'd prefer to go up and join the women." There is a trace of the old irony in his voice and a spark behind the faded blue.

"No, I don't mind," I say.

"The husbands have all gone off fishing. I'm getting too old for that. Two hours in a pirogue nowadays, and the damp settles into my bones for weeks."

"And Mrs. Rivaudais?"

"My wife's up the road taking care of her people. She does that now, like any good Creole housewife. Always in the end, if you live long enough, you come back to the old ways. As for me, about a year ago, I actually talked to a priest. Haven't talked to a priest to say anything other than 'Hello, Father, how are you?' in something like forty years. Know what the bastard asked me?"

I shake my head.

"He asked me if I believed in God. I didn't know what to say for a minute there. Then I said, 'Well, yes.' First time I'd thought about it since I was a boy. God! You believe in God, Mr. Conti?"

This is the second time I've been asked this question in as many months. I consider for a

291

moment, still hesitating, but the old man doesn't give me the chance to answer. He takes a deep breath that rattles in his throat and leans forward.

"You ever hear tell about this Frenchman Pascal?" he says, and he draws a carefully thumbed copy of the *Pensées* out of the deep pocket of the khaki hunting jacket hanging off the back of his chair.

Pascal? I am stunned. I had always pegged the Rivaudais family for one in which any ideas beyond the purely practical were not tolerated. So much for my smug complacency.

"Amazing guy, Pascal," Papa Rivaudais continues. "Highly religious but also a brilliant mathematician and the father of public transportation among other things. He instituted the first horse-drawn bus line in Paris in the seventeenth century. But he started out a skeptic like me, like yourself, and he came up with a proposition for skeptics. Make yourself a bet, he said. Bet yourself that God exists. If he does exist, you win. If he doesn't exist, you win anyway, because it doesn't really matter and you've managed to give yourself something to hold on to in this sad life. Something to keep you warm against what old Pascal calls *les silences effrayantes de ces espaces inconnues*. You know what I'm saying? Here . . ." he says, and hands me the book. "Read it cover to cover three times."

I look it over politely, make a few comments about French philosophy of the era, and hand it back. But I am still a bit surprised. Pascal in the bayou.

"You know, I try to talk to the family about what I've been reading, but they just roll their eyes. They think I'm a crazy old man, even my wife. We're not a stupid bunch, Mr. Conti. Don't make that mistake, no, sir. My *père* and my *grandpère*, they were smart as a whip — I mean in a country way, because they were real country people. Still, seems like we could use a little of this stuff in the family." He taps the book. "I mean, a little abstract thinking . . ."

After that there is another long silence. I hear the water moving against the dock and birds in the bayou. It is possible to sit with an old man without talking and not feel awkward. After a certain age there is the sense that all conversation has been had, all points argued, and it is only the companionship that matters. Like children, old people do not want to be alone. At last we are roused by a tug upon the line.

"Ha!" Papa Rivaudais says. "Sometimes if you don't go to the fish, the fish, they come to you." There is a brief struggle, he is weak, but his seventy-odd years of fishing experience wins out. He reels in a two-pound bream, its dark scales glistening in the diminishing light. "I almost feel sorry for the creatures," he says. "*Lacrima rarum*, as the Romans used to say, how sad it is, but I tell you, split 'em open, clean 'em out, stick 'em on the grill with some lemon juice and garlic butter, and the sadness will pass." He tosses the

293

fish into the basket. Then, fifteen minutes later, he pulls up another one, a two-pound sunfish, all silver and brilliant spots, gasping for oxygen in the thin air.

We sit for another hour like that. I join him in an alcohol-free beer, and he trolls the line as the sun descends, green and gold, through the trees. Then, in the final moments of dusk, two pirogues wind their way from the creek into the lagoon.

"There they are. The husbands," Papa Rivaudais says, and stands with difficulty. I make out four men in the pirogues and hear their hearty shouts as they call back and forth, each to each. I bend to take up the tackle box and basket as Papa Rivaudais folds the canvas chair, but he sets this aside for a moment and turns to me. In the fading light I can hardly see his face.

"I'll tell you a secret," he says. "Antoinette is my favorite out of all my girls. Not a mean bone in her body."

I am silent.

"She nearly killed me when she ran off with that swamp redneck. She wasn't much older than thirteen, you know."

"Yes, sir," I say.

"And I'm telling you, the girl hasn't been the same since. That son of a bitch, he broke something inside her. She's never been able to settle down. She's the only one of my girls who didn't finish college, the only one who isn't married, doesn't have a child. Always so unsatisfied, jumping from one thing to the next. The store's been good for her, but it's just not enough. You know what I'm saying, Mr. Conti?"

I don't, but I nod anyway, and he puts his hand on my shoulder, and we head slowly up the rise toward the lighted cabins.

7

The stars are up, but even here you can see the lights of New Orleans as a pale green reflection in the sky. From the darkness of the bayou now, the reedy chirp of frogs and the occasional plop and splash of fish in the lagoon. An upside-down half-moon throws a sinuous glimmer on the dark water. In the yard the husbands have constructed a bonfire, and the orange blaze lights our faces on the patio. We are all out eating beneath the stars: Mama and Papa, Antoinette and her sisters, Elise, Manon, Claudine, and Jolie, and their husbands.

The baby is asleep. The two little girls, both eight years old, their long black hair done in pigtails, dance like Pocahontas around the bonfire, then roll, fighting and shrieking, on the wood chips of the drive. One is Manon's daughter and half Irish; the other 100 percent Creole, the fruit of Claudine's union with her husband, Paul Sarpy, of the Sarpyville Sarpys, representative from St. Charles Parish to the state legislature in Baton

Rouge, but the little girls could be sisters instead of cousins. They are alike as two peas in a pod. The dark, pretty Rivaudais blood seems to dominate all lesser heritage.

The picnic table is littered with paper plates and casserole dishes. The coals of the barbecue glow white hot, always perfectly ready twenty minutes after the last person has eaten. There was barbecued bream, crayfish jambalaya, Texas caviar, which is marinated black-eyed peas, corn on the cob, mixed greens, red beans, and rice. Only scraps remain. Now we sip Louisiana Lemonade, which is a potent combination of crushed ice, mint, fresh lemonade, and an indigenous sugarcane liquor called Davant, found only in the Plaquemines delta.

I lean against the railing with my drink and listen to the husbands talk about sports. New Orleans is trying to acquire a nice hockey team. The semipro Winnipeg Glaciers might become the NHL New Orleans Revelers sometime in the next six months. I have nothing to add to the conversation.

"I'm telling you what, this city needs a good hockey team," says Paul Sarpy. "I say why not, if the fans will support it?"

Jim Remington isn't so sure. He is Jolie's husband, an old friend of Paul's from the days when they both worked as staffers on Capitol Hill — and they are still two glad-handing Hilloid preps in plaid shorts and pressed Warthog polo shirts from Britches of Georgetown. Their Bass Weejuns are worn without socks. They met their future wives at the same Bush inaugural party in a Republican group house at A and First streets, SE. Jim is a member of the famous Remington gun family and vice-president of a new division that installs alarm systems. Antoinette has told me that he wired her parents' house on Prytania Street and her own apartment in the Faubourg Marigny, free of charge.

"Face it, Paul," says Jim. "New Orleans is just too hot for a hockey team. It's a sun town. Hockey doesn't go in a sun town." He's a tall, handsome fellow with a shock of black hair. He looks quite at home with the rest of the Rivaudais clan.

"Y'all heard of the Los Angeles Kings?" says Charles-François, Elise's husband. "Los Angeles is a sun town, but they've got a tradition of hockey going back to the thirties." A content and balding engineer in his early forties, he sits very close to his wife at the picnic table. She's just a year or two younger than he, but could pass for twenty-eight. Their two girls are off to camp for the summer, and they're cuddling like newlyweds.

"I personally would patronize a hockey team in New Orleans," says Manon's husband, Sean O'Farrell, the Irishman.

"Of course you would," Jim says. "Any sports is good business for you. More drinking."

"That's not it a' tall," he says. "We're not a real sports bar. I like hockey. Fast-paced game. But word around the place is this — team's going to be called the Bayou Blades, and they're going

297

to be based out of Baton Rouge."

"Bullshit."

"Bullshit to you," Sean says.

There is no trace of the hip jazz musician left in this man. He put down his saxophone a long time back, and now he's just one of the boys. The artistic streak he once possessed has been leached out by the Louisiana heat and the easy living afforded by his wife's money. But recently he has gone from being the bum of the family, butt of Irish drinking jokes, to something of a success story: After years of sullen loafing, he opened an Irish bar in the French Quarter, called O'Farrell's Four Provinces. It is an exact replica of a favorite pub in Dublin, down to the Guinness on tap and the gouges in the oak wainscoting caused by an IRA bomb in the seventies. The place has become so successful he's thinking of expanding to Metairie.

"The question is, Where are we going to put a hockey team?" Charles-François says now. "Not in the Superdome."

"That'd be a sight," Paul says. "Zambonis in the Superdome."

"What we really need is a baseball team down here," Jim says. "Now there's a good sun sport. The boys of summer . . ."

Et cetera.

The conversation passes from sports to local Republican politics, then to the state of nutria devastation in the swamp. Thousands of miles of wetland have been destroyed by this small

298

brown muskratlike animal from South America, accidentally introduced to the ecosystem in the 1930s. It reproduces like mad and will eat anything.

This is a topic for everyone, even Mama Rivaudais, who thinks the nutria is a cute animal with just as much a right to live as anything else. Only Antoinette and her father and I hold back. The old man, I know, has come to value his silence. He nods off in his chair. Antoinette keeps quiet for reasons of her own. But I have never been good at such gatherings. Normal folks eating and drinking and talking sports and politics just to hear themselves talk. The husbands are all fine fellows, who express very interesting and well considered opinions, but I am vaguely depressed by the whole thing and bored to tears. I nod and smile and sip my Louisiana Lemonade and make the occasional assenting exclamation, but they don't have much use for me. The very fact that I live in New York seems a threat.

"New York City," Paul says, rolling the words off his tongue like an accusation. It is one of the few comments aimed in my direction the whole evening. He hooks his thumbs in the belt loops of his plaid shorts like a sheriff's deputy and gives me the once-over. "If you want my opinion, New York City has much more influence than it should in the making of national policy." Claudine rolls her eyes at this. Another one of her husband's speeches. "The concerns of New York are not the concerns of the rest of America.

299

New York resembles London more than it does Baton Rouge or even Chicago. All the way down here, we know what New Yorkers are thinking, what New Yorkers are doing. Just because New York is where the media is located and the media controls information and makes policy in this country."

I agree. He seems a little disappointed. He wants more, an argument. I don't feel like saying anything, but I see that I am expected to continue. The husbands watch me in anticipation, drinks in hand. "Yes, New York reminds me of Paris in 1871," I say hesitantly. "A radical place full of radical ideas, ruled by the mob and their newspapers, and defiant of the Prussians. The rest of France capitulated; Paris didn't. Paris had its own mind that was not the mind of France. When the rest of the country made a humiliating peace at Sedan, the Foreign Legion was called in to pacify the Parisians, and there was a terrible civil war. They slaughtered at least one hundred thousand civilians in the streets. Buried them at the barricades where they fell, beneath the cobblestones of most major intersections. They still dig up bones to this day when they do street repairs." I immediately regret my words, but this clumsy historical analogy is the only thing that occurs to me.

An awkward silence follows. Paul seems confused or offended; he doesn't know what to say. Jim Remington coughs. Antoinette looks over at me and is about to intervene, but she shrugs and smiles. The smile is for me alone, lazy and fond. I feel a little jolt to my heart, my awkwardness falls away, and suddenly the night is beautiful, and it doesn't matter. I go back to my Louisiana Lemonade, which at that moment seems an excellent beverage.

"You know, perfect skin is a gift from God," Mama Rivaudais says, breaking the silence at last. It is a comment entirely out of the blue that succeeds in easing the tension. There is laughter and general disbelief.

"What the hell! Has the heat got to you, Mama?" Elise says from beside her husband at the picnic table.

"All of my girls have perfect skin," Mama insists. "Perfect skin even in high school, when girls have a tendency to break out. I can't remember any of you even having one little pimple. Can you, dear?" She nudges her husband awake.

"Huh?" the old man says.

"Perfect skin," she says. "All our girls. What do you think?"

He is puzzled for a moment; then he nods. It is his wife. "Yes, like a baby's butt," he says, and drifts back to sleep.

Antoinette, with her arms crossed at the railing, shakes her head. "Well, I can remember a pimple or two," she says.

"You girls should be grateful for what you have, and you have a lot. The Lord has been very kind to this family. Some girls would kill for perfect skin."

At last there is a murmur of assent and a moment of appreciation for God's bounty. This is as close as we will come tonight to the mysteries. Then the fire burns low; the pigtailed Indians run out of steam around the fire and are put to bed by their mothers. The old folks move slowly to the shadows of the central cabin, and the women and men begin to separate to the wings. That's the way it is on these Rivaudais family gatherings. Women and children sleep in one cabin, the husbands in another, with Mama and Papa in between.

"They get you a good bed?" Antoinette says.

"Yeah," I say. "The pullout couch."

We are standing at the railing, staring out at the lagoon. A light goes on behind the sliding glass doors in the husbands' cabin as they make ready to settle in for the evening with a frat house camaraderie full of farts, cigarette smoke, and bad dirty jokes. We hear a strange hissing sound, and the dark snout of an alligator breaks the ripple of moonlight on the water. Antoinette slips her hand beneath my arm. Moonlight falls along her cheek. Mama was right. Her daughter's skin is indeed perfect.

"I'm glad you came," Antoinette says. "We've got to do this man-woman thing, family tradition, you know. Otherwise I'd stay up half the night talking to you."

"That's O.K.," I say. "I'm really tired. The trip. Can't believe I left New York just this morning. We'll talk tomorrow."

"Thing is," she says, "I haven't been sleeping so well lately. I wouldn't mind talking to someone."

"What about your sisters?"

She shrugs and is silent.

I turn and take her carefully by the shoulders. "Those pills," I say. "Maybe they have something to do with you not sleeping."

She won't meet my eyes. "Don't you worry about me," she says. Then she leans up, kisses me quickly on the lips, and is gone. Out in the lagoon the alligator sinks back beneath the black water, silent as a stone.

8

When I wake the next morning, the cabins are empty, and I hear the click and whine of cicadas from the jungle green of the bayou. A lone nutria snuffles around the patio, then scuttles away. The screen door of the central cabin hangs ajar, creaking in a slight wind, and for a moment there is the creepy feeling that everyone has been kidnapped by Indians. I think for a moment of the famous Lost Colony. How in 1591 the returning English ships found the settlers' homes abandoned, the only clue an Indian name carved into the bark of a tree, and rosy-cheeked Virginia Dare, the first Anglo-Saxon baby born in the New World, vanished forever into the haunted depths of the forest.

I pull on a pair of ragged cutoffs and a T-shirt and go down to the landing, where Papa Rivaudais is dozing in his canvas chair, fishing pole in hand, in the warm morning light.

"Sir?"

He stirs and looks up, pale watery blues focusing with difficulty.

"Huh?"

"The others?"

It turns out they've taken the pirogues and gone off on an early-morning expedition to Coeur de France and won't be back till later this afternoon. "But my daughter, she left you some breakfast in the main house," the old man says. "She's a good girl, Antoinette. Always thinking of somebody else."

I find the Saran-wrapped plate set out on the table in the old kitchen. There's leftover black-eyed peas, cold muffins with marmalade, cold bacon, two boiled eggs, a glass of cranberry juice, and a note.

We tried to wake you at 5:00 A.M., but you wouldn't wake. Guess you'll have to spend the day with the old folks. If you get tired of Papa, Mama's up taking care of her people. Just follow the little trail out behind the main cabin till you come to a white stone that marks the Plaquemines Parish line. Then take a left, and you'll find the place about a half mile down the shell path. I know how you love history. Try to get Mama talking about the family. See you at dusk. — A

The prospect of a day with the old folks is not as tedious as it sounds. I have never been a good traveler because I rely too much on schedules and routine. A good traveler puts his schedules aside with his expectations and lays himself open for whatever comes to pass. I eat and brush my teeth; then I spend an hour with the old man. His eyes are bad today. He asks me to read a few passages from Pascal aloud which I do in a rusty French.

"My father used to read me the comics every Sunday, when I was a little kid," I say when he has had enough. "*The Phantom, Mandrake the Magician, Terry and the Pirates.* Remember the Phantom? He lived in a skull cave in a hidden forest in Africa, and he had this special skull ring. Whenever he punched out the crooks, he left the imprint of a skull right on their jaw."

The old man nods and squints up at the sun. "And now you're reading to me," he says. "It's the wheel. Keeps turning. Pretty soon you're back where you started from."

At about eleven o'clock I grope for a couple of cold Abitas in the ice chest on the patio and head off on the route Antoinette described. The path winds away through the trees for a mile, and there's the sound of strange birds and the thick, loamy smell of the swamp. Crayfish scuttle out of my way, and once or twice I see a snake sinew through the algae-covered water. After a while I pass across a well-kept footbridge and come to the white parish marker and find the shell road. The terrain is wider here and open to the sky. A stand of tall live oaks heavy with Spanish moss moves to the grave and serious music of trees in the wind. Soon the shell road branches off. Then, on a rise overlooking the river and the levee below, there is a white-washed mausoleum surrounded by an ornate wrought-iron fence.

One of the Rivaudaises' shiny Range Rovers is pulled up to the fence, its tailgate open. A variety of painting and gardening supplies lies arranged on the brick walk that circles the tomb. Mama Rivaudais, in white painter's overalls, kneels in the shell border between walk and fence, painting the iron curlicues with a can of black Rust-Oleum. She stands and wipes her hands on her pants when I approach. Green-lensed sunglasses and a painter's cap shield her eyes. The women of this family age well. She's over seventy, but her hair is just now turning salt and pepper, and her face shows few lines.

"You look like you could use some help," I say. She studies me curiously through her green shades for a moment, then nods, and I exchange my last warm beer for the bucket and paint the fence for the next couple of hours as she squats behind in true maternal fashion, handing out much annoying instruction. At about two we break for sandwiches, and she walks me around the tomb to show off the improvements she has implemented in the last few years.

"The first thing you learn as a Creole is you better take care of your people," she tells me. "Your dead got to be tended to just like your children. Used to be every Feast of All Souls, you'd see whole families in New Orleans out whitewashing the tombs, planting flowers in the planters, tidying up. Now you're likely to get shot out there or robbed or whatever. Especially at Old St. Louis number one and two. I feel sorry for those old families with bones in the city. It's a shame. Can't even take care of your dead anymore. We're lucky to have most of ours all the way out here. . . ."

The tomb is a square monolith of brick and plaster. Mama Rivaudais has planted a border of gladiolus, which bow their heads as if in mourning against the mortuary walls. There are narrow iron grille windows on each side, and at the front, a Greek Revival portico surmounted with a cross. The heavy ironbound door is closed with a new silver padlock. On the lintel above the door is a carved coat of arms showing a palm tree and three crescent moons, bar sinister, and the Latin motto *Non duco, non sequor,* which means, if first-year Latin still serves, "I do not lead, I do not follow."

"Antoinette tells me you're something of a historian," Mama Rivaudais says.

"Well, almost," I say. "I'm just an inch away from my Ph.D."

"Good enough. Let's try you out." We step up beneath the portico to escape the hot sun.

"They stuck this on the front in the 1840s," she says. "During the Greek craze, when they were putting columns on everything, even out-houses. The tomb itself was raised about thirty years earlier over the family crypt, which was just a dank hole covered with a slab. It is one of the only below-ground crypts in the whole of South Louisiana; a geologist told me that this here hill is what's left of a huge rock dragged down by a glacier umpteen million years ago. Now, the crypt itself dates back to the late 1730s, about fifteen years after the French came to New Orleans. That was when my people came. They were Franco-Spanish, from Gascony, which is in the south. Been around these parts ever since. See, all this land" — she gestures out toward the bayou and the river below — "used to belong to us. It was the most prosperous plantation along this part of the river. We grew sugarcane and indigo. Not cotton. Cotton was for the no-class nouveau riche bunch, like at Nottoway or San Francisco upriver. There was a beautiful plantation house, one of the largest in Louisiana. Of course, it got burned down during the war."

She pauses, and we gaze down at the river and the concrete levee, which extends into the distance like the Great Wall of China. There is something familiar about the bend of the river here, the way it curves out in a loop and the gentle rise of bank on the opposite side.

"Yes," I say, "the house was down there, where the river bells out . . ." but I stop. I don't know this. There is an odd prickling sensation at the back of my neck. Mama Rivaudais eyes me curiously for a moment.

"You're right," she says quietly. "But I suppose that's obvious to a historian like yourself. The path of the river made a perfect landing for steamboats coming and going to New Orleans."

Suddenly I am very hot, even in the shade, and there is sweat on my forehead.

"You look a little flushed," Mama Rivaudais says. "You should have worn a hat out in this heat if you're not used to it."

"I suppose so," I say.

"Here, let's go inside and cool off." She takes a key from the pocket of her painter's pants and unlocks the padlock on the heavy old door. The air in the mausoleum is stale and full of the charnel house smell of old bones and funerary linens, but it is at least twenty degrees cooler than the ambient temperature. My eyes adjust to the dim light from the windows. The flooring here is made up of worn black and white marble cut into octagonal tiles. An old iron lantern hangs from the ceiling. At the far end there is a small marble altar backed with a slab bearing the palm and crescent moon coat of arms and what looks like an elaborate apple tree hung with tiny worn shields instead of fruit.

"This was the original crypt slab," says Mama Rivaudais, her face in shadow. "The genealogy cut here supposedly traces our family back to Spain, to Rodrigo Diaz del Vivar, otherwise known as the Cid." She laughs at this. "You remember that movie with Charlton Heston, and was it Sophia Loren?"

"Unfortunately I do," I say.

"I know. God-awful. Even if it was about family."

I nod.

To the left of the slab is a shallow flight of stone stairs leading into the darkness. The atmosphere out of that hole is dank and damp as the grave which, in fact, it is.

"It's a little spooky down there," Mama Rivaudais says. "But we've come this far." She takes a flashlight from a steel toolbox behind the altar and leads the way. The steps are slippery with mold. We descend slowly, sticking close to the wall. At the bottom of the steps on a narrow landing, we stop, and she shines the flashlight into the gloom. We are looking at a low barrel-vaulted chamber of brick and plaster. Its floors are covered with a half foot of water. Cinder-block stepping-stones recede in the darkness. The walls are lined with plastered-over niches four to a row, one on top of the other.

"Meet the family," Mama Rivaudais says, a lightness in her voice. She is used to this place, these familiar bones. "We've been meaning to pump the water out of here and get an engineer to shore up the walls, but that's next year. A big project."

"Unh-huh." I experience an odd sensation that manifests itself as a deep rumbling in my bowels.

We cross the cinder blocks carefully to stand on a raised slab at the center. As she shines the flashlight, I make out names and dates ranging from the 1740s through the 1890s. "Look at them," she says. "Scoundrels, slaveowners, duelists, and their ladies. Romantic, eh?"

All the niches are full except for one, a conspicuous gaping hole about waist level, halfway down. Mama Rivaudais pauses her flashlight on this absence.

"Sad story there," she says. "The details are sketchy, but the sense is this — one of the mistresses of Belle Azure just up and ran off one day. This is a good twenty years before the Civil War. She left behind a husband who was famous for being a real bastard and two beautiful girls. It was quite a scandal. Even my aunt Tatie Louise, who knew everything about the family and would talk about anything as long as it was scandalous, wouldn't talk much about it. They never knew what happened to the woman. She never came back to be buried here in her place with the rest. Still, they kept the niche empty, waiting for her. One of those family skeletons you hear about."

All this is very interesting, but I am feeling a little sick. I am used to such sad stories and crypts and graveyards and the bones of the past, but this is my vacation, and just now there is a thick feeling of dread crawling up my spine like a cold hand. I beg out of further explanations, and in the Range Rover an hour later, on my way back to the fishing camp in the cheery sunlight of the afternoon, I can still feel the chill of that place as a shiver along the skin.

9

In the evening there is another family barbecue. The husbands hold forth on some topic of current interest with the pompous assurance of property owners, Papa is asleep again, and the women talk quietly among themselves. I lean against the railing in the shadows, another Louisiana Lemonade in hand, watching Antoinette move from one end of the patio to the other, caught between the green light of the bayou and the yellow light of the house.

She is a member of this healthy, rich, complacent clan, but she is also apart. She possesses a nervousness that the others do not possess, an edge. Perhaps it is a secret ennui that eats at her, or a painful self-awareness, or something as simple as ambition — the same demon that drove her father up from the poor shack-trash bayou town of his birth in the years after World War II. But it's hard for me to tell. I suppose I don't know her that well anymore, and we haven't had much chance to talk alone.

Now the conversation turns to Mardi Gras. The husbands divide the exalted krewes of Comus and Rex between them. Jolie was Queen of Rex as a debutante.

"It must all seem pretty weird to someone from the outside," Paul says to me. "Mardi Gras and all the craziness and the homosexuals dressed as women in the Quarter."

"Nothing seems all that weird after New York," I say, smiling grimly. "Especially the East Village. We've got a few weirdos of our own running around."

"I just bet you do," Jim says.

"You see more and more of that," Charles-François says. "I mean, just in the last few years."

"Of what?" Sean says.

"Of the men dressing as women, that whole thing," Charles-François says.

"No, they always did it," Mama Rivaudais says. "I remember very pretty young men in dresses in the street in the thirties, when I was a girl."

"I honestly don't see the male fascination for panties and bras," Jolie says, and is about to say more but goes in to check on the baby.

"I'm telling you it's really just in the last few years," Charles-François insists. "I grew up in New Orleans, I should know. It's getting worse."

"Shit," Manon says. "The Quarter's always been like that. Full of perverts."

"O.K., Mr. Historian," Paul says to me. "What's the historical perspective?"

"On?" I'm a little confused.

"On the homosexual cross-dressing thing," he says a bit aggressively.

I take a drink of my Louisiana Lemonade. "Well, the ancient Greeks were into boys, even Socrates himself, at least according to Plato. And from a certain perspective, I think you could say they wore skirts. The chiton is a sort of skirtlike garment."

"Something a little more modern," Paul says.

I think for a moment. "O.K., here's something — during the conquest of Peru in the 1500s, the conquistador Pizarro and his men came across a peaceful jungle tribe in which the women dressed like men and the men dressed like women. In those days, dogs terrified the Indians, and the Spaniards traveled with a pack of ravenous mastiffs, kept just this side of starvation. The tribe sent two emissaries to greet the stern conquistadors — a tough-looking woman carrying a shield and spear, and a simpering man with his face painted and wearing feathers in his hair. Pizarro took one look at this pair and set the dogs loose. The whole tribe was torn to pieces. . . . Is that the sort of thing you had in mind?"

For a few seconds there is another open-mouthed silence. Then the sound of Antoinette's laughter. I smile innocently and go back to my lemonade.

10

At midnight Antoinette comes down from the other side of the patio and kisses me on the cheek, an unsettling gleam in her eye.

"What's that for?" I say.

"That's for you being you," she says. Then after a beat she leans close and whispers, "I'm bored to death with this family shit. Let's get the hell out of here."

"Where are we going?"

"A bar," she says.

We slip unnoticed off the patio into the darkness as the husbands debate the finer points of their 401(k) plans. The Saab is parked top down, leaves on its seats, around the side with the other expensive vehicles. Antoinette turns the key, the engine ticks into life no louder than a clock, and we crunch slowly over the shells and out onto the bayou road. It feels like we are escaping a minimum-security prison where the wardens are friendly and the food is good. When we are at a sufficient distance from the fishing camp, she lets out a whoop and cranks up the radio. Cajun music is all we can find in this vicinity, and I recognize the song by Papa Languenbec and the Cajun Allstars that was playing the first time I saw her dancing up on the bar at Spanish Town so many years ago. It seems a sign, though I'm not sure of what. Immediately I regret the notion. I have become as superstitious as Molesworth.

Antoinette reaches across me to the glove compartment, and her breasts brush my arm. "Excuse me," she says, and takes out her small black purse. She snaps it open in her lap, pulls out the pillbox, and pops a couple of the yellow pills into her mouth.

"Here," she says, and hands the box to me.

"What do you want me to do with this?" My impulse is to throw it over the side.

"Take two of them," she says.

"You're crazy," I say.

"Are you tired?"

"Not really."

"Well, you will be tired soon, and I don't want you to get tired. I don't feel like sleeping tonight, and I want you to stay up with me. I haven't seen you, really seen you, in years."

"I'll stay up without the pills."

"You won't."

We pass out of the tangle of bayou now and into the regular shadows of the orange groves. The moon is rising toward its zenith above the river. "Please," she says, and puts a hand on my thigh.

I take two of the pills. They don't kick in until we are bombing up the Belle Chasse Highway. Then it feels like I am floating, and the lights of oncoming cars trail like streamers across the neutral ground, and the sound of the wind is the sound of many voices in my ear, and everything is moving very fast and nothing matters anymore.

"Whoa," I say. "There's more in those pills than speed."

Antoinette smiles a lazy smile from the driver's seat. She doesn't seem to have her hands on the steering wheel. "I still keep in touch with a few folks from the old days," she says. "Dothan's crowd. That old boy Hash Davis, the chemist who made the nasty-ass LSD I used to eat like candy. Now he's come up with these things. Yellow Pollys, he calls them, after his wife, who is a light-skinned black woman from Tallahassee named Pauline. It's a pinch of speed mixed with a smidgen of something hallucinogenic. Not much more potent than your average martini. But you've got to balance them out with alcohol. They're designed for that. Beer's in the backseat." She jerks her thumb over her shoulder, and I see a six of cold Abitas in Papa's Styrofoam cooler. Also, nestled in the shadows behind the seat, my shoulder bag.

"It's my stuff," I say. I pull up two beers from the cooler and hand her one.

"Yeah," she says. "I took the liberty of packing for you. We're not going back."

"How far is this bar?"

"Don't you worry about that."

"What about your parents? I didn't get a chance to thank them —"

"Just sit back and relax, O.K.?" Antoinette says, and slugs down half the beer in a single open-throated gulp, lights of the highway refracting through the brown glass.

I sag back into the seat, resigned, and let the gravity and the forward motion and the yellow pills take me where they want to go. At a certain point Antoinette's hand finds my thigh again and stays there, a warm, insistent pressure. She drives carelessly with the other, one-handed at incredible speeds. We inch eighty-five, one hundred, coming up behind tractor-trailers, flashing the high-beams and blasting by into the night. In two hours we are halfway across the state on 90, through Paradis and Lafourche and Thibodaux and Morgan City and Calumet. Then we are through Broussard and upon the lights of Lafayette, its streets crowded with pickups full of drunk Cajuns at this late hour of a Saturday night, the bars open till dawn. Then we are through the city, and there is the great summer stink of the swamp all around. We glimpse houseboats on the bayou, little more than shacks floating on fifty-gallon oil drums, and there is the sound of an accordion drifting up from somewhere in all that vast darkness.

At last Antoinette points to an exit sign that says "LA 10 — Bayou Nezpique, La Flange Landing — 15," and we break off and follow secondary roads, and then the secondary roads become gravel, and the vegetation closes in densely on both sides. In a few minutes we come to an open flat of hard red clay upon which about fifty cars are parked, mostly pickups, though I spot a new BMW and a Cadillac or two. Beyond this makeshift parking lot, there are reeds and the moon glittering over a lake clotted with more reeds and the small humps of muddy islands. On the air, which smells slightly of sulfur, there is again the sound, faint as hope, of distant music. The clock on the dash reads 2:37 A.M. in green digital letters.

"Come on," Antoinette says. "Let's go get drunk," and she hops over the side, spry as a gazelle.

"My bag," I say when I am beside her. "Shouldn't we lock it in the trunk?"

She shakes her head impatiently. "This isn't New York, boy," she says. "It's Louisiana. Cajun country. Folks are honest out here. Quit your worrying."

I shrug and follow.

At the water's edge there is a cement wedge of a boat landing and a tin hut manned by a shriveled-looking local. His face, revealed in the light of a storm lantern, is lined and weathered as an old saddle.

"What about the next boat?" Antoinette says.

The old man looks up at the moon hanging over the lake as if the answer resides there.

"Be along," he says, and spits a dark splot of tobacco juice onto the ground.

We wait, crouched down by the reeds. Antoinette steadies herself by a hand on my shoulder.

"How do you feel?" she asks, turning toward me, her eyes shining out of the darkness.

"Fine," I say. It is true. The pills and the beer do balance each other and heighten the senses. Details emerge, sharp and hyperreal: A hermit crab shies into his shell in the reeds; Antoinette's lips stand out dark as a wound against her skin; a soft wind blows against the outer edge of my ear.

"About the pills," Antoinette says, "I don't want you to worry too much. I'm going to get off them. This weekend is sort of a last gasp. I used to take twice as many as I take now."

"Jesus," I say to the night air. "How many was that?"

"I don't know. I used to eat them all the time. I used them to get off the coke about eight months ago. There was this guy, Victor. I didn't really like him, but he had a lot of coke. I met him at the bar at Mike's on the Avenue. He wore these expensive Italian suits and he had a lot of coke, and we would snort and then he would fuck me. We never made love. He was the last in a long line of assholes. Then something happened, and I just got sick of him, of everything. Sick to my soul."

"What happened?"

Antoinette is silent for a moment, and she is about to answer, but there is a sudden flat wind through the reeds and a loud whirring like the sound of a large fan.

"Here she comes," the leather-faced local calls from his place in the shack, and we stand and move down the landing. It is a flat-bottomed airboat, propeller facing out behind. The pilot sits up on an elevated chair like a line judge in a tennis match. A single spotlight sweeps the water. I have only seen such a craft in childhood movies about docile bears and the Everglades. A few minutes later Antoinette and I board and clutch on to each other as the airboat backs up and roars out through the reeds and over small, muddy lumps of islands in a straight line toward a light glowing on the horizon. It is a harrowing ride. Goose bumps rise on Antoinette's bare arms, and her hair is whipped back in the wind.

Soon our destination becomes clear: The light is a roadhouse up on stilts at the center of the lake. It is a sprawling, ramshackle affair, with a gallery all the way around, and a large open patio set with bare wooden tables full of men and women drinking and eating. Pirogues and outboards are tied up to the dock and along the railing. There is the sound of Cajun dance music and the rise and fall of many voices. At about fifty yards the airboat pilot switches off the propeller, and we glide the rest of the way up to the dock. He is a lanky fellow in blue overalls and a blue baseball cap. He wears clear goggles to protect his eyes from the wind.

"That's it. I'm off," he says. "You people are stuck here until dawn, unless you want to swim back." Then he tosses a rope over the piling with a twist that seems shorthand for a real knot and heads up the dock to the bar. Antoinette and I crawl carefully onto the rough wood and sit on the edge to catch our breath.

"I've been out here a dozen times," she says,

"and every time that ride scares the shit out of me."

I am too stiff to speak. Above the peopled hum of the bar I hear the dull stutter and pop of a gasoline generator. The blue tinge of carbon monoxide fumes floats in the air.

"You ready?" Antoinette says.

In the window neon script announces Cold Beer, Crawfish, Crabs, and Good Times. Another sign says SUCK THE HEAD with an exclamation point that winks on and off. Inside, the bar is packed three deep to the rail. On the other side of a low wall, a dance floor of red and white linoleum squares is full of two-stepping couples. A three-piece zydeco band — accordion, mandolin, and stand-up bass — reels away on a triangular bandstand in the corner. The walls are covered with stuffed fish and outdated hunting paraphernalia, including a duck punt the size of a cannon. In a less sensitive age this blunderbuss would be filled with anything — bits of scrap metal, nails, gravel, even pennies — and used to knock entire flocks out of the sky. I shout over the music into Antoinette's ear.

"What is this place?"

"Yeah, great!" she says, not hearing.

The crowd is heavily Cajun. Their black hair and high cheekbones betray the dark hint of other races: Choctaw Indian and field slaves escaped from plantations 150 years gone. But I also see other types: preppy couples from Baton Rouge in J. Crew ensembles; LSU college kid hipsters in recycled sixties thriftwear; even a businessman or two, tie loosened, briefcase lying amid a clutter of beer glasses on the table.

I spot him from across the room at the waitress station. One hand holding up the wall, his bulk is bent down over a petite waitress who stands, face tilted up, eyes wide, like some small hapless mammal in the hypnotic gaze of a python. A full tray of beer bottles is propped uneasily on her hip.

"Look who's here," I say into Antoinette's ear, and gesture. She nods and signs that she'll get the drinks and goes up to the bar.

I push my way through the crowd and stand to one side. It's the usual spiel. I can tell by his body language. I've heard it all before, in countless bars across the Lower East Side. Will they sleep with him or not? But this one is resisting. She shakes her head no. He tries a different tack. He is wheedling, which is usually fatal, but now he has an advantage. He is the boss. This could go on forever. Finally I cup my hands around my mouth and bellow, "Molesworth!"

Molesworth jerks around, annoyed. If he is surprised, he doesn't show it.

"I'm busy here, Coonass," he says, as if he just left me yesterday. Then he turns again to the waitress, but she has taken this opportunity to slip back to her section. "Dammit! You ever hear of timing?"

I push a finger against his meaty chest. "Molesworth, I want my six hundred dollars!"

He looks me up and down, considering, then shakes his head. "No way," he says. "Not till I see that phone bill. Itemized."

"Look at this place," I say. "You're making money hand over fist! This crowd drinks more than six hundred dollars in a half hour and you can't afford to pay what you owe me? You miserable cheapskate!"

I am resolved. His red, jowly face sags for a moment. He blinks away toward the band, winding into the last song of their set, and blinks back. There is a slightly hurt expression in his piggy eyes.

"That why you came all the way down here, Coonass?" he says. "To get your goddamn money?"

"Actually I'm visiting Antoinette." I gesture toward the bar, where she is already holding court, surrounded by three handsome, muscular men, with a fourth on the perimeter.

Molesworth frowns. "Never learn, do you? That woman's like an albatross around your neck. You're the Ancient Mariner of Love!"

"My money."

He sighs and motions to a huge brutish-looking man sitting on a stool at the end of the bar. The man is wearing a bandanna around his head and a leather jacket with no sleeves. A sideways 8 is tattooed on his shoulder — the infinity symbol.

"Yeah, boss?" he says to Molesworth.

I look up at him. His head is larger than life.

"Puddin', give this coonass here six hundred dollars," Molesworth says with a pout.

The man mountain called Puddin' takes a wad of hundreds from his pocket, counts out six, and hands them to me impassively. Then he lumbers back to his post at the bar.

"Puddin's my walking cash register," Molesworth explains. "Anything over a twenty. The man's safer than Fort Knox."

The bills feel nice and crisp between my fingers, and I am placated. "So how you doing with the place, Molesworth?" I say.

He shrugs. "I'm not complaining. But I can't talk now. Stick around. I'll buy you a beer when things quiet down a little around here."

"When's that?"

"Seven A.M."

11

A Saturday night spent in a good crowded bar is like a whole century of history in microcosm. The evening divides itself up into eras and events: There is the fight you witness between two Jefferson Parish bruisers over an undiplomatic comment, the twenty-minute conversation with the blonde who might know someone you know from Tulane, then the conversation with her roommate, a redhead who has definite opinions on the political situation in China. Then, blonde and roommate forgotten, there's a group from your hometown at a table in the corner and trips to the photo booth and more pitchers for which no one seems to pay, and the dark waning toward another bleary morning.

At 5:30 A.M., I find myself at one of the tables outside with a crowd of men and women I do not know, watching the sun rise out of the bayou to the east.

"There it comes," a woman says as the first glow clears the tree line.

"Yeah," a man says, "happens every morning just like that."

"Not quite," another man says. "The sun rises at a slightly different time each morning and the light is different depending on the season."

"We've got a budding physicist here," someone else says.

"Yeah," the first man says. "Ask Mr. Science."

"Fuck Mr. Science," the physicist says. "Here it is."

And it's true. The sun has filled the horizon in the short space of this conversation, and the water is gold and red with it, and there are more birds than I have ever seen rising from the swamp into the morning sky.

Then the table clears and there's the sound of powerboats from all around and the stench of diesel fumes and the light splash of paddles. The place is clearing out. A few minutes later I am joined by Antoinette.

"Where've you been since four-thirty?" she says.

"Out here watching the sunrise. You?"

"Ran into some people I know from New Orleans."

She sits heavily beside me and takes my hand, palm up. "I'd read your future," she says, "but I'm drunk. Can't read the future when I'm drunk."

I look over, and her eyes are swimming in alcohol. "That's all right," I say. "I don't want to know the future." Then our eyes meet and we are both drunk and it is morning and the sky is clear and beautiful.

"Uncle," she says. "I give in," and we are leaning toward each other and her lips are very close when Molesworth picks this moment to interrupt.

"All right, kids," he says. "Time for breakfast." He steps up carrying a cork-bottomed tray set with an odd array of fixings. I see Tabasco sauce, tomato juice, cajun spices, onions, eggs, lemons, tequila, a bottle of Benedictine, glasses, and a few other odds and ends. He sits heavily on the wooden bench and proceeds to mix three complicated drinks. The end result looks like a Bloody Mary with a brown layer of brandy at the bottom. I can smell the tang of tomato juice and the tequila and lime from across the table. At last, with a flourish, he breaks a raw egg on top of each and hands out the glasses.

"Voilà," Molesworth says, looking from Antoinette to me and raising his glass. "Shall we say, to love?"

Antoinette gives a lazy smile. "Why not?" she says, and, smiling still, downs the concoction in one long quaff. I almost gag on the egg, and then there is the spiced burn of the tomato-tequila mixture, followed too quickly by the smooth warmth of the brandy, but at the end of it I feel fine. This is a drink like a long and arduous journey after which you feel glad to be home again. My head and sinuses clear suddenly. I take a deep breath, amazed. For the moment I am not drunk or hungover.

"My God, what was that?" I cry.

Molesworth smiles mysteriously, his huge red face puckering up like a country ham. "That's old Molesworth's Cajun restorative, patent pending," he says.

"You've got to bottle it," I say. "You'll make a fortune."

"I thought about that," he says. "But the secret is this" — he leans close — "the ingredients must be absolutely fresh and natural. Stick it in a bottle, and the zing is gone."

"Yeah, that was great, Lyle," Antoinette says. "But I've got a restorative of my own." She produces the pillbox from her little square purse, but before she can pop one of the yellow pills into her mouth, Molesworth snatches it away. He's quick for a man with such meaty hands.

"What is this shit, honey?" he says, examining the yellow pills.

"You know," Antoinette says.

"Get them from Hash Davis?"

Antoinette nods, a bit nervous.

"You shouldn't be eating anything that bastard mixes up," Molesworth says. "You'll be having babies with two heads, let alone the more immediate consequences." Then he tosses the box over the side into the tea-colored waters of the lake.

Antoinette is quiet for a moment. Then she snaps her purse shut and stands with the aggrieved dignity of a southern matron whose honor has been offended. "Lyle, you are a bastard," she says through her teeth.

"You been talking to my daddy," Molesworth says.

"You didn't have to do that," she says. "I am not an innocent high school girl or an addict," and she walks, stiff-backed, into the bar toward the bathroom, screen door slamming in her wake.

"Sorry, Coonass," Molesworth mumbles to me when she is gone. "She's better off without that shit. We had some fast-living college girl in here writhing all over the floor last month from those things. A bad batch. The chick almost swallowed her tongue. One more incident, and I'm turning Hash over to the state boys."

"You don't have to apologize to me, Molesworth," I say. "I was tempted to get rid of those pills myself, except —"

"Yeah, except you let her run you around like a pig with a ring through the nose."

"You're a pessimist."

"Unh-huh. Just be careful you don't waste the second half of your life on that woman. You already pined away the first half."

A half hour later Antoinette emerges and, without looking right or left, marches down to the airboat, its prop thumping into life at the mooring.

I stand up. "This is me, Molesworth."

"Yeah." He lumbers up, huffing, and we shake hands.

"Well . . ."

He looks over his shoulder as if in consultation with an unseen deity, then back at me. "Don't give me that shit, Ned," he says. "It was only a matter of time. I'll be seeing your ass for the rest of your life."

"What do you mean?"

"I mean, it's in your blood."

"What?"

He grins. "This," and gestures toward the lake and the sky and the bayou beyond the dark fall of water, and the cypresses and live oak trailing with Spanish moss, and the whole state of Louisiana receding into the grainy blue distance to New Orleans, just waking up now by its coffee brown river, in the sun.

12

Antoinette doesn't say a word. We are on the dirt road in the Saab, bumping through the bayou to the highway. Her Italian sunglasses reflect the trees and the sky. I cannot make out her eyes.

"O.K., maybe Molesworth shouldn't have thrown away your pills like that," I say, "but you're too old to be playing around with drugs like a kid."

She makes a small, strangled noise in response, and I look over to see that her hands are trembling on the wheel.

"Are you all right?"

"Shit!" she says, and suddenly her lips are splotchy and parched-looking. Then she begins trembling in earnest. She lets go, and I reach over quickly and take hold of the wheel.

"No, it's O.K.," she says, but I steer the car onto a grassy patch shielded from the road by a cluster of pine. The sun comes down thick and full of pollen through the leaves, and there is the heavy croaking of frogs from the swamp. Just beyond the Saab's glossy hood, an algae-covered tributary of the Nezpique gulps and bubbles.

"I swear I'm going to kick the pills," Antoinette says as we come to a halt. "But not like this. This is too damn hard." Then she reaches under her seat and takes out a Ziploc bag containing an aspirin bottle full of the yellow pills. She fumbles with the childproof cap and cannot get it open.

"Please," she says. It's almost a whimper.

"All right," I say. "Give it here." I open the bottle for her and watch as she knocks out two pills, brings hand to mouth, and swallows. In a minute or so the shaking subsides, and she leans back and stares up at the blue sky through the leaves. Finally, face slack and lazy, she turns to me.

"Don't look at me like that, Ned," she says. "I'm not as bad off as I seem. Look in the glove compartment. I've kept careful records."

"Records?" I fumble in the glove compartment and pull a small datebook out from behind the spare signal bulb, maps, tire warranties, and other junk. In the datebook each day is marked with a series of red *x*'s.

"Start with April and flip to August," she says.

The *x*'s, six and seven a day in April, dwindle to two or three in August.

"Those little *x*'s are the pills," she says. "I'm trying to do this thing gradually. I don't want to rely on some clinic detox and then relapse a year later. And I don't want any Prozac. This is something I need to do myself. I'm going to clean out and stay clean."

I consider this plan. "Why do you do them?" I ask quietly.

"Oh, the usual reasons," she says, with an airy wave of the hand. "Because there's not enough going on in my life. The days — they're long, they drag. All those minutes."

"Maybe you should get married," I say. "Children. I hear they have a tendency to take your mind off things."

"Ha," she says, but then she is serious. "There is no one. No one like that."

"Come on," I say. "Not a single eligible man?" A cracking sound comes from nearby. I look up to see a woodpecker, his throat blue, his wings scarlet, drilling a hole into the nearest tree. He stops, blinks at me with beady bird eyes; then in a second he is gone, a scarlet and blue flash in the greenness.

"There are plenty of men sniffing around as usual," she says, "some of them quite beautiful to look at, but no one I can talk to. I've been celibate for eight months now, if you want the truth. And you know how hard that is on me. . . ." She takes off her glasses and looks at me, and her eyes are dark gray today, and there is sunlight on her face.

I feel something snap inside like a twig. "Aw, hell," I say, and reach for her. Her lips are rough, and her mouth tastes sour, but in a minute her breasts are in my hands, and when I push up her skirt, I find that her thighs are wet.

"Yes," she breathes, "please, yes," and it is awkward across the gearshift, so she climbs over and straddles my hips and lowers herself onto me, her knees pressed into the leather of the passenger seat, her arms around my head, and her breasts and her hair smelling of cigarette smoke and faintly of perfume, and her ready smell, which comes back to me now, pungent and familiar. It is over far too quickly, but I am there again soon, and we climb into the back-seat and struggle out of our clothes and go at it the old-fashioned way, she moving beneath, solid and warm as sand, as the hot sun dapples through the leaves in light and shadow on my back, and all the years in between, the long, melancholy years, melting away like a bad dream.

13

For old times' sake, we get a room at the Bienville House in the Quarter. We make love beneath the starched sheets as businessmen and conventioneers congregate in the lobby below, and the noise of the bars and clubs along Bourbon reaches us, a carnival whisper through the thick plate glass, and the river shines dull and heavy with the mud of a continent beyond the low tops of the buildings. I make love to her, then I make love to her again, then I fuck her, because she asks me to and there is a difference, and afterward we lie slick with sweat, cooling in the blast of the air conditioner, two bodies tangled up in the sheets and in the past.

It is a little strange making love to her now. Sex in our youth had innocence, but it was also clumsy. Now the innocence has been wiped away by too much experience. Her body moves knowingly beneath my fingers; she adjusts herself to the right angle; she bids me wait for the moment. Perhaps what was lost in sweetness is made up in pleasure. Is this worse, better? I can't say. We are no longer the same people. As a youth, despite what I once thought, it was not possible to fuck. It would have broken our young hearts. Now it is difficult not to.

Antoinette doesn't talk at first because it is hard for her to talk, there is so much locked up inside her, and because her mouth is busy elsewhere, and then busy smoking, cigarette after cigarette, ashtray balanced on the slight round hummock of her belly. But at last after two days, desire is exhausted, and she runs out of cigarettes, and it is dusk, the sky a blush beyond the crescent curve of the city, and she is compelled to speak. This is the first thing she says to my questions, hair in a black and fragrant tangle on the pillow, last cigarette stubbed out: "I don't really want to talk right now, O.K., honey? Why don't we just leave it alone for a while? Not think. Just be with each other for a while."

I frown, twist in the sheet, drum my fingers against the mattress. Then I say it is O.K., we don't have to talk now, and I settle against her, but she sighs and says: "All right. What do you want to know?"

"Nothing," I say. "Everything."

She wags her foot nervously. "I need a cigarette," she says.

"Send down for room service."

She considers this, then ends up eating one of the yellow pills, the first today, and it is almost seven in the evening. "I'm getting better," she says as her body absorbs the pill and a sly purplish look, now familiar, comes into her eyes.

"Even one pill is one too many," I say.

"I tell you what let's do," she says, ignoring me.

"What?"

"Let's order up a drink."

"No."

"Just a little drink."

"No."

Her lip curls out in a pout; then she brightens.

"All right, let's fuck."

I'm not sure if there's anything left in me, but she is insistent, and I put my hand on her breast and feel the nipple harden and there is the corresponding reaction, and a half hour later, we come out of it, stuck to each other again. "Ouch," I say.

"I know," she says.

"This is a good way to catch a urethral infection," I say.

"I know. Honeymoon cystitis, they call it. From overindulgence. That's why you have to pee afterward. Clears out the pipes. Go, pee." She pushes me off her, and I go to the bathroom. She follows, and then we are back in bed, spoon fashion, my arm around her stomach.

"It's nice to be here with you," she says, covering my hand with hers. "Hell, it's nice to be with anyone after eight months."

"Great."

"I'm sorry. That's not what I meant." She is silent for a while. There is the barest flush in the sky now, as the day drowns itself in the river like a suicide jumping off the Huey Long Bridge.

"Since you want to know, things have been bad with me for a very long time," she says quietly when there is nothing left out the window but the green dark of the city.

"What do you mean?" I can't see her eyes.

She shrugs. "I loved Dothan, I guess, although that seems so far away now. I was so young, too young. And I was crazy about you. You were only the second person I slept with. You may not believe it, but I actually cried my eyes out when you left."

"I believe it."

"Yeah, you up and walked off through Jackson Square, all beat-up and mad as hell. Didn't even look back."

"Unh-huh." I cringe, remembering.

"So after you left, there was Dothan again. Then I got rid of him finally, and there was everyone else. I can't remember half their names. Just sex. Nothing more than that."

"O.K."

"So, a while back, I met this guy, Victor. He was born in Caracas or some such place. Tossed money around like it was water. Sold coke, among other things. He had a big villa out on the lakeshore, a yacht, and a lot of sleazy friends. I don't know how I got hooked into that crowd."

"Probably the drugs."

"Maybe . . . So it got bad. I was snorting all the time, taking money from the till at work. Then, last September, Victor threw this wild party at his house. It was like something out of the seventies, with little silver bowls of coke on the tables and people having sex all over the place, right in front of everybody. I was too stoned and coked up to care. Like, here was this couple fucking on the couch not two feet from me, and I was just — I don't know — absent."

"Unh-huh."

"But Victor, he got all worked up and took me upstairs and we're going at it on the bed when the door kicks open, and it's three cops in flak jackets and combat gear, with guns. I mean, Victor is literally, well, in mid-stroke. It was like a scene from a bad action movie. They pulled him off me and hit him a bunch of times till he was bloody and handcuffed him naked and threw him on the floor. And they wouldn't let me get off the bed or even pull up the sheets. They walked all around, making these crude comments, and I'm laying there, trying to cover myself with my hands. It was horrible. Finally they start asking me if I'm a prostitute, because it turned out most of the women downstairs were known prostitutes. I kept saying no, no; then I started to cry, and they allowed me to wrap the sheet around myself; then they arrested me and took me downtown. So there I was sitting in this wire cage in the Third Ward Precinct house, wearing a sheet, surrounded by hookers and junkies, and the cops wouldn't let me go because they're trying to book me with prostitution and possession and I don't know what."

Antoinette is silent for a while. Ear pressed to her back, I hear her heart beating faintly through the thickness of flesh. I try to turn her toward me, but she won't turn, and at last I must urge her to go on. Her voice is different when she does, descended to a low, sad register.

"I was in there for twenty-seven hours. They wouldn't let me call a lawyer till they finished processing my paperwork. But that was O.K., because I didn't want Papa to know — he's so sick now — and all my lawyers are Papa's lawyers. I just sat in there with these women, the absolute dregs, and did nothing but think. Finally one of Victor's mob lawyers got me out, and there was a limousine waiting and flowers and a bottle of expensive champagne on ice, and Victor kept apologizing, but that was enough for me. I went home and scrubbed myself three times. Then I dug my aunt Tatie's mantilla out of a chest, and I covered my head with it and took my rosary, the one I got at my first communion, and I went down to the St. Roche shrine. I got on my knees and begged the saint to ask God to forgive me, because I wasn't good enough, clean enough, to ask God myself, because I felt, I really felt just then, that He had turned His face away in disgust, and I was so ashamed of the things I had done. Then I made a pledge to the saint in the dark of the chapel. First, I swore I would stop using cocaine, and I was pretty far into the stuff then, which is why I'm using the yellow pills now. Second, I swore I would stop having sex like that, as if it didn't matter who I had sex with. I promised I wouldn't have sex again until I had it with someone I cared about."

She stops talking abruptly and lies in my arms stiff and nervous. I wait for her to go on, but she does not.

"So what about this?" I say after a beat.

"What do you think?" she says gruffly. "I care about you. I've always cared about you. We're good friends, right?"

Then she gets up without looking at me and steps into the bathroom cubicle. Soon I hear the bathwater running, then in a half hour, the tub draining. Ten minutes after this she comes out smelling of soap and talcum powder, naked except for a towel wrapped around her head, and she leans over and kisses me and turns off the lights and gets into bed. In five minutes she is asleep, her damp turban on the pillow. Leaving me to ruminate in the half-dark hotel room, the ceiling lit now by reflection from the Quarter, like sun striking water at an oblique angle through an opening in a cave.

14

The next morning we check out of the hotel and separate for the day. Antoinette goes home to the Faubourg Marigny and thence to her store on Treme, and I dedicate myself to the afternoon of research that will make this trip a deduction on my taxes.

The Convent of the Nursing Sisters of the Cross occupies an ancient town house on Chartres Street, a half block up from the old Ursuline School. The Nursing Sisters are a strict order, requiring severe discipline and mortifications of the flesh. They are not allowed to eat meat, they are not allowed to enter the streets unless in the service of the sick or dying. They are not allowed to speak for the first two years of their novitiates and must subsist entirely on water ten days out of every month. They must divest themselves of all property and renounce all friends and family. When this is done, the order pays for an education at the best nursing school in the country, and many of the sisters go on to become medical doctors.

Their sole mission is the care of the critically ill and the violently insane. Contagious diseases are a specialty, particularly leprosy, a heritage from the Middle Ages. It was the yellow fever epidemics of the last century that led the order to New Orleans. Until the 1860s yellow fever raged in the town every few years, with death rates as high as seventy out of every thousand. The building housing the convent was left to the sisters by a wealthy exporter of cotton, cared for by them as life burned out of him during the terrible epidemic of 1825. Today the convent functions as a retirement residence for old nuns and the order's administrative headquarters in the United States. Its home base is Cigli, a tiny island off the Adriatic coast of Italy, once a notorious plague island, or lazaretto, where the victims of smallpox were shipped off to die. The sisters operate a hospice for terminal AIDS patients in San Francisco and five hospitals in equatorial Africa, a region famous for its virulent diseases. They seem happiest wherever human suffering is the worst. Assets in 1990 dollars were estimated at a hundred million, not bad for an organization with a membership of 3,020 celibate women.

Armed with this information out of Standard & Poor's *Index to Catholic Religious Orders*, 1990 edition — an indispensable reference volume consulted in the reading room of the Brooklyn Library — two mechanical pencils, extra lead, a notebook, and a letter of introduction to the mother superior from Father Rose, I call at the porte cochere of the convent at twelve noon, sharp.

As I press my nose against the bars, the bell rings somewhere in the cool interior. A lizard runs up the stucco. I make out shade trees and large urns full of flowers in the inner courtyard. This pleasant feature of Creole architecture was borrowed from the French. The old houses of the Vieux Carré do not show their best side to the street. Instead they open in on themselves in secret luxury. Rooms with eighteen-foot ceilings and ancient gilt mirrors shun the heat of the city and look out upon the fountains and quiet lawns, the garden patios of domestic life.

Presently, a woman in her late twenties turns the corner and comes toward me down the uneven brick passageway. Blue eyes, a pretty, open face, hair cut short as a boy's. She wears jeans and a ratty Wisconsin T-shirt, splattered with paint. I think of certain Irish Catholic girls I knew in college at Loyola. Pert and saucy, cute as the girl next door, but achingly unavailable. They had boyfriends elsewhere and always kept a sisterly distance, but it didn't matter. Their natural sarcasm made any thought of sex impossible. In bed there is nothing worse for the mood than a well-timed wisecrack.

"Excuse the clothes. I've been painting," the woman says, and bends to fumble with the heavy latch. When the gate swings open, she extends a hand. "You're Mr. Conti?"

"That's me."

"Sister Gregory."

"The mother superior?"

"I'm afraid so," she says with a laugh.

I try to keep the surprise off my face. A nun. Of course. The boyfriend elsewhere was Christ Himself.

"I spoke with Father Rose this morning," she

343

says. "You're doing a parish history? Wonderful. But as I told him, we don't have much in the way of records here. It's a sort of tradition with our order. You could say we don't believe in history. But what we do have, you're welcome to take a look at."

She waves me to follow with the quick elbow and wrist gesture of a tennis player, and we step down the porte cochere, our shoes making familiar hollow sounds against the stone.

In the courtyard a dozen or so ancient nuns are taking the sunlight. They wear the full black habits of a stricter time and those clunky black nun shoes much like the orthopedic footwear pre-scribed for flat-footed children. (Where do they get such ugly footwear! Are they mail-ordered from the Vatican?) A few of the nuns lie trans-parent as wax in lawn chairs. Mouths open, asleep, they snore or mutter. Three more pursue a slow game of croquet on the narrow lawn; I can almost hear their bones creak. At a round café table in the shade of the live oak, two others play a hand of stud poker with buttons for chips. One of them, her face shriveled as a carved-apple granny doll, smokes a cigarette in short, grunting breaths.

"I try to get the girls to wear more casual clothes," Sister Gregory whispers to me. "They are retired now, and the rules of the order are relaxed for them. But most have been wearing the wimple and skirts for more than sixty years. After that much time it is impossible to imagine wearing anything else."

We pass the poker game, and Sister Gregory pauses to borrow a cigarette. They are French, Gauloise Bleu, from a pack stuck with tariff stamps.

"Sister Jerome is one hundred and one years old," Sister Gregory says in exactly the same tone as you might say, "Junior is two!"

The nun squints up at us for a disapproving second. Then she goes back to her cards, which she shuffles accordion fashion, like a dealer in an Atlantic City casino.

"I only borrow a cigarette from Sister Jerome so she'll smoke less," Sister Gregory says when we are out of earshot. "Of course, you figure what can it hurt at one hundred and one?" But she lights up and blows a furtive cloud of smoke up the old facade before scraping it out in the gravel of the walk.

The North American archives of the Nursing Sisters of the Cross consist of twenty-five leather bound parchment ledgers dating back to 1817, the year they came from Italy to Baltimore. On each parchment page is entered the date of entry, holy name, date of birth, and birthplace of the novitiate, followed by a short statement in the novitiate's own hand. At the bottom, the date of death and a stock phrase in Latin. That is all. I flip through the first volume, its pages spotted with mold.

"I had hoped for more," I say. "Letters, documents, that sort of thing." Sister Gregory sits on the heavy library table, arms crossed beneath her breasts, swinging her leg like a sorority girl.

"That's all there is," she says. "All documents of an administrative nature are routinely destroyed at the end of each year. Personal correspondence is not allowed. To join our order, you must dispense with the familiar, shun the world. I'm afraid we don't think much of history here, Mr. Conti. History is for the vain, since the hand of God will sweep it all away in the end. This single page is all that we are allowed. We are not even permitted to write our birth name, just the holy name we choose for our new life, which must be the name of a man. When we die, it is another law of our order that we go to an unmarked grave in potter's field. No stone to mourn over. Just another one of the countless victims of the epidemic called life." She smiles, but the effect is chilling. Such grim pronouncements out of such a sweet face.

When she leaves me alone with the ledger, it doesn't take long to find the page I am looking for, dated November 30, 1840: Novice born May 2, 1819, New Orleans, Louisiana, died Brooklyn, New York, October 11, 1919. The short inscription in a young, elegant hand is written in very correct French and rather easy to translate:

I have chosen the name of Januarius for my life with the good sisters here, after the Martyr of Benevento whose congealed blood they say liquefies eighteen times during the year in the cathedral at Naples. According

346

to the *Lives of the Saints*, this poor soul was thrown to the bears in the amphitheater of Pozzuoli and then beheaded. The sheer violence of this fate attracts me. I long for such an end, though God reserved a similar death for the man I loved and lost.

The sisters here have asked me to write down in this book the reason I wish to take the veil with their order. And they have asked me to write nothing but the truth. Very well. I bury myself in this terrible way not because I love God but because I cannot stand to look at my face in the mirror after the part I played in certain tragic events. I acted out of weakness and wounded pride and jealousy. The man I loved is dead now, and in the end he loved another. Perhaps I shall come to love God in the way the kind sisters love Him. I do not know. I tried to join the Ursulines, but they would not have me, also the Carmelites. The sisters here take me as a novice only because too many of their numbers drop dead every year with the fever of the black vomit and they cannot afford to be choosy.

Let me say now that I was not without dowry or offers of marriage, and I have been told I am pretty. I am the daughter of a proud family, and like my beautiful, sad cousin, I cherished my pride as I cherished my spite. But all of it will be forgotten in time. Now it is merely for me to obey the rules of the order and to make myself suffer as the others suffer. These things I can do. It is easy to follow rules, to live on bread and water. I do not fear death. Life is the troublesome thing. Good-bye.

Not a promising beginning for a saint. I copy this odd statement in my notebook and flip through the rest of the volume, but there is nothing more of interest. Then I go to find Sister Gregory.

She is painting one of the nun's cells down the hall. The color scheme here is white and blue. Blue to the shoulder, white above. The white part is done.

"One of my older sisters passed away in the room last week," she says as we head to the first floor down a set of freestanding spiral stairs as elegant as any in the Quarter. "The poor old girl, it was a terrible death. Sometimes you wonder why God allows such things. A hemorrhage, she threw up lots of blood. Couldn't get the stains out of the walls. That's why we're painting the place."

I shudder at this and am silent till we reach the gate. Then I turn to her on impulse.

"Sister, I want to ask you something."

"Yes?" She is wary suddenly, as if she thinks I am about to make a pass at her.

"What did you write on your page?"

She looks down and scrapes her paint-splattered Doc Martens along the gray brick. "You're asking why I became a nun?" she says at last.

"Yes."

She looks back up at me, her eyes blue and fine and Irish, and I think I know the reason.

"It was *The Sound of Music*," she says quietly.

"What?"

"You know, the musical with Julie Andrews. The Von Trapps. Maria, the nun; Rolfe, the Hitler Youth; the kids; the puppet show. Remember? 'Climb Ev'ry Mountain.' "

"Yes, of course."

"For me the saddest part of that movie was when Maria left her nuns behind. They loved her without reservations; she belonged with them. And then, when the Nazis were looking for the family in the graveyard, I always wanted to shout, 'They're behind the tombstone!' so the captain and those odious kids would get shipped off to Treblinka or something and Maria would have to go back to the convent. Of course, this was a bad impulse, and I confessed and did penance for it. But at least I realized at a young age that I wanted to be a nun."

I don't know what to say. Is she serious? This is just the sort of smart-ass answer the girl next door might give when you ask a question that is none of your business. But before I have a chance to ask another question, there is the hard little tennis player's hand again and the freckled smile.

"Good-bye, Mr. Conti," she says, and the iron gate closes heavily behind me and I am cast out into the muzzy sunshine of the afternoon.

15

I meet Antoinette at four o'clock at 'Tite Poulette's Oyster Bar as we had planned. We stand shoulder to shoulder at the zinc counter with tourists and locals, for Poulette's is something of a landmark and one of the few places frequented by both. I hear the broad upriver accents of farmers and fertilizer salesmen in town for a day on business, the flat vowels of midwestern conventioneers, the affirmative "eh" of a couple from Winnipeg, Canada. With these voices, I contrast Antoinette's — soft, almost shy in my ear. Hers is an accent without being an accent at all. It is the accent of Uptown New Orleans, sophisticated, citified, without the twang, but southern nonetheless.

"You can't leave without having a couple of sliders," she is coaxing. "Come on, now."

I have been drinking a Dixie, watching her polish off a half dozen of these big glossy Gulf oysters and dreading the moment. You have to be in the mood for oysters. I haven't been in the mood for over ten years.

"I'm naturally suspicious of food you're not supposed to chew," I tell her. She shakes her head, imperious. Not liking oysters in New Orleans is treason.

"Don't be such a Yankee," Antoinette says, and flashes a smile at the shucker behind the zinc counter. *"Lagniappe,"* she says to him and winks in my direction. The man smiles back, recognizing one of his own. He shucks an oyster and places it before me. *Lagniappe* is a Creole word of uncertain etymology that means roughly "a little something for free." I stare down at this gray quivery bit of *lagniappe* helplessly, as Antoinette stabs it with her three-pronged oyster fork, swirls it in the hot sauce and horseradish mix, and holds it up to me, one hand under my chin like a woman feeding pablum to a baby.

"O.K. now, son," she says. "Open up." The oyster shivers in the air before me. The Canadian couple, just to our right, finds my reticence amusing; the oyster shucker looks on with a twinkle in his eye. I have no choice but to open and swallow. The spicy taste of the horseradish cannot cover a certain green flavor as the thing goes down my throat like a lump of phlegm. And when it is gone, there is a residue of grit in my mouth. I reach for my beer and gulp a few mouthfuls to get rid of the rotten fish taste and to keep myself from retching.

"Your boy looking a little sicklylike," the oyster shucker says to Antoinette, resting his big rubber glove on the metal of the counter. "Not used to our food down here." In his speech, *our* and *here* have two syllables: *aw-huh* and *he-ah*.

"Hell, what we need is another dozen," Antoinette says. The shucker gives a gap-toothed grin and goes to select twelve good-sized oysters from the trough.

"I think that last one was bad," I say when

I recover my breath. "Gritty. Don't they say that gritty oysters —"

"Old wives' tale," Antoinette says. "Wouldn't you be a little gritty on occasion if you spent your life buried in the mud?"

When the second dozen arrives, I eat two more, just enough to preserve my honor; then I stand back with my beer.

"Okay, this is my dinner," she says as she lifts another viscous muscle to her lips. "You want to stop for something else?"

"I'm not really hungry," I say, and I'm not. My stomach is filled with panic. The plane leaves in three short hours, there is nothing definite between us, and I do not have the courage to speak. It seems Molesworth's prediction will come true, and I will fly off for another ten years of exile and regret.

"Now let's talk about you, honey." Antoinette seems to sense my agitation and pauses after five oysters. "I've been talking about myself all along. You always get me to talk about myself. I go for ten years without a word and you show up and it's one long blabfest. Now a little of your own medicine. What's been going on up there in New York?" It is perhaps only out of politeness that she asks. Not because she doesn't care but because she prefers to live in the immediate, in the touchable, in the particular moment of sunlight. The rest of it, the past, the future, lies vaguely delineated and half submerged like the roots of a mangrove beneath the black waters of the bayou.

I have been hoping for this moment, but now I don't have much to say. I suppose I am still waiting for my life to happen. This is a terrible thing to admit at thirty-two. So instead I tell her about the ghost.

She swallows the last oyster and listens in silence. Then she pays the tab — "Don't worry, it's on me, honey" — and she takes my arm and escorts me out into the street. I cannot tell what she thinks; her Italian shades are down like a curtain. When I finish my story, she is silent, and I am prodded to say, "Well?"

She tosses her head. "I don't know."

"You don't believe in ghosts?"

"Not saying one way or the other. Never saw a ghost."

"You think I'm crazy?"

"So let me get this straight, your life in New York, at least recently — we're talking suicide, muggings, and ghosts. Know what I think, honey? I think you ought to get the hell out of that city. That's what I think."

"O.K. Where do I go?"

She hesitates. My heart is in my throat for a moment.

"Somewhere else," is all she will say. "Come on." Then she's got my arm tight, and she's pulling me down Bourbon Street toward Esplanade, through the crowds.

We turn up Dumaine to avoid an old-fashioned spasm band of young black children banging on pots and pans and dancing on the street corner, go past the house of the cornstalk fence — beloved of architectural historians, though it never did much for me — make a right on Dauphine and make a left on Esplanade. In the middle of the block between Dauphine and Burgundy, there is a crumbling pinkish house of plastered brick standing alone on a narrow lot. It is inconspicuous here, surrounded by statelier homes that better suit this wide avenue, once the grand boulevard of the Creoles, but it would be a landmark in any other American city. The sagging balconies and wrought-iron work place it in the first half of the nineteenth century. A weedy porte cochere leads back into an overgrown courtyard shaded by a single large oak.

We stand for a moment arm in arm on the banquette, looking up. The windows are boarded up from behind. Broken panes of glass glint in the afternoon light. Antoinette has an odd, expectant look on her face. She searches the facade as if for a clue.

"What are we looking at?" I say.

"See the green shutters?" she says eagerly. "There was a time when green was the only color for shutters on Creole houses in the Vieux Carré. Everyone had green shutters. If you didn't, you were déclassé — or an American."

We squeeze through the gate of the porte cochere, rusted half open over the weedy cobbles, and go around back into the courtyard. Here there are two blackened bronze urns depicting classical scenes, and a rusty fountain. A few steps lead up to a wide brick patio littered with broken appliances.

"It's sad how little time it takes for a house to fall apart if no one lives there," Antoinette says. "Only been abandoned for a couple of years, but to look at it, you'd think centuries. What is a house, you know, without the people inside it? The people are the glue and the nails and the wood that keeps old places together."

She leans a garden chair against the bricks at the French doors, climbs up, and retrieves an age-blackened key from a nook above the lintel. At first the lock won't give, then a heavy chunk and the old machinery turns, and Antoinette hips open the door, which scrapes over the mottled flooring of hardwood. Inside there are high, empty rooms with cobwebbed plaster rosettes staring down from the ceiling like eyes. The fanlight over the front door illuminates a curving stairway that leads from the entrance hall into dim upper regions. Dust is piled in the corners. The air is hot and thick. I feel as if we have entered an Egyptian tomb. On the mantel in the front parlor, a stilled clock. Antoinette leads me by the hand in a silent inspection of the first floor. I have never seen her so serious. We cannot go upstairs because a few of the steps are rotted out, and we end up back in the parlor, slashes of yellow light coming through the cracks between the boards overlooking Esplanade.

"Well, needs a lot of work," I say, digging

my heel into a hole in the floorboard.

"Of course," she says impatiently, "but that's not the point. The point is that this is my house now. Mine." She does an odd little pirouette in the middle of the floor, then settles with a delicate movement of rump and thigh and a cloud of dust on a low worktable against the far wall. I find what seems my natural place across the room, leaning arm and elbow against the mantel as if I'd just come in from a hard day at the Cotton Exchange.

"I love this house," Antoinette says, with an unexpected fierceness. "My great-aunt Tatie left it to me in her will when she died three years ago, because she knew I loved it. She was the coolest old lady, lived to be a hundred — can you believe that? Born in the big room upstairs, and she would have died there except she fell down one day and broke her hip and they took her out to Metairie, to this sort of Confederate old ladies' home, poor thing. And she never did come back from there; no one does."

"How old is the place?" I say.

"That's a little bit of history I do know." She smiles at me across the room. "The house was built in the 1820s by some ancestor of Mama's, when Esplanade was one of the most fashionable streets in New Orleans. Except for the land right around the fishing camp that used to belong to the plantation, this is the oldest property still in the family. It was their in-town house. Mostly they lived out at the plantation, of course,

356

but they would come and stay during the winter months for parties and suchlike. The opera, the Olympus Ball, the races. Yeah, I know it's a wreck now. Wiring bad, floors eaten by termites, leaky plumbing. I started to have work done a while back, but it's expensive, and I ran out of money when I got heavy into coke. But you know, sometimes I think that this house is the real reason I kicked that stuff. The only thing that kept me going. Because I belong here, because —"

Suddenly I can't take my eyes off her. She is wearing a floral-print sleeveless sundress cut just above her knees. Her legs are slightly open, and a bit of yellow light from the window falls across her hair and against the wall like a halo. She looks beautiful, but it is more than this. There is something in her voice that has been missing in the last few days, something irresistible. Hope.

"— because it's my house, Ned! My house. Generations of my family have lived here. You remember that painting, the one of the lady in the white dress you saw in the museum in the Cabildo years ago, that you said looked like me? The first time you met me you saw the resemblance, and I was impressed. That's what I liked about you then. You never met me before, but you seemed to know right where I came from. Well, my guess is that lady used to live right here in this house, because they found the painting rolled up in the attic upstairs. O.K., the house is a shambles now, but by God, with some work, it could be beautiful again. Five bedrooms, and fanlights, and the curving staircase and the porte cochere and the courtyard, and the dust of my family in the walls. What's the word I'm looking for, a word you might use . . . ? Continuity! Sometimes I dream of it all fixed and painted and there's carpets on the stairs and the floors are sanded, and there's no Dothan in my past and no yellow pills and no cocaine, and I'm calm and sane and the world is calm and sane, and there's mass on Sunday in the St. Louis Cathedral, and summers down at the camp, and children, five bedrooms full of children. . . ."

She barely speaks this last part, it's a whisper, a secret breath, and without knowing how, I'm standing in front of her, and my hands are on her thighs, and she leans back and pulls up her dress. Then her legs are around me, the heel of one shoe dug in at the small of my back, and I'm inside her, and she's laughing and biting at my ear and saying, "Yes, oh, yes, those oysters, it's the oysters . . ." and then she arches against me as the spasm takes her and the old house is loud with us, the sound of passion echoing off the walls for the first time — who can say? — in a hundred long and dreary years.

16

On the way to Moisant Field we get stuck for an excruciating hour in a traffic jam. There is

an overturned tractor-trailer, two flattened se-
dans, blood and glass on the pavement, a half
dozen police cars; and the grace we found making
love in the old house is lost to the heat and confusion and carbon monoxide fumes somewhere
along the Airline Highway. I am nervous because
I am always nervous when it comes to travel.
Antoinette is enervated because she is high-strung
and impatient by nature. She shakes my hand
off her knee, reaches beneath the seat for the
aspirin bottle, and pops one yellow pill, then a
second.

"Antoinette . . ."

"Goddammit, don't!"

And we don't speak till she pulls the Saab up
to a No Parking zone at the terminal and she
turns to me, eyes cloudy with the stuff. There
is so much I want to say to her, but the panic
wells up, blurring the right words, and there isn't
enough time. My plane leaves in five minutes.
I have a horror of missing planes. She gives me
a hug and a quick closemouthed kiss and pulls
away as if regretting the excesses of the last four
days. Her enthusiasm has faded; her face is sal-
low-looking in the fluorescent light of the terminal.

"O.K.," she says. "Have a good trip."

"We can't just d-do it like this," I say in a
stuttering rush. "I've got to tell you . . . every
day for the last ten years I thought about you,
every day I wished —"

But she puts a hand over my mouth. I can

hear the loudspeaker announcing the departure of my flight. She takes her hand away slowly and clasps them both in her lap. The sky is streaked with sunset and green-gold above the city.

"I need to think about this for a while," she says quietly. "We had fun. Let's not spoil this right off by raking it over the coals." Her voice is softer now, but her tone implores me not to ask the wrong questions, not to insist.

My shoulders slump. I acquiesce.

"I'll call you," she says as I step out of the car.

"Right," I say. "Thanks for everything." Then I shoulder my bag and turn toward the terminal, and I hear the Saab rev, speed down the ramp, and grow faint, a single whiny note lost in the voice of the traffic.

I am the last passenger aboard. As the plane lifts off the tarmac, nosing out across the dark waters of Lake Pontchartrain, I pull down the window curtain to avoid a glimpse of the city slipping away below, the brilliant lit crescent receding in the distance. Soon New Orleans is gone under the dark belly of the plane, and there is only New York blooming like a monstrous black flower on the horizon.

Part Five:
Madeleine's Ghost

I have a fever.

Yesterday I bought a fifteen-dollar digital thermometer at the Drug Loft on Second Avenue to monitor its progress. The fever hovers around 100, though it has been as high as 102.1 and as low as 99. My new thermometer, a beige plastic instrument in a clear plastic slipcase, beeps and displays the correct body temperature on a tiny green screen after barely a minute in the mouth. I know it is no more accurate than ordinary mercury thermometers, but there is something very comforting about its precise digital display and clear plastic slipcase. Every fifteen minutes or so I am able to monitor my temperature without the inconvenience of waiting or the uncertainty of shaking out the mercury and squinting to read tiny numbers etched on glass. Somehow, the digital thermometer, cheery and professional as a candy striper in an old folks' home, makes the sick person feel less alone.

I have had this fever for a few days now, since about a week after my return from New Orleans. It is not enough to make me miss work, but it adds an additional dose of ennui to my labors in the crypt. I seem to have lost all interest in the piles of brown documents, deeds and letters of decades past — just at the point when my efforts need redoubling. Father Rose's deadline is fast approaching, and I have yet to turn up anything that might help with the Congregation of Rites in Rome.

At night the fever gets worse, and I lay prostrate on the couch, TV noodling in the background, a cold compress over my eyes. In the mornings I awake shivering, my sheets stained with sweat in the shape of my body like the impression on the Shroud of Turin. Antoinette has not called. She will not call. I must face this fact.

2

The feverish afternoons drag in these last days of August. Even the crypt, which is usually cold and clammy as the palm of a dead man's hand, has become oven hot. The brittle documents break apart at my touch. Outside in the churchyard the headstones stand stark and white in the sun, the black obelisk casting a blacker shadow across the enclosure like an accusing finger.

The ghost is keeping a respectable distance, perhaps because I am sick. I wonder if ghosts are prone to spiritual sicknesses; are there phantom microbes, supernatural viruses on the other side? I once saw the picture of a virus magnified ten thousand times on a science show on PBS. It was a magnificent thing, a snowflake spiral all ghostly white, floating in the human ether in the darkness between the cells.

Rust thinks I've got a touch of the flu, something I picked up down South. Summer flus can be the worst, he says, particularly August flus, because they are flus outside flu season, ignored by the media, and there are not many people around to share the misery.

We are at the Horseshoe Bar having a beer as he explains this theory. I drink three beers, then feel too exhausted to move, light as a feather, chills and fever running up and down my spine like electrical currents. This expedition to the Horseshoe Bar was unwise, I now know, but I've already been cooped up for five days and thought I could risk going out.

Rust looks concerned. His face is half hidden in darkness. The other half is illuminated in garish reds and blues from the neon beer signs in the windows. The Horseshoe Bar is a seedy Lower East Side dive, scarred and stained from years of drunkenness and despair. Rust likes the place. People come here to hide in the smoke and darkness. One of the beer signs advertises Hamm's with the slogan "The Land of Sky-Blue Waters." I would like to find this place wherever it is and make my bed in a cool stream there. I would sleep, breathing slowly through a hollow reed, as the sky blue waters caress my fever away on the sandy bottom. Suddenly disgust and nausea wash over me in a dirty wave.

"Why are you here, Rust?" I say. There is a petulant edge to my voice.

He squints at me through the gloom, waiting patiently for an explanation.

"This seediness, this same old life," I say, waving a pallid hand. "This city. It's no place for decent human beings. Did you see the news last night? Yesterday morning, during rush hour, a young woman was assaulted on the four between Fourteenth and Grand Central. She ran down the cars, screaming for help, pursued by an ax-wielding madman released from Bellevue last year when they ran out of funds to keep him incarcerated. . . ."

"I got it," Rust says. "No one helped her, right?"

"Wrong. The morning commuters in their suits and dresses with pearls beat the attacker to death with their briefcases and Franklin Planners. Not because they cared about the woman who was attacked but because they were pissed off about being made late for work. Someone actually said that."

"And this disturbs you?"

"What do you think?"

"I don't think it disturbs you as much as you'd like it to," Rust says quietly. "I'll tell you why I'm here, Ned. Like the song says, I love New York. I had enough of wide-open spaces and clean air and so-called decency out West to last me a lifetime, and I can tell you people are pretty rotten everywhere. But you . . ." The rest of his words are lost in the general hum, the traffic on Avenue A, the ceaseless headache drumbeat of the natives in Tompkins Square Park. The next thing I know, we are out on the sidewalk and Rust is flagging a cab. He puts me in the backseat and hands the beturbaned driver a twenty-dollar bill.

"Molasses Hill, Brooklyn," Rust says, and gives directions. The driver hesitates. As usual he does not want to go into Brooklyn, but it is too late. I am in, and money has changed hands.

"Rust?" I say as he closes the door and steps back onto the curb.

"You were passing out on me in the bar," he says. "Go home and get some sleep." Then I see his face slide away, a white blur through the glass as the cab pulls off around the park.

3

I lie in bed for the next three days.

According to my digital thermometer, my fever has steadied at 102.6. My room is little larger than a coffin, just over six feet long, wide enough for a single mattress and a bookcase full of clothes, carefully folded. The ceiling is made of tin and pressed with the elaborate floral patterning popular in the 1880s. It was once the walk-in closet for the apartment, but anything with a door and a window in New York qualifies as a room. I stare up at the whorls and leaves, trace the convolutions with a trembling finger. I try to sleep but am caught most of the time between an uncomfortable exhaustion and a prickly torpor. It seems something terrible is happening. My pee darkens the water in the toilet, and on the evening of the third day I am visited with a persistent nausea, like a low earthquake in the stomach.

Soon the bed is no longer comfortable. I spread Molesworth's old sleeping bag in the middle of the living-room floor, and if I lie just the right way across the red flannel duck-and-hunters quilting, the nausea will go away for a few minutes. On the morning of the fourth day I begin to vomit. There isn't much in my stomach, just a bowl of Ramen noodles and a few stale saltines, but I keep vomiting until I vomit up mucus and bile. At last it occurs to me that I might have something other than the flu. I call a doctor in Manhattan whom I'd seen once for boils, but he is on vacation, and I get the temp filling in for the receptionist. I ask her if she can recommend anyone for an immediate appointment.

"Are you kidding?" the temp says. "There's even a two-day wait for the walk-in places. The whole city's sick."

"With what?"

"The usual," she says. "All the ills that flesh is heir to." An unemployed actress. She tells me to go to the emergency room of any hospital, but I have no health insurance and am without the five hundred dollars necessary for such a visit.

"Then you're up shit's creek," the temp says, and goes to another line.

After this call I vomit again and, when my strength returns, call an ex-girlfriend who is now a nurse. Her name is Clara, and she lives in Los Angeles, where she assists surgical procedures at Mother of Angels Hospital. During the first three months of our acquaintance several years ago, she was a tempestuous dance major at Columbia University. Then she ran out of funding from her parents and dropped out to get her head together and later applied to nursing school. I caught her at a hard time in her life when she was beginning to understand the futility of her artistic aspirations. I always catch them at a hard time: on the way down. When they start back up again, they seem to lose me, an anchor stuck in the muck.

We used to lie in that muck in apartments all over the city, blinds drawn in the afternoon, going at it with a desperate urgency. She didn't have a place of her own the whole time I knew her, but apartment-sat while other people were out of town. All her possessions fitted into one small suitcase. We fucked among other people's stuff on unfamiliar futons, family photographs full of strangers smiling on the dresser, used other people's bathrooms, looked through their drawers for clues to an unknown life. It was a depressing period for her, though I rather enjoyed myself. She didn't shave her armpits for six months, and she didn't bathe all that often. I didn't much mind her smell, which had a certain spicy pungency. Then, when she got accepted to nursing school, she cleaned herself up, and the affair was over. We parted friends. She's engaged to a doctor now and allows me to call her for medical advice whenever I'm sick.

It's three in the afternoon in Los Angeles, but she is home and answers the phone.

"Clara?" I say.

"What's wrong this time?" Clara says.

I give her the symptoms, unintentionally leaving out a few of the most important ones, as you always do when speaking to any medical authority.

"I'm not a doctor, you know," she says. "I just fuck one."

"Yeah," I say. "Why don't you ask him to come to the phone."

"He's not here. He left for work. We're both on the night shift."

"Are the blinds drawn?"

She giggles. Nothing like a nurse or a dancer for sheer lustiness, both professions sharing a certain intimate understanding of the workings of the body.

"So you've got the chills and fever, right?"

"Yes."

"And now nausea?"

"Yes."

"And you feel weird all over?"

"Yes."

"Sounds like the flu to me. Actually there's been a weird one going around out here all month. From some Asian country. If it's out here, I'm sure it's out there. You know, the New York–L.A. incestuous thing."

"Yes."

"So keep yourself hydrated. People who die of the flu don't keep themselves hydrated."

"Die?"

"That's right, honey. They still die of this stuff, just like they did in 1919, because their electrolytes become depleted beyond the body's capacity to deal with it. So drink plenty of liquids, and try to eat some crackers. . . ."

"Yeah, yeah . . ."

"And relieve the symptoms. Go get some over-the-counter remedies. Mylanta, Tylenol, that sort of thing. Relieve the symptoms, and you give your body a little time to recover. O.K.?" Then, there is a pause and a sigh. "You know, honey, I worry about you. Sometimes it seems like you just can't take care of yourself."

"I'm sick, Clara," I say. "Everyone gets sick from time to time. Even successful, independent types."

"I'm just expressing my concern, don't get defensive."

"O.K., Clara. Sorry. And thanks."

She sighs again and hangs up the phone, and in the silent minutes afterwards I feel worse. There's always a melancholy tug when talking to old girlfriends. The road not taken, a whole different life. Perhaps that's what infinity is for. All the possibilities.

4

The next morning, on Clara's advice, I drag myself out of the apartment and struggle down to the F. It's like walking in a dream. Though I give it all my strength, it seems I'm barely moving down the street. Nausea forces me to stop several times and vomit in the gutter. Finally I get the train into the East Village and go to my favorite Drug Loft on Second Avenue. I'm hobbling past a bewildering array of decongestants, one footstep at a time, when an attractive, plump woman in a conservative blue business suit turns down the aisle. I step out of the way, but she stops and puts a hand on my shoulder.

"Are you all right? You look terrible," she says.

I must stare for a full ten seconds to recognize the face.

"Jillian?" I say.

She smiles sheepishly. In her other hand is an E.P.T. early-warning pregnancy test. Our eyes find it at the same time. Weird possibilities flash into my mind. There is that story about the two lesbian lovers, the brother, and a turkey baster. Then Jillian does the unexpected. She blushes.

"Oh, well, things change," she says, indicating the pregnancy test.

"So fast?" I say. It has been little more than six weeks since Chase's funeral.

"Here," she says, and takes my arm. "I think we should talk for a minute." She helps me over to the row of five chairs where the old people wait for their prescriptions. A shriveled octogenarian wearing the type of cap that used to be known as a Sneaky Pete dodders over his cane on the second chair from the end.

"I wanted you to know that I felt pretty rotten about the way I acted at the funeral," Jillian says as we sit. "I tried to call you, but I didn't have your phone number. I was hysterical after Chase . . . died. Just freaked out. It seemed like I was headed for the same dive off the Manhattan Bridge if I kept going the way I was going. Poor Chase, she . . ." Jillian swallows hard at this and finds it difficult to continue.

I give her a moment to compose herself and lean back to get a good look. All traces of the anorexia are gone. She's as plump and sleek as a German housewife, and the weight doesn't look bad on her. She is *süsslich*, as the Germans say, rosy-cheeked. The fluorescent lights in the ceiling begin pulsing a hallucinogenic green. I fight down the urge to vomit and ask a few questions about her new life.

She's taken an entry-level job in her family's PR firm, Sumner and Phillips, one of the top five on Madison Avenue. She's going at the business from the bottom up as a management trainee and learning a lot about how the public can be manipulated through the careful use of images. She finds it all very interesting.

"It's something I should have done right out of college," she says, looking away. "Now it seems like all those crazy years were wasted. I was unhappy, addicted to one thing or another — to shooting heroin or eating or not eating, to fucking strangers on film for money, or whatever debauchery came along. And I wasn't happy during any of it. Now, you know, I think I'm finally on the right track."

"So you're dating someone?" I say, a tinge of regret in my voice.

She blushes again and laughs behind her hand as if she is ashamed of it, like an old lady with bad teeth. "Yeah, my man Harold," she says. "He's an old friend of the family, nearly fifty, but shit, the guy can really put out in the sack."

"What does he do?"

"He's a lawyer on Wall Street. Mergers and acquisitions, that sort of thing."

A lawyer? Even in the depths of my sickness, I'm shocked. "What about Inge?" I manage.

Jillian shrugs. "We're still friends. She's going back to Germany soon."

"How's she taking all this?"

"Inge was always bi, you know. It wasn't me she loved so much as that big dildo I used to strap on when we made love. Anyway, she always had a boyfriend — this lunkish proletarian type who works as a foreman in a coal mine in the Ruhr. Every month he wrote her these illiterate, passionate letters begging her to come home. Now she's going back to him."

"And now you're straight?" I snap my fingers. "Just like that?"

Jillian thinks about this for a minute. "You could say that currently I'm into the penis."

At this the octogenarian in the second chair leers up at her through his bifocals. "Or the penis is into you, sweetie," he says, and gives a phallic thumbs up.

Jillian frowns. "Come on," she says, and supports me up and down the aisles like an invalid as I complete my choices and fill my basket full of pricey over-the-counter remedies, going for the name brand over the generic every time. I will not skimp on medicines.

Fifteen minutes later, on the curb at the corner of Second Avenue and Third Street, we shake hands, and I stand for a moment, not knowing what to say. Her palm is moist as a sponge. The city is hot and insufferable today. The air quality is mud. A thin coating of grime covers every outdoor surface. The flat, stained facades of the tenements show their broken faces to Third Street. On the sidewalk a half block down, a man with no legs or rump, an actual human torso, begs from a board with wheels. In a moment he scoots off across the street and disappears into a bar.

"I've seen that creature before," Jillian says idly, following him with her blue eyes. "He works the subway at rush hour. He's amazing on that board, really gets around. A while back on one of the West Side lines, I felt something touching the back of my knee, and I turned and looked, and there he was, grinning up my skirt. I wasn't sure whether to kick him or scream or give him a buck. I gave him a buck."

There's another long silence, but it doesn't seem our conversation is over. She's got something else to say and is fighting for the words. Once or twice she opens her mouth but then shakes her head. I stand shivering in the heat, buoyed by her uncertainty. It is only this awkwardness that keeps me from collapsing on the sidewalk.

"I'm going to a therapist now," Jillian says at last, "like every other unmarried thirty-year-old woman in the city." She avoids my eyes; her long lashes touch her plump cheeks. "But that won't last long. I'm already O.K. It was your séance. I had never admitted that stuff about my father at the beach to anyone." She looks straight at me, her eyes brilliant blue stones. "I hadn't even acknowledged it myself. I confronted him with the whole thing a month ago, and he cried and came clean. Turns out he was molested as a kid, and now he's in a program for that sort of thing. It's the same old story, I guess. But the night of your séance, something clicked, like a train connecting with a car that's been idling on a side track for twenty years. I heard a scraping like rusty metal and then a solid clank — I literally heard this noise in my head — and it all came back to me. There was something, a funny pressure in that room. I don't believe in ghosts, but . . ."

She bites her lip and shrugs, then reaches up to put the back of her hand against my forehead.

"Shit," she says, "you're burning up. You better get home to bed." Her voice has the ring of new brass. In her blue eyes I see the too-green lawns of her parents' mansion. Somehow, I almost preferred the other Jillian, the depraved anorexic who had abandoned all certainties, who wore her rejection of middle-class morality like a scar. Now she glances at her watch, a new ladies' Rolex, and takes a step toward the curb.

"Good luck," I say.

"Right," she says. "Got to get back to work." Then she hails a cab and vanishes from my life.

5

The night screams with sirens. My digital thermometer reads 103.5. I lie spread-eagled and nude on the flannel quilting of the sleeping bag, panting in the heat like a dog. Once again the rattle of automatic-weapons fire sounds from the Decateur Projects. I tried a cold bath but vomited in the tub. The over-the-counter remedies do little to alleviate my suffering.

With some effort I am able to turn my head to the TV. On the news they are showing a seventy-five-pound lobster caught in the nets in Boston Harbor. The thing is a monster, black as coal, its beady alien eyes milked over and blind from nearly a hundred winters at the bottom of the sea. There's enough lobster here to feed a hundred people, the news commentator quips cheerily, though the lobsterman plans to save his catch and display it in a specially built tank in a popular seafood restaurant. For a moment the camera focuses on the creature, its antennae and claws moving with the jerky unreality of Gamera, the giant fire-breathing turtle of Japanese movie fame. What is this strange, bright world? the lobster seems to ask. Who are my cruel tormentors? And where are all the fish?

The digital thermometer now says 104. I think I am beginning to hallucinate. The walls are covered with a strange white sweat; the furniture wobbles like jelly. My pee in the toilet is black; my shit, when it comes, a single ghostly white nugget. I want to call my mother, to tell her I'm sick, but she died three years ago. I want to call my father, to ask for advice about my life, but he, too, is dead. I haven't spoken to my sisters in years. We were never a very close family. The oldest is married to a naval submarine officer and lives on base in San Diego, California. The other, after two miscarriages and three divorces, moved to an ashram in Fairfield, Iowa. It strikes me only now that I am an orphan, and I begin to weep. Of course, it is the fever, but I weep until the news is over and I must struggle up to vomit into the bathroom sink. Out the bathroom window Manhattan burns like a nightmare, and behind the skyline I see a new darkness that covers the world.

When I emerge from the bathroom, I wobble

straight into an odd cane-bottomed chair, placed at an angle to the door. It owes something to the style of early Quaker ladder backs, is obviously of the same era, and has an intricate woven seat. I do not own such a chair. I have never had a chair like this in my apartment. And just now, the back and seat and supports are haloed faintly in blue static.

I circle the chair with suspicion and make for the sleeping bag at the center of the room, but this, too, is gone, replaced by a sort of animal skin rug that I have also never seen before. Then I realize that the TV is gone, and the couch and the bookcase and the rest of my possessions are gone, replaced by unfamiliar heavy furniture of the late Federal period: a low horsehair settee; a bombé chest, its drawers hanging open and stuffed with gaudy shawls and petticoats. In the fireplace, where the ineffectual gas heater usually stands, a few coals smolder on an iron grate. At either side of the carved mantel drip ornate candelabra full of a half dozen flickering candles. The whole place reeks of tallow and smoke.

My panic is dulled by the fever. I can only gape at my apartment, which is now somehow not my apartment. Long drapes of worn brocade stand open over the windows. The floodlit facade of the power plant has been replaced by an ocean darkness. I make out the vague cross-hatching of the masts of sailing ships down at the river. The air is still and watery. Only a few lit windows dot Manhattan across the way. Then I hear a rustling like the sound of thick skirts dropping to the floor, and I turn to see a crack of yellow light shining past the door to Molesworth's room, which stands slightly ajar.

"No," I say out loud, "I am sick. This is the fever talking," and to reassure myself of this fact, I take my temperature with the digital thermometer, which is still grasped in my hand. The thing beeps cheerily after a minute and reads 104.7 on the tiny screen. "Shit," I say to the unfamiliar air, "tomorrow I'm going to the emergency room. To hell with the five hundred dollars." Then I move purposefully toward the door to my bedroom, which seems farther away than it ought to be, but when I get there, I am relieved to find everything the same. I step inside and slip the latch and put my back to the door. The bedroom window gives out on the power plant as usual. Blue sparks jump between the transformers, and Manhattan blares like a jazz band of light across the river.

"You don't know how much you miss something till it's gone," I say to my photographs and posters smiling down from the wall. After a moment I open the door a crack, and out in the apartment everything has returned to normal: my stuff in place, the TV blaring a late-night talk show. It's amazing what fever can do. Then I close the door, turn off the lights, and, exhausted to my soul, fall to the mattress and am soon taken by nameless, shadowed dreams.

6

In the dark hours of the morning I sweat awake to a small scraping sound that is both familiar and dreaded. I refuse to open my eyes, but there is the odd weedy smell of a foreign cigarette and a voice gently calling my name. I cannot feel the fever or the nausea now, and a peculiar calm has settled down over my limbs. I wiggle my tocs and cannot feel them wiggle. The voice calling me fades to a whisper, gets loud again.

"Ned, Ne-ed . . ."

In a corner of my darkened room there is a phosphorescent glow. At the center of the glow, a human shape.

"There, that's better," the shape says when I open my eyes, and gradually I make out hair, a face, like tuning in a distant station on the UHF dial. Finally I see a young woman squatting in the corner, her back to the street wall. She's barefoot, wearing a low-cut sundress and a cute hat, half baseball cap, half kepi, with gold tassels dangling jauntily off the brim. One elbow is propped on one knee. The smoke of her cigarette works toward the ceiling in an elaborate phantasm of human faces, some smiling, some laughing, like the comedy and tragedy masks of the theater. She's charming, all elbows and knees, a gamine, a girl-woman. I make out the curve of her breast as she leans forward to flick a little ash off her tongue. Her face is celluloid-smooth and heart-shaped, like the face of a movie star of the twenties. When she removes the cigarette, the ghost of a smile plays around her lips.

"Hello, Ned," she says in a voice like a golden bird.

"Who are you?" I say without feeling my lips move.

"I am a messenger."

"A messenger from who?"

She shrugs, then stubs her cigarette out on my windowsill and rises in the way a marionette rises without any visible effort, as if the strings are being pulled from somewhere else. When she is up, she hovers a full foot or so above the floor.

"We've got to go," she says. "There isn't much time."

"I'm not going anywhere," I say. "Especially with someone who's floating around in midair."

Through a gap in the curtain I can make out a faint fluorescent star that I know is one of the lights of the power plant. I concentrate on this light, and a little of the pain and fever returns to my body, and there is a low buzzing that could be the sound of traffic on the BQE, busy as ever with speeding vehicles bound for the dark heart of America.

"Don't do that." I hear her voice now faint as a dream, and the phosphorescence that surrounds her body seems to grow dim. "Please. You will need all your strength to follow me."

Then a sudden gust of wind, and the drape blows closed, and I am in darkness again with the apparition. Now she has lit up another cigarette, and the tragedy and comedy masks of smoke go revolving around the room like a carousel. "Neat trick, don't you think?" she says.

I ignore this. In the next moment the bedroom door fans open on soundless hinges, and out there in low candlelit relief is the other apartment, to which more details have been added: On the wall a gilt-framed painting of a plantation house done in a naive style. Above the fireplace, embroidered in petit point, a coat of arms showing palm tree and crescent moons, bar sinister. Even from this distance and in the reedy light, I can see the place is a mess. Clothes lie everywhere; the floor is littered with squat bottles of blue glass, plates of half-eaten food. Hat boxes an uneven pile in one corner. A newsprint broadside thrown aside on the settee stands up like a tent. Its huge block headlines announce VICTORY AT CONTRERAS!!! and MEXICAN ARMY IN ROUT!!

The apparition hovers in the doorway. "Come with me now," she says.

I try to squeeze my eyes shut but find them frozen in a lidless stare. She waves her cigarette impatiently in a gesture that I recognize.

"I know you," I say. "You're Chase. You've come back cute."

"That name sounds familiar," she says, "but I do not remember it."

"Are you Chase?"

"I don't know."

"Who are you, then?"

383

She is confused for a moment and sinks slowly to the floor. "Don't ask me to remember," she says. "I have forgotten all of that, the sufferings of clay. This is what I looked like all along, in life. Funny how no one could see me this way, no one could see through the shell. The living are so blind." But for a moment superimposed on her death-perfect face is another one, broken, familiar, half eaten by deformity, uneven as a Picasso.

"Is there more to death, Chase?" I say. "Or do you just waft around like that all the time?"

"I don't know."

"Am I dead?"

"No. But close. That is why we can talk like this."

"Will I die soon?"

"I don't know."

"Where are we?"

"In your apartment, of course."

"Chase . . ."

"Stop. You must come with me. They want me to help her before I go on."

"Help who?"

"The one who lingers here. She's asked for your help many times. In your dreams, along the secret ways. But you have refused to listen to her. So they sent me to help you listen, to help you across the threshold for a little while."

"Why does she want me?"

"She has been waiting years for you to come. She will only talk to someone from home. You two are tied together on the loom."

"What loom?"

"You ask too many questions. Come . . ."

And there is something warm in her voice, a memory that makes me rise. She holds out her hand, and the phosphorescence drains from the rest of her body to cup there in her palm. Soon that's all there is, a handful of light in the darkness.

I take hold of the glowing hand and feel a happy looseness as I pull away from the body in the bed. It lies there, stretched out on the stained mattress, eyes half open in an unconscious glitter, breath a faint raspy sound, lips black with dried bile. A horrible sight, but I don't feel anything except relief and a little bit of pity for human frailty. The glowing hand of Chase or the young woman who was Chase leads me across the living room around the piles of stuff on the floor.

Now I hear the low, sexy sound of a woman singing in French and the strumming of a guitar coming from Molesworth's room. Through the half-open door I can see a large four-poster bed and an oval standing mirror reflecting rumpled sheets and more clothes in piles. The woman singing is just out of sight to the left of the door, but behind her voice and the vibrating sound of the guitar is an utter black stillness that is the stillness of death.

"Remember, she is very confused." Chase's voice comes close in my ear. "She does not know if it is today or yesterday. She does not remember her own death or the years in between."

Then the glowing hand winks out, and I am standing alone in the wedge of yellow light, and the woman inside the room stops singing and says, "*Vient'ens* . . . I am ready now, monsieur."

The last few feet seem to take an effort I do not understand. I step into the humid yellow of the bedroom drained of everything. In here there is the thick burnt tallow smell of candles and the familiar smell of sex. Beside the big bed, in one corner, the woman sits at a low stool before a vanity crowded with bottles of perfume carelessly uncorked, and ceramic jars of powder. On either side of the mirror, bronze griffins hold candles, the wax trailing slowly to the floor between their claws. She wears a thin shift, which is open over her breasts. A small Spanish guitar is cradled in her lap.

Now she bends forward in concentration, her fingers picking out a fast Spanish melody full of dramatic chords. Her thick black hair obscures her face. I stand for a while, politely, and listen to her play. She hesitates on a difficult part, picks it out slowly, and goes on. In the moment before she speaks again, I notice that I am not reflected in the mirror of her vanity. The doorway is empty. Here it is I who am the ghost. At last she flips her hair over one shoulder and looks up. Her gray eyes are cloudy and curiously unknowing. Her skin is white and hollow. But I'd know that pretty face anywhere.

"Antoinette," I say.

She smiles; there are thin, unfamiliar gaps between her teeth which have never experienced the miracle of orthodontics.

"You may call me by that name if you like," she says. She is not so much talking to me as through me. "Some of the sailors off the ships like to call me by the names of their wives or sweethearts who are waiting in ports far from here. It makes them feel they are not lying with a whore. Last week one brought a bonnet and a calico dress for me to wear while we lay together so I would remind him of his wife. He paid me in gold, so I wore the bonnet and the dress, but I detest calico."

The likeness to Antoinette is remarkable, the same eyes and cheekbones and hair, the same mannerisms, but now I see differences around the chin and mouth.

"I'm sorry," I manage to say at last. "You look very much like someone I know."

"Your wife?"

"No."

"Your mistress?"

I am silent.

She frowns and strums the guitar a bit. When she looks up again, her eyes are confused and frightened. She puts the guitar aside suddenly and crosses to the window, where there is nothing but a boiling blackness. The boards creak beneath her bare feet.

"This night," she says, a terrible despair in

her voice, "this same night always. No stars and the moon hidden by clouds, and not a light burning except for my own. I am so far from home, monsieur." Then she swings toward me, and she is angry. "You are late! My girl, Mimine, said eight o'clock, and I canceled another appointment because of you. It is now past midnight! I had a supper ready as you requested, but it has long since gone cold." She steps forward, faltering, clasping her hands together, the white fingers intertwining like snakes. "Please, you must forgive me, I am not myself. It's just that sometimes, I feel so terribly lost. . . ."

"Don't worry about it," I say.

She takes a breath and in a moment is calm. "Mimine told me that you are from home. I did not need to be told. I can see by the way you carry yourself that you are a Creole gentleman, one of my own people. Please, do you mind if we sit and talk awhile before we lie together? *S'il vous plaît, parlons notre propre langue.*" She goes on in French, and I respond in kind,

"*Certe. C'est juste . . .*" but it makes no difference; the language we are using has no real words.

"Of course, I am just a whore," she says, "and one does not pay a whore to talk. I am usually strong and cruel — many of the men like it that way — but tonight I am weak, and I am yours, body and soul, if you will only talk with me a little while."

She steps over and takes me by the arm and leads me to the bed. Her touch is not cool and feathery, as you would expect from a ghost, but warm and solid. She puts me between the sheets and goes to get a shawl from the vanity.

"There is an old axiom that clothes make the gentleman, but not in your case, monsieur," she says as she wraps the shawl around my shoulders. She lifts up the sheet for a moment, and we both look down at the erection thumping against my stomach. It is only now I remember I am naked. With a coy smirk she reaches down and gives me a squeeze that I feel in my guts. "Still, it will be that much more pleasurable if you restrain your gamecock for the present and hear me out."

She is eager as a child. She disappears into the dark outer room and returns with a squarish bottle and two small crystal glasses. She hip slides her way onto the mattress and tucks her legs under in the same way I have seen Antoinette approach a bed. She sets the glasses on a flat pillow between us, pours out the thick red wine from the bottle, hands me a glass, and fills her own. The stuff is strong and sweet and like fire. She readjusts the shift to reveal her breasts more completely and leans back against the carved baseboard, stroking a nipple with an idle finger.

"I like to get drunk," she says. "It is the whore's solace. But only on good wine, so you don't feel so terrible in the morning." She takes a greedy gulp of the wine. "This is a fine Madeira, don't you think?"

I nod.

"The captain of a merchantman who sometimes comes to lay with me brings a few bottles as a present when his vessel puts in from Spain. My father was very fond of Madeira. He used to have cases of the stuff brought downriver from New Orleans. Did you know my father?"

"I don't think so."

"My father was well liked. They respected him up and down the river from Natchez to Pointe de la Hache. He was that rare thing, an honest and successful man. But he put too much faith in the inherent goodness of people. And he betrothed his daughter to a monster, and now his daughter is a whore."

We drink for a while in silence. She refills our glasses several times. I am getting drunk. The walls of the room are painted a vaginal pink. There is little by way of decor except for the vanity and the bed, and I recall Molesworth's old Z.Z. Top poster with some nostalgia. Above the headboard hangs a small oval portrait of an arrogant and familiar-looking olive-skinned man in the uniform of the Spanish kings. He stares down at us with malevolent black eyes. On a sash across his chest are pinned the platinum and diamond stars of a few forgotten aristocratic orders. Two dueling pistols stand in an open box beside him.

Soon the bottle of Madeira is done, and there

remains only the sediment, grainy and bitter as coffee grounds at the bottom of the glass.

The ghost is waiting, her eyes as lightless as stones.

"Tell me," I say at last.

"What do you wish to know?"

"Everything."

Madeleine's Story

My name is Madeleine Hippolyte Félicité de Prasères de la Roca. I was born to riches at Belle Azure Plantation in Plaquemines, Louisiana, a few years after General Jackson defeated the English at Chalmette and sent Pakenham's body home in a barrel of rum from which, as the story goes, his soldiers drank unknowingly on the way back to England. I am told we are all equal under the wings of the American Eagle, and I have seen a painting in the governor's house to this effect, but I don't believe it. I insist with pride, as my father insisted, that the royal blood of both France and Spain runs in my veins and that I am better than most. Strange words from a whore, but my story is a strange and sad one.

My mother, Emmeline Françoise d'Aurevilley, was born in France in Normandy in an ancient château and came to Louisiana with her family during the Terror of the Revolution. She met my father at a ball at the old Marigny Plantation in the second week of May, five years before the Americans bought Louisiana from France. At seven in the evening they danced once to an old-fashioned gavotte à la polonaise and were married on the lawn the next afternoon, as the sun went red over the river. All the guests cried when my parents knelt before the priest, because they were both so beautiful and so young — and you know the open way our people have when they are happy or sad. Always the tears and the hand-kerchiefs.

My father was tall and robust with reddish hair. My mother was both fair and dark, with the thick black tresses and gray eyes that you can see I have inherited. Mandeville himself gave his own bedroom for the wedding chamber and a thousand Spanish gold dollars as a wedding present. And the Spanish governor, Señor Salcedo, who was present, exempted the newlyweds from taxation for a year.

Unfortunately I have no memory of my mother except for vague impressions, much like the dreams of a very young child. She died of the fever of the black vomit when I was barely two years old. The only picture of her that remains is a small cameo painted on bone by Mazzini, the famous miniaturist, during my parents' honeymoon in Europe. This is the single item of any value that I took with me when I left Belle Azure for the North. I have the miniature hidden here beneath a loose board in the floor and remove it on occasion when the last man has left my bed in the evening.

As I gaze at my mother's soft face, I think had this woman lived to temper my father's judgments, my life might have turned out differently. When she looks down on me now — if we can indeed look upon life from the blackness of death — she sees a whore and not the virtuous daughter she had hoped to give the world. I am saddened by this fact alone. The rest I brought on myself, through jealousy and passion and pride.

But I was not always a whore. My story is first the story of two little girls. Myself and my cousin Albane d'Aurevilley. As a child I lived in the big house at Belle Azure — it seems like paradise now — surrounded by fields and bayou and river, by the green gifts of the Plaquemines delta.

When I was ten years old, my cousin Albane came from the city to live with us because her father and her mother, who was my father's first cousin, had died of the fever. A terrible epidemic swept through New Orleans that summer, and the streets were full of wagons loaded with corpses. I heard the house slaves talking about this, and some said it was the curse of God on that city for its wickedness. Perhaps this is true, for it is a wicked city. From the top gallery, if the wind blew downriver, you could hear the plague cannon going off and see the smoke of the tar barrels rising into the sky like black ribbons on the horizon.

I remember that summer well because of Albane and because Papa returned from his trip to Paris unexpectedly in early June. He had been gone many months. He was mostly gone from Belle Azure in those days, and though I did not know it then, I was a very lonely child. I was surrounded by people, it is true. There were at various times in the house maiden aunts and spinster cousins who made a show of affection for me, but who really did not care one bit whether I lived or died, and of course, there were always the house slaves.

Zetie, the light-skinned mulatto who nursed me when my mother died, possessed, I think, some genuine feelings for me, but the condition of bound servitude is not one that fosters untainted emotions. Sometimes, when no one was looking, she was very cruel indeed. She beat me where it would leave no marks, and she stole my pretty things — little trinkets and bits of lace — and gave them to her own children, who lived in the quarters behind the house with the rest of the slaves.

Once, when I asked Papa why he was so often away, he replied that life at the place where he had been so happy with my mother saddened him greatly. But he never took me with him when he went on his travels, and I suspect that it was not the house or the plantation that saddened him but my own countenance, for it resembles my mother's almost exactly. We are all alike, the women of the d'Aurevilley line. We are both fair and dark, an unusual combination of qualities. It has been so since the days of Marie de France and shall be so as long as there are women to look beautiful and men to chase after them.

But this time, when he returned from Paris, perhaps because he felt a little guilty, Papa brought me many fine gifts: painted fans and dresses, a mechanical bird that sang when you wound it up with a silver key, and a splendid china-faced doll purchased at Joquelin's, the famous toymaker of the Faubourg St.-Germain. The doll came with a box of fitted gowns, all satin and frills in the latest fashion, and her hair was black, like my own. I named her Emmeline after my mother and carried her with me everywhere. It seems ridiculous now as a grown woman to be talking about a child's doll, but the fate of that doll is a cipher for what happened afterward.

The day Albane came to live with us, Papa took the doll away from me and gave it to her. Not an hour after she set foot in our house, Albane saw the doll in my arms, coveted it, and merely asked Papa in that quiet, mysterious voice of hers if she could have the thing. He consented without a thought for my feelings because, as he said later, I had so many playthings and poor little Albane had nothing. What he did not know was that I loved the doll very much and would have given up everything else I owned to keep it for myself.

I can still recall the peculiar light on the afternoon Albane came to us. The sky was purple over the river, and rain lashed the lattices, an appropriately theatrical entry for the creature who would become the villain of my young life. She was unattractive, pinkish and pinch-faced and all bones. The mourning dress of cheap black tulle hung limp and wet on her sharp frame and dripped stains of dye on the Gobelins carpet in the front hall. I stood on the polished stairs, clutching my doll as Papa took her to his bosom, and I shall never forget the look on her face over his shoulder — arch, possessive, and preternaturally wise. I shivered at the sight of her, and I could not meet those eyes which were an odd, unforgiving shade of blue and which even then concealed unknown powers of persuasion.

Within a month Papa moved Albane into the large bedroom opening on mine, which had been my nursery and playroom. He gave her half my clothes and had Zetie tailor them to fit the child's skinny limbs. He gave her the extravagant gift of a body slave, a young Negro girl of her own age, and he gave her his unadulterated affection.

And in the sad years that followed, Papa seemed to become even fonder of that miserable little orphan. He took her twice to performances at the French opera in New Orleans. I went with him to the city but once, and just to see a poor play of marionettes in a stall in the Place d'Armes.

When we grew older, more for Albane's benefit than my own — as the child showed a scholarly bent — he brought a pedantic young man from town to teach us Latin and mathematics and music.

It was only the music that I mastered. To this day I can play any stringed instrument, including the violin, and I can also play the piano and sing tolerably well. But Papa never praised my singing, while he praised Albane's sums and her tedious Latin compositions, usually moral tales of a falsely pious nature.

Papa was always a great reader of books. He respected knowledge more than he respected money, an attitude that is tenable only if you already have enough money to support yourself in a fine style.

Two rooms off the front gallery of Belle Azure on the second floor were set aside for his library. In one of the rooms alone stood four thousand volumes, neatly arranged on shelves along the walls. I counted them one day when I had nothing else to do. In this room also were a long table of dark wood and a map of Louisiana and a globe that showed all the countries and continents of the world.

For hours Papa would sit in there, the lattices drawn against the heat, reading and annotating several volumes at once open before him on the table. He loved Molière, Racine, the poet André-Marie de Chénier, who was guillotined during the Revolution, the philosophic works of Pascal and Rousseau, and of course, the contemporary writer Chateaubriand, whom he had met once in Paris, though he often complained that the latter's *René* and *La Nouvele Atala* were full of poetic distortions and lies about the red Indians in general and the Louisiana tribes in particular.

When he became overexcited about something he was reading, he would fling open the shutters, step out onto the gallery, and declaim passages in a loud voice to whoever was passing below. The slaves thought him mad. He would make them stop and listen to him, sometimes for hours in the heat. He always wore a pair of yellow slippers and a yellow waistcoat when he read and a sort of round Turkish hat with a tassel hanging from it, which he called his reading hat.

I can see him standing there on the gallery, even now, book in one hand, gesticulating wildly with the other hand and shouting some speech from Racine at the top of his voice. Sometimes, when he came to a favorite passage, he would close the book and recite from memory. It was thought among the slaves that he made it all up, that he wrote the books himself and imagined the words on the spot out of his own head.

Soon the pious pinch-faced little brat Albane grew into a smug and pious pinch-faced adolescent. But she was always an abnormal girl. There was something strange about her from the beginning, something that made you think she was still looking at you when her back was turned. A few of the house slaves who had been brought from St.-Domingue during the terrible uprising there knew the ways of the Vou-Dou religion, and thought that Albane had the gris-gris on her — that is to say, the evil eye. This is the power possessed by witches to affect the very nature of the things around them: to curdle milk in the pail fresh from the cow, to turn the baby in the womb upside down and dead with the cord wrapped around its neck.

Indeed, a supernatural power existed in Papa's family, passed down through the women of his line. There was an old book from France in the library written in Latin that told the story of several women of our family in the days of the great witch La Voisin, and the scandal at the court at Versailles when they tried to poison Louis the Fourteenth himself. One of them, a certain Marianne de Vaubran, was tortured and executed in the Bastille, two days after La Voisin went to the scaffold.

Our slaves were after a while much afraid of Albane. They would turn to the wall and cross themselves when she passed. Papa heard about this and whipped them for it many times. He was not a whipping master and until then had been known for his kindnesses, but this behavior offended his pride and his foolish love for the girl. I would like to say that because of the whippings, Albane was hated by the Negroes at Belle Azure, but hate is not exactly characteristic of the reaction she produced among them.

You do not worship something that you hate.

Slaves have to be watched always; this is one of the conditions imposed by our peculiar institution. To keep a man down, you must know what he is thinking, what he will do next. As a Prasères I was born with this knowledge; it was imparted to me in the womb. The consequences of being lax with the Negroes or not watching them closely enough are fatal, a fact impressed upon us by what went on at other plantations upriver and down. There were stories of poisonings, insurrections, slaves with knives between their teeth crawling beneath the baire at night.

One of our cooks, a sullen light-skinned girl with tribal markings on her face, let a basket of deadly snakes loose in the house not long after Albane came from the city. The act had nothing to do with us but was part of a complicated vendetta between the house slaves. She had spent months catching the snakes out in the bayou and fed them on milk from her own breast, for she had recently given birth to a child that died. When it came out that the cook had done this thing, she was not whipped. Whip marks on her back would have lowered her value. Instead she was locked up, fattened on sweetbreads and corn mash, and taken to the market in New Orleans.

The snakes were small bright bracelets of color, and their bite was fatal. We found them in the oddest places over the next several months. Curled up inside shoes, swimming happily in freshly drawn bathwater, in bonnets left upside down, in plates of food at the dinner table, in the bedding. Every night we had to beat the sheets out for ten minutes before going to sleep. At last Papa called in a snake catcher from the bayou. He was an old half-blind Negro who had bought his freedom from the master of Fleury Plantation several years before. The man had tribal scars on his face just like the cook's. He put out bits of raw meat dipped in molasses in the corners of every room and small saucers of sweet cream in the hallways. He intoned certain spells in his own unknown language, and tiptoed around like a shadow. One morning I saw seven snakes sipping at the cream in one of his saucers as the snake catcher came up behind, quiet as a cat.

When he had the snakes in his canvas bag, I asked him what he was going to do with them. He smiled, and I saw yellow teeth filed to points. "After you strain the poison out of their heads, they make a very powerful magic gumbo, mademoiselle," he said. "Good for the ague and the gout."

In the end sixty-six snakes were taken from the house and the galleries. The man was paid in gold for his skills, which were quite amazing. Then he left, and it was assumed that all the snakes left with him, but later Zetie caught Albane playing with three of them. The strange child had kept them as pets. She fed them on dead flies and housed them in a basket full of grass. One afternoon Zetie found the snakes curled up asleep in the child's hair. When the snakes were taken away, Albane cried for a night and a day.

Out of this incident the slaves began to worship my cousin as a Vou-Dou goddess.

I am referring now to a particular night in August 1829, when Papa was away at Mobile attending to business, and I was fourteen.

I don't need to tell you that fourteen is not so young in our part of the world. At that same age all the Bringier girls were married and the mistresses of great estates of their own upriver, and it is certainly not uncommon for Creole women of any age to take a hand in the day-to-day business of running a plantation. I had already sometimes directed the labor of the slaves in the fields and made sure they were not either worked to exhaustion or unduly spared by the overseers, who are a conniving and untrustworthy breed of white men. I also saw the cane and indigo loaded onto the ships, and made sure that proper receipts changed hands, for thousands of dollars can be lost at this point through forged or incorrect bills of lading.

As you know, August is a month of great restlessness for the Negroes, the time of many midnight and secret rites in honor of their various Vou-Dou deities. Accordingly I slept beneath the mosquito baire with the shutters open on the gallery to catch any odd noises from the yard. For on other plantations, where the slaves are not watched so closely, there have been in this dreadful season reports of human sacrifices: slave children cut open to appease the savage Vou-Dou goddess and then reported missing, or dead the next morning of some convenient accident. Remember, the loss of a single slave is the loss of a valuable piece of property.

That night a wavering moon shone above the yard. The live oaks around the house rustled and whispered in a hot wind from the swamp. I was woken from an uneasy sleep by the heat and a sound of chanting from the jungle of underbrush behind the slave quarters. I listened for a while, put on the suit of boy's clothes I used in the fields, took two loaded pistols from the gun cabinet in father's room, and went out into the darkness. You may scoff at my accounting of this incident, but let me tell you that no Prasères, man, woman, or child, has ever been afraid of their slaves.

I now directed my footsteps to a wide clearing in the jungle. Sometimes on Sundays the slaves are allowed to dance there, free of leg irons and shackles, as they dance at Congo Square in New Orleans. Tonight I found them assembled, about a hundred fifty Negroes, writhing and baying beneath the moon, their attentions fixed upon my cousin Albane. This wicked girl now stood in her nightgown on a wooden table at one end of the clearing, her arms outstretched like some goddess of antiquity, a dozen snakes coiling at her feet. The overseers were loitering about in the background, leaning back in their boots, very drunk, and enjoying the spectacle. I went up and asked them to halt this obscene ceremony and bring my cousin inside the house. "No, mademoiselle," they said, their tongues swollen from the liquor. "Too dangerous now." And they professed themselves afraid to interrupt the slaves at their devotions.

I turned from them in a high rage and took the pistols out of my belt and went myself to remove Albane from the table. One of the slaves, a big field hand, made to stop me, and I shot him through the lungs, a wound from which he did not recover. Albane screamed and whimpered at this, and the snakes around her feet slithered off into the darkness. Then I dragged her through the underbrush and up to her room.

Once there, the girl's spirits revived and she became bold. "I am the goddess Nokomu. Touch me, and I will turn you into a snake," she said, or some such nonsense.

"Interfering in slave ways is wicked," I said, "and you are ordered to desist." Then her face got twisted up and ugly, and she told me that she would behave as she pleased because now she had as much a right as I to be called mistress of the house.

"The last time I went with your papa to the opera in New Orleans," she said, "he took me over to Royal Street, to the offices of M. Levallier, the lawyer. I watched as M. Levallier wrote up a paper signed by your papa and two witnesses that said when he died, this whole place will be divided up equal between you and me." And she laughed, and the sound of it was weird in the room.

But when I heard this scandalous lie issue from her lips, I was seized by a madness I cannot name, and I took up a horsewhip from somewhere and whipped her as I would whip a slave who had thieved from me or spoken with insolence. I whipped her up and down the gallery till her nightgown was in shreds and her back and her arms were covered with great red welts. Neither her screaming nor her tears nor her piteous importunings could stop me. Not her power to curdle milk or charm snakes or steal my father's heart.

When my arms were tired and I could whip her

no more, I called the house slaves, who had been cowering at the bottom of the stairs, and I said, "Here is your goddess now. Take her and put some grease on her wounds." Then I went to my room and closed myself in and slept or did not sleep until Papa came back from Mobile, several days later.

Allow me to pause a moment in my narrative to describe the setting of the dramatic events that I have been relating to you. I mean, the place I love most in the world — Belle Azure Plantation on the Mississippi.

It is situated at a wide bend along the river, at the center of seven thousand square acres of good black-soiled bottomland granted by Louis the Fifteenth of France to my ancestor Antoine Raoul de L'Isle de Prasères for an unknown bit of gallant service to the French crown. His secret action has passed into obscurity, not recorded at the time for high reasons of state, though one may surmise it had to do with the preservation of the dignity of the king himself.

The house itself was built tall with slave-made bricks and cypress wood cut out of the swamp. The brick walls of the ground floor are so wide that as a child I could barely span them with my arms outstretched. They enclose a dark, cool cave of arched doorways and barrels of wine and coiled rope and other odds and ends, where I used to play on the hot summer days. The two upper stories are constructed of cypress timbers with sand and moss and horsehair mixed with plaster in between the posts, and in all the bedrooms you can see the stout timbers of the beams, which bear the mark of the carpenter's adze. A set of horseshoe-shaped stairs lead from the ground up to the first gallery, which wraps in French style around the house, while the second gallery above is reached by a freestanding staircase of curving cypress just inside the front hall.

We are famous upriver and down for these features and for the second gallery, which is unique in all of Louisiana. My mother placed many plants along the length of this gallery. It was once her favorite place to cradle me when I was an infant and suffering from the colic. The plants remain there today, ferns and banana trees and flowering bushes in pots. They give our top gallery the aspect of the famous Hanging Gardens, which a Babylonian king once built for his mistress, and which was one of the wonders of the world.

You have no doubt seen the plantation home of Jean Noël Destrehan, who was a friend of Bonaparte's and who they say once received the gift of an imperial bathtub, slightly used, with imperial grime from the emperor's fat body still visible around the rim. In any case, Destrehan Manor is generally regarded throughout the region as a dwelling of striking beauty and elegance. I understand that since my hasty departure a Scotsman has wed Lelia, the daughter of the family, and improvements have been completed, with the addition of Greek-style columns to the facade.

This is a pity. Destrehan was a house built after the French fashion, without the pompous Grecianisms favored by the American planters.

Belle Azure resembles Destrehan before the recent grotesque additions but is much more beautiful and a good deal larger. The Prasères family was once known for its generative power. My great-grandfather, Étienne Charles Marie de Prasères, sired twenty-two children off two wives. Twelve of the children survived infancy and lived comfortably at Belle Azure until marriage. The great house was meant for broods of this size. We are lucky today to see a family that exceeds eight children. Perhaps our forebears were better, stronger people than we are today, as many insist, but I do not believe it. The real reason is simple: You must first have a happy marriage to bring such a lot of children into the world. And happy marriages, for one reason or another, are rare in these complicated times.

Listen, this is a whore's piece of wisdom: Nothing makes a better aphrodisiac than happiness.

Even now in the sordid exile I have come to, I can close my eyes and picture Belle Azure, down to the last detail.

From the top gallery in the spring, you can smell the countryside blooming just before dawn, then the sun rising hot over the fields spread like a brown furrowed cloak down to the river. In the diminishing light of a winter dusk, the blue walls of the house glow the remorseful blue of the sky after a storm. In summer, seen from the windows of the second gallery, the horizon toward the Gulf is all lilac heat shimmer and the air is dense and still. Then there are the vessels — sail and steam — coming and going upriver and down day and night, whistles blowing as we light the great first-floor gallery for a party and the music spills out over the yard. And the gray of dawn in the fall, hunting friends of Papa's waiting impatiently below, their horses pawing the gravel of the drive, breath rising as white clouds into the air. And always, the green margins of the bayou and the halo of birds rising out of the swamp.

Belle Azure is my beautiful blue star above the river. Everyone must belong somewhere. I belong there. I love its very wood and brick and plaster. Perhaps in the end true happiness in life consists of knowing where you belong and staying put. Circumstance and ill fortune and the necessity of my revenge have taken me away from my home for too many years. But I have made secret plans. And one way or another design and tenacity will take me back again.

At noon on the fifth day after I horsewhipped Albane on the gallery, I heard Papa's tilbury turn up the drive. An hour passed. Then he came up the stairs and entered the brat's room, where he stayed just long enough to examine her welts, which were even then receding into harmless pink bruises. Then he went away a second time. He did not come in to see me; he did not even say a word through my door. I stepped out on the gallery in the dusk and watched him drive off toward New Orleans. This is when I first began to be afraid that something terrible would happen to me. Two weeks later Papa came back, and this time he ascended to my room without even bothering to remove his traveling clothes.

As I feared, he would not let me speak. When I tried to explain my actions, he struck me across the mouth with the back of his hand. Then he told me that I had developed a malicious and spiteful temperament that had caused the death of a field slave worth five hundred dollars, that I had beaten an innocent orphan girl who had received such a shock from it that her life still hung in the balance. He appeared to be in anguish, and I trembled because I had made him unhappy and because I did not want to be punished.

Then his demeanor changed, and he sank down on a stool and put his head in his hands and began to shed tears. These frightened me more than anything I had yet seen.

"I have been unmindful of you for a long while," he said at last. "I thought that it was your cousin who needed looking after, not you, Madeleine. You have always been my strong one. Even when you were an infant and death took your mother, you were strong and you did not cry. I should have remarried or sent you to the convent school with the Ursuline nuns, like other girls of the province. Perhaps the sisters would have given you

410

some moral training, cooled your hot temperament. Now it is too late for such measures."

Then he was quiet a little while, and his tears
ceased, and he stood and went to the door. But
before he stepped into the hall, he turned, and
there was a great sadness in his voice. "I have
betrothed you to Don André de la Roca, a wealthy
gentleman of New Orleans," he said. "The con-
tracts are signed and agreed upon, your dowry
fixed. I may have cause to regret this thing, but
it is too late. You will be married in September,
a week after your fifteenth birthday."

The day of my wedding a sudden and vicious
squall of hail swept across the Place d'Armes.
This was entirely in keeping with the spirit of the
event. The fist-size rocks of ice bounced off the
cobbles and sent the surprised citizenry running
for the covered walkways of the islets. Dogs were
knocked senseless in the street, gulls fell out of
the sky over the river, and a black cloud like the
smoke from a terrible fire blossomed over the
Cabildo.

The St. Louis Cathedral stood mostly empty,
as if for the funeral of an unpopular minor official.
I remember a wrinkled old lady with a yellow face
who sat in the front row — my husband's duenna.
She had been with him since his early youth in
St.-Domingue, was of mixed blood and entirely
mad. We knelt, and the priest droned on and on
in Latin. My dress was beautiful, covered with tiny
freshwater pearls and silver thread-work that

shone even in the dull light. No one noticed my dress. I kept sneaking looks at my new husband out of the corner of my eye. This was the first time I had ever seen the man, and my impressions now confirmed my worst fears. He was old, narrow-faced and cruel-looking, but most of all old. He could not be described as handsome in any way. And my heart grew small and still and withered as the priest said the final words of the sacrament.

Later, in my new house on Esplanade, only fifteen people, all business acquaintances of my husband's, came to the wedding party. My father did not attend, citing a touch of the gout, though he was perfectly healthy. The mad duenna crawled around the floor as if looking for something she had lost. People stepped over her, ignored her as you ignore a dog. My husband did not speak a word to me, barely looked in my direction. I found my way upstairs to the wedding chamber and wept into the embroidered coverlet of the bed, as downstairs the men ate and drank spirituous liquors and smoked cigars, the stench of their smoke rising through the floor. It was more like the sale of a prize mare than a wedding.

After a few hours passed, the guests went to finish their drinking elsewhere and my new husband came into the room without so much as a knock at the door. He instructed me in a cold manner to remove my clothes and lie back on the bed. I was too stricken with fear not to obey him. When I lay naked and trembling there, he told me to put my hands on my breasts, to knead them like so and to pinch the teats. Then he dropped his trousers and stared at my hands at work and stroked himself until he was hard enough to penetrate me. This done, he began to thrust back and forth, oblivious to my cries of pain and with a look of disgust on his face. He left the chamber immediately after he was finished. I was just fifteen, remember, a virgin and quite innocent in these matters.

Don André came back the next night and the next, staying only long enough to complete the act. He repeated these conjugal visits as many times as necessary to get me with child. That is all I saw of him until the day, two weeks before the birth of my first girl, when he turned up in the middle of the afternoon and requested an interview in the front drawing room.

The jalousies were drawn against the heat. I wore a black dress, as if in mourning. The room was full of shadows. Two small coffees were brought. He asked me how I was getting along. I was too stunned to offer a reply to this man, my tormentor.

He went on, polite enough, and spoke to me as if he were a reasonable fellow and not a monster.

"Allow me to be candid," he said. "I have contracted this marriage for two reasons. First, because of your family and antecedents, who include among them Rodrigo Diaz del Vivar, El Cid, the great Spanish knight. Second, I am a man of much wealth but in possession of little land, and your father is a man of much land but in possession of little wealth. Our union has thus united both cash and property, which is as firm a basis for a good marriage as any. Do I wound your feelings? No? Good, then I will continue in a more delicate vein. You must of course understand that while I bear you no malice, I do not love you and am not interested in your body as a thing of pleasure. In any case it is unseemly for an aristocratic white woman to find any enjoyment in this area. It is a compliment to your family that I look for my pleasure elsewhere. From now on I will come to your bedroom once a month, though I urge you not to attach any sentiment to the generative act. . . ."

It was my husband's desire that I should bear him sons to carry on the illustrious name of de la Roca, which he informed me was among the most honorable in Spain or elsewhere and was one of the few families of sufficient antiquity to remain with their heads covered before the king. Outside of my simple reproductive duties, I was free to do as I liked as long as I conducted myself in a manner befitting the wife of a grandee of Spain. I must not allow myself a familiar demeanor in public or in private with the servants. I was not permitted to cultivate the friendship of members of the opposite sex. My virtue must be of the stainless variety, unimpeachable. He would speak of these things only once. The honor of his family, which was as precious to him as blood or air, depended on my strict adherence to the codes of formal behavior. Then he took his leave, polite as you please, and did not return till three months after my girl was born, and I was ready to be raped again.

Honor! Virtue! The man made my skin crawl! It does not take long for a sheltered girl to learn the nature of evil in the world. Cynics say that evil is banality, that it resides mostly in not acting, as when Pontius Pilate turned Christ over to the Jews. I say evil is something different. It is an active force and has as its main component an absolute belief in one's own worth and singularity. Think of Satan cast out of heaven with his dark angels. What was his sin? Pride.

That my husband, Don André de la Roca, is a callous and prideful monster is well known in New Orleans. You have no doubt heard many cruelties attached to his name. I am here to tell you they are all true.

This is one story. Many years before I was born, and before the slave uprising on his native St.-Domingue, Don André was a very rich young man and possessed vast and prosperous estates there. But he so mistreated the slaves in his possession that one day they grew bold enough to kidnap one of the overseers. They did not kill the man but only asked him to take a few simple requests to Don André. They asked for more to eat for strength during the long hours in the cane brakes, and they asked to be allowed to walk for a brief time on Sunday without their shackles, as was the custom on surrounding estates. All this was in accordance with the Code Noir, which I believe still regulates the treatment of slaves in most parts of the West Indies.

My husband replied to these reasonable requests by lashing to death the slaves who had kidnapped the overseer. Then, as an example to the rest, he selected ten at random from the ranks of the field laborers and crucified them along the road leading to his estate, like a Roman general out of Plutarch.

Esplanade, which is now the fashionable street of the Creole population in New Orleans, was in the first days of my residence there just a swampy trail at the edge of town. I was one of those who gave the thoroughfare its reputation as an elegant place to live.

As you can guess, left to my own devices in a town as riotous and pleasure-loving as ours, I became a woman of fashion, noted for my entertainments and my extravagant style of living. The terms of the wedding contract allowed me a substantial private income and the living off certain properties, including the town of Coeur de France, built on land belonging to the family. True to his word, my husband left me to my life as long as no scandal was attached to my name. He visited my bedroom once a month as he had promised and left by the back door as if he had just committed a shameful deed.

I soon discovered that his conjugal interests lay

in the darker quarters of the city — I mean, in a particular small but well-appointed house beneath the ramparts.

Like many aristocratic gentlemen — and I use the term with contempt — my husband kept a quadroon woman and a second mulatto family. He had several children by the woman, whom I saw once or twice around town. She was a common-looking creature, favoring garish yellow silk dresses, her hair always done up with feathers and colored beads. Don André had met her at one of the Quadroon Balls in that place on Chartres Street where the pretty light-skinned quadroon girls paint themselves up to attract the attentions of wealthy white men.

It is a disgusting institution, which leads to a disgusting double life and sorrow for everyone in the end, at least everyone who has a heart. And if there is one thing I can't stand in the world, it is the life of lies. Be a villain if you choose, but at least be an honest villain. You may raise your eyebrow, monsieur. I am a whore. Still, I know the difference between right and wrong.

True, many men tried to make love to me after my marriage, and it is not so unusual to take a lover in New Orleans, but I spurned them all. A perverse sense of honor kept me aloof from all offers of affection. Out of a twisted sort of pride, I wished to show my husband and my father just how honorable a woman I could be, even when surrounded by the corruption and cruelty of our age. In this way I kept my heart barren and empty until my twenty-third year.

Often our lives plod along, each day like the one before. Then, in a single moment, everything is changed. This is the way it was with me. In August, a month before my twenty-fourth birthday, I received news that Papa had been killed in a hunting accident in the bayou near Belle Azure. The slaves bore him up from the swamp on a bier of cane and saw grass, and there was much weeping on the plantation. He had always been a just master to his slaves, never unnecessarily cruel or a lover of the whip. Though I did not know it then, everything changed for me with this event, and I was rocked from pride and apathy into a new life.

Don André and I traveled downriver to the funeral in a barge draped in black, as is the custom. I saw Papa interred in the crypt beside my lost mother, and I shed a few tears for the world that might have been and for my papa, who, despite his hasty judgments, had never been a cruel man.

The next morning I had a table and some chairs brought out to the upstairs gallery, and the funeral party assembled there for the reading of the will. There was the lawyer, M. Levallier, his clerk, myself and my husband, various relations, and finally my cousin Albane d'Aurevilley. She was now a thin girl of nineteen and, I observed, not without a certain colorless and ephemeral beauty. Her fine straw-colored hair set off those odd blue eyes. But the whiteness of her skin was her chief attraction. Beneath its translucent china surface, you could see, even at a distance, the slight tracery of veins.

I had not laid eyes on Albane since the horse-whipping of almost eight years before, and I watched her now from behind my fan while the will was read. She sat dressed in black as at our first meeting, straight-backed, her eyes downcast, her pale lips trembling. For it became apparent from the particulars of the will that Papa's feelings had cooled toward the girl in the years of my absence. Instead of half his property, he left her only a modest sum for a dowry and an acre or two of land bordering the Prasères lagoon where he had his fishing camp and lodge. But even these small bequests were not hers outright. He asked that first I accept my cousin as my ward and see her properly married. Only then would the terms of the will be put into effect.

I received Albane later in Papa's library. I sat patiently in Papa's chair as she knelt and wept well-rehearsed tears over my knuckles and begged my pardon for any past offenses and commended herself to my care. Here was a girl who knew on which side her bread was buttered! "If there is any ill feeling between us," she implored me, "let it be forgotten at this sad time. Let us come together as sisters in memory of the man who loved us both too well." Then she bent and took my foot and put it on her neck. It was a gesture worthy of La Magdalene! Against my own better judgment, I was moved by her

419

pretty speech and her biblical gesture. I took her into my arms then, told her that the past was indeed forgotten, that we were now friends. My father's wishes would be honored, I said. At the end of the proper mourning period we would see her made a bride.

The following September I moved down to Belle Azure, while my husband remained in New Orleans with his quadroon wife. And I threw myself into the arrangements with some zeal. The old house's many rooms were opened and refurbished. I even regilded the ancient French fire screen in the front hall which bears the arms of the Prasères family. Then I planned a lavish season of entertainment, culminating in a grand ball just before Christmas. I contacted friends in New Orleans and announced that my cousin Albane d'Aurevilley would be coming out. Also, in the most discreet manner possible, I let it be known that the poor girl's dowry and holdings would be augmented substantially from my own pocket in the event of a suitable marriage.

The parties I gave were written up in the New Orleans papers in two languages, in *L'Abeille* and the *Louisiana Gazette*, and much talked about in society. My husband was obliged, to his dismay, to leave New Orleans and come downriver for a time. He stood by my side in his pompous and seignorial Spanish manner in the uniform of a king who no longer held sway over the province, and deigned to join the dancing for an old-fashioned gavotte or two.

Each party lasted a week, with various entertainments, including a carnival masque and a sort of historical tragedy from the hand of the young dramatist Victor Hugo, which had been recently performed at the Comédie Française in Paris. Bachelors journeyed from miles around, from as far away as Mobile and Natchez. All the bedrooms of the great house were full, sometimes with a half dozen sleeping to a room and others in hammocks on the galleries. I spent a fortune, which came largely from my husband's bank account in New Orleans. Musicians and actors and extra cooks lived in tents in the backyard. We had Madame Lecoute, the hairdresser of Royal Street, to fix Albane's hair, and for the girl's party dresses Mademoiselle Annabelle Loury, the well-known modiste, who was herself in communication with the most fashionable dressmakers of the European continent.

Still, it was a very difficult task. Albane was not naturally witty or much of a conversationalist. Her pale charms were popular only with a certain morose, intellectual type of young man whom she naturally despised as weak. She was made four proposals of marriage from bachelors of this effeminate type, but of respectable means, yet she found some fault with all of them. They were too fat or too lean, or their faces were pocked or they were losing their hair, or they spoke with annoying lisps or did not speak much at all.

Sadly, the more robust young men whom she admired from a physical standpoint would have nothing to do with her. Her manner was gloomy, and when she turned those strange blue eyes on you, there was a chill that went down your back. You thought of priests and winding sheets and the wages of sin and other uncomfortable things, not of weddings and the pleasures of the marriage bed. I exaggerate, but there was definitely something. Perhaps she still had the gris-gris on her, as the house slaves had once insisted.

Esteban de Vasconcellos came to Belle Azure for the last and grandest party of the season, just before Christmas. He arrived alone at dusk, without manservant or valet, on the packet from New Orleans. He brought with him only a small valise and a letter of introduction from my husband, who had remained in town — so he said — on business.

Most of the guests had arrived the preceding Saturday, and the house was full. Esteban was an unforeseen addition to the company. Frost covered the ground in the morning, and it was too cold to sleep on the galleries or in a tent in the yard. At the last minute Zetie found a place for him beneath the eaves at the back of the second gallery, which is reserved for the house slaves, an irony that did not escape me later. But Esteban did not complain. That evening in the drawing room before dinner, he approached and introduced himself, bowing over my hand in the best European fashion. He thanked me for my hospitality and complimented me on the expansive view of the river from the small window of his room. "It's a pity," he said, "that such a vista is wasted on slaves." I was charmed.

His hand was soft, but not without muscle, as one would imagine the hand of a violinist or a fencing master. He was about my own age, quite dark, his skin a deep olive tone. His side whiskers were long and thick, and they framed his face in a wonderful manner, like those I had seen in engravings of Chateaubriand in one of Papa's books. His hair seemed a single black curl, and his eyes were a princely opalescent green. He was beautiful. Later this physical beauty struck me as inferior to his intellectual accomplishments. For he spoke five languages, played the guitar and mandolin, sang beautifully, and could discuss Molière and mathematics as easily as the latest advances in the refining of cane sugar.

Women fell in love with him instantly. Men were suspicious of him, because the contrast was not in their favor. You will agree with me that many of the young men of today are shallow, interested only in horses and gambling and conventional love affairs. It is a commonplace to say that modern love is little more than the exchange of two whims and the contact of two epidermises. Not so with Esteban. He possessed depth of soul and an undeniable ardor for the things in which he believed. He was New Orleans born, of a family originally from St.-Domingue, but had been educated in Madrid and Paris. It was obvious to all present that here we had a fine example of a well-bred gentleman, though no one could say if they had heard of his family in society.

Albane herself, so far reticent and tongue-tied around the young men whom she found pleasing, engaged Esteban in conversation almost immediately and contrived a way to sit beside him during that first night at dinner. He had a certain manner that put even plain women at their ease. He talked and joked prettily; his witticisms were pointed but not too sharp. Albane blushed at almost everything he said and seemed overcome with emotion at his presence. But this dinner was torment for me. I was seized by a strange giddy sensation, and whenever I looked in the direction of Albane and Esteban talking together, I felt a peculiar squeezing to the pit of my stomach, so that I could hardly swallow a mouthful.

I excused myself early from the company, leaving Albane and Esteban singing a duet at the piano, and retired to my room. There I studied the vague letter written on Esteban's behalf by my husband.

"This is to introduce Don Esteban Ramón de Vasconcellos," he wrote, "the son of a friend of my youth from St.-Domingue. Señor de Vasconcellos has great education and is related to one of the oldest families in Spain, but alas, his is only a modest fortune. I commend him to you as a suitable match for your ward, Albane, and ask you to see that they are often together. — Don André de la Roca."

Without my knowing why, the idea of marriage

between the pair revolted me. This beautiful and courtly young man wasted on Albane, who was such a wan and nauseating creature! I threw myself down upon my bed and wept bitterly. Then, in the morning, I awoke to the sound of laughter from the gallery, and when I looked at my face in the mirror, I knew that I was in love with Esteban. It was like falling prey to a terrible disease. At first I could hardly breathe. Then I unloosed my corset and was sick in my water basin. My heart — untouched since the death of my mother, a woman whom I did not even remember — now filled itself with fury and fire.

Still, my sense of honor and family pride made me determined to resist these new, painful emotions. Over the following days I complied with my husband's wishes and saw that Esteban and Albane were constantly together. I suffered. My suffering was sublime, the only thing that made my empty life bearable. Then, by the end of the third week of his stay with us, Albane sought me out to acquaint me of the obvious. She was deeply in love with Esteban, and she put it rather blasphemously.

"I love the man more than I love God or my own salvation," she said. "He has returned my affection eagerly, if not yet with the matching enthusiasm that will come as we are more and more together. And lacking only your permission, dear cousin, we hope to marry in the spring."

I paused at this revelation as if considering it

carefully. The girl positively quivered in terror at the thought of a rejection. When I gave my consent, she threw her arms around my neck and embraced me with great feeling.

"You have been so kind to me," she said. "You have at last become the sister I never had," and she covered my cheeks and my hands with kisses and both laughed and wept from joy. But each kiss, each tear hardened my heart against her. Why should this miserable orphaned girl, who had already stolen my father from me, now steal the only man I would ever love?

The prospect of her happiness, unearned as it was, seemed more terrible than death itself. I confess to this cruelty and this selfishness and can only excuse myself by saying that love had been too long denied my heart, which now fell prey to a passionate and sinful jealousy.

Later that same night I donned my most revealing dress, touched a little scent of verbena behind my ears and between my breasts, and went to Esteban.

I did not know what I would do until I saw him there smoking a last cigar on the gallery before the door to his new room on the second floor. Most of the other guests had departed just after Christmas. Only Esteban and a few others had consented to stay on for the New Year. He was a little shocked to see me there at such an hour and, as he was attired in his dressing gown and ready for bed, sought to excuse himself. But I put my hand on his arm and would not let him go. I asked him if he loved my ward, Albane. He smiled and shrugged, as if to say — She will do.

"An offer of marriage has been related to me through my ward," I continued. "It is considered good form in these matters that such an offer be addressed to the guardian first. I am Albane's guardian, and I have heard nothing from you concerning your intentions."

Esteban apologized; the whole thing was somewhat hastily done, he said. And he expressed his intentions to approach me with a proper proposal in the morning.

"Nevertheless, I am prepared to accept the offer now," I said. "And if it is made, I will increase my ward's dowry with an additional contribution of ten thousand Yankee gold dollars." Then I stepped back to see the expression on his handsome face in the dim moonlight.

If he was surprised, he did not show it. He nodded his thanks complacently, as though prepared for such an act of generosity. I waited a full minute without saying anything else. I heard the mournful splash of a side-wheeler down on the river, and the cry of loons from the bayou, and the quick sound of my own breath. Then I took him by the arm again, and this time my hand was a claw.

"I had thought you a gentleman," I hissed, "and supposed your affections too precious to be sold for so mean a sum as ten thousand dollars. In this matter you have shown yourself the lowest sort of opportunist, trading for gold on a poor girl's affections. But if you dare go through with the cheap transaction, monsieur, I shall with my own hands slit your throat on your wedding night."

I did not give him time to react to my violent statement. I leaned up and pressed into him with my body and kissed him on the mouth with such longing and such passion that we went immediately into the bedroom and lay together on the bed. After we had committed ourselves once to each other, we closed the shutters against the night and stayed in the bed together as man and wife. During those dark hours Esteban repeated many times that act which until then beneath my husband's bulk had been without meaning or pleasure. Let it suffice to say that I loved Esteban with my heart and my body, and my love was returned.

At dawn, after again experiencing his love, I put Esteban's dressing gown over my nakedness and went down to Albane's room. She lay asleep, dreaming perhaps of the bliss of married life, a look of peace and contentment on her face such as I had not seen there before. I waited quietly by the side of her bed until she awoke with a start to my presence. When she was lucid, I told her that I had reconsidered my consent of the night before.

"As your guardian," I said, "I must forbid a marriage with a man as penniless as Esteban de Vasconcellos. You had better accept one of the other willing, richer bachelors in this one's place."

Poor Albane went very white at my words. She did not weep or make a sound. Then her eyes took in the disheveled state of my appearance, the man's dressing gown I wore. And she said in a small voice, "I know what you have done. You do this to me because I came to your house once as an orphan, alone in the world, and asked for love and your father gave it to me. You have never forgiven me for my need. Your soul is black. You will pay for your sins in the darkness of eternal night." Then she turned away from me and pressed her face into the pillow.

I felt a momentary chill and thought of the gris-gris, but I left the room and made immediate arrangements to get away from Belle Azure with Esteban. I dismissed the remaining guests, with the excuse that I was going on a journey to look over some family property at St. Francisville. Esteban bade me good-bye in front of the house slaves, boarded the packet to New Orleans, but had himself put ashore just a few miles upriver. And that evening, at dusk, we met at Papa's old hunting lodge in the bayou, a crude rambling structure of cypress logs that overlooks the Prasères lagoon.

Secreted away from the outside world in the heart of the jungle with only the wild birds for company, we lived as man and wife for two months, engaging in conjugal union as many as six or seven times a day. He hunted and fished. I traded small bits of my jewelry with the Acadians at Coeur de France for cornmeal and molasses and eggs. We were like Adam and Eve before the fall, surrounded by the bounties of the garden and wed in the eyes of God — an idyll that would last until M. Levallier could dispose of a significant portion of my property, enough to allow us to take ship for Brazil and live comfortably there. But our arrangement was blind, clumsy. We should have fled immediately to some other country, money be damned. We knew in our hearts that disaster could strike at any time and were too enraptured with each other to care. Pride, conscience, caution — all of these were thrown aside for the sake of our primeval love.

The sky burned a clear blue the afternoon they came for us. I stood waist-deep in the lagoon, washing our clothes with a brick of lye soap like a good Acadian housewife. Esteban lay asleep in the hammock strung between two of the beams of the porch, one of Papa's books open over his stomach — Montesquieu's *Esprit des Lois*. I had kept my sweet lover awake half the night with my desires, as indeed I did every night, and he was indulging in a well-earned siesta.

Then I heard a crashing through the bayou and the barking of dogs and the shouts of men. I left the clothes floating in the water and ran up the slope through the underbrush to the lodge, a thick humming that was the sound of my own blood in my ears.

There were seven men in the hunting party — my husband, four huge Negroes from the fields, and two white men I did not know. A dozen blood-hounds growled and frisked nervously about the yard, tails down, as dogs will do when they know something is up. Esteban knelt trembling before Don André. I was too far away to hear their words. My husband made an impatient sign, and I watched in horror as one of the bucks took Esteban around the neck with his huge hands and snapped his spine in a second as a child would snap a twig. I heard the awful cracking sound and saw my love's eyes bulge out and go dark. I started to scream and screamed until I went faint and fell to the ground.

A few minutes later, revived by a mouthful of brandy, I found myself on the porch of the lodge, arms held fast behind my back by one of the big buck Negroes. Don André looked me up and down, expressionless. When he saw that I was fully awake, he nodded gently at the buck who had killed Esteban. This one took out a heavy curved knife, cut Esteban's body down the middle as you cut open a calf for the roasting, and reached inside and fumbled about as if it were an old sack. In another moment he pulled out a dripping red organ that I saw was my lover's heart.

It was then I begged them to kill me, so I could fly to my beloved Esteban in death. But my husband turned to me with a weary and understanding smile that was all the more horrible considering the circumstances.

"You are my wife," he said, "and you will remain

my wife. That is the more sublime torture." Then he told the buck to throw Esteban's heart to the dogs so that they might devour it before me. At this I begged and pleaded most piteously to be allowed to eat the heart myself. If I could eat his heart, I thought, I could keep Esteban's love inside me forever. Even Don André was surprised at this request and hesitated for a moment. "If you love the traitorous bastard that much," he said at last, "then fight the dogs for him."

The buck threw Esteban's heart to the dogs, and the other let me go, and I scrambled into the mud of the yard and fought the dogs for the heart. But these beasts have hard claws and sharp teeth, while I am made of softer flesh. I received many bites and scratches and only managed to get a single mouthful of my lover's heart, still warm from his body. It tasted of his love, of salt and life like the fluid of his seed. But one of the dogs tore the precious organ from my grasp and trotted off into the woods to devour it in private, and I fell into a swoon from the pain and horror of my ordeal.

I lay sick for many days, caught in a fever between sensuous dreams of my dead lover and monstrous visions of gore and riven organs. When I awoke from this madness, I found Don André at my bedside, his hands clasped, calm as death itself. My cousin Albane stood by his side, dressed in the mourning that always seemed to suit her so well. She looked skinny and paler than usual. Her eyes, ringed with dark circles, were fixed on the floor.

Helpless and weak as I was, I cursed my husband and informed him that I would have M. Levallier contact the government prosecutor in New Orleans with the particulars of this odious crime. "Unless you kill me now while you are able," I said, "you will be arrested and dragged in irons before the court, where they will convict you for the murder of my beloved Esteban."

But he listened calmly to my threats, and I could see in his face that his revenge was not yet complete. At last he informed me with a cold smile that the quadroon slave called Esteban de Vasconcellos had been disposed of legally and in the presence of the sheriff of Plaquemines Parish and his appointed deputy for the crime of violating a white woman. The punishment for this crime, as everyone knows, is death.

I looked from Albane's white face to my husband's black eyes, the eyes of an unfeeling animal mistakenly endowed with intellect, and I saw that this statement was true. He then went on to tell me that the quadroon slave called Esteban de Vasconcellos was in fact his own son, born on St.-Domingue out of a youthful union with a mulatto slave woman of his former estate.

"Yes, the boy looked like a white man and showed a quick wit," he said. "But he was still a Negro and a slave under the laws of the United States and under the regulations of the Code Noir. Long ago, out of a mistaken affection for his mother, who died during the uprising, I promised to send the boy to Europe, where he might be educated properly. This was a terrible mistake, which I realize only now. It is always a mistake to educate a Negro above his station. For that alone I am responsible. But your whorish and base passions are to blame in every other respect. If you had encouraged this marriage between your ward and my son, no one would have been the wiser. Instead you took the slave for yourself and lay with him in fornication, and in so doing sullied the precious honor of the de la Rocas. The slave is dead. You will live on to ponder your misdeeds."

Don André then paused for a while for this terrible information to sink into my brain. But if he waited for me to express regret or horror concerning my love for the person whom he identified as a Negro and a slave, he waited in vain. For in that instant I abandoned all conceptions I had of the differences between Negroes and whites, between slave and free. Esteban was a slave and I had loved him, and I still loved him. Don André was white and a monster and a murderer, and I hated him with the full force of my passion.

When Don André saw that I was not moved by his revelation, he let loose one final arrow.

"You should know that it was your own dear cousin who informed me of your perfidious adultery," he said. "As soon as she discovered your whereabouts, she sent for me. But now the poor girl appears distressed at the outcome of her efforts. Pity. Allow me to leave you two alone to commiserate over the death of a Negro slave."

And he bowed with ultimate contempt and left the room.

After he was gone, Albane tried to speak to me. She pleaded for forgiveness and expressed herself with much emotion, but I cannot tell you now what she said. I turned my face to the wall and did not hear a single word of it. And at last she, too, fell silent and left me alone with my grief.

In the months of my recuperation I lay propped in a chair on the top-floor gallery at Belle Azure, watching the light change over the river and plotting my revenge. The thought of my revenge was the only thing that kept me from taking my own life.

Since the law would not touch my husband, I must be the one to drive the dagger into his heart. I imagined this scene many times — armed with a knife or a pistol, walking up to him in his coffeehouse on Bourbon Street and ending his life in a second with a single bloody eruption. But I came to consider that this assassination would be too quick an act. He would suffer little, and at his age he was no longer much afraid of death.

By and by I discovered through correspondence with a few friends in town that Don André had fabricated a near-fatal bout of cholera to explain my prolonged absence from society. News of my affair with Esteban, and of his death, were not known in New Orleans, having been hushed up by my husband and his agents. This detail revealed my husband's weakness, put the true weapon in my hand. The place to wound him was in his pride. I must bring dishonor to his precious family name, drag it in the mud once and for all. And after it had been dragged in the mud for a good long time, all Louisiana would come to know the dishonorable circumstances of my life. A woman may perhaps be excused one affair, or even two, but thousands? Only from such a mortification would Don André truly suffer.

So this is the reason I have become a whore, the common prostitute you will share the bed with tonight. Understand that I am a whore now only because I alone have willed it. I was not driven to this vile trade through need, like all the other poor sluts. I am a whore out of spite, to work my revenge on the only person in all Louisiana whose pride is greater than my own, that monster of arrogance, my husband, Don André Villejo de la Roca. It is his portrait you see there, staring down at us now from the wall over my whore's bed. He has watched like a guardian demon over the sweating backs of countless men. Watched as I opened my legs for them and took their pleasure into my body. My body, which is the weapon I shall use to strike him in the heart of his pride, for there alone is he capable of sustaining a mortal wound.

When I was well again, I left Belle Azure in the middle of the night and fled north, to reach a place beyond my husband's reach. As you know, he is too powerful in Louisiana to allow me a free career of harlotry in that province. I stopped for a while in Savannah, in Charleston, in Baltimore and Philadelphia, but in each place received intelligence that my husband's agents were on my trail and under orders to end my life.

At last, four years ago, I arrived in New York City and from there crossed the river to Brooklyn and this dingy neighborhood near the docks. Here I believe I have escaped him utterly. I put my card on the door, as is the fashion with whores, and installed myself in these squalid rooms. I am famous among the sailors for my looks, which are better than those of the common prostitute, and for my willingness to sleep with anyone. Negro or white, man or boy, I treat them all alike. I take them inside my body, into the wound that is my love.

But you are the first man I have met from home in many long years, one of my own people. This is why I have told you my story tonight. You have been very patient with me, kind enough to listen. Also, you are a gentleman, and I think you are sympathetic to my plight. Because after all my suffering, something has gone terribly wrong. My plans have been interfered with, and I think you know who is responsible. Monsieur, please, I am in desperate need of your help . . . please. . . . You must help me. . . .

7

Hours have passed, or days. It should be dawn out the windows of Molesworth's room, but there is still the same impenetrable blackness, still the same night, endless, vast, that holds us in its dark hand.

Sometimes I am naked and alone, blind with fever and lying prone on my stained sheets, digital thermometer beeping in alarm beneath my tongue. Sometimes I am with a prostitute named Madeleine in a rope-sprung four-poster, in a room that is much like Molesworth's room, in a house that is like my own, in a town that is not Brooklyn, that is instead Brooklyn lost in a terrible darkness.

Now she is begging me to help her. She is weeping; she is tearing at her hair. The lamentations fill my ears; they are loud and have lasted for more than a century. Now I can see her tears glinting in the dim light of the tallow candles; now I can see them fall from her cheeks to her bare breasts. Now she is naked, and on her shoulder a blue scattering of marks that might have been made by the teeth of a dog.

And as I press against the headboard, I can see the portrait of the olive-skinned man staring down with his cruel black eyes, and I can feel the smooth roughness of the muslin sheets on my back, and I can smell the rank human smell of the bedding and the strong odor that comes from between her legs as she crawls toward me slowly on hands and knees, the straw mattress creaking on its ropes. She does not cease her pleading, which comes in erotic gasps now, and her eyes are filled with tears, but she is ready for me because she is a whore, and I am as hard as I've ever been.

Soon I feel her mouth on mine, her lips wet with tears wept in the darkness between worlds, and if I see the walls of my room again, and hear the power plant grinding out the window, and the digital thermometer beeping its warning, it is only for a moment. All that is gone when she settles on top of me at last and we connect like the pieces of a puzzle; when I feel the weight of her breasts and the familiar slickness, my hands tangled in her thick black hair as she begins to shift and jerk; when I hear the sad, passionate sound of her voice imploring in my ear, her voice, which becomes a whisper, which becomes an echo, which becomes the wind, fierce at first, then fainter, fainter, which becomes a dead leaf falling through the dead air, which becomes a pale exhalation, which becomes a breath, which becomes a last dead sigh and then becomes nothing. Nothing at all.

Part Six:
A Miracle

I hear a faint hushing sound and, farther off, the solid muscular thud of waves on a beach. There is also an occasional mechanical beeping, much louder than the digital beep of my thermometer. I am prodded, stuck with sharp points. My wrists are tied to something I cannot see because my eyes are clouded by an inky blue membrane. It is like looking up from the bottom of a fish tank into a dark room. Lying in the red and yellow gravel, I can barely make out squiggles and reflections and bits of fish food floating on the surface. Water fills my lungs. This seems all right to me; I prefer the water to air.

After a while, I can't tell how long, the blue begins to break up with more and more light, and at last I open my eyes to a spotless white wall decorated with an excellent full-size reproduction of Raphael's *Madonna and Child*. It's the famous one in the Vatican, with the bored putti looking up from the bottom foreground. To my left a small aluminum frame window gives out on a gray and empty ocean sky, heavy with low clouds.

A long, clear tube is connected from a vein in my arm to a plastic bag full of clear fluid hanging overhead. The hushing noise comes from an important-looking medical machine which displays a parabolic graph and a fluctuating series of numbers on a screen the size of a small television set. A thick ribbed plastic tube runs from this machine across the bed into my mouth and down my throat, which hurts terribly. My wrists are fixed to the chrome rails of my bed with yellow hospital bracelets. The room is silent except for the sound of the sea and the painful hushing of the machine.

Then I hear a feminine voice to my right. Soft and full of harmonies, it vibrates in the air like a tuning fork.

"Is that bothering you? Here . . ." The tube is removed from my throat, my hands are unfastened, and the bag of fluid is unhooked. For a second I have forgotten how to breathe, but I take a gulping breath, and my lungs are full of air again.

"That's very good. That's right. Breathe."

I turn toward the voice. It is a young nun wearing the robes of an order I do not know. They are of celestial blue and snow white. The style is old-fashioned with full skirts and wimple. A gold crucifix hangs around her neck on a heavy chain made of interlocking gold links like the ones worn by the mayors of provincial towns in France. This nun is very beautiful with piercing blue eyes, delicate features, and skin like bone china. Beneath its smooth surface, the faint network of veins. I am silent. There is something about her, a brightness, a stainless quality that is dazzling. She smiles, and I can't help smiling back.

"Hello," I croak. "Who are you?"

"You've had a hard time of it," she says. "You've been a long way. We had some trouble getting you back."

"I'm in the hospital?"

"You are."

"A Catholic hospital?"

"Yes."

"How did I get here?"

"Shh. There will be plenty of time for questions later. Now, how do you feel?"

I must think about this for a moment to realize that I feel pretty bad. A general, indescribable prickling fills my body. A painful lassitude.

"Actually, not too good," I say at last.

The nun nods and leans closer. I can't quite meet her blue eyes, which are clear and perfect. Her breath smells like wildflowers. In a moment I feel her cool hands on my chest under my hospital gown, on my neck. "Lie calmly," she says, "and let your thoughts wander a little."

I sag into the pillow, and some of the prickling goes away. In a moment she's got my gown up and her hands are on my stomach. My face is turned to the side, my eyes on the Raphael Madonna. Mary looks sweet and a little bewildered in this picture, as would any virgin who has just given birth to a child.

"Ah, here it is." The nun's hands stop at a place halfway up my right side. "This is where the pain comes from, am I right?" And when she presses down, I gasp.

"Yes," I manage. "It's pretty tender there."

"Your liver," the nun says. "You've been abusing this organ these last fifteen years. Spirituous liquors. Lagers and bocks."

"And stouts," I say, thinking of a full glass of Guinness. "Don't forget them. You know, in Ireland they supposedly feed pints of the stuff to pregnant women in the hospital."

"That's not funny," the nun says, and presses down again, and I stiffen in pain. "Riotous living, lethargy, and excess. These things are mortal sins. I don't need to tell you which ones. And they endanger your immortal soul."

"My immortal soul?" I fix for a moment on those blue eyes, which are like the flame at the heart of the fire.

"You do believe in an immortal soul?"

I am silent.

"It exists," she says quietly. "I have seen yours pass through the darkness, a poor rag and very faint. Almost as sick as your body."

"Wait a minute —"

"Shh. Listen. One thing has saved you."

"What?"

"Guess."

I think for a minute. Her hands press cool on my stomach and form a triangle of flesh between thumb and forefingers. It feels as if she's got my liver there, drowned for so many years in grease and alcohol and despair, pickled in regret, and she's wringing it out, kneading away the poisons of life.

"Well, it's probably the vitamins," I say. "I always make sure to take them religiously, every day. Two Es, two Cs, and a multivitamin."

Her laughter, when it comes, is like a silver bell. "I am not talking about your body now. I am talking about your soul. Do you know what has saved it?"

"No."

"Love."

Suddenly I see a picture of Antoinette in my head, so vivid she could be in this room. And I know that she is sick and sad like me and that she will not make it alone.

"Antoinette," I barely whisper.

"But be careful," the nun says, a sharp warning in her voice. "Do not confuse the Maker's intent. Order is a divine gift. There are rules. It is only the devil and his legions who live in anarchy. Love must be sanctified by the sacrament of marriage. Love must be of the spirit first and the body second. Remember, the body will fade and grow weary of the earth, while the spirit, properly nourished on love, will rise up free and shining to God."

At this she raises her hands as if to show me the way, and for a moment they are two white doves in the air. Then she lets them down and bends to kiss me on the forehead. The touch of her lips feels like the petals of a rose. From the place where her hands were pressed, I can feel a curious warmth spreading through my body.

"Now close your eyes," the nun says.
I close my eyes.
"And sleep."
I sleep.

2

When I wake up again, the day is sunny and bright beyond the aluminum window, and the sound of the ocean is strong. For some reason, they have taken down the excellent reproduction of Raphael's Madonna and put up a cheap Sears-style still life of flowers and fruit in a frame that's bolted to the wall.

A doctor and nurse are standing over my bed, an expression of surprise — no, shock — on their faces. The nurse, a large-boned woman with dyed blond hair, wears a white hospital smock and white pants of a cotton-poly blend. On her feet the thick, squeaky-soled white shoes favored by nurses everywhere. The doctor wears his hospital smock over a raucously flowered sports shirt and khakis held up with an expensive-looking woven leather belt. He's a handsome man with chiseled features like a doctor in a soap opera and resembles the popular magician David Copperfield. A small black tag on his chest reads "Morris Abrahamson, M.D."

"Hey, Doc," I say. "Where's the Raphael?"
The doctor looks too stunned to reply.

"You took down the Raphael Madonna," I say, "and put up that sofa-sized thing there." I gesture toward the Sears painting on the wall.

"Excuse me?" Dr. Abrahamson says at last.

"There was a Raphael on the wall, just a while ago . . ." but I see from his face that I should not go on. This man has other matters on his mind.

"Mr. Conti," he says, "who took you off life support?"

I look over at the impressive machine with the TV screen, which is silent now, blank.

"And who unplugged you from the glucose and took the breathing apparatus out of your mouth? And who unloosened your restraints?" He points to my wrists, which I flex appreciatively.

"The nun," I say.

Dr. Abrahamson and the nurse exchange a frightened look.

"What nun?" Dr. Abrahamson says.

"The nun who was in here earlier," I say patiently. "She works here, right?"

Again the doctor and nurse exchange looks. The nurse steps forward, tentative. "We have no nuns that work here, sir," she says.

"Is this a Catholic hospital?"

"Well, yes, nominally," she says. "But really it's like any other hospital. We have doctors and trained nurses. Nuns are a thing of the past."

"Not this one," I say, crossing my arms.

"We have no nuns, sir," she says, a little angry now. "I should know. I'm in charge of the nursing

449

staff. If a nun has somehow infiltrated the hospital and has gone about treating patients, we need to know about it!"

At this Dr. Abrahamson turns to the nurse. "That's O.K., Ms. Kelley. I'll take it from here."

The nurse flushes, hesitates, then pivots on her squeaky soles and leaves the room. When she is gone, the doctor scratches his chin in the way he's seen doctors do in the movies and walks over to the window, hands clasped behind his back. He's there for a minute, thinking things out and staring down at the beach I have not yet seen. On an impulse I get out of bed and stand behind, looking over his shoulder. The linoleum floor is cold on my bare feet. I'm a little dizzy from lying in bed, but other than that, I feel fine and quite jolly.

Just below, there is a wide and dirty boardwalk littered with scraps of paper and the usual Jersey-type lowlife beach scum. Hooligans on stolen mountain bikes, tattooed rednecks toughing around shirtless, bimbos in bikinis with high-heeled flip-flops and big hair, alongside the usual bewildered octogenarians who can't believe the beach has changed for the worse since the heady days of their youth in the 1920s. Beyond the boardwalk, sand covered with a gray layer of car exhaust dwindles into the sea. A trawler rides the horizon. Closer in, the low-hulled profile of a garbage scow. From somewhere comes the faint rancid smell of frying meat.

"This looks like Far Rockaway," I say.

Dr. Abrahamson jumps a full three feet to the left and twists around to see me there, grinning. His head bangs against the frame of the flower painting. "Shit! Get back in bed!" he almost yells.

I shrug and get back in bed, where I feel like a mischievous child. I fidget, tap my fingers on the chrome railing to the cadence of "Dixie." "You know I'm pretty hungry," I say. "How about a bacon cheeseburger?"

Dr. Abrahamson has some difficulty regaining his doctorly composure. At last he comes to sit somberly on the edge of the bed. "If anything, clear liquids," he says. "Then we'll see. But I think you should continue the glucose for a while until we can determine exactly how you are doing. The nurse is getting another bag."

"Come on, Doctor," I say. "A gourmet pizza, with artichoke hearts, basil, and prawns. An omelet with shitake mushrooms and goat cheese. Sushi — Ama-ebi, that buttery raw shrimp, then the deep-fried heads in a bowl. Soft-shell crabs done Thai style with mint and ginger. A T-bone steak. Biscuit tortoni. Bouillabaisse."

The doctor smiles tightly, but there's a look in his eye that reads "Shut up." "Mr. Conti," he says in a professional tone, "you were brought into this hospital three days ago with a fever of one hundred and six, your skin as yellow as the sunflower in that painting. We checked and found your liver expanded to the size of an eggplant. At that temperature your body was literally burning up from the inside out. We did a blood test

451

and determined that your liver count — that is, the presence of bilirubin in your blood — was sixty-seven hundred. The bilirubin count in a normal human is somewhere around fifty. Accordingly, given those symptoms, I diagnosed you with one of the worst cases of hepatitis that I had ever seen."

"Hepatitis?"

"Yes. Whether A or B or C or some other strain, we don't know yet. The tests are still out. But that was immaterial at the time, since your body was beginning to shut down. You were frying in your own juices, Mr. Conti. No human being can survive for long with a temperature of one hundred six. Do you understand what I'm saying here?"

I nod, puzzled. "I guess that I was pretty sick?"

"Sick?" All of a sudden, Dr. Abrahamson's doctorly demeanor crumbles from the chin up, and he begins to laugh. He covers his face with his hands and laughs a good hard minute till his ears are red. Then, suddenly, he is serious.

"We only had you on life support till we could notify your next of kin. In layman's terms, Mr. Conti, you were dead."

3

September. The sea is high today, the sky azure blue at the horizons with a faint brownish layer of smog halfway up. A stiff wind full of sand and litter blows at our backs, blows the dirt of the city out to the open ocean, where it will be dispersed amid the swells. Fall is in the air. The lifeguard chairs are empty. Two odd creatures in windbreakers lunch among the dunes. Behind us, St. Luke's Geriatric Hospital towers over the boardwalk, the first of the long row of twenty-story towers — cheap condominiums, low-income housing, old people's homes — planted up the beachfront like tombstones.

Rust is visiting. He kicks the flaking metal railing of the boardwalk with his scuffed cowboy boots, then flips around and leans back on his elbows. I can see the stitched-up bullet hole in his left boot. Jacket collar up, wind blowing his hair into a pompadour, he looks like an older James Dean who has lived through his sports car crash and the turmoil of youth to attain wisdom. I am sitting a few feet away on the concrete bench, eating a funnel cake covered with powdered sugar. Since my sickness I've been very hungry, haven't stopped eating. The hospital doesn't feed me enough, just Jell-O and a bit of boiled chicken for dinner, so I sneak out and gorge on fried food.

They're still doing tests on me and have had a hard time figuring things out. Dr. Abrahamson cannot reconcile himself with the fact that I am alive. His current theory is that I contracted an unusual strain of hepatitis that goes acute rapidly, then vanishes, leaving no trace. When all the tests are done, he plans to write up an article on my case for the *New England Journal of Medicine*.

Rust squints up at the ugly brick monolith of St. Luke's Geriatric. A five-story neon cross decorates the facade. Its steel mountings catch the light, flashing signals in the afternoon sun. This hospital was the only one that would take me as a charity case with no health insurance. Father Rose has a connection on the board and arranged the whole thing, though I must be the only patient here under seventy-five.

"That priest fellow came down looking for you," Rust says now. "Lucky for you. He said you hadn't been to work in a week. I said, 'Let's break the door down.' Otherwise we wouldn't have found you upstairs till you started to bloat and stink."

The last lump of funnel cake sticks in my throat. The image of myself as a rotting corpse is not good for the digestion.

"Sorry, buddy," Rust says. "But are you sure this is O.K., you eating this shit? What do the people in the hospital say?"

"To hell with the people in the hospital," I say. "I'm fine. I'm only sticking around as a favor to Dr. Abrahamson. In fact, I'm still hungry."

We walk back up the boardwalk to Rockaway Boulevard, the main drag, a dilapidated street of bars and retirement hotels, divided by a burned grass median. It's hard to imagine a time when Far Rockaway was new, when the restaurants served good food and the hotels, just built, were full of clean rooms and good cheer. Hard to imagine it as anything but what it is now — a last-chance greasy beach resort at the end of the line, the distant suburb where the suburbs end, blighted with working-class ennui and endless side streets of sand-blasted salt-box houses. There is nothing more melancholy than a low-class beach at the end of the season. The smell of three-month-old grease in the fryers and empty bottles of suntan lotion in the sand, the long shadows of the parking meters on the cracking blacktop, a lone broken thong sandal left stranded on the dirty median.

Even Rust feels it. He shivers and rubs his hands together as I munch a chili dog, extra onion at the last stand left open on the boardwalk. Then I follow him up the street into an Irish bar, marked by a fritzing neon harp. Inside, it's a cavernous room with pictures of long-dead boxers on the walls and a jukebox full of Irish sentimental favorites, including, as always, that damn song about the unicorn. Halfway down, through a swinging door, is the lobby of a residential hotel for old men. As Rust gets his Guinness from the bar, I take a look back there: dusty couches, a rubber tree, an old front desk of dark wood, a yellowed photograph of Myrna Loy on the wall. It could be the set of a 1940s era detective movie.

When I join him at a table near the front, Rust is half done with his pint. It is the good stuff, shipped direct, nonpasteurized, from Ireland, and leaves telltale rings on the side of the glass with each sip.

"You were a goddamned sight, Ned," he says, wiping the froth off his mouth with the back of his hand. "When the priest and I busted in, we heard these weird panting noises coming from your bedroom. And there you were, sprawled half off the mattress — hot as a poker, buck naked, your dick sticking straight up into the air, and moaning and squirming around like you were getting the lay of your life."

I pick some lint off the sleeve of my sweater, embarrassed. "I had a fever of one hundred six; that's what Dr. Abrahamson said," I mumble.

"So we dragged you into the bathroom and threw you into a tub of cold water and ice cubes. That's probably what saved your ass."

"No," I say. "That wasn't it at all."

"O.K., so what was it?"

"A miracle."

He puts the empty pint glass down on the table with a firm click and restrains himself from comment. Like the rest of them, he thinks I'm still sick, that the fever has affected my reason.

"O.K., whatever you say." He pushes up from the table and pulls on his jacket. "But right now we need to get you back to the hospital before the doc knows you're gone."

Rust doesn't believe in miracles. Nor does he believe in God, whom he sees as a big fat lie invented to help people sleep better at night. And while he accepts the existence of ghosts, he believes they are a natural phenomenon, a sort of photographic imprint of past traumatic events on the magnetic field, which will someday be quantified by science. I heard the story of his early disillusionment one night over too many beers at the Horseshoe. Some people get goofy, some violent; when drunk, Rust gets philosophic.

"I was a kid," he told me, "this is Carswell, Nevada, 1956. My oldest brother, Cyrus, was in the hospital with leukemia brought on by one of the nuclear tests they were always doing in the desert in those days. It was this rinky-dink hospital, primitive, you know. I got bored with watching the kid die, which didn't happen fast like in the movies, and I wandered away while my parents were talking to the doctor. Well, I ended up down at the morgue just in time to see them dump a barrel full of fetuses into the trash. That was it for me. How could God sit still and watch them dump a barrel of fetuses into the trash? Was life worth about as much as a rotten old orange peel and some coffee grinds? The whole thing didn't make sense. Then in a second I knew there was no God at all. Just an emptiness filled up by people's fears."

I can't argue with him now because I'm not prepared to examine the consequences of belief myself. Does this mean that I'll have to start going to mass on Sundays and holy days, take communion and confession with the old ladies, stop using profanity as casual punctuation for my sentences, and make use of sex only for the purpose of procreation? And worst of all, will I have to drop my cynicism and cultivate a positive attitude? People live in darkness because they want to, the poet Dante tells us, because they love their sins. For so long the malaise has been my constant companion in life. Can it be that men and women are meant to be happy in the world? It seems unthinkable.

4

These considerations are far too metaphysical for Dr. Abrahamson. He comes into my room twice a day to draw blood, ask a few questions, record a cool scientific observation on the pad clipped to his steel-backed medical clipboard. But this afternoon the doctor has his hands behind his back, his clipboard under his arm, and a pensive look on his face, as if he's trying to get to the bottom of something big.

"And how do we feel today?" he says.

"We feel fine," I say. "Just like yesterday and this morning."

"Oh, yes, I forgot . . ." His voice trails off.

I have managed to get the aluminum-frame window open and sit on the bed in a breeze from the sea, reading a copy of Eugène Sue's *The Wandering Jew*, checked out from the hospital library. It's an unwieldy tome of some twenty-five hundred pages written by a man who for a time during the nineteenth century was the most popular writer in the world. Dr. Abrahamson leans against the windowsill now, blocking my light and air.

"What are you reading?" he says absently.

"*The Wandering Jew*," I say.

"Yes, that's exactly how I've felt these last few days," he says. "I've been wandering this hospital, chasing down your tests, trying to figure out what the hell happened."

"The book's not what you think," I say. "It's a ridiculous nineteenth-century romance in which the lovers get separated and circle the world in opposite directions, only to catch one last glimpse of each other across the Bering Straits —" But he's not listening.

"I just can't figure it out," he says.

"The nun," I say, and put the book aside.

He waves his hand. "A hallucination, a particularly vivid hallucination caused by the fever."

"And the machine and the tubes and the bracelets?"

"One of the nurses must have thought you were dead and disconnected you. She's just afraid to come forward."

"Come on, Doctor. That's pretty negligent. Sounds like lawsuit material to me. Malpractice."

He winces at this comment.

"Just kidding," I say.

"Another thing," he continues. "We can't quite pinpoint the strain of the virus, which depends on successive tests. Your blood was black with the stuff; now it's —"

"Perfect?"

"— normal. You were down South recently, am I right?"

"New Orleans."

"I'll get in touch with public health officials down there. Maybe they can help out with identifying the strain. New Orleans is a port. It could have come from anywhere. A new strain, or mutated. Hepatitis M, hepatitis Z!" He is excited at the prospect. "Did you drink any polluted water on your trip?"

I shrug.

"Eat any raw shellfish?"

I feel a sinking in my stomach. "Shellfish?"

"Yeah, you know. Oysters, clams, mussels, et cetera."

"Yes. An oyster bar."

For a moment he seems disappointed. "O.K., that could explain where you picked up the virus, but it's how you got well that worries me." Then he leaves the room abruptly, still pensive, hands behind his back.

The next day I am released. Dr. Abrahamson walks me downstairs and out into the hospital parking lot, where Rust is waiting with his new-used pickup truck, bought from an artist friend who has just moved to Williamsburg from Austin, Texas. It's a dented 1959 Ford F-100, dusty red and still wearing its Texas truck tags.

Dr. Abrahamson is a good sport. I've stumped

medical science, but he shakes my hand anyway.

"Thanks for your patience, Mr. Conti," he says, "and good luck."

When I am halfway to the truck, he calls me back for a moment. This is difficult for him. He looks up at the neon cross on the facade, looks out at the ocean, then looks back at me.

"Ned," he says, "I am a man educated in the scientific method, I went to Columbia, graduated top of the class in geriatric medicine, I'm a skeptic, a nonpracticing Reform Jew, and I do not believe in miracles. But humor me."

"O.K."

"This nun, did she wear a white and blue outfit and was her skin very, very white?"

"Yes," I say, surprised.

"It's just that a few of the older patients reported seeing her that same night. This woman on the sixth floor, Mrs. Castafiori, says a nun visited her room and helped her get out of bed. Only thing is, the woman's ninety-three, on intravenous and hasn't walked in six months because of a disintegrating hip joint. Now she's walking up and down the terrace under her own steam, eating solid foods. Says she wants to live to see her great-grandson born, and her granddaughter isn't even pregnant. What do you make of that?"

"I don't know," I say, and shrug. It's almost too ridiculous.

"What is this nun, the Virgin Mary or something? Who was, I might add, a nice Jewish girl."

461

"No," I say. "I'm not sure. A saint."

"Which one?"

"She's new," I say. "An unknown."

"There are new saints?"

"Yes. They're coming up all the time."

Dr. Abrahamson and I shake hands again, and I climb into the truck. Rust nods, and we pull out of the parking lot and head back toward town, the beach sky bleached out and mysterious with haze behind.

5

We loop up the Long Island Expressway, the sun setting red behind Manhattan's daunting profile in the distance.

Rust is silent for a while. Then he takes a pair of sunglasses out of a cubbyhole beneath the dash as if they've always been there. This gesture is like a whole conversation. The truck smells of gasoline and brake lining and old truck, is very loud, and vibrates as if it's got a loose engine mount, but just now there isn't any place I'd rather be. I settle happily into the cracked old vinyl as we rattle over the Kosciusko Bridge and Brooklyn lowers just ahead.

"You know, I've been chewing over some of the things you said," Rust says, breaking the loud silence.

"Yeah?"

"I don't mean the crazy stuff about the nun. I mean what you've been saying about getting out, leaving New York."

I wait for him to continue, but I can already see it through the windshield of the truck, prairie storms blowing against green buttes in the spring, red-gold mesas, long, unbroken rows of fence posts, a big dome sky overhead, and the land rolling off to the horizon through air fresh and pure as the breath of a child.

"Thing is, I got a letter from Wyoming the other day. My kid brother just got tossed into jail. They gave him twenty-five years. Supposedly he's out in five with good behavior, but who knows?"

"Jesus," I say. "What happened?"

"Bastard got himself a gutful of whiskey, went into Cheyenne, and shot an Indian in a bar."

"I'm sorry to hear it."

"Yeah, well, I tell you what. My younger brother — Mitch — is an asshole. He's a hell raiser and one ornery drunk. And when he's sober, he's worse. Turns into a smooth-talking, oily son of a bitch. Been married six times now."

The story comes out in bits and pieces. It seems Rust and his brother had a falling-out years ago over the most beautiful girl in Wyoming, Ella Slater, who was elected Miss Wyoming in a contest in Cheyenne in 1967. There was a rivalry that ended in a drunken fight during which Mitch got a gun and shot Rust in the ankle. Rust lifts his foot off the gas for a beat to show me the

463

patched hole in his boot. We slow; a white limousine behind us honks, swerving wildly into the next lane.

"Got a metal pin in my ankle now," he says. "Damn near blew my foot off. But Ella, she still went ahead and married the bastard. I was wearing these same boots at the time. Keep them around just to remind me. Been resoled a hundred times, and every time I put them on, I think about that woman. Mitch and her barely lasted out the year. He beat up on her or some such shit, and Ella wasn't the kind of woman to take it. She went off to Texas and married an oilman. Thing about Mitch, he could always make the ladies laugh. Always telling a joke, pulling some stunt. I'm honest, you know, but I'm a glum son of a bitch. The ladies will take laughter over character any day."

"So you were in love?" I say. The sentiment appears to be universal.

He shrugs. "I was young. She had this blond hair. Wore it in a thick rope down the middle of her back like an Indian girl. In any case I left Wyoming and I stayed away. Because in the end I would have killed the bastard. But now . . ."

"You're going back."

"We've still got fifty-seven hundred acres along the North Platte, west of Douglas, in Converse County. Barley and sugar beets. Belongs to both of us equally, but I left the whole damn spread to him when I took off. It's going into receivership if I don't go back and take care of things. Thought

464

I might try my hand at farming again."

"How long has it been?"

"Shit. Twenty-five years, more."

"Sounds risky."

"Life is risky, pardner. The day you're born, they start figuring the odds."

"Might be right."

"Hell, like you said, how long can you hang out in the same damn bars on the East Side, listening to the same damn songs on the jukebox, watching the same damn cockroach crawl across the same damn tabletop? This city gets dirtier and more dangerous, I get older, and soon I'm one of the lost souls. It's no country for old men, Ned. Look around, and you'll see them by the thousands. Lonely old men riding the subway, sitting on the stool at the end of the bar, nursing the same fifty-year-old beer, same delusions of grandeur running around their head. I've been here fifteen years now. Written four unpublished books. Always told myself that fame and fortune were just around the next corner. Shit. Time to give up. Time to go home."

"You're lucky," I say quietly. "You've got a home to go home to."

He grunts; then he is silent.

6

We pull down the ramp off the BQE as the last light fades. It's just September, but the evening comes quickly, and the violet heat in the sky at dusk is gone, replaced by a mellower, permanent blue, and the city is like an oven cooling. In this part of the country, extremely hot summers are often followed by the deep freeze. Long winters of ice and snow, record colds. September gives New Yorkers time to meditate upon disasters to come.

When we get to Portsmouth Street, I climb up the stairs slowly and open the door to the apartment and stand on the landing for a second, feeling the atmosphere. The place is a wreck, furniture knocked over, sleeping bag still spread out in the middle of the floor, vomit stains on the pink bathroom rug. And only now, home again in the quiet dust in the first gloom of evening, do I think about the ghost, Madeleine. Her story is vague now, like the details of a nightmare, but I don't need the details to know the truth, which is in my bones. She died in this place the year Sister Januarius came to Brooklyn from New Orleans. She died here horribly and unavenged.

Then, directly following this terrible intimation, I know what to do. I clean myself up as quickly as possible, go downstairs, borrow Rust's truck and drive over to the cathedral on Jay Street. The windows of the rectory are dark. I park on

Concord and go around to ring the bell and keep ringing until the housekeeper, whose name is Mrs. Schnadenlaube, pulls back the little glass window peephole and stares out with her usual suspicion.

It appears that Father Rose is off on vacation playing golf until Sunday.

"He'll be back in time for mass," the woman says. "If he's not back, the bishop will have his head." I get the feeling that Mrs. Schnadenlaube does not approve of Father Rose's golfing, and I tell her so.

"What the good father does with his spare time is up to him," she says. "But I've known him to cut services short on holy days so he can watch a tournament on TV. Someday it's going to catch up with the man." She's about to shut the peephole when I tell her I need to get into the crypt.

"To finish my work," I say. "I've been sick, you know, and the deadline for my research is September fifteenth."

Mrs. Schnadenlaube eyes me suspiciously through her thick glasses. At last she wrinkles up her nose. "You're up to something," she says.

I put on my best smile. "Just my work," I say.

The crypt is dark and full of darker gradations of shadows. Out in the vault, the red glimmer of electric votive candles illuminated in honor of the dead by the quarters of the living. Mrs. Schnadenlaube unlocks the iron grate and steps in beside me. Three boxes of archives left unsorted sag in a row against the wall like the monkeys who see, hear, and speak no evil. The rest of the space is covered with piles of documents, labeled and arranged in chronological order.

"Twenty-eight boxes of moldy paperwork cataloged since June, not bad," I say, half to myself.

"And not good either, if you haven't found what the father wanted you to find," Mrs. Schnadenlaube replies tartly.

"Maybe it's not here," I say.

"Maybe you haven't looked hard enough, young man," she says.

"Thank you, Mrs. Schnadenlaube. I'll call you to lock up when I'm done."

"Don't make it too late. At my age, contrary to what they say, you need more sleep, not less."

When she is gone, I drag the three unsorted boxes into the center of the room. Then I crouch down and concentrate. I imagine the sheets of paper buried in the darkness of the boxes, the old solemn phrases scrawled across them, the individual letters of the alphabet hooked together in an archaic hand, all of it one vast cipher, a labyrinth of pen and ink and paper and words.

"Hey, St. Januarius of Brooklyn!" I say. "Thanks for saving me at the hospital. But I've also got one other request. I know there's something here. A scrap I've overlooked. Please show me where it is. Understand, this is for your benefit more than my own."

I squeeze my eyes shut and wait. Nothing. Not a peep from the Other Side. Soon my foot begins to fall asleep, and along with the numbness, I feel rather foolish. Here's a grown man talking to a heap of moldering paper. But just as I am about to rise, defeated, I feel a slight wind on the back of my neck. I turn slowly on my haunches to see one of the neat stacks of correspondence — second pile from the end, front row on the left — begin to flutter and rustle in the cool air. In a moment the pages are blowing across the room, sheet after sheet turning over in a slow, steady breeze which comes from everywhere and nowhere. The other piles are motionless, undisturbed.

I have grown so used to ghostly happenings and miracles and such in the last six months of my life that I feel only the faintest chill at this marvel. Instead I rise and watch the sheets float through the air, hands in my pockets, and begin to understand why God put an end to the Age of Miracles. We mortals have a low tolerance for such things, loaves and fishes multiplying, the dead raised, rods turning into serpents. Life needs to be hard for us, or we will take the marvelous for granted. At last the wind dies down, and there is a dead calm in the crypt. At my feet a single manuscript page flutters, sepia against the dark stone. I bend down to pick it up.

It is a page out of a missing volume of the parish record, written in faded blue ink sometime around the turn of the century. At a glance, in the dim light, I can see that it contains a straightforward account of the death of Sister Januarius, written by Father McCarty, who was the pastor of St. Basil's from 1890 to 1925. Of course, no mention is made of the secret interment or the fresh blossoming cultus. "Sister Januarius, an old and pious nun of long service to the Parish, died in her sleep on October 11, 1919," Father McCarty wrote. "Knowing that death was nigh, in accordance with the rules of her order, Sister Januarius instructed that she be buried in a simple pine box in an unmarked pauper's grave in her nun's habit, along with the Bible she had used for her devotions in life. . . ."

Nothing out of the ordinary here. Certainly nothing to advance Father Rose's case before the cardinals in Rome. Not a single clue or possibility. Not a whisper. Then I pause and read the sheet again.

In the crypt the silence drips like water.

7

The next afternoon I find Mrs. Schnadenlaube watching *The Guiding Light* in the basement of the rectory. This is where they store the seasonal hangings, those bedspread-size appliqué banners which decorate either side of the altar during the mass. They dangle on curtain hooks all around the walls here like the tapestries of dogs playing cards you see hanging on clotheslines at country stores along the Blue Ridge Parkway. Mrs.

Schnadenlaube is perched on the edge of the green tweed couch, one hand clutching the handle of a battered blue Hoover convertible, the other holding a cigarette, its ashes burning unnoticed toward her fingertips.

She's caught up in the florid action of the soap opera with the full devotion of her being. Right now, from what I can tell, there are two plot lines going. A fey young man with a drinking problem has wrecked his parents' Mercedes and is afraid to tell them. Meanwhile, a handsome older man with a beard and a beautiful young woman who apparently hate each other are stranded together on a desert island where, it seems, shenanigans will ensue. A copy of *Soap Opera Digest* is spread open across the coffee table with certain pertinent passages underlined in red ink.

When I try to speak, Mrs. Schnadenlaube doesn't even acknowledge my presence. But she turns toward me angrily during the commercial break. "This is my private time," she says. "The priest himself wouldn't bother me when I'm watching *The Guiding Light*! What the hell do you want?"

"Your help," I say, as earnestly as possible.

She gives me an odd look, and is about to respond, when the soap comes back on the air, and it is as if I have vanished from the room. During the next commercial break I prey on her weakness and ask about the characters and plot. She knows I am patronizing her but, like any

471

true fanatic, cannot resist attempting an explanation. The plot is baffling, as complicated as the sums in an advanced physics textbook. I understand nothing but feign interest. At last it is over, and Mrs. Schnadenlaube clicks off the set with the automatic channel clicker.

"Well?" she says.

I clear my throat and try to sound as official as possible. "I assume that you are responsible for cleaning the rectory and the church?"

"Me and a few others," she says warily. "I've got a crew of Mexican girls comes in on Wednesdays. It's a big place, you know."

"Of course. And what about the crypt? Do you clean the crypt?"

Mrs. Schnadenlaube hesitates. Then she says, "We sweep it out every other week. You'd be surprised the dust that collects down there. But if you're insinuating that somehow, one of us messed up your precious piles of papers —"

I shake my head. "The secret vault," I almost whisper. "I've got to get in there. Do you have the key?"

It turns out that Mrs. Schnadenlaube, Helga, as she tells me to call her now, is a strict Lutheran who has little respect for Catholic superstitions. She attends a bare white Lutheran church in Park Slope, with hard pews and no decorations whatsoever on the walls.

"If you ask me, they should have buried that withered old thing eighty years ago, when she died," she says as we step down into the flagstone corridor which leads to the vault. "It's indecent to keep a human corpse around like a stuffed bird. And those wax eyes. Ugh. They give me the creeps every time."

We are before the door with the Chi-Rho, and she finds the key on her ring and swings it open. There's a protesting creak and that strong smell of must and old bones, but Mrs. Schnadenlaube seems unaffected. She flips on the wall switch, and the Christmas lights wink on around the ceiling, giving the room its cheap tinsel air. The mummified body of Sister Januarius lies still and shrunken in its glass coffin at the center of the room, wax eyes staring into space. Mrs. Schnadenlaube shakes her head at this ghastly relic and steps over to plug an extension cord into a socket in the corner. In a moment we are illuminated in a hard green glow.

"Can't see a thing in here without those on," she says, indicating the fluorescent tubes concealed in an alcove, "but you know Father Rose, he likes the mood lighting. Helps him imagine he's got something here besides a mess of old bones." Then she walks over to the coffin, runs her fingers along the top, and comes up with a thick coating of dust. "Where does the stuff come from, ever ask yourself that? I use Endust and Formula 409, we've always got the door bolted, there are no windows, but . . ." She wiggles her finger in my face.

"Entropy," I say. "Tiny particles of everything.

Dust is the visual evidence of the world itself falling apart."

For a moment her eyes go blank on the other side of the spectacles. Then she shakes her head. "You're just as crazy as the priest," she says.

The lid of the coffin is secured to the sides by eight elaborate bronze brackets held together with alan screws in the leafy engraving. Mrs. Schnadenlaube produces an alan wrench from the band of her orthopedic socks and bends over the first bracket. Then she catches sight of the spider-web strung between the nun's clumpy black shoes and knocks an angry knuckle on the glass. The spider hangs placidly in his web, unaware of the holocaust to come.

"I vacuum in there once every two months," Mrs. Schnadenlaube says, more to the spider than to me. "And still there are bugs. How do they get in there? I'll tell you how! Dead bodies attract all kinds of vermin. The sooner the dead are in the ground, the better!"

I have managed to convince Mrs. Schnadenlaube that as a result of my investigations, Sister Januarius's body will soon be laid in a grave in the churchyard. This suits the woman just fine. We all have our petty annoyances, the irritating details that, added one to the other, somehow conspire to make our life miserable. The removal of even one of them can make it seem like the world is becoming a better place. As Mrs. Schnadenlaube looks at the situation, Sister Januarius's mummy is her responsibility, and she will not let me near the sarcophagus as she works on the screws with her wrench. She bids me lean against the far wall beneath the Christmas lights. It is fifteen minutes before she calls me over to help with the heavy glass lid.

With some effort, we slide it half off one side to the teeth-gritting scrape of glass against glass and surprisingly, the scent of wildflowers.

"I put in one of those stick-um things," Mrs. Schnadenlaube explains. "You should have smelled the old girl before."

"Where did you put it?" I say.

"Don't ask. Now, what is it you want out of here?"

I try not to see the shriveled brown skin, the skeletal teeth. "The old Bible," I say, dry-lipped. "There . . ."

Mrs. Schnadenlaube nods and reaches in to knock out the spiderweb and retrieve the book. We push the lid back into place, and as she once again busies herself with the alan wrench, I step back to examine my treasure.

It is a heavy Douay-Reims translation of the New Testament, printed in Paris toward the last half of the eighteenth century, bound in black morocco and trimmed with cracking gilt. The inside covers are marbleized; the sacred text is three-columned and close printed to save space. And as I suspected, it is a study Bible, printed on heavy vellum, with more than half the pages set aside for private notation and commentary. A cursory look shows these pages are covered from top to bottom with a minuscule feminine hand — large chunks of writing broken only at odd intervals by the interpolation of a few blank spaces and a date. There are many such dates from beginning to end, covering a period of some forty years. Not a day-to-day chronology, exactly, but a diary just the same. The diary of a saint.

I feel the weight and density of this book in my hand. I carefully blow a faint layer of dust off the textured cover and smile.

8

Saturday.

The day is bright and clear and beautiful. September, with its luminous days fading into the amber twilight of last barbecues. The air in the morning is a bit chilly, just enough for a light jacket. The jet stream trails high impassive clouds. The cars of the Long Island Railroad train smell dusty and old.

I get on at Flatbush and get off at Jamaica, Queens, to wait for the transfer on the platform with the rest: mothers and children with umbrellas and picnic lunches; retirees in golf caps; young, attractive Jewish girls, their hair a tangle of curls, hiding behind sunglasses and books; yuppies fresh from the office bringing briefcases full of legal documents, squash racquets under their arms.

Now, sitting on the concrete steps in the shade, I have a vague and comforting sense of déjà vu. This is one of those great repetitions of bourgeois life. Getting out of the city for the day to the countryside, the train pulling into the last station, the dunes near and achingly white, scooped out of light.

I look around and watch the faces. New York faces, hard and yellow and worn by life in the city. They haven't had much time to get away this summer, to breathe some fresh air. The rat race has kept them pent up in the offices, in the stores, on the subway. They seem like characters out of Maupassant, tragic and ironic at the same time. Once I was one of them. Just yesterday. But now I am different, and I fancy that difference burns like a star. In my shoulder bag, padded between a new paperback history of the Mississippi Bubble scandal of 1720 and a two-month-old copy of the *Voice* — the key to my life. The diary of a saint. I want to embrace strangers, shout my discovery from the top of the train. I can hardly suppress my glee.

Suddenly a clean wind blows from the direction of the sea. I fill my lungs with it. The train comes clattering around the curve and slows into the station. The passengers line up along the platform. I hesitate, then push my way toward the front. Do I imagine this, or do people move aside to make way? And the attractive, young Jewish girl with the mop of gold-brown hair, does she lower her copy of Camus and flash me an approving glance above the dark half-moons of her sunglasses?

9

The small station at East Hampton is decorated with a large banner advertising the Rushwick Country Club–Long Island Pro-Am, with the dates in big green letters. Rushwick Country Club is a new facility, opened just two years ago on the grounds surrounding the turn-of-the-century mansion that once belonged to one of New York's oldest families, the Van Rushwicks. The last heir died insane in the late 1980s. After a long court battle the grounds and house were sold to a golf enthusiast–real estate developer who carved eighteen holes out of the property and put up the most modern golfing facility in the state, full of superfluous conveniences like digital ball washers and electronic scorecards.

I board the shuttle bus to the tournament with a small group of golf fanatics, older men and women wearing green-visored caps and exaggerated golfing attire. They seem quite excited and hold hands like teenagers. We roll for twenty minutes through the green and even countryside and approach the Van Rushwick estate through an alley of oaks that reminds me of plantations in Louisiana. There is a great iron gate between brick and mortar posterns, the glimpse of green lawns extending to the horizon, and somewhere the sound of cheering.

When we disembark, it is like stepping off the bus into paradise. We advance in awe to the ticket booth and pay the thirty-five dollar admission fee without blinking an eye. It seems a reasonable price on such a beautiful day, in such a green and precious park. Then I follow the crowds around the brick bulk of the old mansion, its dark side sladdered with scaffolding. "They're turning the place into a fancy hotel for golfers," I hear one of the old ladies say, "with close-circuit monitoring of the greens and underground parking, so as not to spoil the effect." We pass through a second set of turnstiles, where a dour young man with a walkie-talkie and a Rushwick CC polo shirt checks my bag.

"What are you looking for?" I say as he paws through my books, a scowl on his face.

"Automatic weapons, explosives, alcoholic beverages. In that order," he says.

"Have you had problems out here?"

"You never know, sir," he says, eyeing me narrowly. "There are lunatics everywhere." Then he pulls Sister Januarius's Bible out into the air.

"Be careful with that," I say.

"What is it?" he says.

"A Bible."

"You're not one of these born-again Christian nuts, are you? They can be dangerous. We had one start witnessing last year from the gallery in the middle of the seventh hole, and the golfer missed his putt. That really sucked."

"Don't worry," I say. "I'm a Catholic. We're pretty quiet."

He scowls and flips through the Bible and hands it back. "A book like that, you could use as a weapon. Don't they make smaller editions?"

I shrug. He hesitates but lets me through.

For the next two hours I wander the course, dazzled by the sumptuous landscape. Along the way I see several birdies, two eagles, and three bogies. On the greens the pros lean over their putters as if in prayer, caddies bowed at a respectful distance. The sand traps loom like open mouths. It's not so much the game itself, the primitive sexual dynamics of ball and hole and club, as the whole beautiful setting: gemlike greens in oceans of grass, trees swaying in the breeze, the warmth of the last sun, and the spectators hushed and respectful, like the crowds at a coronation.

When I find Father Rose, he is stuck in the dogleg of the thirteenth hole, trying to hack his way out of the rough. He has abandoned his mock-Jesuit simplicity today. Indeed, there is nothing of the priest about him. He wears a fashionable 1920s-style golfing ensemble, with tweed knee pants, yellow argyle socks, two-tone brogues, an argyle sweater, and a tweed cap. He studies the lie for a few minutes, gestures to his caddie for a nine iron, and knocks the ball into a clump of willows seventy-five yards to the west. He swears, goes red in the face. I can almost imagine him breaking the club over one knee. On the big board he ranks 110th out of a field of 112.

I wait till he's up on the green, three shots later, and staring down a double bogie, his next putt a nearly impossible forty-footer. I tear a page out of my notebook and write, "Father Rose: It might help your game to know that Brooklyn has its saint, with a miracle or two thrown into the bargain — Ned C.," and send it through a greensman.

Meanwhile, the famous Armenian golfer Pulan Lazikian, who's playing along with Father Rose, bends for his marker and replaces his ball for a twenty-foot putt. He squints at the hole for a moment, then putts with the calm assurance of a professional. The white ball inscribes a gentle arc on the grass, looks good up to the last foot or so, but jogs off to the left. The gallery lets out a disappointed murmur. Lazikian's just lost himself a half million dollars and the tie for first. Father Rose pulls himself away from this drama to read my note. Then he scowls, takes a pencil out of his pocket, scribbles a response on the back, and sends it back to me.

"Right now I'm not a priest, I'm a golfer," the note says. "And as a golfer, I resent the intrusion on my game. You can talk to the priest following the tournament this afternoon on the terrace of the clubhouse."

After this he seems nervous but, moments later, sinks the impossible putt in a single dazzling stroke.

10

The terrace of the clubhouse is kidney-shaped and half an acre wide, paved in polished fieldstone of alternating grays. The clubhouse itself, a massive bungalow of timber, stone, and glass, recalls Frank Lloyd Wright's Falling Water. There is the smell of night in the air, of cut grass and the loamy dark beneath the bushes. The tables are packed with golfers and entourage, relaxing over drinks in the first calm light of dusk. For some reason, mariachi music filters through the loudspeaker as if one of the Mexican busboys has commandeered the sound system. The rattle of the tinny horns and accordion mixed with the sound of male laughter and the clink of glasses makes me think of a cantina in a border town and the raw stink of tequila.

When I find Father Rose, he is slumped alone over a Bloody Mary at a small table in the far corner. Lithe girls in aprons move back and forth, silent as elves with their trays full of glasses. A cold wind blows from the sea. He motions for me to sit down. He stirs his Bloody Mary with a celery stick and will not meet my eyes. I wait for him to speak.

"It's been a rough day," he says after a while. "I've got to face it. I'm not much of a golfer anymore."

He finished 108th, improving his standing somewhat in the latter part of the afternoon.

"Come on, Father," I say. "There were a couple of good shots there. I saw one excellent putt."

He waves me off. "Sometimes I think golf is a worse vice for a priest than having a mistress from his congregation or sleeping with the altar boys," he says. "Wanting to win as much as I do, it's a sin. I tell myself the obsession won't matter if I pledge my winnings to the church. No, that's not true. What I really think is that if I pledge my winnings to the church, a miracle might happen and I might make the top five."

"A miracle did happen, Father," I say, smiling.

He raises his eyes wearily. "All right, what have you got for me?"

I pause dramatically, then take Sister Januarius's Bible out of the book bag and set it on the table, where it sits heavy and dark as a slab of beef.

Father Rose recognizes the book instantly and is aghast. "You didn't" — he can hardly find the words — "desecrate the resting place of —"

"Please, Father, hear me out." I tell him about the miracles in the hospital, and I tell him about the ghost, about Madeleine de Prasères de la Roca, and about Albane d'Aurevilley, how one became a prostitute and the other a nun who took the name of the martyr Januarius. The light fades in the west over the dark hills. The night comes on. The lithe girls bring out heat lamps and place them here and there on the patio to take the chill off the ocean breeze.

"Mr. Conti," Father Rose says at last, "I've got to tell you that I don't believe in ghosts."

"How can you believe in saints and miracles and not believe in ghosts?"

"Let me put it a different way. The Congregation of Rites in Rome, they don't believe in ghosts. They're a pretty hard-nosed bunch. Lawyers in red hats. 'You heard all of this from someone who heard it from a ghost?' they're going to say to me. 'What kind of proof is that?' I'll be laughed right out of the Vatican."

"Don't worry, it's all down here, the whole thing," I say, tapping the Bible. "In nineteenth-century ink, in a nineteenth-century hand on eighteenth-century paper, authentic, verifiable. A saint's own story, a valuable historical document. She turned stones into cheese, made the blind see, the lame walk. She started out a weird little girl in the possession of unfocused spiritual powers and hoed a long row to God. God came to her in little bits, in flashes, like artistic inspiration. She groped her way toward Him; she made many mistakes. But there was one big, unforgivable mistake when she already knew better, right at the beginning of her saintly career in Brooklyn. And because of it, she kept a soul imprisoned between the four walls of my apartment for a hundred and forty-odd years."

The priest drains off his third Bloody Mary

and munches noisily on his celery stick as I open the Bible to the relevant passages and summarize.

Remorseful over her part in the murder of the quadroon Esteban de Vasconcellos, Albane d'Aurevilley took the veil in New Orleans in 1842 and became Sister Januarius of the Nursing Sisters of the Cross.

At first Sister Januarius's faith was weak, and she thought only of Esteban, her lost love: how he betrayed her with Cousin Madeleine and how he was brutally killed because of her own vindictive jealousy. But during the rigorous novitiate she changed. Gradually Sister Januarius's heart emptied of despair and self-interest and filled with selflessness and religious ardor. Then, one night in the spring of her second year as a novice, she was visited in her dreams by the Virgin Mary and told that St. Benedict and St. Teresa of Ávila would be her patrons and that it was required of her to use her special abilities for the glory of God. So she prayed and fasted and was granted the power to heal and work wonders.

Meanwhile, Madeleine de Prasères de la Roca's unexplained absence from society was the talk of New Orleans. Her husband, Don André, let it be known that his wife had gone to a spa in Europe for the treatment of a nervous condition. But there were still many rumors, and Don André killed two young men beneath the Dueling Oaks for idle speculation on the matter.

The night before Sister Januarius's final vows, St. Benedict and St. Teresa of Ávila visited her in the shape of hummingbirds and revealed to her the whereabouts of her cousin. Madeleine languished in a place far from God called Brooklyn, they said. Go to her and help her to know that God is merciful.

A year later Sister Januarius received permission from the bishop to serve as an uncloistered nun at St. Basil's, then an impoverished new parish with a congregation of Irish immigrants. Guided by the voices of her saints, she traveled north and eventually found Madeleine in squalid rooms in a prostitutes' quarter near the Molasses Hill docks. But poor Madeleine was in awful shape, already half eaten away with a suitably biblical disease — leprosy.

"What's the point of this gruesome tale?" Father Rose interrupts. He waves to the waitress for another Bloody Mary.

"You'll see, Father," I say, and bend my head to the crabbed handwriting in the dull light of the terrace and begin to read.

11

1847 — 6 Aug. — *I have done my best to alleviate my poor cousin's suffering, a task set before me by the Almighty to strengthen my soul for the work which is ahead. The doctors will not come any longer & have ceased sending their medicines because there is no money left & I must wrap and bathe her* *lesions myself. The stench is terrible. Poor Madeleine's limbs are rotting on the bone; her hair is falling out. She clings to her hatred of her husband like a drowning man to a bit of wreckage & she no longer believes in God or Salvation. I tell her that suffering should not deter her faith, that even suffering is a gift from an Almighty & Merciful God, so that in the next life we may appreciate Paradise more thoroughly. She laughs at me, and the sound of her laughter is terrible, the sound of the Prince of Deceivers laughing in the Wilderness of Hell. She also uses profane language and abuses me in the most licentious manner possible — blasphemies learned in her life as a whore.*

Try as I might, I cannot feel Christian Love or Sympathy for her & I know that this is a grave & perhaps a mortal sin; we are abjured to love those who have wronged us, as is written in the Scripture. I have not turned my mind to my dear lover Esteban in a long while, but now I think of him again daily, and I think of the seven times we had carnal union — twice in the garden, once in his room on the upper gallery, once in my dressing room on the lower, twice on a couch in the library, once in Papa Prasères's tilbury the afternoon we took a drive through the countryside — all before Cousin Madeleine seduced him away and took him from me. Yes, I know I endangered my soul with these acts of physical love — indeed, of adultery — and I have repented of them, yet I can't help it. I still despise Madeleine for her treachery.

Yesterday I walked with glass in my shoes until

my feet were bloody to repent for my failure to forgive her.

8 Aug. — *In the few lucid hours she still possesses, Cousin Madeleine is engaged in a bizarre and copious correspondence with Mr. Bleekman, a lawyer who keeps offices on Manhattan Island across the river. She lost the use of two fingers yesterday and now asks me to tie the pen to her hand. This correspondence — which she will not let me set eyes upon — she lowers out the window in a basket to a slatternly Negress who conveys it to Manhattan on the ferry that docks at the base of Fulton Street. The gentleman's replies are delivered by a young clerk who refuses to come any closer than the foot of the stairwell.*

I have inquired many times as to the purpose of all this frantic note carrying, but my cousin will only smile in a most sinister manner and reply that she is making arrangements for her journey home to Louisiana. God deliver her from such painful delusions! She would never survive such an arduous trek. I fear she has gone mad. Then I see the fierce light in her eyes, and I think instead that she is plotting something terrible to take place upon the event of her death.

12 Aug. — *Madeleine is now in the grips of the most hideous pain, which I see as God's judgment upon her. I offer an opium elixir to dull her sufferings, but she refuses & says she prefers to keep her intellect clear for her work, which is not yet done. Such incredible strength of purpose! Yet she refuses to accept God's Mercy & confess her Sins. This ob-*

stinacy greatly troubles me, for by it she shall lose her Immortal Soul! I explain to her that she will be denied the Sacrament of Extreme Unction at the End & consequently suffer the torments of Hell, but she does not appear greatly moved by this warning. The stench grows worse here; the air full of the reek of rotting flesh and excrement. And I console myself with these words from the prophet Isaiah — "My decline draws near speedily, My Salvation has gone forth, Lift up mine eyes to the Heavens!"

15 Aug. — *Much to my shame, Cousin Madeleine still denies the Light of God's Mercy. O Saints and Angels, give me strength to wrestle with the Prince of Deceivers, who holds sway over her weary soul! I have many conversations with her on the subject of her Salvation, all to no avail. She mocks me as I kneel at her bedside to pray for her & she often taunts me with descriptions of her lovemaking with Esteban — tho I do not believe she has any intelligence of my own activities in that realm & shall keep silent so as not to add to her suffering. St. Benedict and St. Teresa of Ávila have not come to me in the guise of hummingbirds for some time. I think they have been driven away by the stink of my Cousin's evil & unrepentant heart.*

17 Aug. — *Today I discovered that Cousin Madeleine has added suicide to the long catalog of her sins, which include whoring & adultery, & as always, I tremble for her immortal soul. She has told me that she contracted the leprosy last year, by whoring with sailors on a clipper from China quarantined in the harbor; the sailors have all since died of the*

489

disease. Every night for weeks Madeleine spirited herself out to the ship & threw herself upon her back & whored & whored until she had carried off all the gold the poor wretches possessed. A month or so afterwards she began showing the first signs of putrefaction, which appears as hard red welts up the skin. Tears in my eyes, I begged her to reveal her motivations to me. Had she grown tired of life? "I did it for the money," she said, & turned her face to the wall & would not hear anymore, tho I took out my New Testament and read from Matthew 8, in which Christ Our Lord heals the sinful and the sick — "Behold a leper came to him and knelt before him, saying, Lord, if you will, you can make me clean. And immediately his leprosy was cleansed."

20 Aug. — My cousin grows daily weaker and less observant & I have at last intercepted a few pieces of her correspondence with the Hon. Mr. Bleekman Esq. of Manhattan & am beginning to apprehend the shape of her awful plot. My soul is frozen by this intelligence! It is too horrible! Madeleine has sacrificed her life on the altar of vengeance & intends to wreak a terrible punishment upon her husband for the death of my dear Esteban! The plot is diabolical, worthy of the Great Deceiver himself! She mentions a large sum put aside to assist her efforts, profits gained from her whoring over the course of these last black, sinful years. I believe it to be more than five thousand dollars in gold coin, which she keeps in a strongbox beneath the bed.

As I understand them, the particulars are these:

Madeleine has already purchased the construction of a peculiar funerary memorial, an obelisk of black marble inscribed only with her name and profession in no uncertain terms — WHORE — & she has entered into an agreement with this lawyer Bleekman to arrange all other salient details after her death. The obelisk will be shipped alongside her corpse back to New Orleans, where the newspapers are to be provided with a lurid account of her sinful life and putrid death. Once she is there, the agreement calls for the memorial to be raised with great pomp in the St. Louis Cemetery on Royal Street. Masses are to be said at the cathedral while her corpse, installed in a magnificent coffin, journeys downriver in a grand funerary flotilla to its final resting place in the crypt at Belle Azure.

Cousin Madeleine has calculated all this for the greatest possible public notoriety. She rightly supposes that our city will long talk of these events, for which good Creole would miss such an ostentatious funeral? And who will not read the account of it in L'Abeille and Le Courier de la Louisiane? In this way Madeleine's fate will become generally known & her fantastic revenge achieved in a single stroke. Don André's monstrous pride will be wounded beyond repair & his family honor destroyed. A descendant of the grandees of Spain married to a whore! The populace will talk of nothing else! He will be made a laughingstock, this proud and pompous Spaniard! His challenges will not be accepted — & that alone is a mortification worse than death to such an avid duelist as Don André; he will be ridiculed out of

Society. Madeleine's plot is indeed ingenious & will pierce that puffed-up, murderous man to the quick. But bought at such a terrible price! Bought with sin and with death! Bought with her body's horrible sufferings & with the doom of her immortal Soul!

I weep for her and meditate upon these words inscribed in Lamentations, 3:25 — "The steadfast love of the LORD never ceases, his mercies never come to an end, they are new every morning. The LORD is my Portion, says my Soul. Therefore I will hope in Him —" Oh, St. Benedict & St. Teresa, come to me! Why have you been so silent? Give me the strength to make Madeleine see the error of her ways!

25 Aug. — My cousin's affliction has taken a sudden turn for the worse. She cannot lift her arms & her extremities are little more than Gangrenous stubs. A fever rages in her body & she lies in her own filth without moving. I swoon from the stench & must wear a cotton mask soaked in camphor to bear a moment at her bedside. The end is only a day or two away, & still she fights fiercely for life. Such resolve! Were it only put to good use! Did our Lord suffer as much upon the Cross? This thought is sheer Blasphemy, but it seems Madeleine's suffering could redeem a thousand souls from Hell — though now it suffices to send one soul to its Eternal Perdition.

St. Benedict & St. Teresa keep their Holy Silence. Is it because they know there is no real Love in my heart for my cousin Madeleine? I saw two hummingbirds yesterday hovering about one of the fig trees that spring up along the sidewalk in this poor neighborhood, and my heart leapt — I held out a hand as a perch, and the delicate, feathery creatures hovered above my palm there for a moment, so close I could feel the breeze stirred by the beating of their tiny wings, but they had nothing to say & were only poor feathered creatures of this world.

26 Aug. — *Today I see the terror in Madeleine's eyes & I must confess to my shame that it gives me a satisfaction that blackens my soul. It is not the terror of death that has her by the throat. No, she is brave, far braver than I! Instead she is haunted by the fear that she will die before her plans for Revenge come to full fruition & I say to her, Yea, the Almighty often intervenes in the best-laid works of men, and at these words, she trembles with fear. For the disease has now caught her with a singular necessity still undone — namely, this — She has yet to pay for any of her complicated arrangements! The lawyer Bleekman she maintained till now on a retainer, intending to transfer the bulk of her monies presently. But Death has no respect for schedules, no regard for carefully made plans & the five thousand dollars in gold coin rest as yet in the strongbox beneath her bed.*

Today she was too weak to compose any more of her letters, and begged me to send for Mr. Bleekman's messenger or, failing this, to hand over the gold to him upon her demise. I refused her sinful request outright. I cannot allow her plot to go forward — Revenge is mine, saith the Lord! D.V. tomorrow

I shall call in Father Collins from St. Basil's to hear her confession. D.V. perhaps we may yet save her immortal soul.

27 Aug. — *My cousin lives, though she is out of her head with fever most of the time. In rare periods of lucidity she calls on me in a most piteous manner to pay the lawyer what is still owed. She pleads with me; then she turns face & abuses & berates me in the foulest manner imaginable; then she weeps like a child. She blames me for the wrongs of her life. She tells me that I stole the love of her dear papa from her the day I entered the house at Belle Azure, a poor and friendless orphan; she tells me I am responsible for the death of Esteban & that now I steal away her Rightful Vengeance. It is useless to protest against her, to tell her if I have wronged her, I have repented of it, to tell her not to doom her immortal Soul on my account, but her heart will not hear the words. She utters many blasphemies as I try to offer her comfort in her last hours, and I reply with a verse from Acts 8 — "Repent therefore of this wickedness of yours, & pray to the* LORD *that the intent of your heart may be forgiven you. For I see that you are in the Gall of Bitterness & in the Bond of Iniquity."*

31 Aug. — *It has happened. Madeleine is dead at last.*

She died unshriven of her sins & painfully in the black hours of the morning, and I fear that her soul will know the Torments of Hell. She fought with me to the last, and before she died, heaped more insults & curses upon me. Of course, God's

Mercy is infinite, only He knows where True Justice lies & perhaps he will find a way to bring Madeleine to the Light.

I walked in the garden of the church afterward, beneath a brooding sky, praying to the Saints for advice again. They were silent. As I am Madeleine's closest surviving relative, her whore's gold is mine now, to dispose of as I will. I am convinced of the simple truth that it is immoral to spend five thousand dollars on a single woman's Vengeance when the sum might be used to alleviate the suffering of so many families in this poor parish — & yet my conscience is troubled and confused.

The boy came yesterday from Bleekman, asking for the first payment of monies. I hesitated, then told him to return on Tuesday next for my answer. I cry out to the Saints for guidance; they will not speak. Is this a test of my own Soul? Oh, Lord, what shall I do?

12

The last light has sunk under the dark bulk of the continent to the west. It is too dark to read anymore. I close the Bible, its heavy vellum pages stiff with age.

"You can't just stop there," Father Rose says as I put the book away. "What did she do?" His eyes are red in the red light of the heat lamps.

"We have a restless ghost on our hands and a saint that never became a saint. What do you think she did?"

Father Rose considers for a minute. He folds and unfolds his hands on the metal tabletop. The Mexican music floats into the darkness. The clubhouse is lit up like an ocean liner. "I think that Sister Januarius acted for the good of the parish community," he says at last. "She put the needs of the many over the whims of the one. She did the right thing."

I shrug. "Sister Januarius took money that did not belong to her, money earned through great suffering and marked for a special purpose. As a consequence, Madeleine de Prasères is buried in the churchyard at St. Basil's and not at Belle Azure, where she belongs. You know the black obelisk; it looks so out of place among all the other, humbler tombstones. You've hit the thing with many a practice ball. I went out to look at it yesterday. The word *Repentant* was added to the word *Whore* by Sister Januarius after Madeleine's death, carved in a different hand by someone unaware that the addition was something of a grim joke. The five thousand dollars were used to rebuild the church when it was burned down again by the anti-Catholic mob of Know-Nothings in 1848. You know the rest."

Father Rose hesitates, but his mouth is drawn down stubbornly at the corners. "According to you, Sister Januarius is currently working miracles," he says. "Appearing in hospitals. Appearing to you" — he seems a little rueful at this — "curing diseases, fixing hip joints. These are the actions of a woman blessed by God, a saint."

"Yes, but she's not a saint yet," I say. "You know better than I do that's up to Rome. She made a bad mistake with Madeleine, an unsaint-like error in judgment. And it seems to me she has been working for a long time to repair the damage caused by her error. To tell the truth, I felt something when I moved into the apartment years ago, something I did my best to ignore. Not just the ghost, something else waiting. A guiding presence. Now I know it was Sister Januarius, waiting patiently for the pieces to fall into place. Waiting for human agents to help her finish her work in the world, to help her repair the wrong she did to her cousin in life. Those agents are us, Father."

"You're kidding," he says.

I shake my head.

"You're talking about an exhumation."

I am silent.

"That sort of thing requires a dozen different permits and is very expensive."

I am silent.

"But who is going to care if a skeleton comes home to rest? Everyone concerned in this terrible story is gone. Dead a hundred-odd years! The woman's husband, her friends, her family —"

"Madeleine de Prasères de la Roca's descendants live in Louisiana still," I say quietly. "I've seen the crypt at Belle Azure. I know the family pretty well."

Father Rose is surprised at this. "You do?"

"Yes. And I think that's why I was chosen for this . . . work. I think you'll agree there is something here, Father. A divine symmetry. A coming together of lives."

Father Rose thinks this over for a while. He drains the last of his drink. The sky glows faintly orange in the direction of New York. Winter is coming.

Then, suddenly, he throws up his hands. "What do you want me to do?" he says.

I smile.

13

The apartment ticks quiet and empty at midnight. They've changed the bulbs in the spotlights on the facade of the power plant across the street, and now an opal fluorescence floods my dusty rooms.

For a while I sit in this bright darkness with a beer in the orange Naugahyde chair and watch a baseball game sound off, on television. The Detroit Tigers are playing the Cleveland Indians in an unlikely pennant race that sounds like something out of *The Jungle Book*. I can still smell the dark moon of the golf course in my clothes, and the priest's uncertainty. But now I know that everything the last ten years has led up to this quiet midnight, this dusty silence. I hold my breath. What next?

It is not till I am in my striped pajamas and about to retire that I notice the number flashing on the answering machine. A single message. I replay it three times, then make ready for a journey in the morning.

14

The 8:20 A.M. train from Penn Station pulls into Philadelphia Thirtieth Street at ten o'clock. I am forced to use the public bathroom in the station and find to my dismay that some madman has taken a crap in the urinal.

Philadelphia is a gloomy city, mute and crumbling, its great days as the first capital of the Republic long forgotten. One hears of the most gruesome murders committed here — remember the man who mutilated and ate a half dozen retarded girls in his basement? And the other one, in whose apartment they found nine bodies buried in waist-deep trash? It is no longer possible to imagine the calm cobbled thoroughfares upon which Dr. Franklin once walked, munching his crust of bread, the future like a bright animal waiting just around the corner from Chestnut Street.

On impulse, I decide to catch a cab from the

station. This proves to be a mistake. The driver takes me on a long and roundabout route through bad neighborhoods and over half the rutted streets in town. According to his registration, he is a Rwandan named Mboku Himombatu. Tribal scars slash across his cheeks. He refuses to answer questions and plays weird music full of wooden gongs and silences at top volume as we bump over nameless streets, beneath the rusty elevated and past bombed-out buildings rotting on either side like bad teeth.

I see half naked urchins playing in piles of garbage, police in leather jackets arresting a dozen suspects lined up against the wall. A man wearing only boxer shorts and combat boots walks barefoot along the stained concrete median, a nickel plated automatic strapped to his waist. From all around comes the high wail of sirens, and I reflect that our cities have become as foreign and dangerous as Kabul was to Cavagnari in the last century, as unknown as Timbuktu to Mungo Park. Blank spaces on the map under the sway of strange and savage tribes, where life is cheap, law is unknown, and wild, inexplicable passions rule the mob.

But at last we are out of the city on the Main Line, and we turn down a fine neighborhood of tree-lined avenues, Saabs and Mercedes-Benzes parked casually on the drives of beautiful large homes. The sky above is overcast, heavy as lead. A light rain begins to fall, speckling the windshield with tiny black beads. We stop before an ivy covered gate. A guard post and high brick wall follow the curve of the street. The tops of mimosa trees inside wave over barbed wire. The driver turns around.

"Sixty-seven dollars," he says. The Bryn Mawr train stop is no more than five blocks away. I could have made the same trip for a lot less. I tell him so.

"You come over here," he explains. "Main Line swank, you know? I figure you for a rich white man. Sixty-seven dollars is nothing to a rich white man."

I pull out my pockets to show him a few crumpled dollar bills and change. After a half hour of haggling, I get the price down to $12.50, plus a 15 percent tip.

They are expecting me at the guardhouse. I am buzzed in and crunch slowly up the long gravel drive. A large Georgian style main building with portico and cupola stands correct as a retired officer at the center of outbuildings arranged around a quad. In the days when Anglo-Saxon rectitude was deemed a virtue, this place used to be an exclusive finishing school for girls of wealthy Main Line families. They were taught how to walk and speak properly, how far to go on first, second, and third dates, which opinions were expressible at the dinner table, which were not. Upon graduation they were given a set of wedding china bearing the school crest and the single-word motto *Modesty* in Latin. All that is gone forever.

The school was sold in the sixties and has since

become one of the most highly regarded and exclusive sanitariums in the country, more fashionable with celebrities than the Betty Ford Clinic. Well known movie stars, whose names shall not be mentioned, check in for the treatment. Rock stars are a fixture, as are certain European princes whose families have been prey to congenital weaknesses since the days of Louis XV. More like a country club than a hospital — with private rooms, valets, and personal diagnosticians — still, the success rate here is undeniable. Two months sequestered inside these ivied walls, stuck with hypodermics, analyzed, and dieted, and the substance-abusing patient is clean for a good decade to come.

Behind the main building a football field–sized oval of grass slopes gently to a pond full of ducks and other migrating birds. I am taken out by a pretty nurse whose name tag identifies her as Ms. Longbutt, though ironically, her behind beneath the tight starched uniform is round and dimpled as a peach. The nurses here look like nurses from a film, down to the white hats, short white dresses, white shoes, and Red Cross pins in their lapels. Such familiarity I suppose is comforting for the inmates, a few of whom lounge outside now in lawn chairs despite the slight pattering of rain.

I find Antoinette down near the water's edge. She's sitting stiffly in a wheelchair, is wrapped in a blanket though the temperature is nearly seventy degrees. A few ducks nestle at her feet.

They waddle away as I approach.

"Antoinette?"

Her head above the rumpled mass of blanket looks small and childlike. Her hair hangs limp and dry to her shoulders. She hardly looks up, her eyes are fixed on the green water of the pond.

"I guess you got my message," she says, a distance in her voice.

"Are you all right?"

"I'm fine."

"Then why the wheelchair?"

"The lawn chairs were all wet, so I got in a wheelchair up at the hospital and wheeled myself down. I kind of like wheelchairs, actually. Makes me feel like I've got something real to recover from."

But I'm still not convinced, so she leaps up, the blanket falling from her shoulders, and swings her arms out and does a chorus line kick toward the pond. She's wearing an old pullover full of holes that used to belong to Papa, and she's lost a lot of weight. She's got that tired, ribby look I remember from Jillian's anorexic days. When she's settled back down again with the blanket, she says, "See? How was that?" but she still won't meet my eyes.

I am silent. I come around and squat in the wet grass by her side, my knees creaking. "I've got a few things to tell you," I say. "A couple of very strange stories. First, let's start with those oysters we ate at —"

"Papa died." She interrupts suddenly. Then she

bites her bottom lip and pulls the blanket tight around her throat.

"I'm very sorry. When?"

"A month ago, right after you left. He just dropped dead, like that." She snaps her fingers. "He and Mama were watching television, and he sort of stood up and coughed, then fell back on the couch, unconscious. Some kind of heart attack. Poor Mama, she didn't know what to do. She thumped on his chest, tried to give him mouth-to-mouth, nothing. It took fifteen minutes for the paramedics to get there, and he had pretty much stopped breathing. But then — and this is the worst part — the bastards, they kept him alive on life support for ten days like some kind of goddamned vegetable. It was awful, Ned. I sat with Mama in the hospital the whole time. We watched him and held his hand, but he wasn't there. He was dead as a stone. Just kept breathing by those awful machines."

"Yes, I know how that is."

"Then Jolie and Manon, they came in and actually started arguing about who was going to get what in the will. I couldn't believe it! Papa lying there, and all they can think about is money. Know what I did?" Now she looks at me, and there is a slight gleam in her eye.

"What?"

"I stood up without saying a word, and I punched Manon in the gut, I mean hard! Then I gave Jolie a nice backhand right across the face, and her lip split open. They took off pretty quick after that, I'll tell you."

Antoinette's glee is momentary. In a moment the gleam fades, and she goes back to staring at the pond. We are silent for a while. The ducks bob motionless on the surface, like decoys of themselves.

"So why are you here?" I say at last. She frowns, squirms in her wheelchair, pulls the blanket tight.

"I OD'd," she almost whispers.

"On what?"

"On Hash's little yellow pills, that's what. After the funeral I just started eating them like candy. It was terrible. Couldn't face things with Papa gone. And no one in the family would talk to me after I socked Manon and Jolie in the hospital. I mean, they were in shock; they thought I was going nuts or something. I can't explain it, but Papa was my standard. I guess I measured myself by what he thought, and when he was gone, I just cut loose. At least that's what the doctors here say."

"What do you say?" My foot is fast asleep, so I take off my jacket and put it on the grass and sit by her side.

"What do I say?" She hesitates. "I guess for a minute there I wanted to die."

"So you tried to commit suicide?"

She squirms in the wheelchair. "Not exactly. I just took a whole lot of the yellow pills."

"How many?"

"Fifty, sixty. I don't know, I kept taking them, just to see what would happen. I just kept swallowing, and before I knew it, I had taken the whole batch. I remember a lot of light and loud noises and wandering around the Quarter at four in the morning. Then I remember this weird blue color, then nothing. I woke up in New Orleans General while my stomach was being pumped. They said it was a good thing I passed out face first in the gutter because otherwise I would have choked to death on my own vomit like Jimi Hendrix. That's what saved me, though. I puked up most of the pills; my stomach couldn't digest them fast enough."

Now from over the wall the sound of a car backfiring, and in a great rush of wings, the ducks rise from the pond into the air like a flock of pigeons. We watch them ascend toward the clouds, flapping and bickering among themselves; then they wheel around and alight in the pond again to float and paddle as placidly as before. In the next minute, over Philadelphia and the Schuykill, the heavy gray shifts a little. A few bright theatrical rays of sun break through here and there; then all is gray and heavy again.

"You should have called me," I say. "I waited for you to call; then I thought you'd never call again. You should have called the minute your father died. He was a good man. I would have come down for the funeral. Shit. You should have called me before you took all those pills. Shit."

"I was scared at first," Antoinette says, a catch in her voice, "because I didn't really know how I felt about you; then I decided and I did call.

I called ten, fifteen times, but all I could get was your answering machine. I called in the morning, and I called at night. I couldn't leave a message until yesterday. I wanted to talk to you, to see if you were mad at me for — for letting you down again like I did ten years ago."

I reach for her hand beneath the blanket and give it a squeeze before she pulls it away.

"No, listen, please." This is very hard for her. "I called, but you weren't there. Then I couldn't think anymore, and I took the pills."

"If you had died, Antoinette, my God! I wouldn't —" But she shakes her head and turns away from me, a flush of color in her pale cheeks.

"I've got something else to tell you now," she says. "Something I haven't told the doctors or the therapists that they keep sending to my room here. Something about Dothan. And I don't want you to talk before I'm through, O.K.?"

"O.K."

"The real reason why I left Dothan the first time when I was a kid and we were living together in Spanish Town is that I got pregnant and he made me get an abortion, and the abortion went bad. We went to the clinic in Baton Rouge, and they scraped it out or whatever they do, and afterwards — I don't know why, maybe because it was a nice day — we went fishing on the river. Fishing, can you believe it! So, there we were in this aluminum outboard in the middle of the Mississippi, and he was spearing some night crawlers on his hook — they were still alive and wiggling, you know — and I started to hemorrhage. I felt this wet feeling between my legs, and I looked down, and the whole front of my dress was red. It was like my insides were leaking out. Dothan rowed like hell for the shore, but the bottom of the boat filled up with blood, and I passed out. Then he threw me in the car like a sack of feed and raced at top speed to the hospital. By the time we got to the emergency room, I was stone white. I had lost half my blood or something. Ruined the car — this stolen Corvette he drove around back then. They gave me a transfusion and patched me up, and I was all right in a few days, but shit, I came this close.

"I'm telling you all this, Ned, not to give you another chapter of my sufferings, but to explain myself to you. Why I have such a hard time being really intimate with someone, what the doctors here call emotionally unavailable. Why I just close up when we start getting close. Ever since that abortion thing, it seems I haven't been able to trust anyone at all. I was close to Dothan, I loved him, and I wanted to keep the baby and get married, but he said I was too young. So I got the abortion and almost died, and it wrecked me. I never told anyone this story, not even Papa. It seems like my life was broken by what happened. Afterward I was old suddenly, and there was this whole half of myself locked away in cold storage somewhere.

"Papa knew something had happened, of course.

I think he sensed that something was different about me, but he never knew exactly what it was. I didn't know myself maybe, until he died. . . ."

She is crying now, the tears rolling off the end of her nose and her chin and spotting the blanket. I try to reach up and take her in my arms, but she holds me off with a hand on my shoulder.

"So I can't promise you anything," she says. "I can't tell you that everything will be all right, that I will ever be completely O.K. I can't tell you that I'll never take any of the pills again, that I'll never feel sad and shut off from everyone —"

This time I won't let her finish. I've got my arms around her up under the blanket, which falls away like a layer of old skin, and I'm holding her as tight as I can, and she's crying into the collar of my shirt now and against my neck, and I feel the sobs rack through her, and I hear her saying, "Oh, baby, oh, sweetheart," over and over again until I put my lips over hers and we fold into each other like the petals of a single bloom, and in the next second, despite the gray and heavy Pennsylvania sky, the horizon to the south seems full of wild light and color, and I can smell Louisiana on the wind.

15

We climb up to the promenade in Brooklyn Heights to say our good-byes to the city we are leaving. Tonight the stars are up in a black sky, and Manhattan lies below, marvelous and wind-swept as a castle on a moor, connected to the reality of the mainland only by the spiderlike trac-ery of its bridges. Now the streets and avenues between the towers are flooded with a brilliant artificial light. This is entirely appropriate. After all, it is the idea of this city that matters. Not the real streets, but the dreams we have of them.

Rust takes off his hat and wipes his forehead with the back of his hand. For him it's been a long day on the range, nearly fifteen years, but he's on his way back to Wyoming tomorrow to pick up where he left off. I've got a week or so, just until I can get things straightened out with Father Rose.

It's a hot night, a small reminder of the tor-turous days of summer. Lovers line the benches along the promenade, nuzzling in the gloom. I hear the snap of cotton underwear, a soft moan. Ice cream melts in paper cups. The nineteenth-century town houses sit back, disapproving in the darkness of their gardens. I lean over the parapet to catch a breeze from the harbor but instead get a lungful of carbon monoxide. The BQE roars just underneath the shelf of masonry, on its way from nowhere to nowhere, a continuous and never-ending loop of taillights and exhaust.

We're silent for a while, each remembering our years in the city, the thousand amazing details, the faces lost in the crowd. For us, New York is like a wreck sinking into deep water. Now the bow is down, now the winch and wheelhouse; soon it's just an oil stain on the surface.

"What will you miss the most when you're gone?" Rust says in a quiet voice, almost to himself.

"What's to miss? The crime, the high cost of living? Eight-dollar six-packs of Genessee Cream ale? Pay phones that don't work?" But I regret this cynicism. "Cawalloway's," I say suddenly. "Remember Cawalloway's, Rust?"

"Whatever happened to that place?"

"Gone."

"That was a good bar, cheap. And the women."

"Yeah."

"But you know, I think I'll miss the subway," he says. "Never knew what you'd see on the subway. Like a moving carnival. Just yesterday this crazy lady comes through, two hundred and fifty pounds of meat in a pink nightgown and fuzzy bedroom slippers, handing out dollar bills to every third person."

"All right. This is going to sound like a stock answer, but I'll miss the Brooklyn Bridge," I say. "A beautiful span. Walking across to the city in the summer at dusk, then up through the crowds of Chinatown and all the fish and squid and eels laid out and reeking, then up into the East Village, and beautiful, hip women getting out of cabs."

"I'll be in Cheyenne by tomorrow night." Rust shakes his head. "Shit. Hard to imagine it after all this time. And the farm. I was twenty-two when I left that dusty-ass place for good. Now I'm going back."

"A change of pace, Rust," I say. "We can't go on like this forever."

For once he doesn't squint toward the horizon but looks down at the toes of his cowboy boots. "I suppose I can write my book back there as well as I can write it here, probably better," he says. "But I'll have a big spread to take care of. And my jackass brother's got a kid. A little girl, seven years old. The mother ran off after a year, so I'm the legal guardian. Way I see it, you can't take care of a little girl without a wife. I suppose now I'll have to get myself a wife."

"Anyone in mind?"

He shrugs.

Suddenly there is a touch of panic in my gut. This is New York. People sacrifice everything to be a part of the teeming life of this city — their dignity, their health, their standard of living — because on certain evenings you can almost imagine the streets are still paved with gold. Who knows what could happen tomorrow or the next day or next year? If we could just stick it out. Maybe then the city will open its doors to us, hand us the keys to the future. Maybe we are giving up too soon!

"You know that story about Dick Whittington, Rust," I say when I catch my breath.

"Used to play for the Yankees. Shortstop, right?"

"No." I smile. "It's a story I read once when I was a kid. A kid's story. About this country boy, Dick Whittington, who leaves his home to seek his fortune in the big city. In this case, London."

"So?"

"So he's there awhile, and times are tough, and his only friend is a stray cat he can't afford to feed. Then, one day, he's had enough of the heartache, puts the cat in a bag, and decides to go back to the country. He's on the highroad a few miles out of town when the bells of the churches start pealing and he hears this voice from the bag saying, 'Turn back, Dick Whittington, turn back.' "

"It's the cat talking?" Rust says.

"Well, Dick takes the cat out, and it won't say anything, so he puts it back and goes on his way. Then he hears it again. 'Turn back, Dick Whittington,' and the same thing happens again, three times in all. But the last time he turns back and eventually becomes lord mayor of London, thrice, as the story goes."

"How's that?"

"The cat is sold for a fortune to a foreign prince from a catless country with a big rat problem. Then Dick marries the boss's daughter and goes on from there. That's not the point, though."

"So what's the point?"

"Come on, Rust."

He thinks it over for a while. "You hearing talking cats now, Ned?" he says.

"Not really," I say. "The point is Dick Whittington turned back and we're leaving."

"I'll tell you what," Rust says, and sweeps his hat to Manhattan. "This is not London. And in New York any man who listens to a talking cat is a fool."

He straightens and puts his hat back on, and his face is lost in shadow, and he turns and walks down the promenade, worn heels of his boots scuffing against the pavement. I take a last look at New York glittering through the haze, breathe in a last breath of New York air damp from the sea and both fragrant and stale from the life of cities, and a moment later turn to follow him.

In silence then, for the last time, we descend together across the park, under the Gothic arches of the Brooklyn Bridge, under the creaking steel of the Manhattan, through the dangerous neighborhoods, and along the cobbled streets of Molasses Hill into the darkness of the warehouses.

16

A dirge full of oboe and trombone sounds low over the Mississippi. This is the first funeral on such a grand scale on the river in a hundred years. It seems the whole parish has turned out to watch it pass. The barge carrying Madeleine's coffin and black obelisk churns up midstream, followed by powerboats full of jazz musicians, journalists, caterers, and a TV news crew. Police speedboats from New Orleans lead the way, their sirens turning soundless and pale in the sunlight. Fishermen and curious pleasure boaters in Chris-Craft are anchored to the sandbars. Spectators watch from the batture and from the roofs of cars pulled over on the Belle Chasse Highway, beer cans in hand. Down this part of the country it's any excuse for a party.

The coffin barge wavers in the current and pulls toward the far bank. A sodden black silk drapery trailing off the stern is churned under in our wake, then resurfaces twenty yards distant like the body of a drowned man. The flat prow is decorated with a black wreath. It is the latter part of October, but hot as any July day up North. Antoinette tells me I'd better get used to the heat, that in Louisiana, it's sweltering three-quarters of the year. I tell her I remember it well, that I'm already shedding my northern skin, taking my siesta and cool bath in the long hot afternoons like any good Creole.

Now I sweat into my new linen suit and peer through my sunglasses into the green distance. At the next bend in the river we should come to Belle Azure. The great house is gone now, but the crypt is there, dug into the faint rise above the levee. And Madeleine's niche, empty all these years, lies waiting to receive her earthly remains.

Antoinette and her family spared no expense

on this funeral. Final cost for the arrangements came to over two hundred thousand dollars. They hired a construction crew and crane in Brooklyn to remove the obelisk from the churchyard at St. Basil's, a special team from the coroner's office to exhume the body, and lawyers to file the papers for removal at the Statehouse in Albany.

I provided the historical research for the project free of charge. The state required a complete genealogy, and there was at first some difficulty in proving the Rivaudais family's claims to the body. It was during the course of my research that I discovered a curious fact: Since Madeleine's day, there have been no male heirs. Not a single one. Descent has passed exclusively through the female line. The odds against this, biologically speaking, are unusually high. If it is a sort of curse, an assessment Mama Rivaudais ascribed to her grandmother, then it is a curse that has long benefited the men of Louisiana. For this sunny part of the world has seen generation after generation of gray-eyed, black-haired beauties, women who as a sort of added bonus are often graced with a languid and pliant temperament.

It is difficult to escape New York, even in death. But finally all papers were stamped and filed, all fees paid, and Madeleine was allowed to come home. Last week she was brought south around the Florida Keys and into the Gulf of Mexico's blue water on a boat full of computer parts and plastic sandals, not too different in spirit from the New Orleans packet of 150 years ago.

A special jetty has been constructed along the levee at Belle Azure, and a road paved with shells and gravel cut through the underbrush and forest up the rise to the crypt. A derrick and flatbed truck wait to transport the casket and obelisk this last half mile. At noon the guests and musicians and journalists and caterers disembark to the green smell of newly cut wood and the wide, dirty reek of the river. I join Antoinette for the funeral procession. We walk hand in hand in the mournful cadence of slow jazz through the heat. The ceremony is short, a bare fifteen minutes. It doesn't take long to put somebody in the ground, especially if they've been there since the 1840s, at least in the flesh.

Afterward, Mama Rivaudais, still healthy and sleek despite her husband's death, stands on a chair, steadied by her daughters, to deliver a short eulogy to the crowd.

"One of our girls has come home to rest," Mama says, her eyes vague and sympathetic through the sea green of her shades. "She has been lost to us for many years. We found her quite by accident through the help of a friend and decided to bring her back to Belle Azure, where she was born and where she fell in love. Her life was not a happy one. She suffered greatly, and resting in foreign soil up North, she has suffered ever since. But now her suffering is over. . . ." With this Mama turns toward the coffin resting on a black catafalque before the door of the crypt. "Sleep well, Madeleine. You're home now, honey. We'll

517

see you again on Judgment Day."

Then the coffin is borne down into the darkness and anchored in its niche. The great stone bearing the arms of the Prasères and the shields of allied noble families going all the way back to El Cid, Pacifier of the Moors, is rolled into place over the opening and sealed forever, and the iron-studded door is closed on the moldy dampness and on the dead that lie within.

Fifteen minutes after the obelisk is raised on a new brick foundation near the gate, the caterers have set up the food, and the liquor flows, and there is livelier music from the musicians and much drinking and eating in true Louisiana style until the sun sets into the river in the west.

Antoinette finds me at dusk, the horizon a thin strip of vermilion over the dark contours of the bayou. She slips her arm into mine and kisses me on the cheek.

"What are you brooding about now?" she says. She takes a taste of my warm gin and tonic, makes a face, and dumps the rest into the grass. "Come on," she says.

"I'm really not brooding," I say, but I shrug.

"I can always tell when you've got something on your mind."

"O.K.," I say. "I'm a historian. I tell stories about dead people. It's Madeleine. Her story got told. Great. But what about all those people who don't get their stories told, who end up in a ditch somewhere, forgotten?"

Antoinette shakes her head. She laughs; then

she is serious. "You've got to pray for them," she says quietly. "Even though you don't know their faces, even though you never heard their voices. You've got to pray for the whole suffering world. But you can't take care of them all, Ned. You know that? You can only take care of your own family. You take care of your family first, and that takes care of the world."

"My family?"

"That's right."

"So how many kids you figure in this family of mine?"

"Well —" she smiles into the darkness — "I'm thirty-two now. I figure we get started right away . . . oh, eight, ten . . ."

"Jesus."

"Why not? Got a great big old house on Esplanade. Might as well fill it up."

Then she leans up and kisses me hard on the mouth and pulls me into the underbrush until we are deep into the bayou, and the music and the sound of human voices come to us faint and far away. It is dark here, I can barely see Antoinette's face, but we go farther still, until there is blackness all around, and we can no longer hear the music or the voices and there is only the reedy sound of the wilderness like a rushing in the water. Somehow, Antoinette finds a dry spot against a tree and lifts up her dress.

"I said I figured we'd get started right away, I meant right now," she says, and when I find her body in the tree darkness, it feels like home.

Epilogue

Six months have passed. Antoinette is six months pregnant, and it looks as if she conceived the night of the funeral — whether in the woods or at the fishing camp afterward is hard to tell.

We were married at the St. Louis Cathedral when she was just starting to show. There was a reception for family and friends at the New Orleans Yacht Club afterward. Given the circumstances, we were going to do a small ceremony, something brief and civil, but at the last minute Antoinette changed her mind, and with the help of four sisters sent out 350 invitations and made all the arrangements in two weeks.

"What the hell," she said to me, "I don't know about you, but I'm only going to get married once."

The wedding made the society pages of the *Times-Picayune*, with pictures of the happy bride and dazed, sedated groom. The paper announced kindly that the groom looked nervous but resolved, that the bride looked lovely and pregnant in her dress of pale blue — it was hard to pull off the virginal white with her stomach showing like that — and that sonograms had revealed the sex of the child as male, the first boy baby in the family in over two hundred years. This came as a shock to me. I was counting on one of those beautiful girls for which they are famous and am secretly a little disappointed. But if we are going to have ten, as Antoinette says, there is plenty of room for several of both kinds.

Father Rose flew down to assist at the wedding mass and looked very priestly indeed in his vestments at the altar. He has given up golf entirely, he told me later at the reception, and has instead gone into the business of saint management full time. The strange case of Sister Januarius has received quite a bit of attention in the press lately. Miracles have been reported in Brooklyn. Cripples are walking; the blind are seeing; crutches litter the steps of the cathedral. A few of the youths of the Decateur Projects have even come to turn in their guns at the altar. Who knows what could happen next? Father Rose says the good sister is already more than halfway toward beatification. The Congregation of Rites in Rome is investigating, but it is now only a question of legal processes and canon law. Still, it could take a year or two or two centuries. The Holy See is inscrutable in these matters, Father Rose says. And the issue is complicated by the fact that Sister Januarius's cultus was celebrated in secret for almost eighty years.

Meanwhile, Father Rose has become something of a celebrity. He has appeared on *Good Morning America* and on the Regis Philbin show. His picture, along with a scandalous close-up of the shrunken, mummified head of Sister Januarius, was featured on the front page of the *New York Post*. The headline read A SAINT GROWS IN BROOKLYN? Perhaps it wasn't success in golf he had wanted all along, Father Rose confided to me as a guilty aside, but a little bit of fame.

Work on the house on Esplanade moves forward at a good pace. Antoinette hired an army of carpenters, electricians, and plumbers to do the specialty work, and last week we moved into the big bedroom on the second floor, which is still a little like camping out. I am having a hard time getting used to the idea that we are rich and still plan to finish my thesis one of these days and apply for a position teaching history at one of the local colleges. After so many years of hardscrabble living, Antoinette's money is impossible to imagine. I find myself making the most absurd economies, though I am told that after taxes our share of Papa's assets comes to something around seventeen million dollars. I say our share because Antoinette has refused to draw up a prenuptial agreement, cutting me out of a share in the loot in the case of divorce or abandonment.

"If we sink, we sink together," she says. "Anyway, what's a million or two more or less to me now?" I have to agree with this assessment, but in my case it is God's truth that I would take her barefoot and destitute without a rag to call her own, and all this newfound wealth embarrasses me just a little. After the child is born, we're going to give some of the money to the poor, I tell her, and she folds her hands across her belly and gives a smile worthy of the Madonna herself.

Still, like Henry Murger, after the success of *Scènes de la Vie de Bohème*, I am lifted from a life of bohemian penury and suffering in a single brilliant stroke.

One of my economies has taken the odd form of landscape gardening. I am redoing the courtyard behind the house on Esplanade, drawing on experience garnered as a summer landscaper during high school. It is miserable, backbreaking work, but it eases my conscience a little. I've got a pile of old bricks from a demolition yard, and today I am rebuilding the planter walls around the live oak when I hear the crunching tire sound of a heavy vehicle pulling into the porte cochere.

It is a vintage fifties era Bentley Continental, with a two-tone paint job of glossy black and deep burgundy and lots of polished chrome. When the chauffeur comes around to open the passenger door, I see the cross keys and miter insignia on the door and begin to brush the dirt off my knees. An older man steps out, wearing the red-trimmed skirts and cape and red skullcap that is the insignia of a cardinal of the Catholic Church. I am dumbfounded as the man approaches. His heavy gold crucifix gleams in the sun of three o'clock. His shoes are patent leather, Italian, handmade. He is short and plump, with odd square sideburns and a mole like a beauty mark on his left cheek. He smiles pleasantly when he steps up, but his eyes are grave and serious and conceal unknown depths.

"Excuse me, I am looking for a Mr. Edward Conti," he says in a measured English that shows its Italian accent through the pronouncement of my last name.

"Yes?"

"I am Monsignor Antonio Ruccia, attached to the Congregation of Rites at the Vatican. Can you spare a moment?"

We sit at the cast-iron table beneath the live oak. Cardinal Ruccia carefully dusts the seat with an embroidered handkerchief, and when he sits, his skirts spread delicately over his knees, but there is nothing frivolous about the man. He has the assured gestures of someone who is used to the exercise of unquestioned authority. He brings out a small cassette player from a fold in his cassock, places it carefully on the table between us, and begins to ask questions about Sister Januarius, about the apparition in the hospital, about the long and arduous progress of my research over the course of last summer.

When I am finished telling him what I know, he clicks off the tape recorder and leans close. His aftershave smells slightly of gardenias, but something about his eyes make me sweat.

"I ask you, Mr. Conti, to swear upon the fate of your immortal soul and on your love for the church, that the things you have told me are true and do not represent fabrications or elaborations on your part."

I am flustered and for a moment think of Galileo

standing before the Inquisition. "Word of honor," I whisper, "it's all true."

His eyes narrow for a moment. Then he nods and seems satisfied, and the tension lifts off into the afternoon like smoke.

"You must forgive me if I am too serious in my work," he says. "But the creation of a new saint is a very serious matter. We must be sure you are telling the truth."

I blink an agreement, and the cardinal is quiet for a moment. He looks around the courtyard, scratches his chin, smiles.

"This will be a beautiful house when you are finished with it," he says. "I like the style of architecture here. It's open yet private. European but not quite."

"Creole," I say. "French, Spanish. With a little solid American Federal style thrown in."

"A felicitous mix," he says.

"Thanks," I say, because I don't know what else to say. The guy makes me nervous. At that moment Antoinette emerges from the kitchen with a pitcher of lemonade and two glasses in hand. She is barefoot, and her skirt is pulled up and tied around her thighs. She's been wallpapering the room adjoining our own that will be the nursery. Her arms are speckled with paste. When she sees the cardinal, she nearly drops the pitcher of lemonade.

"Oh, I didn't realize," she says weakly. "You've got company."

The cardinal stands and gives a slight bow.

"Signora," he says, "I was just on my way. I do not wish to intrude upon your afternoon."

But Antoinette and I prevail upon him to stay. We finish the lemonade, and as the first blush of evening comes to the sky over the river, the cardinal expresses a desire to try one of our local alcoholic concoctions.

"I have heard much of the mint julep," he says. "I saw *Gone With the Wind* in Italy when I was a child, and this always sounded like a delicious drink to me. I couldn't of course be seen going into a saloon, but if you have the ingredients on hand?" He raises an Italian eyebrow.

Antoinette has a wicked gleam in her eye. "Mint juleps aren't exactly a New Orleans tradition; they're more of a plantation drink. But I'll go you one better, Father," she says, and disappears into the house. Ten minutes later she emerges with two Sazeracs in highball glasses.

The cardinal sips carefully and smiles. "Yes," he says. "Very good."

"It's a Sazerac," Antoinette says. "Homemade. None of this store-bought stuff. From scratch. Here, let me take a sip . . ."

"Antoinette . . ." I say.

"I said a taste. Don't be paranoid, Ned. It's not going to hurt anything." She takes a demure sip out of my glass and hands it back to me. "Not bad," she says. "Needs something, though . . ."

"No," the cardinal says enthusiastically, "this

526

is excellent!" and to prove the point, he downs two more.

When he rises to go at last, he is a little tipsy, his cheeks shining red in the twilight. The chauffeur is asleep in the car.

"Thank you both for a very pleasant afternoon," he says. He shakes my hand and kisses Antoinette on the forehead, but as he turns to go, she whispers something in his ear.

"Yes, of course," he says with the air of a man who has been reminded of something important.

Antoinette comes over and takes my arm, and we both kneel together on the flagstones and the fallen leaves of the courtyard. The cardinal raises his hand, makes the sign of the cross over us, and intones a brief blessing.

"The hardest thing is to find happiness in this world," he says. "But the recipe is simple. We tend to our goats, so to speak; we take our children by the hand. And as the Scripture says, we walk humbly with our God. Be happy, my children."

Then, with a flourish of cloak, he is gone into the dusk.

Later Antoinette and I lie drowsing together in the big bed, talking quietly of the future. My hand is pressed to her belly, but the baby will not kick for us tonight.

"So what did you think of the cardinal's recipe for happiness?" she says to me.

"Everybody's got their own version," I say.

"A ghost once told me that happiness consists of finding out where you belong and going there."

"Hmm. And where do you belong?"

But I don't answer. And soon we are asleep in each other's arms.